GREEN WITH ENVY

A FRANK HARPER MYSTERY

GREG ENSLEN

GYPSY
PUBLICATIONS

Published in 2020, by Gypsy Publications
Troy, OH 45373, U.S.A.
www.GypsyPublications.com

Copyright © Greg Enslen, 2020

First Edition

This story is a work of fiction and, while based on actual events and locations, is entirely fictitious. All names, characters, locations, and incidents appearing in this work are fictional or have been used in a fictional context and in no way are meant to reflect actual events, incidents or locations. Any resemblance to actual persons, living or dead, is entirely coincidental.

All rights reserved
No part of this book may be reproduced or utilized in any form or by any means, electronic or mechanical, including photocopying, recording, or any information storage and retrieval system, without written permission from the author or publisher.

Enslen, Greg
Frank Harper Mysteries Series
Green with Envy / by Greg Enslen
ISBN 978-1-938768-99-6 (paperback)

Cover by Jennifer D. Magro
Cover Design by Pamela Schwartz
Cover photo by shayes17 via iStock

For more information, please visit the author's website at www.GregEnslen.com

Author's Note

First off, welcome back. I always feel a weird mixture of emotions when I'm finishing up a new book, an amalgamation of relief and dread. Relief that the book is done, obviously, and dread that it won't be received as well as my previous books. Often, these books are very difficult to write and take years to produce. Frank Harper is back to his old ways, investigating things and sticking his nose in where it doesn't belong.

As I'm writing this, it's September 2020, and the world is experiencing a global pandemic brought about by the Covid-19 virus. Needless to say, it's been a strange time over the past seven months, but things are starting to settle down. My kids are heading back to school, and my oldest is just staring his freshmen year at college. So far, so good—school is in session, everyone is healthy, and things are starting to move in the direction of normalcy. Finger's crossed we get through the rest of the year without an invasion of locusts or a zombie uprising.

I've been trying to stay busy writing. I'm working on this book and several others, including a Binge Guide to one of my favorite TV shows, the 1970's classic "Emergency!" I also wrote and released the final Binge Guide for "Mr. Robot, Season 4" and I've been working on some screenplays.

Six Years

I've been working on this book, in parts, for about six years. Folks will notice that this isn't the first mention of Jessica Mills in the Frank books—in fact, she keeps cropping up in the background.

I'd love to claim that this is a result of my amazing talent, or my ability to write several books in my head ahead of time. Alas, that is not true. But Jessica's been a background character since the beginning. I kept coming back to her, hoping to expand her story into a large part of a future Frank book. Well, here we are, and I have to say, I'm very happy with the outcome.

I often explain to people that when I finish writing a book, I'm wrapping up a year-long (or multi-year-long) process of solving a puzzle. A puzzle of my own creation, to be sure, but still a puzzle, with strange pieces that I'm trying to cram together in a way that makes sense. It's like doing a huge, 10,000 piece puzzle, making all the parts fit right and rotating some sections and leaving other sections until the end because they're just too damn hard. I have to get all the pieces to fit together in just the right way or it doesn't feel right.

But the Frank Harper books are getting easier to write, I feel. I know Frank like the back of my hand, and fall back into his voice without much trouble. I'm always working on different projects, one of the reasons I've rarely had to deal with writer's block, and switching projects can be a challenge. Different projects lend themselves to different voices, and I emulate Steinbeck and Clancy when inspired to write long, descriptive passages and pages and pages of painting scenes. For other stories, like the Frank Harper mysteries, I tend to write in a choppier, more Hemingway-ish style, with short paragraphs and less description.

I'm working on launching another series, and I find myself describing things in longer passages that just wouldn't feel correct when writing about Frank and his breathless, take-no-prisoners style of police work. To me, Frank wouldn't be interested in long, descriptive passages. He just doesn't have time for that.

Jessica

I like Jessica Mills. She's been rattling around my head for a while, and every time I read about a Hollywood starlet dealing with her fame—and the problems that come with it—I think about Jessica. She's an amalgamation of Lindsey Lohan and Brittney Spears, but with a little Drew Barrymore and Brittney Murphy thrown in. I can't even imagine what it's like to be a child star in Hollywood, with careers managed by parents and other adults, and the children likely having very little say in the direction of their careers.

I mentioned Jessica in the very first Frank book, "A Field of Red." He's working out in his hotel room in Chapter 5 and there's a story about her on the television. She comes up again in Chapter 52 of "White Lines," when Tavon's on a stakeout and bored and reading a

People magazine article about the "troubled Hollywood Starlet." She's mentioned by name for the first time about half-way through "Yellow Jacket," when Laura reads about her, also in a People magazine.

She was a challenging character to write, and I'll leave it to the reader to decide if I got it right or not. She's not that likable at the beginning, and that's fine with me. Hopefully, she grows on you the way she grew on me. As for her stalker, the less mentioned, the better. He's a "piece of work," as they say.

Locations

As usual, Cooper's Mill is the setting for much of this Frank Harper book, and the town is based on Tipp City, Ohio, where I live. My wife and I moved to Tipp in 2005, looking for a small town after living in the frenetic suburbs of Washington D.C. It ended up being a very good decision—Tipp is a great place to live and a great place to raise our three children. We live near the downtown and can walk to the bank, several restaurants, churches and plethora of shops and activities.

Frank's "Cooper's Mill" is a fictionalized version of Tipp, with much of the city preserved and reflected in the stories. Public locations, like the parks, schools, and street names, all retain their "actual" names, so if you're keeping track, there is a real Kyle Park and a real Broadway Elementary. Portions of this story take place in City Park, a particularly uninventive name for a beautiful downtown park which hosts, among many other events, the annual Mum Festival, held every September. The Mum Festival is a central part of Jessica's story in this book, so you'll recognize the location—and the swings—if you ever happen to visit Tipp City.

Another location in the book is the underground garage. Suffice it to say that yes, that's a real location, and yes, it's located under our local furniture store. Drop by and see them at the corner of Main and Fourth Streets, buy a couch, and maybe, if you ask nicely, they'll let you tour the dark basement. Watch out, though—you never know who might be down there.

And a little plug—I run a website dedicated to Tipp City, which lists all of our awesome shops, restaurants, and area activities. It's at www.visittippcity.org. If I get around to it, I might add a page for Frank Harper tourists—I'm sure there are a few out there.

Until then, drop by our great little town, visit the coffee shop and the soap store and Coldwater Café, which in fact does feature a bank vault. I often get complements on how "real" my fictional town of Cooper's Mills feels—and I have to confess, sometimes I'm just describing the real-life setting here in town. I don't know if I'm clever enough to come up with Freeman's Prairie, a real place east of town that gets burned every year. And stay tuned for more "secret" locations in upcoming Frank Harper books.

Writer's Block

I'm lucky—for me, I rarely run up against this issue. People ask me about it all the time; in fact, it's the second or third most-asked-question I get when I'm hunched over my table at some event, selling and signing copies of my books. The first question is almost always "Where Do You Get Your Ideas," which is a story for another time. But Writer's Block? No, not often. I tell people that if they're getting writer's block, in my experience they're likely working on the wrong project. It's burnout, plain and simple, and switching to another project, even if it's just to outline another story or to get the creative juices flowing, can often fix the problem.

Or it doesn't. Right now, I'm stuck on an issue with my other series, and I've found "free writing" to be the best way to the help with that. What's "free writing," you ask? I sound like Gollum. "What's taters, precious?" Free writing is the process of literally sitting down and typing whatever comes into your head.

A few years ago, I was having trouble coming up with the ending of "Black Ice" and stumbled across this notion of just typing. Type your ideas, type your problem, type what you like about the story and what you don't like. I started by literally typing "I'm working on Black Ice and I can't seem to come up with a good ending that I like" and continued typing, capturing several different ideas I was bandying about along with my thoughts on the weather and a half-dozen other topics. I was writing at one of my book shows, typing away on my laptop between customers, and wrote down everything I could think of related to the show. I made a list of things I needed to do, and created a Costco grocery list, and added more ideas for endings. Eventually, I eliminated a few endings and narrowed it down to two I liked, then brainstormed more "details" about those until I found one I liked.

If you're having writer's block, I'd try working on something else. If that doesn't work, I'd free write about the project and what you don't like about it, brainstorming goofy solutions until you find one you can live with.

And you might just have to live with it. Finish the book, finish the story, move on. Don't get bogged down in making it perfect, or you'll never send it out into the world.

Thank You

Well, that's it for this time. I'll get to work on the next Frank Harper book and let's all try to avoid the Covid-19. Stay healthy out there, and I'll see you soon,

— Greg

Green with Envy

CHAPTER 1
Driving

Frank Harper sat in the front seat of his old Camaro, driving the back roads east of the small Ohio town of Cooper's Mill. It was late in the day on July 28, 2012, and his mind was barely on the road.

The ex-cop looked much younger than his 56 years, with a thin body and ropey arms that betrayed his obsession with working out and the Israeli form of martial arts known as Krav Maga. It was something he did for fun, a piece of information that few people believed. He'd somehow managed to avoid putting on the "Donut 30," those extra pounds every aging policeman seemed to accumulate once they stopped working in the field and parked themselves behind a desk. At this point in most people's lives, it seemed just staying thin was an accomplishment.

Frank was deep in thought. It had been a rough day already, and it was barely noon.

The funeral for his friend and colleague, Deputy Peters, had been held this morning. His daughter, Laura, had attended with Frank, both out of moral support for him—Frank blamed himself for Peters' death—and because she'd known the young deputy as well. They had been friends, or had at least started down that road, before the man had died so tragically.

After the funeral, they had driven to her apartment, where Frank was crashing. He'd moved up from Alabama only a week before, looking for a change of scenery. Now, he was doubting that decision, as he'd doubted so many before.

Sensing his mood, his daughter had gone out of her way to change the subject. As they drove to her home, she asked about his "plans" to start a private investigation business in town. And they were plans, certainly, though they seemed so much less important than they had only a few weeks ago.

After he'd dropped her off, Frank had put the car in drive and headed out to clear his head. To gather his thoughts. He often drove, alone, piecing things together in his head, or pondering the clues of some mystery. He'd gotten in the habit as a beat cop in New Orleans, driving the streets and thinking. Sometimes he even talked out loud to himself—if he was alone—and verbalized his different theories and clues, looking for a solution to some problem.

Today was different. The funeral, the other cops, the blistering sun beating down on them. Frank, sweating, standing there in that quiet cemetery, wishing to be somewhere else. Anywhere else.

He'd buried too many partners, too many friends. Just another hazard of being an old cop. But the worst had been the look on Chief King's face.

Deputy Peters' funeral had been difficult, of course. It was difficult for everyone involved, standing around the open grave and saying goodbye to one of the most popular members of the Cooper's Mill Police Department (CMPD). It had been hard for Frank, too—Peters was the closest thing to a friend he'd had in town, and they'd partnered on several cases while Frank "helped out" with the local cops. Frank would miss him, miss being a mentor to Peters.

Laura had been crushed, too. She and Peters had become friends, and there had even been the tiniest possibility it could grow into something more.

But, of course, Deputy Peter's death was hardest on Chief King. Peters was his cousin, and King had encouraged him to go into law enforcement, bringing him onto the Cooper's Mill Police Department.

As they'd all stood around the open grave this morning, Frank couldn't help but feel King's eyes on him. The Chief blamed Frank for Peters' death. Hell, every member of the CMPD probably blamed him.

Get in line, boys. Frank blamed himself, getting caught up in Joe Hathaway's web. Chasing the clues the man had dropped. Acting like an idiot. But the situation had spun out of control. Laura and Jackson, Frank's daughter and grandson, had been kidnapped. Frank had been searching for them, following a set of clues dropped by Joe Hathaway, an escaped murderer on a mission to destroy Frank. Joe was a genius, and an evil one at that. Frank had been instrumental in catching him for three murders, and the guy should have been rotting in jail. Instead, he'd escaped and, somehow, surrounded himself with a cult-like following of useful idiots. Frank finally tracked Joe and his people to an old farmhouse north of Troy, Ohio, a farmhouse that Frank had a history with.

As he drove, Frank pondered the absurdity of the whole incident.

Frank had done the right thing, telling Deputy Peters, who had insisted on coming along. Who was Frank to stop him? Deputy Peters was a grown man, a police officer. He knew what he was doing, knew what he was getting into. He'd saved Laura and Jackson and a dozen others once the bullets had started flying. And Peters would have survived, as well, if he'd followed precautions. A stupid, $200 Epi-Pen would have saved him.

Apparently, only a few people knew that Peters had a deadly bee and wasp allergy. Frank certainly hadn't known. When the shooting started and civilians were fleeing, Peters had put himself in harm's way to protect them. By the time Frank found him, Peters would have required immediate and extreme medical care to save him.

But now Deputy Peters was dead.

Frank drove, trying to distract himself. He was near New Stanton, a small town east of Cooper's Mill. Frank was getting more familiar with the area, driving the roads often when he needed time to think.

Or search. Frank's eyes trailed over every stand of trees. Joe Hathaway was out here somewhere, escaping the shootout at the farmhouse by playing dead and floating away. Frank could see it all so clearly in his mind's eye, watching Joe's "body" wash down the river to disappear around the distant curve. How was Frank supposed to know the guy had survived getting shot? At the time, Frank had bigger concerns. Worried about Laura and Jackson hiding in the trees near the river. Worried about Peters and the other cops in the area and the civilians fleeing the scene.

They didn't find Joe's body. As the days had stretched out, the cops dragged the river but found nothing. And it finally dawned on Frank: Joe had gotten away.

So now, whenever he got a chance, Frank drove the back roads, searching for Joe. His eyes scanned the cornfields and distant tree lines, searching. Surely, the old man was long gone. Why stick around the area? Joe was smarter than that.

But it wasn't fair: Deputy Peters was gone, and Joe was out there somewhere. But was that all it was? Was Frank obsessed with finding Joe? Or was Frank just running away from Cooper's Mill, trying to avoid the looks he got from the local cops? How would they ever forgive him? And how could he forgive himself?

Frank shook his head, driving on, his eyes searching the fields that stretched around him to a flat, Midwestern horizon.

CHAPTER 2
Nightclub

On the same evening, 3,000 miles away, Jessica Mills sat by herself in a corner booth. The starlet sat alone, hiding in a dark corner of Liquid, a West Hollywood nightclub, desperately trying to not be seen.

Jessica was 23, thin, with long blond hair that cascaded down around her shoulders. She was incredibly attractive in a classical way, the kind of beauty that drew eyes and stares no matter where she went.

Jessica was wearing a tiny dress that hugged her thin, lithe body, the result of years of workouts and private fitness coaches and a steady routine of near starvation. It was the "Hollywood girl" fitness plan, typified by coke and bland foods in tiny portions and studio-funded gym equipment. She was always hungry. She'd been hungry for the last fifteen years.

And she was a magnet for attention.

Jessica had always been "cute," but after years in TV and movies, her level of attractiveness had become so honed that now she was practically a commodity. She was one of two dozen recognizable "young Hollywood" women who were currently—and desperately—trying to make the difficult transition from kid star to serious actress. She saw her "compatriots" everywhere. They grabbed at any role they could find to legitimize their "serious" credentials, and some were doing better than others. One had won an Oscar last year, but two others were in rehab. She hoped to fall somewhere in the middle, at least.

But, on this particular evening, things weren't going well.

Jessica looked around the interior of the humid, overcrowded nightclub, wishing she could literally be any other place in the world. The club smelled like old beer and desperation. The music pulsed around her, shaking her bones, making her body vibrate. She could feel it in her teeth. She just wanted a moment alone. That was it, really.

But everyone else wanted something from her, it seemed. Show up here, be pretty there. Endorse this product, appear at this gym opening, speak out on this social cause. It was all exhausting. Right now, all she really wanted was to sit in a dark booth with her watered-down Tom Collins. The drink was gross, but at least she was alone, if only for a few precious moments.

A group of intoxicated people passed her booth and she turned away, lowering her head. The movement, one she used often, allowed her long blond hair to spill down over her face. The drunks passed her booth without giving her a second glance.

Jessica relaxed, sipping her drink. She realized how weird it was, using her hair like a shield. Somewhere along the line, flopping it down like that in front of her face had worked. It kept her from being spotted, and now the movement had become almost second nature. The "flop," as she called it, happened a lot, especially when the cell phones came out. They inevitably appeared wherever she went, sprouting from people's hands.

People always took photos of her without her permission. When had that started? Somewhere along the line, it was as if her image had fallen into the public domain. It wasn't hers anymore. Jessica's image belonged to whatever TV show or movie she was promoting at the time. Her face and body were trotted out to support TV shows or movies or brands of ice cream or car batteries.

Her face wasn't her own anymore. It had become a separate entity. Maybe her face should get its own publicist. That made her smile. What if her face could just trot off on its own to make a career for itself? Would she then be free to have a normal life, whatever that was?

Cell phones. Whenever she saw the telltale shimmer of a black screen, she instinctively turned away. Her stylist Ferrara, noticing the "flop," had tried to get Jessica to cut her hair. "Do a short bob," Ferrara would say. "People would love it. It would look so cute!"

Jessica wasn't interested. A bob wouldn't protect her from the world of cameras and screens and paparazzi that seemed to hide like rats behind every tree and bush and car in Los Angeles. They were completely unavoidable.

It was ironic, of course, trying to hide her face from the public, when it was her face that was her moneymaker. It always had been, back as far as Jessica could remember. It was her meal ticket, but it was also a curse. She couldn't go anywhere without being "seen."

Accosted, recognized. But admired? Respected? Not even close.

Everyone wanted to look at her, show her off to their friends, be seen WITH Jessica. But no one knew her. Aside from Ferrara, no one really even talked to her anymore. But they all "loved" her. That's what the studio stiffs and branding people and fans always said: "I LOVE YOU JESSICA!!!," they screamed from behind the velvet ropes. "I LOVE your clothes—you always look so FABULOUS!!" At dinner, they said "I loved you on that show," or "I loved that movie you were in" or "I'd love to introduce you to my friends."

It was a love-fest all around.

But Jessica didn't feel loved. She felt used. Used by everyone around her, used by her mother as an ATM whenever the drunk woman came up for air between bottles of scotch. Used by faceless corporations to sell their crap.

Used by the entourage of slackers and hangers-on she'd managed to accumulate around her.

Jessica chugged the rest of her drink and set the empty glass down. In her fleeting moments of sobriety, she understood that it was her fault. She'd surrounded herself with them, including the person she was hiding from right now. How long could she disappear until they—

"Jessica! There you are!" Scott Rubin whisked into the booth, always a flurry of activity. Scott settled into the dirty seat across from hers, smiling. The guy ran on coffee and Hollywood "sugar." "They're all looking for you!" Scott shouted over the music. "EVERYONE wants you! The band's ready, the sponsors are here," he said in his rapid-fire speech pattern that made all his words jumble together as if they were in a hurry to get out of his mouth. "You need to introduce the brand, talk it up, introduce the owner guy—he's the CEO. And then the band."

"Why?"

He shook his head, confused, his perfect hair momentarily out of place. He brushed it back, tucking it behind one ear. "Wait, what?"

"Why do I have to introduce this crap, Scott?" Jessica looked at him. "I hate their vodka, and I hate that band. I don't want to—"

Scott glanced around and leaned in, pointing at the glass between them. "How many of those have you had? It's a little early in the night for you to be this sloshed—"

Jessica looked at him. "I'm not 'sloshed,' Scott."

"So, what's the problem? You asked me to set up these things for you, especially with money so tight."

"I'm sick of being paraded around—"

"I know, honey. I know."

She hated it when anyone called her honey. And she'd asked him on multiple occasions—

"But the vodka people paid you to be here tonight," he continued, looking around. "With your finances the way they are, Hank said you can't pass on these kinds of events."

"I know," she said. Hank Jennings, her agent and business manager, had been harping on her about money.

"Just talk up their swill," Scott said. "Introduce the band. Then we can leave."

"I need a smoke," pointing at the back doors.

"No time, honey. We gotta go."

Scott stood, all smiles, as usual, and helped her to her feet. Sometimes his relentless "happy" act made her want to strangle him. He was right, of course. Money was tight, and this gig would help. And they'd already paid her. And it was true, Jessica had had "a few" to dull the anger she felt. But not enough that she couldn't walk on her own. She jerked her arm away.

"I can walk."

Scott nodded and led her toward the side of Liquid's main stage. To one side of the empty, darkened stage, a DJ worked behind a music rig, spinning records and keeping the crowd moving until the presentation started.

Scott turned and looked at Jessica, reaching up to straighten her hair.

"Stop it," she said, swatting his hand away.

"We need you to look nice, honey. I'm just tidying up—"

"I'll do it. And don't call me honey."

Jessica stalked away, finding a lighted mirror and makeup table nearby. She settled into a tall chair and opened her little white purse, getting out a makeup kit.

She cursed under her breath as she powdered her nose. She didn't need any help, especially not from someone like Scott. The man was good for little but setting up photoshoots and keeping other people's publicists at arm's length. Besides, Jessica had been doing her own makeup since she was nine. In the sweaty, close club, she did what she could to freshen up the look that everyone was here to see. Get in line folks, here she comes. Take your pictures.

Ferrara would not approve of the slapdash job Jessica was doing, surely. But she did the best she could with the small bag of makeup she kept in her purse. In between the bottle of mascara and the other makeup containers, Jessica spotted a small bag of white powder. Her little pick-me-up. It couldn't hurt, right? She glanced around, and no one was looking. Amazing. Jessica tipped out a little "sugar" on her finger and sniffed it up, her body shivering.

It never felt as good as the very first time, but it was close. Close enough to get her through this crap.

The sugar twins rarely disappointed—they knew where to get the good stuff Jessica needed. It was half the reason she let them hang around and leech off of her career.

Jessica shook her head and looked around, the room spinning suddenly. Jessica steadied herself with one hand and looked at the face in the mirror, a face she barely recognized anymore.

"OH MY GOD, it's Jessica Mills!"

The voice, unbidden, drifted from somewhere in the backstage area. People were always saying things like that around her. And so loudly. They wanted Jessica to acknowledge them. They were desperate to talk to her. Tonight, Jessica ignored it. These clubbers were so desperate to be acknowledged, to have their stupid, pointless little lives validated, if even for a second.

Jessica pushed the mean thoughts from her mind and finished her face, freshening her mascara and lips. The DJ's music pumped around her, through her. In the vibrating mirror, she could see Scott waving her over, but she ignored him and spent another minute fixing her hair. She felt like she didn't have much control over her life anymore, but she could at least make them wait, even if it were only for a few seconds. She'd seen it with other famous people, especially on film sets. They made the crew wait, getting a reputation as a diva. But, really, it was one of the few things in their lives they could control. It felt good to reassert control over your life, every once in a while.

Finally, she bagged up the tools of her trade—makeup, hairbrush, cocaine—and stood, walking to the side of the stage where Scott was waiting with some old guy who looked completely out of place in the dark club. The old man looked like someone's grandfather, or even great-grandfather, standing backstage in an ill-fitting suit that was easily ten years out of style.

Scott nodded and gave her a thumb's up. "That's better, honey." She shot him a look but he'd already turned away. "Jessica, this is Donald Locklin. CEO, Advantage Vodka."

"Nice to meet you, Ms. Mills," Locklin shouted, shaking her hand. His hand was a cold, moist fish. "I'm…happy that the distributor put this together. Thank you for coming."

Jessica smiled at him, hoping to dazzle him, but she didn't get the reaction she expected. Her smile always worked, breaking any ice. But Locklin was cold, distant. Jessica nodded and leaned in, trying a different tactic. Something in her NEEDED him to like her, even though she really couldn't care less. She hated this innate need of hers, the "requirement" that she be liked by everyone around her. Jessica hoped someday she'd outgrow it.

"Don't worry, Mr. Locklin. I don't want to be here either," she whispered, leaning in and smiling again. "But I'm excited to introduce your vodka. It's wonderful."

He leaned back and looked at her and part of his face slid into something approximating a smile. She'd always been good at reading people, even as a kid. Good enough to navigate her way through the cut-throat world of television and film, where you had to be able to read people.

"Thank you, Ms. Mills," Locklin said, his shoulders relaxing. "And I'm sorry if I seem out of it. I'm completely out of my element here." He looked around like he'd found himself standing in ancient Rome— or on the moon. "Put me in a board room, I'm a happy camper. But this? All of this craziness? I have no idea what I'm doing."

Jessica smiled again, taking his arm and leaning closer. "Don't worry, we'll get through it." She could see hairs growing out of the tops of his earlobes. It was gross, but she ignored it. She'd spent a lifetime pretending to like people. "After I introduce you, just say a few words and then introduce the band. Do you remember their name?"

Locklin nodded. "Dumpster Fire. Hard to forget."

Scott touched her on the elbow, getting her and Locklin's attention. "Okay, here we go."

He led her and the old man over to the stairs up to the stage, then waved at the DJ, who nodded from behind his rig. A huge white dude wearing a polo shirt and absurdly-large headphones, the DJ changed tracks and brought up the house lights, switching gears with ease. As the lights came up, a staffer set up a microphone in the middle of the small stage, while another man pushed a wheeled table of ornate-looking alcohol bottles out, front and center, the glass clattering.

"How is everyone doing tonight?" the DJ asked from backstage, eliciting a loud cheer from the tipsy crowd. "I SAID how is everyone doing tonight?" the DJ asked again, looking for a louder reply, but what came back was even less enthusiastic than the first. Cutting his losses, he moved on. "Okay, we've got a huge announcement tonight. HUGE!! You guys are SO SO lucky to be here for it. AND free booze, right? And we've got a HOLLYWOOD LEGEND out tonight to kick things off!" He let that settle over the crowd before continuing. He also kept the beat thumping under his words, low and feral, building the excitement. "STAR of MOVIES and TELEVISION, including her LATEST MOVIE, "KNIGHTS OF THE TEMPLE, in theaters THIS NOVEMBER NINTH. You know her, you LOVE her! Give it up for JESSICA! MIIIIILLS!"

The music swelled as she climbed the stairs and made her way out onto the stage, surrounded by applause. She smiled and waved, doing a fist pump in the air.

"Yeah, great crowd! HEY everyone! Thanks for coming out tonight!"

She gave the crowd a moment to applaud again. Jessica had it all down. She knew the timing, the rhythm and cadence required to speak in front of a crowd. She'd been doing it most of her life. It was all about give and take, saying something and then giving them a chance to respond to whatever you were saying. You talk, then let them respond, then you talk some more. It was like breathing, in and out, slow and steady. It came second nature, now. It was easy, once you got past the nerves of all those eyes on you. Of course, the "sugar" helped. And Tom Collins.

"Okay, glad you guys are all HERE tonight," she shouted, gripping the microphone. Her voice sounded good, steady, surprising her. Too much coke could make her voice sound weak, almost brittle, but she sounded fine. "I wanted to be here TONIGHT to introduce you to something I love. Seriously, it's a favorite of mine. I was so EXCITED to hear they're LAUNCHING NATIONALLY next week. So, who likes VODKA!!"

She let the crowd respond, then pumped her fists, eliciting another round of cheers. Jessica relaxed, settling into the pre-written speech the vodka people had provided. They'd sent it over last week. Jessica had no trouble remembering it, even half sloshed. She'd been memorizing other people's words since she was five. Jessica let the words flow out of her, smooth, steady. She tried to make them sound unrehearsed, spontaneous, speeding up and slowing down her cadence, varying her tone. That's how you made it sound natural, off the cuff.

As she spoke, Jessica studied the faces of the kids in the crowd. She thought of them as 'kids,' even though they all seemed to be around her age.

But they were different. They seemed happy, free. Unencumbered by anything, unencumbered by the weight of success. Sometimes she longed for no more shoots, no more casting calls. No more weird auditions with strange men, no more traveling to foreign places and spending the whole time in a hotel because it wasn't "safe" for her to be on the streets of Dublin or Detroit or Dubrovnik.

"—and he's produced some top-notch spirits, I'm telling you. Now, do me a personal favor and help me welcome DON LOCKLIN, founder and CEO of ADVANTAGE VODKA!"

She waved the old man up on stage and applauded with the crowd as he shuffled over, clearly petrified. Jessica hoped he wouldn't puke—she'd seen enough people with that look on their faces to know it was a possibility. TV sets, movie locations, public events like this: it was all the same. The nerves could take over, intimidating even the most confident person in the world.

Jessica let him face the crowd for a moment. Was she torturing him? He looked desperate for rescue, stammering, unsure if he should be saying anything other than repeating "thank you" so quietly no one could hear him. It was nice to let him sweat, if only for a few seconds. Part of her mind chastised her for being so childish. Hell, this man's company was paying the bills. Don't torture the sweaty guy…

"Okay, okay!" she yelled, holding up her hands to quiet the crowd. "Thanks for joining us, Don!"

He stood next to her and leaned over, talking awkwardly into the microphone.

"THANK YOU, JESSICA!" He was way too close to the mic and the feedback echoed before she could pull the mic away.

"Whoa, cowboy, back off a bit," she said with a smile, and the crowd laughed.

Ten minutes later, the whole presentation was over. The old man had relaxed, settling into his pitch after a minute of awkward banter with Jessica. When he was done, he introduced the band, managing to get the name right.

The lights went dark and stagehands helped her and Locklin off—it was dangerous to walk around in the dark like that. It was very easy to fall off. She'd learned a long time ago to trust the local people—they knew the venue best.

Nearby, other stagehands moved the table of vodka out of the way while others got the band set up, pushing a drum kit forward and setting up the guitars and mic stands. Moments later, the band ran out and greeted the crowd, waving and launching into their opening number.

Jessica took advantage of all the noise and confusion to slink away. Now, ten minutes later, Jessica was in another empty booth somewhere near the back of the club, alone at last. She didn't want to show her face at the bar to order another drink. Instead, she'd picked an empty booth with some half-finished beers on the table. Making a face, she sipped at one of them, trying not to gag. Nope, this was not the life she'd always dreamed of.

Chapter 3
Search

"Have you seen her?"

Sofia Ferrara turned around. She was a short, thin young Hispanic-American woman with a blue streak that ran through her long dark hair. Her makeup was immaculate, as it should be. People knew she was the stylist to some of Hollywood's biggest stars, including Jessica Mills. Ferrara had to look the part, even if she was from the Midwest.

She saw Scott Rubin, Jessica's publicist and event coordinator, approaching and shook her head.

"No, not since the band started, when she left the stage. Is she drunk?"

Scott scowled. "When isn't she drunk?"

Ferrara shook her head. "At least the sugar twins aren't around. Why do you need her?"

Scott shook his head and looked around. "I need her because I need her. That's my job. She doesn't need a publicist—or an agent. She needs a babysitter."

"Maybe," Ferrara said. "Or a smaller entourage."

"No chance of that."

"I've been telling you she needs a security guy. She still talks about that stalker guy. Remember him? That creepy scared the crap out of her. She was freaked out for months—"

"She can't afford one, Ferrara. You know that. She can barely afford me. Or you."

She scowled. "A 'handler' could keep her out of trouble. And keep the paparazzi away."

Scott was still looking around, then turned back to Ferrara, exasperated. "Look, I need her backstage again, schmoozing with the vodka people. Especially the old guy. Jessica bailed as soon as the band came off stage. They want to meet her. They were in the green room. And the old guy, the CEO, wants to take her out for a late dinner or something."

Ferrara shook her head. "She'll never agree. You know she hates that kind of stuff."

"I don't care," Scott said, looking at her seriously. The music pumped around them. "Why do you? She's not 'Jessica Mills' the person. She's 'Jessica Mills' the brand."

The music was so loud, Ferrara missed part of what he said. "What? She's in a band?"

"She's a brand? A BRAND," he said, leaning closer. He smelled like sweat and hair gel. She tried to keep her reaction to herself. "I'm gonna go look for her. If you see her, send her backstage."

Ferrara nodded, relieved to see him go. She seldom never got to tag along on any of Jessica's outings and was trying to enjoy this one as best as she could, even with Scott sniffing around. If only her friends in Ohio could see her now...

Jessica Mills was like a big block of cheese. Scott was always nibbling around the edges, taking whatever he could. Just like all the others in Jessica's entourage. Ferrara liked to think that she was the only one that actually cared about Jessica, but now, enjoying the party and the free drinks and the attention, Ferrara started to doubt herself. Was she really a friend? Or was she just as enamored with living the "Hollywood life" as everyone else? Ferrara wasn't sure. Maybe the fact that she was feeling bad meant she was different from the other members of "Team Jessica."

Ferrara shook her head and started around the perimeter of the bar, looking in the dark recesses. It's where she would hide if she were looking to disappear. A few minutes later, Ferrara found Jessica hiding in a booth in the back.

"Jessica, what are you doing?"

The starlet looked up at Ferrara, her makeup streaked. By the looks of it, she'd been crying.

"Hiding."

Ferrara slid in next to her and put her arm around the woman. Jessica was both an incredibly famous childhood actress that Ferrara had "known" since she could remember and, at the same time, a scared young woman Ferrara hardly knew. Even though she'd been with Jessica for almost two years, Ferrara still had trouble reading her. Maybe it was Ferrara's Midwestern sensibilities, but sometimes, California people were ciphers.

"You don't need to hide, Jessica," Ferrara said. "If you want to leave, we'll leave."

"Oh, but I'm having so much fun."

"I can tell." Ferrara flipped her hair out of the way and pulled Jessica's head down onto her shoulder. "What's wrong?"

"Oh, just everything," Jessica said into Ferrara's shoulder. The words were hard to hear. "I hate it. All of it."

"Being rich and famous? Yeah, what a drag."

Jessica looked up. "Shut up. Don't you start, too."

Ferrara smiled. "Kidding."

"You know what I mean."

She did. Ferrara had heard it before, many times, during quiet hairstyling sessions or while waiting for Jessica to finish up in the tanning bed in her little Hollywood house, perched on a hillside overlooking Melrose. She kept a tanning bed there to keep her color.

"Scott's looking for you," Ferrara said. "More schmoozing with the vodka folks. And the old guy wants to take you to dinner."

Jessica shook her head. "That's what I mean. Gross. I'm just a thing to these people." She reached for the half-finished beer and sipped from it.

Ferrara nodded. Jessica was, at least in her own mind, navigating a world of rats. "Is that your beer?"

"No, I just found it here."

"That's gross."

"I know." They shared a laugh. "I just didn't want to go to the bar and order. They'll recognize me."

"I can get you a drink—"

"That's not the point," Jessica said, staring at the glass.

Ferrara changed tactics. "I'm telling you, you need another dress down day. Remember when we went to the Grove? Or the afternoon at that pier?"

"Oh, that horrible wig."

"Right?"

"It smelled like cheese. It was a disaster," Jessica said with a wistful smile.

"It was not a disaster. You loved it. Walking around, shopping, no one bothering you."

"Because I looked like a freak."

"Yup. You need another day like that. Or a whole week," Ferrara said quietly. "I'm serious. I'll do your hair and makeup, and no one will recognize you."

Jessica smiled and looked at her. "Where'd we go, Santa Monica Pier?"

"Yup. And no one recognized you."

"And no one recognized me. It was wonderful. But that wig—"

"It was pretty hideous."

They laughed together, the music of the club pumping in the background. For a moment, Ferrara thought Jessica might be happy. And then Scott appeared out of the darkness and broke the mood and dragged Jessica off to finish the "meet and greet."

Ferrara watched Jessica disappear into the club and felt sorry for her. Even if money was tight right now, Jessica was richer than anyone else Ferrara knew, especially compared to most people. And she was famous. She was free to do nearly whatever she wanted—money in the bank did that. But she felt trapped, and in a way that Ferrara didn't think many people would, or could, understand.

Chapter 4
A Date

Half a nation away, Penny Halderson was sitting at her desk, getting ready to go out on a date. Outside her windows, New Orleans sparkled in the late July heat. Even at dusk, the city lay swamped under a dome of heat, an invisible pressure cooker that would trap the city in sweat until relieved by the first cool breezes of fall.

"So, which guy is it tonight?"

Penny looked up at the bedroom door and saw Tina lurking there, watching Penny get ready. Spying on her, again. Penny was too busy to get up and shut the door, so of course Tina had settled in. She had nothing better to do.

Tina was a carpy little bitch, in Penny's opinion. Always giving Penny crap about dating too many men at the same time. Like that was even a thing anymore.

Standing, Penny finished pulling on her sundress—it was a thin little yellow thing she'd gotten at Samuel's a few weeks back. They'd been having a sale and she loved the way sundresses hung, especially when it got hot out. She ignored Tina for a long moment, looking in the mirror.

"Not that it's any of your business, but I'm seeing Blake again tonight," she finally said, focusing on fixing her hair. She'd put it up earlier and now let it out of the curlers. It bounced down around her shoulders in a satisfying way. She loved curling her hair, but it was always such a hassle. She didn't usually take the time.

"Which one is he again?" Tina asked, her voice dripping with jealousy. "Oh, Penny, you know I can't keep them straight." It was bullshit—she knew exactly who Penny was talking about.

Blake Oleander was hard to forget.

Tina was trying to be snide, probably assuming Penny wouldn't understand. Penny got that a lot—people didn't think pretty people could be smart. She wasn't narcissistic, but she'd been told she was beautiful for so long, somewhere along the line she'd started believing it.

In her awkward high school years, before college and before moving to New Orleans, Penny had never thought she was pretty. Or even cute. But if enough people tell you something, you start to believe, right?

"Blake Oleander. The BMW."

Tina nodded. "Oh, I remember. The guy with the scar."

Penny didn't say anything. Yeah, Blake had a scar on his face, a car accident from when he was a kid. It ran down one side of his face, but she kinda liked it. It made him look wild, crazy. Dangerous."

Tina plowed on. "I love guys in Beemers. You're lucky—the Oleanders are loaded. His family's been in New Orleans forever."

"I guess."

The silence dragged out, and Penny could practically hear the wheels in Tina's head turning. "You been to his house yet?"

"A few times."

"Is it big?"

"What?"

"His house," she said, brushing. "You know."

"Huge. Pool, greenhouses, back yard as big as a football field."

She glanced at Tina, who looked sufficiently jealous.

"Where's he taking you for dinner? Assuming you're having dinner and not just skipping right to the—"

"We're going to Three Sisters."

Tina screwed up her face. "Oh God, how boring. I've been there so many times, it makes me sick just thinking about it."

"I like it," Penny said, trying her hand at being snippy. "Especially when someone else is paying."

Tina gave her a look like she was eating lemons straight from the bowl. Tina wasn't the most attractive girl—probably the reason she was home alone on a Saturday night, while Penny and Tracy and all the other girls were out with men. Her sour look didn't do her any favors.

"Penny, you know that place will be full of tourists."

"I don't care," she said, looking for her clutch. It was true; Penny didn't care. She liked Blake, at least enough to allow him to take her out. He was always polite and respectful, and he always paid.

Penny wanted to tell Tina that she could go jump in a lake, but Momma always said to be polite, "especially to the mean ones."

And Tina had been extra mean to Penny lately. She was probably mad because Penny had lucked out and gotten Becca's old room when she'd moved out. The bedroom was the largest in the group house. Becca had been dating some guy for half a year and things had gotten serious. She'd had moved out a month ago.

Group homes were like that, apparently. Becca Taylor was a pretty brunette with short hair, cut in a bob. She'd been swept off her feet by some rich boy from Virginia and had sent an email about how things were going. She'd moved to some town named Liberty, her new beau sending a moving van and two burly men for her things. The girls had sat around and watched the muscular men pack up Becca's stuff, making faces and mooning over them.

Penny heard a honk from outside. Tina was off in a dash, peeking out the window.

"He's here," Tina shouted. "Okay, that is a nice car."

Penny checked her mascara one more time. She was fine with making Blake wait. Anticipation made the heart grow fonder, or something like that. She checked her purse for the Big Three: mace, money, and condoms. More advice from Momma. Never go on a date without the Big Three. A girl needed to take care of herself.

Tina was still staring out the window. "Wow, he's a big fella, isn't he?" she said before scampering out of the room.

Penny smiled to herself. Yeah, Blake was a big boy, but he knew how to take care of her. And Penny didn't care what Tina thought. Of the four men Penny was currently seeing, off and on, Blake was the richest. He was nice to her, although maybe too clingy. Once he'd showed up at the gallery where she worked, unannounced, to take her to lunch. She'd spotted him, nervously hulking in one corner, trying to get her attention. He'd said he was just passing by, but Penny got the impression he'd been keeping an eye on her.

She left her bedroom, closing her door behind her. She liked her privacy and didn't need people in her stuff when she wasn't around.

Penny headed down the wide staircase that took up most of the foyer of the old New Orleans mansion, now serving as a home for female college students and young professionals. Tina was peeking out the curtain next to the door.

"Tina, cut that out."

She turned and looked at Penny. "My dates always wait in the car, but yours is on the porch. Have fun!"

She scampered away and Penny rolled her eyes, then pulled the front door open and walked out. Sure enough, Blake was leaning casually against one of the white pillars that framed the wide steps that led down to the walkway and, eventually, the street. He was a large young man, dressed nicely in expensive, tailored clothes, his eyes dark and full of fire. The scar stood out in the dark, a jagged line across his otherwise handsome face. Whenever she spoke to him, Penny always got the impression he was deep in thought, like his mind was full of plans and elaborate ideas.

"Hi, big boy," she said with a smile.

"Wow, you look amazing," he said. His voice was low, deep. "Is that a new dress?"

"Yup, Samuels." Blake looked great tonight, a nice suit and new shoes. He'd spent more time than usual on his hair, Penny could tell.

"It's nice," he said as they walked to his car. He walked ahead and opened the door for her. Ever the Southern gentleman, and something few men did anymore. Somehow, the whole women's lib thing was lost on most men, Penny thought as she settled into the BMW's lush leather upholstery. We still want to be treated like a woman, right? We want a level playing field in life, but we still want to be treated with care. Most men didn't get that.

Chapter 5
Mirror

The band played their second set as Jessica and the others stood in a VIP area, and she nodded and pretended to converse with the people around her. The paps were scurrying around like rats, taking photos of Jessica and the CEO together.

She'd spent a half-hour meeting the band and avoiding the sweaty advances of Locklin. The CEO with the hairy ears had his own gaggle of hangers-on, and she'd started to feel sorry for him—right up to the point where he'd insisted she join him for dinner. She explained that she was tired, and unlike many men she'd met, he took the "no" with a degree of class.

Finally, Jessica slipped off to the ladies' room. She timed it to leave the VIP area just as "Dumpster Fire" was coming off stage for the second time, wrapping up their evening. All the paps rushed to stage left to catch pictures of the band, and Jessica bent down and covered her face with her hair and scooted away through a crowd of sweaty twenty-somethings, looking at the dirty floor between her feet, searching for the bathroom.

Most nice clubs and other happening places had a separate VIP bathroom, but this place didn't. Jessica would have to tell Scott to stop booking places that didn't have separate facilities. It was a joke, being forced to use the public bathroom. High-end places knew to keep the stars separate from the riff-raff. If this place didn't add private bathrooms, it wouldn't attract many celebs.

She found the bathroom and cut in at the front of the line, ignoring the shouts.

"Bitch! You can't just jump the line..."

Jessica Mills, Hollywood starlet extraordinaire, turned and looked straight at the girl. Half of the people in line gasped. Everywhere she went, people were always gasping. Maybe it was just because she was famous, or because these people finally had something interesting happen in their pitiful lives.

She looked at them and smiled, flipping her hair. "I gotta pee. You all don't mind, do you?"

The women in the line smiled and shook their heads. Even the girl who'd yelled at Jessica changed her tune. The girl at the front of the line, right where Jessica had cut in, shook her head. "It's fine. Go ahead, I don't mind."

Jessica turned and waited with a smile. Sometimes, fame was helpful.

When the door opened, she went inside the tiny, one-person bathroom and locked the door behind her. Jessica Mills did her business and then stood, looking in the dirty bathroom mirror, which was streaked with black paint and something that looked disturbingly like dried blood.

Close up, Jessica didn't really look like herself. Her hair was a mess, despite the fact that she had spent close to an hour on it earlier in the evening. Well, she hadn't spent an hour on her own hair. She had people for that. But now her once-perfect makeup, so expertly applied by Ferrara, was smudged and uneven. A line of wet mascara ran down one cheek.

At least in here, there were none of the telltale flashes of the paparazzi cameras. The photographers, swarming like rats, yelled out her name to get her to look in their direction for a photo. She never saw a penny, of course, but they acted like she worked for them.

She stood up from the sink slowly, unsteadily. She needed a Purple Monster, her other favorite drink. A good Tom Collins was fine, but Britney Spears' favorite concoction could turn any night around. Vodka, Red Bull and Nyquil. Elixir of the gods. Two or three of those could always keep Jessica moving and happy.

Finally, she turned to leave. Privacy for her was like a transient state of bliss. Like the feeling she got from a Purple Monster, it was short-lived. She unlatched the door and pulled it open.

Ignoring the women in line, Jessica searched for a door outside. She needed a smoke, and there were no smoking areas inside. Thanks, California.

Passing the bar, keeping her head down, Jessica found a back door. The cool blast of air that came in as it was being closed caught her attention. She moved in that direction, only to be stopped by a huge bouncer.

"Sorry, miss. No exit."

She looked up and his face changed.

"Oh, I'm sorry, Ms. Mills. I didn't recognize you."

"It's okay," she said, smiling. It was the most winning smile she could manage in her present mood. She leaned in, resting one hand on his thick arm. "Any chance I can duck out for just a minute? I would kill for a smoke."

The bouncer, a huge black man with a nametag that read "JESS," looked around. "I'm not supposed to, ma'am. Not allowed. It's an emergency exit. I'll get fired."

"You're not going to get fired."

The bouncer looked at her and smiled.

"You don't know my boss. He's kind of a dick."

"You're not gonna get fired. Worst of all, he'll yell at you."

Jess shook his head. "Nah, he'll fire me, just to make a point."

"What?"

"He'll make a point about me letting you in and you bringing in friends and how I broke the rules."

"So?"

He leaned down. "I need this job."

"I feel like I'm going to faint. It's so hot in here, isn't it?"

She could tell he was wavering, thinking about it, considering the options. He was looking around and she knew he was looking for his boss. She leaned closer. "Look," she said quietly. "No one is going to know." She touched his chest gingerly—that usually worked. "I'll be back in a minute. I just need a smoke."

Finally, Jess nodded and stepped aside. "Okay. Just knock when you want back in."

He smiled and let her out into the cool Los Angeles night.

Chapter 6
Smokes

Jessica Mills enjoyed three whole cigarettes, making them last.

It was a special treat, one she always had to sneak off to enjoy. Ferrara and Scott both frowned on her smoking. "It'll turn your teeth yellow," Ferrara would say.

Out in the chilly alley behind Liquid, it didn't matter. She was alone, and no one cared who she was. The dark alley was lined with barred doors and very few lights, trash skittering past her. The narrow road down the middle of the alley was cobblestoned, broken up only by a shallow gutter that ran along either side. Boxy trash dumpsters huddled together in the darkness.

The Tom Collins was really starting to kick in, and the beer, and the "refresher" of coke she'd enjoyed in the bathroom. Jessica was smart enough to not take bumps in public. What would the tabloids pay for a photo of her snorting coke?

Jessica took her time—it was at least twenty minutes before she was done. She wasn't excited to get back inside. Her third cigarette smoldered in her hand. Finally, she took a long drag on it, then dropped it to the sidewalk and stubbed it out with her high-heeled shoe.

Walking back to the emergency door, she knocked quietly. When there was no response, she knocked louder. She didn't want to get the bouncer in trouble—she'd already forgotten his name—but Jessica needed to get back inside.

Exasperated, she gave up. The guy must have wandered off—she could hear the thumping bass of the music as it vibrated the heavy metal door. She pulled on the handle, but the door would not budge.

Down the alley, she heard voices approaching, rough shouts.

"Shut up!" a man yelled.

A woman responded. "No, Jeffrey! I saw how she was all over you!"

"She was not. You're imagining things."

"And you're a douche-bag," the woman answered.

The people approached and Jessica turned away, moving off. She didn't want to get involved. She heard their voices fade out as the argument continued—apparently, the woman was drunk and they were searching for their car.

She realized, in a moment of sparkling clarity, that this wasn't a great neighborhood for her to be in, alone and wandering around half-drunk.

Jessica needed to get back into the club, so she started up the narrow alley that led back to the front of the building. Stepping off the curb, she walked up a street paved with cobblestones. It was hard to walk on, especially in heels. Who made roads like these?

After ten feet, she stumbled and fell onto the rough stones of the alley. She heard her dress tear, the hem ripping. One of her hands landed in mud.

"God DAMMIT," she said.

She crawled over and plopped down on the curb next to a light pole, her shoes in the dirty gutter. The concrete felt cold against the backs of her legs. The white dress was tight—the uniform in Los Angeles wasn't very creative—but poofed out at the bottom. Now it was torn as well. The gutter between her shoes stank of vomit and piss. She watched a rivulet of water flow beneath her heels and turned to watch the water run down the gutter and into a nearby sewer grate.

Thank God the paparazzi didn't see her fall, she thought. They'd get top money for a photo of that.

Finally, she stood again, rallying. The world swam around her, and she steadied herself against the light pole, brushing the mud and dirt from her torn dress. Her hair was in her eyes and her stomach felt heavy, queasy. Down the street, she heard more rough shouting. The man, yelling at his girl.

She started up the alley and remembered something. Squinting, she looked around.

"Where's my purse?"

Her clutch sat in the middle of the cobblestone road. How did it get all the way over there?

"Christ, there you are."

She didn't notice the headlights flashing down the alley to her left. If she had, Jessica would likely have discounted it as another pap who had finally found her and was taking pictures of her: dress torn, skinned knee, no purse.

Instead, Jessica was concentrating on walking, and her purse, and the cobblestones under her feet. She did okay for the first two or three steps, but then she stumbled sideways. As the car approached, she fell heavily into the middle of the road.

Chapter 7
Dinner

Blake Oleander wove the BMW through the narrow streets of downtown New Orleans. Rain had moved through the city, and the roads were slick and shiny.

"My sister Gertie loves to wear sundresses, and a large white bonnet," Blake said, settling into his favorite topic, his family. Penny thought there was something sweet about the way he always talked about them.

She glanced over at him, taking in his face, his hair, the scar that ran along his cheek. He'd said it was from a car accident when he was a kid. "She's the one that went off to California?"

"No, that's Paula, my other sister. Gertie loves sundresses, but Paula always wears bulky clothes, grays and blacks and the occasional burgundy. Goth, I guess you could say. She works for the Park Service in San Francisco. And Gertie's at Yale."

Penny nodded, barely following. He talked about them a lot. It was clear he came from a moneyed family, like the way he just casually mentioned that his sister was attending an Ivy League school. Of course, rich boyfriends weren't hard to find in New Orleans.

They were driving through the fanciest part of NOLA and every house was huge, much bigger than the group home Penny shared with six other girls. These were the families that have been rich since the war. And, in New Orleans, when anyone talked about the "war," they meant the Civil War. These were monied families with enough wealth to last generations.

But Blake was nice. Quiet, a little strange, but nice.

It was their eighth date and she liked him. So far, he'd been respectful, a nice change from the louts and sex-crazed hounds she'd been meeting on Tinder. They pawed at you like dogs. Penny didn't know where things might end up with Blake, but at least he didn't seem like a total creeper. He did have a weird fixation with Jessica Mills, the Hollywood starlet. What kind of grown man had posters of her on their bedroom walls?

They slowed in front of a massive gray and white Victorian mansion on Ryder Street and Penny realized they were parking in front of his family home. It was a huge, multi-storied, gabled hulk that looked like it had been soaked in money and time. She'd been here several times, always sneaking in the back and up to his room, and had never gotten a good look at the front of the house. The inside of the place smelled stuffy and old, like it needed a good airing out.

"I thought we were going to dinner first," Penny said, giving him a knowing smile. She was fine with skipping right to the screwing, if that was what he was up for, but she wouldn't have minded a nice meal first.

"Oh, sorry," he said, parking. "I thought we'd walk over to Bourbon from here. Save time with parking. It's only three blocks, then back here for drinks after?"

She glanced over and saw the lights of Bourbon Street in the humid night, not realizing how close his family home was to this part of the French Quarter. "Oh, that's fine. I didn't realize it was so close."

"Plus, I have a surprise for you," he teased, smiling.

"Oh? Do tell."

"Not yet. But it's a good one. Don't worry."

He locked the car and they walked, hand in hand, leaving his family home behind. They strolled the two blocks over and one up to Three Sisters, talking and enjoying the humid evening.

The restaurant was packed, but, of course, Blake had made a reservation.

Dinner was great. He spent most of the time talking about his parents. It was clear how important family was to him, if only based on the fact that the topic dominated every conversation. And she was happy to listen—they were nice, his family stories, although they often veered into the darker aspects of human nature.

His mother, an elderly matriarch from an old New Orleans family, always wore black and apparently had a thing for hats, frilly numbers that she balanced precariously atop her head. Blake went on and on about her hat closet, a room she'd had specially built for them. Penny wondered what it was like to be that rich.

Blake's impressions of his late father were different, quieter. Apparently, the man had died ten years ago or so. Penny could tell Blake was affected by the man's passing, a story he'd touched on before. Tonight, she got the unabridged version as they enjoyed their etouffee and escargot.

Blake's father hadn't been born wealthy—he'd come from the "swamps." That was the term people used for families that grew up in the rural areas north and west of New Orleans, families that lived off the land and scraped together whatever life they could. Jon Oleander, Blake's father, was in the gator business, a weird and uniquely "bayou" occupation that involved raising, breeding, and training gators. Few people seemed to have a knack for it.

Jon was good at it, though, and good enough to establish himself as a going concern with several employees. People sourced gators from the Oleanders for shows and exhibitions, and called them when wild gators needed catching or killing. Jon grew the business, buying out competitors and creating a name for himself. It was at some point that he became well-off enough to start dating the eligible daughters of the rich. He ended up marrying Blake's mother—and into her wealthy family, the family that had owned the beautiful mansion on Ryder Street for several generations.

When he finally got to Jon's tragic death, she'd interrupted, even though she was curious.

"Blake, you don't have to," she said, setting down her drink and taking his hand. "If it's too much..."

He looked up at her, his eyes shiny. "No, I need to tell you. Tonight is important."

"Why?"

"It's part of the surprise."

She nodded, unsure of what to say. She'd heard bits and pieces before, but not the whole thing. Should Penny push him, or let him come out with it in his own time? Finally, her curiosity was too much. "What happened to your father?"

His smile faded. Blake went back to eating, and Penny started to think maybe she'd pushed too hard.

"They were in the swamps near Jackson," Blake said finally, setting his shrimp fork aside. "They were tracking a group of gators that had been hassling some farms in the area. They had them pinned into a creek, and Dad's second-in-charge, an old swamper named Tarn, was driving the gators toward Dad, who had a long pole with a loop of rope on the end."

"Tarn?"

"Yeah, I don't know," Blake said. "Bayou people have weird names. Anyway, Dad was using the snare pole—that's what they call them— and Tarn was waving an ax around to scare the gators. Tarn slips on the mud, swings the ax. Catches Dad right in the face."

"Oh, no."

Blake nodded. "He bled to death before Tarn could get him to a hospital."

The rest of the dinner was quiet. He asked Penny about her job at the gallery, about what it was like to live with six other young women in a group home. He seemed most fascinated with the bathroom sharing, and wanted to know how they decided who got it when. Blake also smiled like an imp and pressed her for stories of when Penny saw the other girls naked or walked in on them in the shower. Men. Even when they were polite and thoughtful, they could still be pigs.

They finished up dinner and Penny offered to pay. She didn't always make the men pay—it made her feel like she owed them some tail. But Blake got the better of her, as usual. It turned out his family had a running "tab" at this and several other downtown restaurants. There was no bill. "They just send us an invoice every few months," he said with a flippant air that betrayed how entitled he was—and just how clueless he was about it.

Penny let it go. She followed him out, passing a line of people waiting to get in the exclusive restaurant. They looked at Penny and Blake with envious eyes, making her smile. Tina was wrong—this place was popular with locals as well as tourists.

She took his arm as they walked away, thinking they did make a handsome couple. She smiled to herself—she sounded like her mother.

Chapter 8
High Heels

Jeffrey was ignoring his girlfriend.

He'd finally found his car where he'd left it, parked in a dark lot behind a nearby clothing store and around the corner from the nightclub. He'd been momentarily happy that his car hadn't been towed, but it wasn't worth it. She wasn't worth it. And now she wouldn't let up.

"I saw her, Jeffrey! I saw that waitress giving you her phone number!" She was in the seat next to him, drunk and pissed and fired up. She slapped at him, at the dashboard, at everything.

"No, no," he answered, trying to keep his voice calm. Why were women allowed to hit and slap without consequence? "I asked her for a napkin after you spilled your drink. I was cleaning up—"

"YOU'RE A LIAR!!"

Jeffrey shook his head and turned down the narrow, cobblestone street that ran next to Liquid. They'd left after she'd made her scene, but she was still yelling and screaming. Jeffrey liked her, or had liked her for the last few weeks, but maybe he needed to rethink this relationship. She was fun most of the time, but she couldn't handle her liquor. He drove the car up the alley, accelerating. Jeffrey wanted to end the date as quickly as possible.

"She didn't give me her number, I promise you."

"I don't CARE," she said, slurring the last word like she was trying to sing. "You can just go home with her if you want. Bang her all you want. I don't care anymore, you're such a—WATCH OUT!"

He had glanced over at her and looked back at the narrow alley and saw a shape lying in the street, a ghostly figure in white. Jeffrey yanked the wheel, acting completely by reflex. The car turned hard, missing the shape in the road and swerving, glancing off a light pole and crashing head-long into the brick wall of the neighboring building.

Jeffrey's head hit the steering wheel with enough impact to trigger the airbag. He had just enough time to see his girlfriend's head slam into the windshield of the car—she hadn't put on her seatbelt—before everything went to black.

Chapter 9
A Mansion

It was cooler outside now, after the rain, and Blake offered Penny his jacket as they walked home. The streets of New Orleans were full of people, noisy and happy, and they passed several clubs. Jazz poured out of open doors and windows, fighting for attention. Drunks stumbled over the rough cobblestone streets. One slept his bender off in a doorway.

"Thanks for letting me talk so much tonight," Blake said as they strolled back to his family home. "I've dated girls in the past, obviously, but it's never really worked out with any of them. They never let me get a word in edgewise," he said, looking at her. "They never wanted to listen."

"What happened to them?"

"Didn't work out," he said simply. "I still see a few of them once in a while. Now they let me talk as much as I want."

Penny nodded, not really understanding. It seemed to be Blake's way—sometimes he'd be talking about someone from his past and get things confused, like he was talking about them in the present.

"So, what's the surprise? I can't wait any longer."

He grabbed Penny's hand and looked over at her.

"Okay, don't freak out, but I'd like you to meet some of my family tonight."

Her stomach did a little flip. Penny liked to think of herself as a free spirit, dating whomever she pleased. She wasn't ready to settle down, not by a long shot, and she'd already turned down a grand total of four marriage proposals so far at the ripe old age of 25. Momma said to be picky and never settle.

Meeting his family? Blake was clearly more serious about this relationship than she was, and Penny felt a shiver of dread run down her back. She would have to think about this more when she got home.

She didn't say any of this, of course. Men were simple, easily offended. They called women the fairer sex, but a man's confidence could be destroyed with a stray word or even an odd look.

"Sounds good," she said finally.

I'll meet them, Penny thought. Be pleasant, say, "hi," tell them a little bit about me, say nice things about Blake. I won't mention that I have a date tomorrow night with a man named Tony, or mention Tony's fascination with urban exploration. They were planning to sneak into the old abandoned Six Flags amusement park on the southern side of New Orleans. The place had flooded in 2005, during Hurricane Katrina, and now it was an overgrown, abandoned mess.

Some people said it was haunted, but Tony didn't care. The man liked to have sex in weird places, mostly outdoors, and Penny was happy to oblige him. It was exciting. She was looking forward to it. Hey, a girl had to sample life before she settled down, right? Get out there and live a little, Momma always said. Just don't forget the Big Three.

Penny was pretty sure neither Blake nor his family would appreciate hearing about her adventurous nature in general or tomorrow's sexual itinerary with Tony in particular. "Yes, Mrs. Oleander, it's going to be so much fun. We're hoping to sneak into the park and bang like rabbits in the old bumper car pavilion."

It was quiet as they walked, Blake leaving Penny alone with her thoughts, only speaking up after a half-block of silence.

"Oh, and don't freak out, but one of my ex-girlfriends might be there tonight," he said. "She was mother's favorite, but don't worry. You've got nothing to worry about. Not anymore."

It was an odd comment and a potentially awkward situation, but Penny let it go. She was thinking about Tony and her date the next evening and how much fun she was going to have.

After a moment, Penny set her mind to wrapping up this evening with Blake as quickly as possible. Introducing her to the family? It was too soon. She decided to be polite, and cute, and say all the right things. Maybe she'd give Blake a goodbye bang, just to be nice. One for the road, so to speak.

They walked the last block to the front of the house—it looked even bigger from this direction, squatting in the middle of a huge yard. Penny noticed for the first time how tangled the yard was with plants and vines and an overgrown Magnolia tree that leaned out over Ryder Street.

She headed for the front door, assuming if she was meeting the family, Blake wouldn't be sneaking her in the back way, but he turned and headed around the back anyway.

"Why don't we just go in the front?"

He shook his head. "They're still having dinner. We'll join them for dessert."

In her previous visits, she and Blake had always entered through the kitchen, taking the servant stairs up to his room on the second floor. People around here stilled call them the "servant stairs." It showed you how little things had progressed, all right. Blake had told her that all the old houses in this part of town apparently had a second, narrower staircase in the back of the house for the "help." Used first by slaves, then by the live-in house staff that had replaced them.

Blake walked up the ornate brick pathway that looped around the back of the house. Penny passed the huge jasmine and lavender bushes that screened the backyard from the street. The fragrance was insanely powerful, and she stopped to smell them again. This was always her favorite part of coming here.

"Come on," he yelled, disappearing around the back.

Penny followed him reluctantly, grabbing a branch of lavender and pulling it free, smelling it as she followed.

The back of the house was as impressive as the front: a wide, sweeping yard with a pool and two other small buildings. The pool was green and brackish. The overgrown gardens stretched to the far stone wall. Closer to the house, natty rose bushes ringed the broken panes of a dilapidated greenhouse. It was all like something out of some twisted fairy tale.

Penny followed him to the double doors—he was holding them open for her. They went through a foyer/mudroom into a massive kitchen. It was old school, and she noticed the equipment for the first time. Every other time she'd been through this room, it had been dark, and the lights were out.

"Wait here," he said, and he disappeared off into another room.

Penny leaned on the massive kitchen island and stared at the wide cabinets. This was the kind of kitchen designed a hundred years ago and meant for feeding twenty or thirty people at once. You could run a catering business out of this empty, underused space. There were two refrigerators and three ovens, and the stove had eight burners. Newer appliances had been added over time, including dishwashers and what looked like a new, massive stainless-steel ice machine. It was the only new appliance in the place—but how much ice did one family really need?

Beyond the kitchen, Penny could see doors leading into what she assumed was the dining room. She could hear classical music coming from the other room.

There was movement off to her left and Penny turned. Blake was there, smiling, and he took her into his arms. He looked excited, like he was getting ready to kiss her. Instead, Blake's hand came up and he put something wet over her nose and mouth, holding it there tight.

Surprised, it took Penny a moment to start pushing him away. Chemicals burned her eyes. She realized the fumes were coming from the fabric covering her mouth and nose. The world went fuzzy around the edges. She pried at his fingers, but her knees buckled and the room went black.

CHAPTER 10
Alley

The elder cop, Hanson, leaned over, nodding at the young woman in the back of the nearby police car. She looked very familiar. Hanson did a double-take and looked at his partner, Ramirez.

"Is that—"

"Yup," Ramirez said, nodding. "In the flesh."

"What happened?"

Ramirez nodded and pointed his pen at the cobblestone alley. He'd been writing notes. "She shoulda died. Seriously. Car came down here, high rate of speed," he said, waving his pen. The car was half-buried in a wall of bricks, which had partially collapsed on the hood of the car.

"Swerved to miss the light pole?"

Ramirez nodded. "Last second. Took out part of the wall. Mills was in the middle of the road, passed out. Good thing they swerved."

Hanson nodded. "I don't want anyone famous dying on my watch."

"Your watch? You just got here."

Ramirez went back to his notes, and Hanson walked over to the EMTs, who were still working to extract a female passenger trapped in the car that had gone into the wall. They were using the Jaws of Life to tear off the door to get to her. A man was on a nearby stretcher, being checked by two more EMTs.

"What we got?"

One of the EMTs stepped over. "Face to steering wheel," he said, pointing at the man on the stretcher. The EMTs were bandaging his face prior to transport and starting an IV. "Broken nose, facial lacerations, blood loss. He'll be fine once we get him stable. The woman's another story—they're extricating her now. Not looking good. Least she didn't bleed out."

"Seatbelt?"

The EMT shook his head. "Went into the windshield. They were probably doing 30, 35."

Hanson looked at the alley. "In this space?"

"Yeah, he was accelerating. On the upside, she was drunk and didn't tense up. No broken arms, so she didn't brace for impact. Probably didn't even see it coming."

"She gonna live?"

"Dunno," the EMT said. "We're leaving as soon as they get her out. We'll try to stabilize en route."

"I'll call the tow. What about Mills?" Hanson asked, nodding at the cop car.

"She's fine," the EMT said. "Not a scratch. They swerved or she'd be dead."

Hanson made a face. "Gotta love being famous, right? She'll get a slap on the wrist," he said. "Happens all the time."

"Yup, the Hollywood shuffle. Happens too much, you ask me," the EMT said, looking at the woman in the back of the cop car. "Oh, driver asked about the ghost."

"The ghost?"

"Yeah, said he saw a ghost in the road. That's why he swerved."

Hanson nodded at Mills. "White dress. Probably saved her life."

Hanson walked back over to the cop cars blocking the alley. Ramirez was off canvassing the gathered spectators, and getting any pictures they might have taken. Hanson doubted if any of them would be helpful. In most of these types of accidents, people didn't see or remember much. Ramirez also shooed off the paparazzi, keeping them away from the car holding the Hollywood starlet.

Hanson radioed in for a tow truck and watched as the EMTs finished extracting the woman passenger. Hanson had to agree with their assessment—she didn't look good. He wondered if she'd even make it to the hospital. The EMTs loaded both of the injured into the waiting ambulance and pulled out, roaring away down the narrow street, siren screaming.

Ramirez walked back over, and Hanson nodded at the cop car.

"You done with her yet? We releasing her?"

The Hispanic cop shook his head and smiled. "No. Drunk and disorderly, at least. Waiting for the DA to call me back. Sometimes they don't want these kinds of cases to touch the books, but I don't see how they avoid that this time. Found this in her purse."

Ramirez held up something to the light: a small bag of white powder. The elder cop whistled. It was a decent amount, maybe enough for Intent to Distribute.

Chapter 11
Cooler

Jessica was scared.

For the first time in a long time, she wasn't sure what was going to happen next.

She was sitting alone on a bench attached to the back wall of a cold jail cell. The cell was surrounded by bars that had been painted mint green at some point in the past, but the paint had faded over time and now the poles looked whitish-blue, the color of melted ice cream. Jessica could hear people moving around in the other cells around her, but she couldn't see anyone else. It wasn't like in the movies with bars between the cells – here, concrete walls separated them.

In the movies, prisoners were always talking to each other, passing stuff back and forth. This was different. Lonely.

It had only been a couple of hours ago that she'd been at Liquid, introducing the vodka CEO and complaining about her life to Ferrara.

Jessica didn't want to go back to Passages. She'd been there, twice. The Ford Clinic, more. She'd hated them, and the other "rest" places she'd gone to, but they had to be better than sitting here. The floor was cold, and the cops had taken her shoes. Jessica had tried to curl her legs up underneath her on the bench to get them under the dress, but the wooden bench was too hard and uncomfortable. And she knew better than to ask for a blanket—this wasn't like flying first class on British Air. Asking for something would only make the cops hate her more.

She looked out of the cell but all she could see was the corridor and the empty cell across the way. She wasn't completely alone. She heard occasional coughs, and snatches of low conversation drifting in from somewhere. Earlier, someone had been crying. Jessica sat with nothing to do and no one to talk to. She kept absentmindedly reaching for her purse and her phone before realizing she had neither.

Another thing that was different from the movies: Jessica hadn't been put into the same cell with a big muscled lady to "rough her up" and get her to talk. The "sugar" in her purse would probably be enough to get her into big trouble, along with causing that accident.

She hoped the people in that car were okay.

Two hours ago, she'd had everything. And now all she had was her white Vera Wang dress. Torn at the hem, probably ruined. At least it wasn't like that Oscar de la Renta she'd ruined at the Emmy's last year with a spilled cranberry tonic. The paps had loved that one.

Jessica smoothed the dress out on her lap and tried to contain her anxiety. The alcohol and coke in her system had seemingly evaporated once she was booked. She felt completely coherent—and scared. She'd been in and out of jail cells before, but it had always been with people she knew. And only for a short amount of time.

And tonight, the cops had treated her differently. In her past "incidents," of which there had been several, they were usually pleasant. Almost reverent. She guessed cops could be starstruck just the same as anyone else. But tonight had been different. The EMTs had checked her for injuries, and she only had a scraped knee from her fall to the ground. One of the EMTs had chuckled, like it was a joke.

And after the cops had read back to her the history of her infractions over the last few years, they dropped their façade of politeness. They went from treating her as a troubled celebrity to how she assumed they treated "actual" criminals: cuffed and put into the back of the police car without any concern over her comfort.

Jessica had a nagging feeling growing in her stomach. It was as if the police were done treating her like a famous person. She'd heard about this—cops had a certain leeway in the way they treated people. Maybe she'd burned through all her chances. When she'd complained that the cuffs were too tight and digging into her wrists, the older cop had laughed at her.

Jessica wasn't used to being dismissed.

She was used to people thinking she couldn't act, or following her around and living off her money. Every star she knew in Hollywood dealt with impostor syndrome—it came with the territory. And everyone had a "crew," right? Publicists, agents, friends, family. "Team Jessica." Folks to carry things and arrange for things and set up things—meetings, auditions, people to "get the car" and fend off the paparazzi rats. And yes, sometimes, people to arrange for "special needs," things like what the cops had found in Jessica's purse. It had been a long time since she had procured her own drugs. She wouldn't even know where to go anymore—she had people for that. Everyone did, right? Sometimes it was good to have a cushion between you and the real world.

Jessica rubbed her wrists—they were sore, red from the cuffs. She'd have to remember that the next time she had a "jail" scene. Screenwriters never got all the details right. It was why actors shadowed actual people to prep for roles—you couldn't read a script and learn to "be" a fly fisherman or professional tennis player. Of course, you couldn't actually "be" any of those things, but you could pick up enough mannerisms and tics and terminology to fake it. Half of acting class was trying to learn how to tap into your natural abilities or pick up new ones from those around you. The other half was learning to cry on command, it seemed.

Jessica looked around the cell, reaching for her phone again to check Instagram and realizing for the hundredth time that they had taken it. She was cut off. No one could help her, and none of her "friends" were around to cushion her from the world.

For the first time in a long time, Jessica was on her own.

CHAPTER 12
Room for One More

Penny Halderson woke up sometime later, her mouth full of a weird taste.

She had no idea how long it had been since Blake had surprised her by holding something wet and cold to her face. Her nose was still burning from whatever the chemical was.

Her eyes were covered, and she realized she was tied up in a sitting position. She struggled to get free of the ropes that were wrapped around her arms and legs. They were too thick; she couldn't make them budge. Penny moved her head and neck around as much as she could. There was fabric pulled tight across her mouth.

She stopped struggling for a moment to calm herself. Obviously, Blake had knocked her out, probably with some kind of fumes, and tied her up.

Maybe it was a sex thing, and maybe the whole thing with his family was a fake-out. Maybe Blake was kinkier than he'd let on, and maybe they were in his room and he was getting things ready for a raunchy bit of the old in-and-out.

But Penny didn't think so.

This was wrong, different. She could hear classical music and wondered if she was in the dining room. Why would she be tied up if she was meeting his family?

Stay calm, Penny told herself. Keep your wits about you, find your purse. Find your mace.

She stopped struggling with the ropes and concentrated on the room around her. She could smell food now. Pie, she thought, and coffee. And something else, overpowering, a different smell under everything else. And lavender.

Penny leaned over, finding that she could bend at the waist, and touched something with her forehead. It was warm and squishy and turned the blindfold over her eyes scarlet. A red stain spread across her vision. The blindfold was made of thin fabric—if she could get it off, maybe she could see.

Penny bent over, more to the side this time, and felt a flat, hard surface with her forehead. A table, maybe. Wooden. Dishes, clinking as she brushed against them. A thick sprig of something itchy, bushy. Lavender. Was it the bunch she'd pulled free of the bush outside?

Finally, she found the edge of the table and started scraping the blindfold against the surface, turning her head from side to side, working it free. The fabric slipped away from her eyes and settled around her neck.

Penny sat up and looked around her. It took her a second to realize what she was looking at. She felt all the blood drain out of her face. Instantly, Penny went cold, numb.

Terrified.

She was tied to a seat, her wooden chair at one end of an ornate, massive dining room table. There were nine other seats around the table. Only the seat at the far end was empty—all the others were occupied.

Everyone else around the table was dead.

Four to her left, four to her right. Rotting. All in varying states of decomposition. All of their heads turned toward her. Some of them stared at Penny with dead eyes. Others stared with only the empty sockets where their eyes had once been.

Penny recognized Blake's father first. It was hard to miss him. He was seated on the left, at the far end. He was dead, a large rusty ax sticking out of the front of his head. The blade was buried in his skull so far that the pointy edge of the blade poked out through where his left eye should have been. He was dressed in ratty, mud-covered coveralls.

She stared at the dead man for a long moment, trying to understand.

Her attention was drawn to the figure next to Blake's father. It was Blake's mother, immediately recognizable by her huge floppy hat, sitting at a jaunty angle. Her rotten arms rested on either side of a formal place setting, and Penny realized the whole table was set with fancy china. There was a fresh piece of pie and a steaming cup of coffee on the table in front of each person, including herself. She looked down and saw the impression of her forehead in the piece of cherry pie. A fresh cup of coffee steamed beside her plate, next to the sprig of lavender.

Penny shook her head, trying to loosen the gag in her mouth. Blake's sisters were also there, watching, seated next to their parents, all on Penny's left. They looked like Blake had described, but both were long dead. Paula, the large sister, had twigs and leaves in her hair. The body closest to Penny was probably Gertie—she was wearing a sundress. It was hard to be sure—there was no head.

Penny grabbed at the ropes again, leaning over and knocking a fork into her lap. She struggled to lean around, bending awkwardly, then got it into one of her hands. She desperately started sawing at the rope.

While she sawed, Penny looked at the figures along the right side of the table. Three young women and a man dressed in a FedEx uniform. They were all dead, of course, but they looked "fresher," if that was the word. All of them were tied up, just like Penny. One looked familiar. She had been strangled—there were red and black bruises around her neck. The other two women were just dead, with no signs of how they ended up that way. The FedEx guy had a plastic bag tied snuggly over his face, which wore an expression of absolute terror.

Penny heard a commotion in the kitchen and the double doors opened. Blake walked in, smiling, then stopped when he realized she was looking at him.

"Oh, Penny. You couldn't wait? I wanted to surprise—"

"LET ME GO!!," Penny screamed, but it came out muffled by the gag in her mouth. She struggled against the ropes as he took the open seat at the head of the table.

"It's like I said at dinner. I wanted you to meet my family," Blake said, pouring half-and-half into his coffee and stirring it ornately with a silver spoon, one pinkie raised. "The coffee is fresh, by the way. Do you want some half and half?"

"NO!"

He looked at her. "That's fine, but you don't have to be rude. Especially in front of my parents. I thought you wanted to meet my family."

"YOU ARE A FREAK!" She screamed, but the words were lost in the gag. Penny struggled with the fork, continuing to work it across the rope that ran over her lap. She needed to get free, to get away—

"I wanted you to meet them, Penny. Here they are," Blake said, waving at them as if she hadn't already noticed the rotting carcasses arranged around the table like a dinner party from hell.

Penny played along, nodding, as Blake pointed around the table and introduced each person, launching into a detailed story about each of them.

After a few minutes, Penny finally managed to cut through the rope.

While he was pointing at his parents, explaining how they thought he would never be able to find a "suitable woman" with his scarred face, Penny jerked the chair back and tried to stand, but her legs were tied to the chair legs and she fell. She pulled her gag out and screamed as loud as she ever had in her life. She saw Blake's legs under the table as he stood and walked around and kicked her in the stomach, knocking the wind from her.

"Oh, you're not leaving. You're the honored guest, Penny. That's why you're at this end of the table. Don't make me drug you again." He pulled her up and placed her back in her chair, retying the ropes. Penny struggled, trying to head-butt him, but Blake laughed.

"No need for that, dear."

"Screw you, asshole."

Walking back to his end of the table, Blake sat down. Behind his chair, Penny noticed a large poster of Jessica Mills on the wall. He'd painted a huge red heart around her face.

"Watch your language, please. I want Mother to like you." He ran one hand down the scar on his face. "She's convinced I'll never get married, not with a face like this. But I will. You'll see."

He looked at Penny as if expecting her to answer, but she just shook her head.

"Okay, I'll start again," he said. Blake talked and sipped at his coffee, going into excruciating detail about what really happened to each of his family members, how he had killed them, how he had preserved their bodies. His father hadn't been killed by a friend while they trapped gators. Blake had hit him with the ax in their back yard, catching his father unawares near the rose bushes. They had fought about the broken window, the one that had given Blake his scar.

His mother and sisters had died at his hands as well, Gertie decapitated and Paula starved to death. Blake had stuffed Paula's dead body with straw to make her fat because that's how he liked to remember her.

"You...you need to let me out of here," she said.

Blake talked on and on and Penny started to cry. Momma had always said it was the easiest way to control a situation, especially with men, but it didn't work in this case. Blake seemed to enjoy it. He seemed inspired by it.

"I thought you'd like to meet some of my old girlfriends," he said, nodding at the young women on Penny's right. "Like I said, it didn't work out with them. Mother didn't like them. She's a big fan of Jessica Mills," Blake said. "Maybe she'll like you, too."

Penny nodded, her energy flagging. "I hope so," she said quietly. She doubted he even heard the sarcasm, her last vestige of willfulness.

"Me too," he said, sipping his coffee and nodding at the woman next to her. "But you already know one of them, of course."

Penny turned, shocked. As if she could be shocked further. She looked closely at the young woman seated directly to her right. She was attractive, familiar.

Becca.

She hadn't moved to Virginia. She'd been dating some guy and now she was here and she was dead and...

"Becca had some very nice things to say about you," Blake said with a smile. "She talked a lot, especially at the end. She said you were the nicest one at the group house. I put all her things in the basement. I'll put your things down there, too, once I collect it."

Penny looked up at him and he smiled and she began to sob. Not to manipulate, not to try to get him to do what she wanted. Penny cried because all hope was lost, and she knew it.

Blake nodded and picked up his steaming cup of coffee, waving it at her like he was offering a toast.

"Welcome, Penny. Welcome to the family. We're so glad you could join us."

CHAPTER 13
Judged

The next morning, Jessica Mills woke up, rubbing her eyes. Someone was coming.

She sat up from the hard, wooden bench, momentarily confused. Then she remembered where she was. The jail cell and the torn dress brought everything back.

It had been a scary night—noises, people crying, someone shouting to be let out. The cops had let her out to use the bathroom twice—other than that, she'd seen and talked to no one. It was brighter now in the hallway, daytime. Morning. Jessica heard familiar voices approaching, talking loudly, and stood, straightening her torn dress.

Two men came around the corner, Scott and Aaron Skilling, her attorney. She rarely saw Aaron unless things had gone south.

"You left me in here all night?" Jessica yelled, hearing the panic in her voice.

Aaron and Scott were followed by a guard. Aaron ignored Jessica and turned to the guard. "Can we get her out of there? We're due in the judge's chambers in ten minutes."

The cop nodded and produced a heavy set of keys that looked like they were straight out of a movie.

"Guys, what's going on?"

Aaron looked at her. "Stay quiet for now, Jessica."

The cop turned the lock and pulled the door open. Jessica started to say something but then thought better of it. She began to walk out into the hall, but the cop stopped her.

"She's supposed to be cuffed."

Jessica looked at Aaron, making a face.

Scott shook his head. "Her? Is that really necessary? Do you know who she is?"

Aaron cleared his throat and gave Scott a look that shut him up. Aaron turned to the cop and nodded soberly.

"That's fine. But we need to hurry."

The cop pulled cuffs from his belt and slapped them on her with a thin smile. As if she could feel worse.

They started off, Jessica following Scott and Aaron, the guard walking next to Jessica. They passed through a glass corridor that led from the jail itself to another building. They passed through two more sets of doors, the last guarded by another cop, who gave Jessica a funny look.

Inside the second building, the halls and rooms were much nicer. The halls were marble, old school.

"Wow, this place is straight out of L.A. Law," Scott said. "Awesome."

Nobody answered him. They walked into a clean, white-walled room with a table and chairs. Aaron waited until the guard was gone, pulling the door closed behind him, before setting his briefcase down on the stark, metal table.

"Aaron," Jessica started, sitting down. "What the hell is going on here? I've never had to stay the night—"

"Jessica, you're in trouble," Aaron said, sitting across from her.

"I was in a cell all night. You couldn't get me out sooner—"

"Jessica, I need you to calm down," Aaron said, looking at her soberly. "First, how much is still in your system? They drug tested you when you came in."

"Is that even legal?" Scott asked.

"I don't know," she said, sitting back. "I'm straight now."

"Scared straight," Scott said, trying to lighten the mood. "Am I right?"

"Scott, shut up or I'll have you removed," Aaron said, pulling open his briefcase and taking out a thin sheaf of papers. "Jessica, we have to talk."

"No duh."

He looked at her. "I read the police report. It's bad. You were in possession of a large amount of cocaine. Is that right?"

"I wouldn't say it was a large amount. Like a weekend's worth, okay?"

"This isn't funny, Jessica," Aaron said. "Most celebrity cases never get to this point. They rarely stay overnight. But you did."

"I know that, Aaron," she started to say. "And you should have—"

"And you have a hearing in front of a judge in five minutes. On a Sunday, which means the judge made a point of coming in. I've only had two other situations that went in front of a judge. Usually, the cases get diverted and are handled by the LAPD liaison."

"What does all that mean?" She leaned forward, setting her cuffed hands on the table in front of her.

Aaron shook his head. "I don't know. We're in a gray area here. The LAPD hate prosecuting celebrities," he said, speaking quickly. "They have diversion for that. The county prosecutors don't like cases like this. Too public. Most times, celebs do rehab or house arrest. Very rarely are they sent to any kind of detention, and then it's only minimum-security."

She sat back, shaking her head. "Wait. You're scaring me, Aaron. Why are you talking about jail—"

"Because this is serious. And the judge—she asked for the case. Remember Judge Watkins? She presided over your last two hearings."

"So?"

"She's taken an interest."

Scott piped up. "That sounds bad."

"It is," Aaron said.

"So, when can I get out of here?"

Aaron shook his head slowly. "You're not getting out. Not today, at least."

"What?"

Scott leaned in. "Aaron, she's got an interview in four hours at KTLA, Channel 5. For the movie."

"She's not going to make it," Aaron said, not even looking up. He flipped open the pages and pointed at something. "Here. This says seven times, Jessica. Is that right?"

Scott leaned over. "What?"

"She's been arrested seven times?"

Jessica nodded soberly, not looking at the report Aaron was showing her. She didn't need to read it. She'd lived it.

"The other times, the cops were lenient. Even when you tested positive for coke, they let you off with warnings as long as you went to rehab. Right?"

"Yes."

He scanned the papers. "Betty Ford, Passages. Once at a place in Palm Springs."

She nodded. Suddenly, Jessica didn't feel like talking.

Aaron looked at her. "I'm assuming they didn't take."

"Aaron, be nice," Scott said quietly. "Don't poke the bear."

It was quiet in the room for a moment. No one spoke.

Scott broke the silence again. "But I don't understand. Everyone in Hollywood parties. I heard some starlet used to drive drunk on the

101 and the cops would give her an escort—"

"That's a myth," Aaron said. "And there's a difference between 'partiers' and drug abusers."

"I'm not an abuser," she said quietly. "I just...I have a lot going on. I needed a break."

Aaron started to say something, then thought better of it. "Look, you don't need lectures from me, Jessica. You're an adult, you know what you're doing. And you've been in this industry long enough to know how things go."

She nodded, not saying anything.

"Some people can handle their drugs," Aaron continued. "But for some, it spirals out of control and they end up dead on the sidewalk in front of a friend's club." He didn't have to say it, but they all knew what he was talking about. Actor River Phoenix OD'ed in 1993 and died on the sidewalk in front of the Viper Room, a happening place partly owned by his childhood friend, Johnny Depp.

There was a knock at the door and the bailiff, a huge black man, leaned in.

"Judge Watkins is ready."

Jessica looked at Aaron.

"What do I say?"

He put a hand up and stood, collecting his papers. "Nothing. Stay quiet. I'll handle it."

They followed the bailiff out and down a small hallway. A doorway led them into a massive, wood-paneled courtroom. She'd never been in a real court—the only ones she'd ever seen were fake ones, sets for TV shows. Judge Judy, places like those. She'd seen plenty, temporary constructions, like everything else in the TV world. Those smelled like every other set she'd ever been on—fresh-cut lumber and coffee.

This place was different. The place smelled old and official, like musty books and old papers. It stank of hopelessness and broken dreams.

Off to her right, Jessica recognized Judge Watkins. She was seated behind a large desk on a raised area. It was much fancier than a TV courtroom. On the wall above the judge, ornate, ominous words had been carved in marble: "JUSTICE WILL BE DONE."

The judge looked down at them as they entered. Aaron directed them to one side of the room, and Jessica recognized it as the table where defendants sat. Another woman, a fierce-looking lady with a tight face, sat at the other table. Next to her was the older cop from last night. He gave Jessica a smile she didn't like.

"Called to order," the bailiff announced, standing, and the prosecutor and cop stood. Jessica and her team hadn't even sat down yet and remained standing. Judge Watkins nodded and spoke into a microphone on the desk in front of her. "On today, July 29th, 2012, official proceedings by the State of California, County of Los Angeles shall be conducted. All come forward and be heard. The court is now in session, case number 4583921-4, State of California v. Jessica Mills. The Honorable Judge Watkins presiding. Be seated."

Sitting, Jessica felt a chill run up her back. This was the real deal. Hearing her name read out like that, in open court…it wasn't good. At least there weren't any photographers in here. Wouldn't they love a photo of her in handcuffs? Jessica glanced around—there was no one else in the courtroom. Scott always said all publicity is good publicity, but right now, she didn't agree.

"At this time, the Court calls this matter to order," Judge Watkins spoke for the first time, looking down at them. "Will the parties state their affiliations for the record, please?"

The prosecutor stood. "Thank you, your honor. The State of California appears by Assistant District Attorney Tarah Simmons. I appear in this case as prosecutor."

Watkins nodded as she sat, then looked at Aaron. Jessica started to stand as well, unsure of what to do, but he pushed her down into her seat. "Ms. Jessica Mills appears, your honor, with her attorney, Aaron Skilling. I will be acting as defense." He nodded and sat.

Judge Wilkins held up a sheaf of papers. "Has the defendant received a copy of the Complaint in this matter?"

"We have, your honor," Aaron answered, standing again. "We received a signed copy this morning. We waive the reading, your honor."

"Good," Watkins said. "Let us begin. Prosecutor?"

Jessica looked at Aaron. "Wait, what's happening?" He shushed her.

"Thank you, your honor," ADA Simmons said, standing. "And thank you for making yourself available on a Sunday, your honor."

The judge nodded, not saying anything.

"The state of California recognizes the defendant's career and her standing in the community. And while we recognize the severity of the charges, including possession of a large amount of a Class 1 substance, we also recognize her social standing. The State, therefore, opts for diversion in this case. We will be seeking 90 days of medical intervention and incarceration, to be served in the facility of her—"

"No, I don't think so," Judge Watkins interrupted.

The room grew quiet. Simmons, the prosecutor, stopped talking and just stood there. No one said anything. Jessica wasn't sure what was happening.

Judge Watkins turned to Aaron, who stood as soon as she looked at him.

"Counselor? This is her seventh arrest, correct?"

Aaron nodded slowly.

"Yes, your honor."

Watkins looked at the paperwork in front of her. "And that doesn't count the other nine incidents when she got off with just warnings. Correct?"

"Yes, your honor."

"And then last night. Car accident, causing the injury of two people. Publicly intoxicated. In possession of twenty-two ounces of cocaine. Is that correct, Simmons?"

The prosecutor stood again. "Yes, your honor. But we—"

"What is the status of the injured?"

Injured? Jessica knew she'd caused an accident, but it had looked minor. She'd seen the EMTs working on the car's occupants. Was someone hurt badly by what she'd—

"Two persons were injured when their car swerved to avoid hitting Ms. Mills," the prosecutor said. "The male was treated and released, but the woman went into the windshield. No seat belt. She's in a medically-induced coma at Harbor General—"

"Oh no," Jessica said loudly, unable to control her volume.

Watkins looked at her. "Oh yes, Ms. Mills. Welcome to the real world." The judge looked back at the prosecutor. "Anything else?"

"No, your honor," she said. "I'm waiting for an update from the hospital.

"That's where they filmed that old TV show, *Emergency!*" Scott added. "Harbor General, down in—"

"Shut up, Scott," Aaron said without even turning.

This was bad, Jessica thought, ignoring Scott and his pointless Hollywood trivia. People were hurt, swerving to avoid running over her. And the drugs? And her record?

"Seven trips to rehab," Watkins said, turning to look at Jessica. "Plus several more warnings. Mr. Skilling, how many chances do you think your client should enjoy?"

"I'm not sure, your honor," he said.

"She's certainly enjoyed the tolerance of the justice system. So, how many chances do you request? An infinite number?"

"Her visits to Passages and the Ford Clinic have proven helpful, your honor. And it's been four months since—"

"Doesn't sound like they've been that helpful," the judge said, looking down at her papers. "And this possession charge? That's enough for distribution. The charge isn't just going to go away."

"Yes, your honor," Aaron said in a tone that reminded Jessica of her mother when she was angry.

"Is your client a drug dealer?"

"No, your honor," Aaron said quietly. "Her...appetites are larger than other users, I would say."

Jessica felt her face warm. This was more embarrassing than she'd ever dreamed, people talking about her like she wasn't in the room. Talking about her weaknesses, addictions.

Skilling continued. "But celebrities such as Ms. Mills are often exposed to elements of society that can have a corrupting influence, your honor. I can assure you that she's on the right path. And we can make sure to cut her off from any access to—"

"That's great," the judge said, looking up. "You're going to keep her off the nose candy, counselor? Personally? I don't think so. And I don't think we're making any progress here. She thinks she is above the law. I think it's time to teach her that is not the case. Prosecution, give me some more options."

The prosecutor looked up, surprised, and stood. "Umm...yes your honor. In cases like this, we would usually place them in rehab or another medical facility—"

"Yes, yes, the 'Hollywood Shuffle,'" Judge Watkins said. "I know it well. But I know where she's been, Simmons, and it's clearly not working," Watkins said. "I want other options."

"Yes, your honor."

Watkins read from her papers. "We're looking at possession, reckless endangerment, and two injuries, one of them serious. The Betty Ford Clinic isn't going to cut it in this case."

"Your honor," Aaron said, standing. "We would request a continuance to look into other facilities that would be appropriate for someone like her—"

"Denied," Watkins said. "I'll decide what's appropriate. Prosecutor?"

"Well, your honor," Simmons said, shuffling papers frantically. "The defendant...she could go into the GP. At a minimum-security facility, of course. Or we could find a smaller local location. But normally she would be placed in a private facility, one more... appropriate for her station."

Aaron stood up. "Your honor, general population? As in 'regular jail?' She'd be a target immediately. You know that, your honor. There would be no way the staff could guarantee her safety or monitor her around the clock. You can't put someone like Ms. Mills in with—"

"In with common criminals?" the judge asked. "No, even if I wish I could." She regarded her papers for a moment. "Simmons, there are plenty of people in 'real jail' serving sentences for possession of less cocaine. Isn't that true, prosecutor?"

"Yes, your honor. But in cases like this, we would tend to divert—"

"Yes, I know," the judge said. "What do you think, Ms. Mills?" The judge looked at her suddenly. "Ready to rub elbows with a few real criminals?"

Jessica felt the hairs on the back of her neck stand up. Real jail? Like "real" real? In a daze, she started to stand but Aaron beat her to it. "No, your honor. She would prefer rehab, of course, if that's still an option. Or some location away from the GP."

The courtroom grew quiet for a few seconds. Jessica was struck by what was happening—a group of people, most of whom she didn't know, were deciding her fate. She leaned over to Aaron.

"I want to speak."

He looked at her. "I would advise against it. Strongly. You don't want to give the judge an excuse to—"

"I'm not worried about it." She stood and turned to the judge. "Your honor?"

Watkins looked up at her. "Yes, Ms. Mills?"

"I just wanted to apologize for what happened," Jessica said. "I was attending an industry event and stepped outside of the club to get some fresh air. I dropped my purse, and when I went to grab it, I tripped. You see, the street had these cobblestones, and I'm not used to walking on—"

The judge put up her hand. "I understand the circumstances. I also understand that you were under the influence of...hang on, let me find the toxicology report." She read it off. "Alcohol, cocaine, and some kind of pain killer." She looked over the top of the piece of paper at Jessica. "Is that correct?"

Jessica nodded.

"You have to answer," Aaron whispered. "Out loud."

"Yes, your honor," Jessica said.

The judge turned and looked at the cop at the prosecutor's table. "Officer? How much cocaine did you find in Ms. Mills' possession?"

He stood quickly and adjusted his belt. He looked nervous. What did he have to be nervous about? "Twenty-two ounces. Your honor."

"In your estimation, is that amount high for personal use? Is that amount more likely to be found on a user or a dealer?"

Aaron leapt to his feet. "A dealer? Officer, your honor, you can't be serious."

The cop didn't know who to answer but he kept his eyes on the judge. "Umm...that's a lot. For personal use. The most I've ever seen, your honor. But it's possible that she's a heavy user and needs more to...you know...get a reaction? Ma'am."

The judge gave him a look but didn't answer. Unsure of what to do next, the cop sat down. It got quiet again, and Jessica sat as well. Maybe Aaron was right and she should keep her mouth shut.

The judge looked at the prosecutor again. "Any other options? Maybe a minimum-security, 'Club Fed' place?"

The prosecutor was on her phone, scrolling through it. "We have a few private cells in a facility in Lompoc. And there's a minimum-security facility in Dublin, up near San Francisco. Both are full right now. She could serve 90 days in either, away from the GP."

Things were moving so quickly.

"You ever been to Lompoc?" Scott said, leaning closer and talking to Jessica. "They grow flowers there for seeds. It's quite beautiful, actually. I was up there for an event at Vandenberg Air Force Base, and—"

"Shut up," Jessica and her lawyer said at the same time.

The prosecutor stood up again. "Your honor? Lompoc and Dublin are both full. It looks like we wouldn't have room at either for at least two weeks. The defendant would have to remain here, isolated, at this holding facility until then."

The judge nodded, satisfied. She looked at Aaron. "Counselor? 90 days in Dublin or Lompoc, including time served here?"

Aaron turned to Jessica. "It's the best deal we are going to get."

She shook her head, starting to panic. Her stomach turned over. "No, no. Aaron. I can't. I can't be in jail. Real jail. I need to go to rehab. Jail isn't going to help me—"

Scott sat next to her, whispering. "The movie comes out in November. She has the publicity tour—"

"That's not happening," Aaron said. "You'll have to negotiate something."

"It's in her contract," Scott said. "The studio will sue—she agreed to perform publicity tours in support of the film. She can't get out of it."

"She can if she's in jail," Aaron said soberly. "This is the best deal you're going to get," he said, glancing at Judge Watkins. "I've been here for two hours, negotiating. Got them down from two years to 90 days."

"Two years?" Jessica said, incredulous. "Are you kidding?"

Aaron nodded. "Possession. And your eighth offense. Plus the warnings. They can look the other way, but only so many times."

The judge spoke up. "Counselor? My patience isn't limitless."

Aaron nodded at her and waved. "Yes, your honor."

He looked back at Jessica. "90 days. You can do it. Scott and I will talk to the studio. And we'll keep it out of the press as long as we can."

Jessica looked at Scott and back at Aaron. Her stomach groaned. What was even happening here?

"Take it," her lawyer nodded.

She had no option, she realized. Not knowing what else to do, Jessica Mills slowly began to nod.

Chapter 14
Stakeout

Frank Harper sat in the front seat of his car, bored out of his freaking mind.

It was Wednesday night, August 1st, and Frank was watching a house on a quiet suburban street. It was one of his first "freelance" cases since moving to town. The lights were on inside, but Frank couldn't tell anything else. He resisted the temptation to check his phone again—it was almost dead.

Frank had recently moved to Cooper's Mill. It had been a big change, and he was still settling in after years in Birmingham. But change was good, right? He'd made the move and now was currently crashing on his daughter's couch, his boxes and furniture taking up space in her place. He needed to rent an apartment, get out of Laura's way.

Add it to the ever-growing TO DO list Frank was building.

Frank looked at the house and sighed. Nothing was happening. Being a "private investigator" could be damned boring.

Technically, he wasn't even one of those yet. His license with the State of Ohio was still in the works, held up in some office in Columbus. Here they approved PI licenses at the state level and were waiting on some paperwork from Alabama. But Frank wasn't going to let the lack of an official license hold him up. He had money to earn and bills to pay. It worked as long as he kept his nose clean, stayed out of trouble, and told the people he was working for that he wasn't licensed yet.

Not that it mattered in this particular case, where he was just shooting some photos and staking out a house. Frank was on a public street and would explain as much to any curious cops. Frank didn't plan on engaging in any fisticuffs. He couldn't legally carry a gun in the state anyway, another thing awaiting the proper paperwork.

He looked up at the house again. The stakeout was for a divorce case—more accurately, a marriage heading for divorce. The wife had hired Frank to tail her husband, Mr. Taylor Robinson. His wife was utterly convinced that her husband was cheating with one or several other women, and Frank was starting to believe her. There was also money missing from their joint account, and Fran, the wife, thought her husband was spending it on his "chickies," as she called them.

Frank was parked in front of the house of one of the husband's female "friends." It was nearly 11 p.m. but the lights were still on in the house, as they had been since the husband had arrived around eight. Frank could see movement in the living room, shadows on the window shades.

The upstairs lights stayed off, so Frank assumed all the "action" was happening on the main floor. Maybe the husband was here to fix the lady's broken sink, but the husband didn't look very handy. Frank had taken pictures of him going in, and this time he'd remembered to turn on the date and time stamp, so it saved a record of exactly when the husband arrived.

But Frank had a decision to make: sit here all night and wait for the man to leave? Photos of him leaving would make the case stronger, but Frank really needed to pee. Leaving meant risking the husband leaving and Frank missing another photo opportunity.

Finally, Frank decided to roll the dice and headed back out to the main road. He could've just found a bush or something to do his business, but he was getting tired as well. He needed a pick-me-up.

After plugging in his phone to charge, Frank guided the Camaro over two blocks onto Main, heading towards I-75. The Speedway near the highway on-ramp was brightly lit, and Frank went inside, relieving himself and picking up another coffee to keep his eyes open. He eyed the bottles of bourbon behind the counter but decided against it. Investigations were boring enough without him settling in and falling asleep.

Frank hurried back, passing the Vacation Inn near the highway. He'd stayed there several times—he'd even been kidnapped from there once. It seemed like years ago, but it had only been a few months. The hotel was the first thing you saw in Cooper's Mill from the highway. Since he'd moved to town, he didn't need a hotel, although he was considering it—he'd been crashing on Laura's couch now for nearly two weeks. While he loved spending time with her and her son, Jackson, Frank knew he was wearing out his welcome.

Back at the target house, Taylor Robinson's car was still there. If he was cheating, then the guy was an idiot—he'd parked right in front of the "chickies'" house, just daring to be caught. Relaxing, Frank settled in for the long wait. Maybe the guy would stay the night and Frank would be here until the sun rose.

Killing time, he checked his phone again, reading through his messages. He was still getting used to his new iPhone, and hadn't even explored half of what it could do.

He checked the calendar, one of the few applications he understood. It seemed like it had been weeks since Deputy Peters' funeral, even though it had only been four days. Frank shook his head at the senselessness of the whole thing. The members of the CMPD blamed Frank, especially Chief King. Frank needed to keep his head down and stay out of the way of the CMPD. He didn't need more trouble.

A half-hour later, around midnight, Taylor Robinson exited the woman's house. He looked sweaty, disheveled. Frank snapped photos with his phone as Robinson kissed the woman on the cheek and awkwardly shook her hand. Who shakes hands with a lover?

The woman returned the kiss, but the whole thing looked oddly professional. But then, who goes to a woman's house alone at night and stays for several hours? They both looked flushed, like there had been some kind of "activity," and it didn't take a genius to guess what they'd been up to.

Robinson got into his car and drove away. With one more glance back at the woman's house—all the lights had gone out now that all the excitement was over—Frank put the car in gear and followed Robinson away.

He trailed the car easily, leaving some distance between them. It was late, and few cars were out. Frank didn't want to tip the guy off and let him know he was under surveillance.

At the Robinson home, Frank watched the man park and head inside. Before driving away, Frank checked the photos he'd taken, then emailed them directly to the client. For some reason, the photos made Frank sad—he hadn't gotten into law enforcement to track cheating husbands. Frank wanted to be doing good, and this didn't feel good.

But the photos would make the wife happy, at least, and they paid the bills, at least for now. And there was no arguing—the husband was stepping out.

Chapter 15
Waiting

For Jessica, the week that followed was miserable.

It was now Thursday morning, August 2nd, and she'd been in this cell since Saturday night. Of course, they'd let her out to use the restroom, and they brought her meals, but she hadn't left this room much in six days.

The first day was the worst. After Aaron and Scott had left, the cops had taken her back to her cell. Jessica didn't want Aaron to leave—she grilled him about what would happen next, what she should do. Aaron didn't have much to say.

"Keep your head down," he said, telling her that he'd keep negotiating with the prosecutor to see if they could get the minimum-security sentence commuted or changed to rehab. ADA Simmons, the prosecutor, clearly didn't want to send Jessica to jail. It would threaten the LAPD's relations with the Hollywood folks—and set a bad precedent going forward.

But Aaron and Scott had to leave. They had fires to put out, fires of her making.

They would be heading to the studio first—her newest feature, "Knight of the Temple," was coming out November 9, and she was supposed to be going on a multi-country publicity tour in support of the film. Without Jessica, the studio would have to rely on the other actors from the film, but the studio wasn't going to be happy. Aaron said they were likely to sue—she had agreed and was contractually obligated to tour and promote the film. He said the studio might settle with a claw-back from her contract. Scott read it off from memory, stating the publicity requirements. He'd been the one working with the studio to organize the press tour.

After they left, the jail staff had come around and removed the handcuffs. They'd led her off to another area of the facility, where they'd let her shower privately and provided her with a clean orange jumpsuit.

She didn't say much but tried to be pleasant. You never knew. The shower felt good, although she was on the lookout for cameras. She didn't need any clandestine photos of her nude body in a jail shower showing up online. She'd policed all of that as well as she could, trying to protect at least that part of her image. Topless paparazzi shots of female celebrities appeared online every day, it seemed, and that was one kind of publicity she didn't need, no matter what Scott said.

When Jessica was clean and dressed, they walked her back to her cell. Two trays of food were waiting when she got back, and she attacked them, famished. She'd had no idea how hungry she was until she saw the food.

The rest of that first day had crawled. She kept finding herself reaching for her phone, for the TV remote. It was so frustrating, having nothing to do. She could be reading scripts or answering the piles of fan mail she got.

Anything that would make the time pass faster.

As hard as it was to imagine, day two was even worse than day one. At least on that first full day, Sunday, she could pretend Scott or even Aaron might come back to talk to her. But Monday was worse.

Jessica had a list in her head of the things she was going to ask Aaron for: first and foremost, she wanted writing materials. Pens, pencils, a notepad. Whatever. She needed to be writing things down, taking notes. And she wanted stuff to read. There was a stack of scripts in the corner of her home office, the room that also held her computer and a few other work-related things. The walls in that room were decorated with posters and photos from her past projects, along with the smattering of awards she'd won over the years. Most of them were from her kid's shows on the Disney channel. The movies she'd made since "graduating" from kid's TV had not been as popular as the air-headed entertainment she'd appeared in earlier in her career.

People weren't sending her many quality scripts to consider, but by Tuesday, she'd have killed for a stack of dumb scripts to read.

Next on her list was her phone, of course. And email. Instagram. Snapchat. The basics.

On Wednesday, Aaron visited for a conference, alleviating her boredom for a time. Jessica was moved to a small meeting room with two chairs and a metal table in the middle. The room was painted a ghastly color that landed somewhere between light green and gray. The room color and the florescent lights and the mirrors on the wall immediately depressed her. She suddenly wished she was back in her cell, a reaction she would not have predicted.

Aaron hugged her and set his things down on the table between them. "How are you? How are things in here?"

"It sucks ass. I want out," Jessica said.

Her lawyer put his hand up. "I know. I'm working on it. I've had two more conferences with Judge Watkins and the prosecutor."

"Good news?"

"No, not really," Aaron said. "Watkins made it clear she's tired of your 'antics,' as she put it. Even with me and the prosecutor arguing against it, she's dead set on you doing time. It's looking like Lompoc will open up first. It's a small facility, relatively new. Not the worst place you could end up. And the max facility isn't too close."

"Great."

"If I were you, I'd get used to the idea. Simmons doesn't want you anywhere near other prisoners, even the minimum-security ones. The prosecutor is stalling, but I guarantee that rehab is off the table."

Jessica didn't know what else to say. They talked for a few more minutes, and she asked for her phone and her stacks of scripts. He laughed.

"You're not going to be getting those kinds of privileges for a while," he said. "I can see about writing materials, and stuff to read. Your scripts, sure. But nothing electronic."

Chapter 16
Coffee

Thursday morning, Frank pulled into the McDonald's parking lot in Cooper's Mill and parked, heading inside.

The place was exactly as he remembered it, looking just like any other McDonald's. He glanced over and saw the collection of old folks at a round table near the entrance to the kid's play area. At the counter, Frank got himself a coffee and an Egg McMuffin, then walked over to the table of people he barely knew.

"Mind if I join you?"

They all turned to look at him with smiles. Murphy Collier, the de-facto leader of the coffee klatch, greeted Frank warmly.

"Hey, no problem. Have a seat!"

Frank was greeted by the table of older folks—they obviously remembered him from his visit earlier this year. He'd sat with them one morning while he had been investigating the disappearance of one of their members, Tom Mercato. Frank had sat at this very table months ago, the snow coming down outside, and asked those gathered around the table questions about Mercato and his possible whereabouts.

Of course, at the time, none of them knew that Mercato's killer was sitting at the table with them.

Joe Hathaway, another member of the coffee klatch, participated in the conversation. The old man had sat there and answered Frank's questions calmly, rationally, being helpful and pleasant. He never gave the slightest hint that he'd been the one to kill their mutual friend—or that he was currently keeping the poor man's dead body on ice at his home. Literally on ice—Hathaway had put him into a large freezer in his garage. But Frank had helped solve the case, and Hathaway had gone to jail—only to escape and disappear after another incident when Hathaway had abducted Frank's daughter and grandson. It was all water under the bridge, although Frank was certain the topic of Joe Hathaway would come up. It had to.

For the time being, Frank settled into the conversation and enjoyed his coffee and the breakfast sandwich—and the company.

When he'd been alive, Tom Mercato had run their little group, but Collier had picked up the reins after Tom's disappearance. "Great to see you, Frank," Collier said. "And bully for you, almost taking down Hathaway. Any word on where he's gotten off to?"

Frank shook his head. "The cops in five states are still out there, beating the bushes, but no leads. It's been almost two weeks. He's in the wind, I imagine."

The couple sitting next to Frank, Will and Janette Duff, nodded along. Will was a bailiff for the county and had been present at Hathaway's trial. He leaned forward. "Yeah, good job, man. At least he's out of our hair, wherever he ends up. He was always strange, but seeing him at the trial creeped me out."

The table agreed, and Janette Duff spoke up. "I still can't believe he sat here every day and none of us figured out how insane he was."

"Hiding in plain sight," said Monty Robinson, the only black person at the table. Frank nodded at him—they had met even before Frank had attended his first meeting of the coffee klatch. Robinson was a night watchman at a construction site in Cooper's Mill, and he'd walked Frank through the location during another one of Frank's investigations. "That's what they do. The psychos. They blend right in. Right, Frank?"

Frank nodded. "That's been my experience. I've seen my share. And people always say the same things: 'I couldn't believe it was him. He was always so nice.'"

"Yeah, the neighbor on TV, right?" Monty asked with a laugh. "They never know."

Janette asked Frank to go through the story again of the events at the farmhouse north of Troy. Frank obliged, repeating what he could and coloring it with his thoughts. Frank also downplayed the gruesome parts. Hathaway had been on trial for three counts of attempted murder but escaped the hospital. Joe had been recovering from a car crash. It was strange, recounting the series of events. To him, it had been real life, but telling it now, later, it all seemed too fantastic to be real.

"How'd you figure out he was at that farmhouse?" Collier asked.

"Text messages, codes to figure out."

"That sounds like Joe, all right," Collier added, nodding. "He was always talking about chess moves, stuff like that."

Frank nodded and continued, explaining what happened when he and Deputy Peters, along with other cops, had raided the farmhouse. Most of the civilians present, along with Frank's daughter and grandson, made it out alive. Frank had shot Joe, who fell into the river and floated away.

Janette shook her head. "Surely he's dead."

"Not if they don't find a body," Frank said. "He's still considered alive—and dangerous—until someone can prove otherwise."

"You said three homicides?" Collier asked. "I thought it was just Tom and his girlfriend, the one who worked at that restaurant downtown."

"She was pregnant," Frank said quietly.

"I'd forgotten about that," Jeanette said. "I can't believe he involved your grandson, Mr. Harper. You must have been so frightened."

He nodded. "Call me Frank," he said. He continued, finally wrapping up the story with Deputy Peters' funeral. They peppered him with more questions, and he answered them each in turn, trying to avoid going down any rabbit holes or getting too far into official police business. People really only wanted to hear the highlights, and that's what Frank gave them. After ten more minutes, the questions petered out and everyone seemed satisfied.

"So, what's been going on around here?" Frank asked, happy to turn the conversation away from him.

They chatted about local happenings, the 2012 Summer Olympics in London, and the upcoming Presidential election in November. Most people were pretty sure President Obama would be reelected. The conversation turned to the July 20th movie theater shooting in Aurora, Colorado. People were stunned at the massacre of 12 people whose only crime was going out to see a movie. Soon, they moved on to the topic of gun control.

Frank let the conversation wash over him, answering the occasional question and enjoying his food and coffee. He got up to get another one, heading to the counter and handing over his cup. It was nice to listen to other people's opinions for a change. Sometimes Frank felt like he was too much in his own head—he needed to get out, hear what was going on in the world. He'd seen an alert come over his phone about the theater shooting and then had forgotten all about it. He hadn't seen the news or read a newspaper in days—he'd been concentrating on his case.

"What do you think about this Colorado mess?"

Frank turned to see Monty at the counter with him. He handed his cup to the McDonald's employee, who filled it with coffee and handed it back. Frank's cup was sitting on the counter in front of him, filled to the brim, the lid next to it. Frank realized he'd been spaced out, not paying attention.

They both walked over to the coffee station, which was stocked with cream and sugar, and fixed their coffee.

"Which part?"

"The theater shooting."

"I don't know," Frank said. "I haven't been following it much."

"Too busy? Heard you were doing some PI work."

"Nothing official, yet," Frank said. "Still waiting on paperwork from the state. I picked up a couple of jobs. You still doing security?"

"Yeah, nights mostly," Monty said, stirring his coffee. "And watching too much TV. Lots of old movies. They cut my hours, so I'm looking for work," Monty said with a smile. "Let me know if you need any help."

Frank nodded as they sat. He stayed another half hour before excusing himself. They invited him back anytime—Collier said they usually got started around 8:00 a.m. or whenever people showed up, going to 10 or 11, depending on the weather. Frank thanked them again and headed out. He'd promised himself that he'd try to make some new friends, and this was a step in the right direction.

Chapter 17
A Crazy Idea

"No."

"Why not?"

Aaron looked up at Ferrara and made a face. He'd already made several during their short conversation. "Because it's literally the dumbest idea I've ever heard."

Ferrara sat back in the chair in Aaron's office downtown. The place reflected his personality—and his net worth. The office looked fancier than any fake office she'd ever seen in any movie.

For one thing, the place was huge. Bigger than the entire hair salon she'd worked in back in Ohio. And the floor-to-ceiling windows made the office even more impressive, with their expansive views of downtown Los Angeles. She could spend hours staring out the windows, watching the cars and trucks moving slowly on the highways and the constant stream of planes winging in to land at LAX. More people, coming to Los Angeles to follow their dreams.

His desk was huge as well, big enough to be a dining room table for a family of eight. It was piled with case files and folders, as were other tables that ran along the wall across from the windows. They were piled up, every folder was marked with a sticky note with numbers and names.

"It's not a dumb idea," Ferrara said. "It's out there. Sure. But you said no one wants her to actually go to jail, do they?"

Aaron looked at her over his glasses. "The judge does. She hates her. And you weren't there—I had to do some fancy moves just to get Watkins to let her off with 90 days."

"She wanted to give her two years?"

Aaron nodded, his pen still in the air. She'd walked in and plopped herself down in the chair a few minutes ago, launching into her pitch while he'd been marking up some document on the desk in front of him. Now, the pen hung in the air, mid-way between the desk and his mouth. Her suggestion had apparently been so ludicrous that he'd forgotten what he was doing.

"Yes. Watkins gave her diversion and time served last time. That was the 60-day rehab. Thirty days house arrest, thirty days at Passages."

"Wasn't Lindsey Lohan there?"

"Not at the same time," he said, going back to his document. He started crossing out words with his red pen, probably assuming she would just get up and leave.

Ferrara had always been intimidated by Aaron, but she pressed on. This wasn't about her. It was about Jessica.

"I know the idea sounds nutty."

Aaron looked at her again, sighing.

"I don't even want to bring it up with Watkins," Aaron said. "She's looking for an excuse to throw the book at Jessica. The idea of mixing Jessica into the general population was a scare tactic, but I wouldn't put it past Watkins if we piss her off."

Ferrara lowered her voice. "But my idea could be a good out for the judge. It also has the added advantage of getting Jessica out of Los Angeles."

"They don't have cocaine in Ohio?"

"That's not what I mean."

"Still, the answer is no."

Ferrara leaned in. "It gets her away from Carrie and Gina. And Scott." Carrie and Gina were Jessica's "friends," the "sugar twins." They weren't good for her. Jessica had met them on one of her TV shows. Bad influences, Ferrara's mom would have said if she were around instead of back in Ohio. Carrie got Jessica her coke. And Gina was always dragging Jessica out to "party." Gina and Carrie were responsible for half of Jessica's problems, to be sure. They got her in trouble and then conveniently faded into the background whenever it came time to pay the bill—or talk to the cops.

Scott was the other problem. It was his job to get Jessica "out there," his term for keeping her in the public eye. "No publicity is bad publicity," all that. But Ferrara disagreed, and spoke up when she got the chance. Jessica needed downtime just like everyone else. Of course, she had to be out in public for press junkets and other things to support her projects. But appearing at bar openings and doing cameos on game shows? It was all too much. Scott worked Jessica to the bone, like a trainer showing off his prized pony.

"It would never work," Aaron said, going back to his document. "Security would be a nightmare, for one. Who would keep an eye on her to make sure she didn't wander off? Or to make sure no one messed with her?"

"Me. I'll do it."

"Sure, that would work," Aaron said sarcastically. "You gonna chain her to you? She needs counseling, actual help."

"She's going to get that in jail?"

Aaron shook his head. "No, but rehab didn't work. She's been to every facility within a hundred miles."

"I could do some investigating," Ferrara said. "I'm sure there are drug counselors in Cooper's Mill."

"Where?"

"Ohio. My hometown," she said. "Where Jessica and I are going. Were you listening?"

"Not really." Aaron put the pen down and steepled his hands on top of his paperwork, looking at her as if he were talking to a child. "Ferrara, it won't work. The judge won't want to have Jessica out of her control, or out of the state's custody. She won't trust you—or me—to keep Jessica on the straight and narrow. And there's no way the whole makeup and hair thing would work."

"It did already. Several times. We went to Santa Monica pier and she walked around. She went to that movie premiere and watched her film with the regular folks—"

"That was for two hours. You're talking about weeks. It would never work."

Ferrara went on for another twenty minutes, pleading her case. She repeated the whole idea again, and Aaron at least paid her the courtesy of listening. She didn't feel like she was making any headway, and she wasn't surprised when he buzzed his secretary to walk Ferrara out.

At least I tried, Ferrara thought as she rode the elevator back down to the first floor and walked out into the Los Angeles sun. Things were so different out here. People in LA were just different. And people became cold once they ended up here. Mean, angry.

Chapter 18
A Friend

"But you're doing okay?"

Jessica Mills nodded slowly, looking down at the concrete floor of her cell. To Ferrara, she looked thinner. Her hair was waxy and dull, and her face, long scrubbed clean of makeup, looked pale. She didn't look like herself anymore. And that jumpsuit wasn't doing anything for her complexion, either.

"I hate this place," Jessica said, looking around at the gray walls. She was still in the local county holding cell, in the building complex that included the courthouse. Ferrara knew she'd been here all week—apparently, the LAPD was reluctant to move her. "But I don't want to leave. This sentencing—she's gonna send me somewhere else. I just know it. And I can't imagine living in a smaller cell—or being in with a bunch of other people," Jessica said with a shiver.

"I know," Ferrara said, shaking her head.

"Murderers, killers. Rapists," Jessica said quietly.

"You'll be in the female population, right?" Ferrara said, trying to sound positive. "At least, that's what Aaron said. Minimum Security. Not in the general...group. Whatever he called it."

"General population. You talked to him?"

"Yeah," Ferrara said, looking away. "I had a dumb idea. One that I thought might get you out of here. But he shot it down."

"What was it?"

Before Ferrara could start explaining, there was movement in the hallway. Aaron and a guard walked up to the metal bars. Jessica stood automatically, like a robot. Ferrara did as well, following her lead. The guard jangled some keys and opened the cell door. Jessica walked over and put her wrists out, waiting.

Aaron looked at the guard. "Is that really necessary? I mean, everyone on the planet knows what she looks like. If she were to somehow escape..."

"Sorry," the guard shrugged. "Rules." He put the handcuffs on Jessica, who sighed.

"It's okay, Aaron," she said. "Maybe it will make the judge feel sorry for me."

He shook his head. "Watkins doesn't feel bad for child murderers and serial arsonists. She won't feel sorry for you."

Ferrara started to say something and then shook her head. Her mom always said it was better to keep your mouth shut and let people think you were stupid then say something and prove it.

Ferrara followed them down a set of hallways, emerging into a much nicer part of the complex. They passed through empty, marbled corridors and finally into a nice courtroom. The judge's podium was to the right and, to the left, tables for the prosecution and defense. Beyond those, rows and rows of seats were lined up like church pews. Ferrara had never been in an actual court before and was surprised to see it was almost as nice as what you saw on TV.

Aaron directed her out through a set of swinging gates and into the front row of seats, where Ferrara sat and waited, nervous. She had no idea what to expect, but she was worried about her friend Jessica. Strangely, Ferrara really did consider Jessica a friend, even though the young woman employed her. Jessica had a "good soul," as Ferrara's mom would have said.

Jessica's problem was that she was rich.

She wasn't the kind of idle rich that didn't have to earn money—Ferrara saw how hard Jessica worked on sets. She was there, putting in the hours. But she'd also surrounded herself with a toxic group of people, enablers that got her into more trouble than Jessica could on her own.

It wasn't that Jessica was an angel, of course. She liked her coke as much as the next Hollywood starlet, and the "sugar twins" were happy to supply it. Carrie and Gina weren't really twins, of course, but sometimes Ferrara had trouble telling them apart. Bottle blonds, skinny from doing enough of Jessica's blow to avoid every other meal.

But Jessica was a good sort, most of the time. Sending her to "real" jail was the worst possible idea. Jessica needed a vacation from Los Angeles. She needed to be around "regular" people, people who didn't automatically agree with every idea she had, enabling all her worst impulses. Of course, the entourage said "yes" to every bad idea—no one wanted to contradict Jessica and get kicked off the "Team Jessica" gravy train. Spending Jessica's money for her came with several conditions. The main one? Don't poke the bear. Don't disagree with Jessica, or ever say the word "no."

That's what Jessica needed. Someone to tell her "no." Ferrara had tried to do that on a few occasions, and Jessica had always looked at her funny, as if she couldn't even remember a time when she didn't automatically get whatever she wanted. Ferrara had actually managed to say "no" quite a few times and still, somehow, stay in Jessica's good graces.

The idea of a "vacation" had given Ferrara her crazy idea. Too bad she couldn't get anyone to take it seriously. Ferrara was convinced Jessica wasn't beyond help—she just needed to be away from troublemakers for a while.

Chapter 19
No Other Option

In the courtroom, waiting for things to start, Jessica adjusted the handcuffs in her lap and turned to speak to Aaron.

"Sentencing?"

He was shuffling papers. "Yes. And final hearing on your location."

Jessica nodded, anxious. She was glad for the break from her cell but worried about what this might mean. Her cell was at least private—what if they put her into the GP? They wouldn't actually do that, right? She was famous, well-known to everyone. She was on TV, in the movies, for Christ's sake. But other actors had gone to jail, too, and lived to tell the tale, right?

She glanced around at Ferrara—thank God the young woman was here. Ferrara was a nice girl from someplace in Ohio. She was a wonder at hair and makeup and a rare calming influence in Jessica's life. And she told Jessica "no" every once in a while. It was refreshing.

Ferrara gave Jessica a smile and a thumbs-up, making Jessica laugh.

Jessica turned back around and glanced up at the empty judge's seat. This judge was sick of her. What would she do this time? Make an example of Jessica? What if she—

"All rise and come forward to the bar to be heard. Court is hereby called into session, presided over by her honor Judge Watkins." The bailiff spoke, loud and clear, and for a second Jessica thought he would be a good actor. Great enunciation, good range.

She realized the others were standing and stood as well. Judge Watkins entered, nodding to Jessica's attorney and his opposite number, the woman prosecutor. Had it only been six days since the club? Jessica felt like she'd been in that cell for a month. She missed her house, her phone, her TV. Everything. If she got out of this, she was going to take things easy for a while. No parties, no drugs. Maybe even cut Carrie and Gina loose.

"Please be seated," Watkins said, and everyone but the prosecutor sat. She waited, then spoke up.

"Thank you for this hearing, your honor."

"No problem. Any objections on the sentence?"

Neither ADA Simmons nor Aaron spoke up.

"Good," Watkins said, noting something on the papers in front of her. "90 days, with time served. Now, as to her location. Simmons, do we have any updates? Any progress?"

ADA Simmons nodded. "Of a sort, your honor. The holding facility in Dublin can take her for the 90-day period, but not for at least three more weeks."

Aaron stood. "Your honor, we'd prefer she could be kept in the local area. She has a press junket coming up and it would be easier to facilitate interviews."

Watkins looked at him for a moment. "Are you kidding me, counselor? There will be no interviews, no "junkets"."

He shook his head. "No, your honor. But she's contractually obligated to carry out—"

"I don't care what she's contractually obligated to carry out. No interviews. And I don't want her up north, Simmons. What about Lompoc?"

"Full, your honor. With the state mandate to reduce overcrowding, they won't accept her. In fact, I had to petition for the Dublin slot, away from the GP. Even that is still pending."

The judge looked down at her desk at some papers the prosecutor was referencing, and Aaron looked down at his copies. Jessica leaned over closer to read them as well—Dublin was near Oakland. The facility was huge, with two wings: max and minimum security. It said they intermixed on certain days but that a subset of inmates could be kept away from the GP.

"Aaron, I don't want to go there," Jessica said quietly. "I don't want to go to prison at all."

He turned and looked at her. "I think we're past that, Jessica. At this point, we're just negotiating where."

The prosecutor stood again. "For the record, your honor, we're still against this. We want to see the defendant punished, of course, but there is no way we can provide 24-hour protection. Lompoc is safer. At Dublin, the other inmates will find out who she is and possibly retaliate."

"Retaliate? Me?" Jessica said out loud, louder than she'd expected. She couldn't help it.

Aaron shushed her but it was too late. Judge Watkins looked at her.

"Yes, you, Ms. Mills. You will not be liked there, I can guarantee it."

Aaron stood. "Your honor, there has to be another option. If Lompoc is full, Dublin is not a good fit. The populations mix on a regular basis and the staff won't be able to—"

"Ms. Mills, you represent everything those prisoners don't have: money, privilege," the judge said, ignoring Aaron and locking eyes with Jessica. "Those people don't get second chances. Actually, you've had...more than a dozen, as far as I can tell. Correct, Ms. Mills?"

"Yes, ma'am."

The judge looked at her. "Does that sound fair? How many chances do you think you deserve? You could've killed those two people in that car. They swerved to avoid you, drunk in the middle of the road, and ran into a brick wall at full speed. Do you deserve to walk free while the woman passenger is still in a coma?"

Jessica shook her head, mortified, embarrassed. Aaron started to stand and defend her, but Jessica put her hand on his arm, keeping him in his seat.

"No, your honor, I don't. I've been to rehab several times, and I've tried to get a handle on this. Really, I have. I'm not sure what to do. Maybe you're right. Maybe this is the best thing."

She sat down and the courtroom grew as silent as a grave. The judge looked at her strangely and said nothing.

Finally, the prosecutor stood.

"As I said earlier, your honor, we're not pushing to have her jailed at this time. Lompoc would have worked, but Dublin is too violent, I fear. We're at a loss for a location for her to serve her 90-day sentence. We don't really have any other good options."

The judge looked at her, then over at Aaron and Jessica, shaking her head.

"I don't really see any other way," Watkins said, lifting her gavel. "The Dublin facility is minimum security. Ms. Mills will be remanded to their care as soon as a spot opens up. They will make every effort to keep her out of the GP. Until then, she stays here in our local cell. Without further exceptions, I'm going to move—"

Suddenly, Aaron stood, knocking papers off the desk. "Your honor, we have another option."

The judge paused, her gavel in the air.

"What, counselor?"

"We have another option," Aaron said. "One that the court may find acceptable."

Watkins set her gavel down slowly. "What is it?"

Aaron glanced over at the prosecutor. "I think it's best if we discuss it in chambers."

The prosecutor, curious, stood and nodded.

Judge Watkins looked back and forth between them, then over at Jessica, who had no idea what was happening. What other option? No one had mentioned anything to her.

Finally, Watkins spoke up.

"Okay, come on back. We're recessed for ten minutes."

Aaron turned. Jessica thought he was looking at her, but he'd turned all the way around and was nodding at Ferrara, who was sitting in the first row, silent as a lamb.

"You, come on. Now's your chance."

Ferrara's eyes went wide. She looked at Jessica, shrugged, and then stood, following Aaron back into the judge's chambers.

What the hell was going on?

Chapter 20
Say What?

"Counselor, you are insane."

Aaron and the prosecutor were sitting in the chairs opposite the judge's desk, where she was seated, her hands steepled on a stack of papers. Ferrara was impressed by the size of the ornate office. Behind Ferrara, one whole wall was taken up with floor-to-ceiling bookcases loaded down with still more books, a massive law library, Ferrara assumed.

Jessica's lawyer leaned back in his chair. Ferrara could tell Aaron was good at this because he'd started with the most ridiculous parts of Ferrara's off-the-wall idea.

"I know, your honor," he continued. "That's exactly what I said. It sounds like a Lifetime movie of the week: 'Unruly Starlet in the Heartland.'"

Simmons, the prosecutor, let out a little laugh.

"But, your honor," Aaron said. "The more I think about it, the more I like the idea."

The judge looked at him. "Okay, let's just ignore all the logistical insanity for a minute. You know, like keeping track of her, making sure she's in custody, etc. How could this possibly be a good idea? Ever?"

Aaron leaned in. "Well, for one, it gets her out of Los Angeles. Away from the paparazzi. Away from the industry. She does her 90 days, of course, and in the custody of the LAPD. A police officer would be with her at all times." Ferrara was watching the judge's face, trying to read her expression. "But she does her time far out of the public limelight," Aaron continued. "Not in a jail cell or another rehab facility, but somewhere she can get the help she actually needs. And away from her enablers—an idea I trust you'll like, your honor. We also will get her professional counseling and assist her in detoxing from any drugs she is addicted to."

Watkins shook her head. "Wow, that's a tall order."

Aaron nodded. "Yes, ma'am."

"In jail, she'd also be away from her enablers."

"Yes, your honor, and she'll be trading in one group of bad influences for another," Aaron said, agreeing. "And a much worse one, I would hazard to say. She could come out of Dublin worse than she went in, mentally. Assuming she survives at all."

"Oh, I don't think it would be that bad," the judge said, shaking her head. She glanced at her desk and pulled out a sheet of paper, holding it up to Aaron. "The minimum-security portion of Dublin has the lowest violence rate in the state. I want to put the fear of God into her, counselor. Not see her get stabbed in the shower."

The prosecutor spoke up. "Actually, that's our biggest concern, your honor. We can't guarantee her safety—"

"As you've said. Several times," Watkins interjected sharply. "I know you're just trying to get off the hook."

"Yes, your honor," Simmons said quietly. "You are right. We want to see her prosecuted, of course, but her safety is a huge concern. Any inmate managing to kill the 'Hollywood girl' would be famous for the rest of their lives."

The room went quiet.

"It puts a huge target on her back. If anything happened to her, it would also change the way we handle all similar future cases," Simmons continued.

Aaron turned to point at Ferrara, who was leaning against the wall of books. "She's from Ohio, suggested the idea. Along with an LAPD deputy or other law enforcement official, Jessica would be under her supervision 24-7." Aaron paused, nodding at Ferrara, who got the hint and spoke up.

"Yes, your honor. I would," Ferrara said, standing straight. All eyes were suddenly on her and the temperature in the room jumped ten degrees. "Jessica…Ms. Mills, your honor, would be under my supervision. My family has a farmhouse out away from town. Nice place. Very quiet. Secure."

Ferrara paused, waiting for someone to say something, but no one did. She looked at Aaron, who was no help. Finally, he spoke up.

"And getting her away from here would be good because…"

"Yes," Ferrara said, smiling. "Right. It would be good to get her away from here for a while, your honor. I'm always trying to get her to come to Ohio, take a break from all of it. You know, it's crazy out here. You guys know how it is, right? And she's in the worst industry. Scott has her scheduled for every publicity thing he can find, and Hank, her agent, sends her on too many auditions."

She paused, waiting, then continued.

"I think, back home, Jessica will be around a lot of good people. Normal people, you see. And my mom works at a grocery store. She could get Jessica a job, let her see what normal life is like for a while. And we can get her counseling. It would be good for Jessica..."

Aaron was making a face and Ferrara realized she was talking too much and stopped, her mouth closing with an audible "click."

The judge scowled at Ferrara. "Right. Jessica Mills, Hollywood star, working at a grocery store. Did Ms. Mills put you up to this? I saw that movie where she goes to live on the pig farm. If this is her idea—"

"No, your honor," Ferrara said. "I haven't told her. I brought the idea to Aaron, who said—"

"Thank you," the judge interrupted. "At least it's not her harebrained idea. But I don't see how it could work logistically. While I would like to see her out of LA for a while, I don't see how this is anything close to 'serving time.' Sounds more like a vacation to me."

"We're fine with that, your honor," Simmons interjected. "We would send an officer with her to supervise. And track her location at all times via an ankle monitor."

Ferrara looked at the prosecutor. It was strange she was agreeing with Ferrara.

"Like I said, we're not looking forward to the disruption of putting her into the system," Simmons said, leaning forward. "While we would prefer a rehab facility, those options have already been tried. Frankly, it's been complicated for the few days she's been here. We've had to keep her isolated, away from other prisoners. Limiting visitors to keep out any photographers." The woman turned to Ferrara. "Where would she be located?"

"My family farm," Ferrara said. She waited but it looked like the woman wanted more information. "It's surrounded by fences and fields on all sides. Do you know where Dayton is?"

Simmons shook her head. "Not really. Central Ohio?"

"Southwestern, not far from the border with Indiana."

The prosecutor looked at her, confused.

Ferrara put up her hands and sketched in the air. "Ohio is like a square. They call it 'America's shirt pocket.'" Aaron rolled his eyes, but Ferrara plowed on. "Anyway, Columbus is in the middle. Dayton's west of there. Cincinnati is south, on the river," she said, pointing in the air. "Anyway, Cooper's Mill is north of Dayton. A nice small town—good schools, summer carnivals. Zero crime."

"Sounds great," the judge said, smirking at Aaron. "Can I tag along?"

"Of course, your honor. We'd love to have you." Only after she spoke did Ferrara realize the judge was being sarcastic.

"Sadly, I'm busy. So, it's Ferrara, right?"

"Yes, your honor."

"Right. I can't believe I'm even asking this. Won't she be spotted immediately, even with this makeup thing Aaron was talking about?"

She started to answer but Aaron spoke up, cutting her off. "As her stylist, Ferrara would also be responsible for making sure Ms. Mills travels incognito, doing her time off the radar and far away from any publicity. We've done this a few times before, your honor. Ferrara can alter Ms. Mills' appearance to the point where she can pass in public without being recognized. They have been out several times at public locations in the Los Angeles area, including attending a movie premiere, and Ms. Mills was not spotted. We're confident it will be even easier in Ohio."

Ferrara nodded, not saying anything. They hadn't talked about any of this, but she knew enough to keep her mouth shut while the man was negotiating.

Simmons spoke up. "We would send a female deputy. To maintain custody around the clock."

"How would that work?" Ferrara asked. "We're going for inconspicuous, right? If she's in uniform, that kinda blows the whole thing—"

"She can be undercover," the prosecutor said, warming to the idea. "This isn't negotiable. I'm not letting Ms. Mills out of our custody."

Ferrara started to say something but Aaron shook his head. He turned back to the prosecutor. "So, 90 days in a 'safe house' in another state, including time served. In the custody of an officer. Ms. Mills promises to serve her time without incident and under the supervision of the LAPD. Ms. Mills will also cover all costs associated with this venture, including compensating the department for the officer's overtime."

The prosecutor nodded. "Yes."

"And Ms. Ferrara here will travel with them and ensure Mills is incognito and out of the public eye. Are those the conditions?"

The prosecutor nodded. "And the ankle monitor."

"Of course," Aaron said. "We agree." He turned to the judge. "So, your honor. Is this a thing that could happen?"

The judge looked at the papers on her desk, and the room went quiet. Ferrara realized the judge was deciding. Like, right now, at this very second. This woman with the dark hair was deciding Jessica Mills' future. If this woman sent her to prison, Jessica might be injured or even killed. This was crazy, right? She wouldn't actually endanger someone as famous as Jessica, would she?

Suddenly all the drama from past movie shoots and television shows, all the troubles Jessica had had with drugs, it had all led up to this moment. It all paled in stark comparison.

Jessica could be going to prison. Or the judge could relent and sign off on Ferrara's insane plan, a plan so full of holes that it would be impossible to pull off. Aaron might have sounded convincing, but could they really keep Jessica out of the public eye for 90 days? Surely someone would find out and spill the beans. Even in Cooper's Mill, every person above the age of five knew who Jessica Mills was and exactly what she looked like. Ferrara would have to come up with a good disguise, something foolproof—

Finally, the judge nodded slowly.

"Okay. This whole thing sounds insane, but I don't see any better alternative." Judge Watkins looked at the prosecutor. "You sure this is what you want, Simmons? If it comes out, we're all going to look like idiots."

Simmons thought about it and nodded. "I don't see a better way, your honor. If we can keep this quiet, it might work. If not, Lompoc will have openings in three weeks. We can bring her back from Ohio and incarcerate her."

The judge turned to Ferrara.

"You and this deputy will be responsible for her, got me?"

Ferrara nodded.

"I'm guessing Ms. Mills can be a handful," the judge continued. "She had coke in her system, according to the drug tests, so she'll be coming down off of that. Moody, angry, more than a little entitled. Can you handle that?"

Ferrara nodded, putting on her most serious face, the same one she'd used when she told her parents she was leaving Ohio and moving to Los Angeles to pursue her career as a stylist. They had looked at her like she was crazy.

"Yes, your honor. I can do this."

The judge agreed, reluctant. "I hope so," she said, looking at Aaron. "Ohio? Really?"

The lawyer started to answer but Ferrara spoke up, cutting him off. "She needs a break from LA. I love it out here, but it's all so fake, you know? Fake and artificial."

"Those are the same things," the judge said with a smile.

"Yes, your honor," Ferrara said, plowing ahead. "But they're not really, are they? Fake is pretend, made up for the appearance. I know all about that. But artificial is something worse—like we all know that it's not real and we just play along. I always say LA is like a shared delusion. Everyone agreeing that things are awesome, even when they're not."

The judge nodded soberly. "You're saying we're all suffering from mass hysteria?"

"Maybe, your honor."

"Well, maybe a break from all of that will help Ms. Mills. You're going to be spending some time with her, one on one. I have a message for her."

"Yes, ma'am."

Watkins looked Ferrara dead in the eyes. "Let her know that I said this is her last chance. And I don't mean that in a pissy, finger-wagging sense. It's literally this or prison."

Ferrara nodded, keeping her mouth shut.

"Rehab is out, and no more house arrest," Judge Watkins continued. "Next time, it's Lompoc or Dublin, minimum security. No questions asked. And she might not have you or Aaron looking out for her. It seems Ms. Mills has a habit of burning bridges."

Ferrara started to argue but then thought better of it and simply nodded.

"Yes, ma'am. I'll take good care of her."

"Good," Watkins said, looking at her desk. "Where is that thing? Oh, here it is." She grabbed a leather book and flipped through a calendar of dates. "Okay, 90 days in jail translated to house arrest, which is what this is turning out to be. Does anyone have a problem with that?"

The prosecutor and Aaron looked at each other and shook their heads.

"Okay, I'm flipping and I'm flipping," the judge said, narrating her page-turning. Her voice sounded resigned. "Looks like—October 29 is her last day, assuming things go well." She looked up at Ferrara.

"Summer in Ohio. Yippee."

"That should work," the prosecutor said, checking her own calendar. "I'm sure we can find a female deputy. I'd rather pay one person for the summer than turn an entire jail upside down."

"Great," the judge said. She looked at Aaron and Ferrara. "Have her back here in my chambers on Monday, October 29. I hope to God she's a changed woman. Agreed?"

The judge looked at them all one more time, but no one had any objections. She nodded and stood, going to the door and pulling it open.

"Bailiff? Go get Ms. Mills."

He scowled and scurried off. Watkins turned back to them.

"You guys can have the fun of explaining it to her."

Chapter 21
The Plan

Jessica didn't even understand the whole idea the first time through. Aaron explained it in front of Judge Watkins, glancing at her every once in a while. He was also looking at Jessica strangely, clearly trying to get her to agree to everything quickly, saying things like "we'll get into the details later."

From what she could understand, the judge was on board, but the whole thing was on shaky ground. Jessica got the distinct impression she should just agree to it, whatever it was, and did so, nodding, apparently to Judge Watkins' satisfaction.

They were out of there in a matter of minutes, and Aaron and Ferrara walked her back to her jail cell as they explained the idea again. In front of the judge, Jessica hadn't objected. She'd kept her mouth shut, for once, and kept her opinions to herself. But now, in her cell, she could actually think about the deal that Aaron and the judge and the prosecutor had all worked out.

To say it was ridiculous was an understatement.

Traveling to Ohio, going incognito. Ninety days at a "safe house" under house arrest. Staying with Ferrara's family. An undercover cop with them every step of the way for security and to "maintain custody." An ankle monitor.

And then the agreement they'd made about Jessica's appearance. Ferrara's makeovers were fun distractions, a chance to go out for a few hours without being harassed by the paparazzi rats. But three months? With Aaron egging her on, Ferrara had run down a brainstormed list of bad ideas: long wigs, new and unflattering makeup, several different kinds of glasses. Fake teeth, fake ear piercings, even a port-wine stain. A dressed-down wardrobe, bad shoes to make her walk different. All to make Jessica Mills 'disappear' for a few months.

She would become a completely different person, a young woman with a different look, voice, history, one that Jessica and Ferrara would invent together.

It all sounded crazy. But would it work? Of course, anything was better than staying in jail, and even the minimum-security facility near Oakland sounded like hell on earth.

Jessica Mills spent the next forty-eight hours going through every part of the plan with Ferrara, who visited twice a day. While Aaron worked with the LAPD and prosecutors to set up "the plan," Jessica and Ferrara worked out Jessica's new look. They decided on Jessica's new name—"Sydney Green"—and created a biography of the fictional woman.

Jessica dove into the sudden and welcome distraction, talking about Sydney like she was a real person. Part-way through the second day, Jessica felt a chill run up her spine—this might actually work.

One of Jessica's previous incognito events was when she'd attended one of her movies to get an authentic reaction from the audience. Two nights before, she'd attended the glitzy Hollywood premiere, stepping out of a limo and walking up the red carpet. The movie was well-received, with all the industry people laughing and clapping and congratulating her afterward.

But at the showing where she'd been anonymous, the reception was decidedly more muted. Did the audience like it? They laughed at the right places and even clapped once, but it was hard for her to gauge their reaction. And it was nothing like opening night, when everyone involved with the film was there, congratulating each other in that Hollywood self-affirming way, a circle of people patting each other on the back. "Aren't we all amazing!"

But her nervousness at being discovered faded immediately—no one was looking for her, and, therefore, no one saw her. It wasn't where she was expected to be and therefore, she wasn't there. She was just another face in the crowd, albeit a crowd somewhat disappointed with the movie they were watching.

A few other times, Jessica had snuck out with Ferrara and gone to the Santa Monica Pier to ride the rides and stand by the ocean. It had been wonderful fun.

But this was serious. After they talked, Ferrara left and Jessica stared out through the bars and wondered how long she would be here. The place drained her spirit. When she'd tried thinking about her career, or her future, all she could ponder was how quiet the place got at night, nothing but muted crying and anxious silence.

A few days later, things were looking up. Ferrara had cleared things with her family, and now Jessica had a plan. She missed Starbucks and TV and choosing the best Instagram filter. She missed the little things. Jessica just wanted to be Sydney, if even for a day.

Sydney Greene. The name sounded made up, but Jessica didn't care. She just wanted to be someone different, even for a little while.

Chapter 22
Living Conditions

Frank was still asleep on the couch Sunday morning when his grandson, Jackson, ran into the living room of Laura's apartment. The place was small and, at the moment, overstuffed with items that belonged to both her and Frank. Jackson jogged around a stack of cardboard packing boxes and ran up to the couch, waking Frank up. "Grandpa! Wake up!"

Frank turned over, groggy, and looked at the little kid. "I was out late. Grandpa sleepy."

"You can't be sleepy. We're going to the pool today!"

Frank leaned back. "They don't open until noon, you know."

"I gotta get ready!"

The little kid ran off as Laura walked in, already dressed for work. She was smiling.

"No sleeping in for you, Dad. Not with him around."

He sat up with a smile. "I know."

"How late did it go?" She sat in the chair across from him. The furniture in her apartment was "lived in," as the kids said nowadays. To Frank, it looked like she'd found every piece separately at the curb in front of someone's house.

"Got in around 3."

"I heard."

"Sorry about that," he said. "I was trying to be quiet. Of course, you've always been a light sleeper."

She nodded and handed him a coffee. "Here you are. GO juice."

"Thanks."

"Did you catch him?" Frank had a tendency to talk about his cases, especially with Laura. It wasn't strictly protocol, but she was a smart kid and picked up things.

"Got some more pictures."

She sat back in the chair.

"Good to see you're working cases," she said. "How many is that?"

"Two active. Not bad since I've only been working a week."

"Does that include looking for Joe?"

He looked at her—she didn't miss a thing.

"Okay, three."

"I know you've been out driving around," she said. "I figured that's what it was."

"He has to be somewhere," Frank said. He started to run through the cases in his mind, wondering how to keep them organized. He needed to start tracking the cases by number or something, at least to keep them straight. And for invoicing and such. "Juggling multiple cases comes with the territory."

"Just make sure you track your receipts," she said. Sometimes her accounting background broke through. "And apply them to each case for billing."

This was nice. He and Laura hadn't spoken for years until last summer, when he'd taken a chance on rekindling their tattered relationship. He'd been in a bad place, both in his personal life and at work, where he'd felt trapped in a dead-end job.

Now, not only were he and Laura closer, but he'd done something he'd never expected. Frank had picked up stakes and moved to her little Ohio town. Years ago, he'd retired from the police force and taken a civilian investigator job in Birmingham, Alabama. But his visits up to see her in the Dayton area had convinced him to move north.

Technically, the move was still ongoing—he glanced around at the corners of her living room, which were stacked with cardboard boxes labeled with words like "HARPER CLOTHES" or "HARPER PAPERS AND FILES." The handwriting was unfamiliar—back in Birmingham, he'd hired a couple of guys to help him load up a rented van with his belongings, and one of them offered to label Frank's stuff.

"Actually, that reminds me. Once things get up and running, I'm gonna get swamped with paperwork."

"Tracking cases?"

"No, billing. Invoicing. Never had to do any of that as a cop, obviously. We just worked the cases and locked up the bad guys."

"Or shot them."

"Sometimes," he said with a smile. "On the good days."

"Shut up."

"Anyway, I'm not good at the paperwork side," he said, looking at her. "Any chance you can help me out if I get overwhelmed?"

"Sure," she nodded. "$15 an hour, in between my other work. And believe me, that's a bargain."

"Good," he said. "It's a deal."

She sighed and stood up. "Okay, I gotta run. I'm at the salon again all day today. You sure you're fine with taking him to the pool? It's a whole thing: towels, water slides, suntan lotion. Take a book. And the music—just hope it's not one of the days they play country music at maximum volume."

"I'm looking forward to it," he said, making a face.

"Liar."

She bopped him on the shoulder and headed off.

He stood and stretched and went off to make some more coffee. After his short night, he would need it.

Chapter 23
Paperwork

Monday morning, Ferrara reappeared, carrying her big makeup kit and another bag. This time Aaron was with Ferrara, and Jessica was happy to see them both. She hugged them and sat down on the hard bench.

"Okay, what's happening?"

Aaron smiled. "Today's the day. You're leaving."

"Today?" She grinned. "Really?"

He nodded. "We figured out how to get you out of here without the paparazzi finding you. The LAPD is on that. But first, we have to go see Judge Watkins. She wants to talk to you, lay down the ground rules."

Jessica nodded. "But I'm out today, right?"

"That's the plan," Aaron said.

"I'm ready for anything."

Aaron shook his head. "You've got this 'Sydney' business down?"

Jessica nodded.

"Good. But don't get cocky, Jessica. Remember, this has to go perfectly. You got lucky—if Lompoc and Dublin hadn't been so overcrowded, you'd already be at one of them," he said.

Jessica nodded, mollified. "This will work, if I have anything to say about it."

Aaron looked at his watch as the guard unlocked the jail door. "Okay, here we go," Aaron said as Jessica stood, holding out her wrists, but the guard shook his head.

"No cuffs this time," Aaron said as he walked out. Jessica followed.

They walked through the facility, escorted by the guard. They ended up in an office area. Aaron knocked on one of the doors, waiting.

"Come in," someone said, and Jessica followed him in. Judge Watkins was sitting at her desk.

"Ah, Ms. Mills, come in," she said. A moment later, someone else knocked and entered—it was ADA Simmons, the prosecutor, who greeted them.

"Okay, so how's this thing going?" the judge asked.

The prosecutor took out a notepad and looked at it.

"Well, step one is to transfer 'Jessica' to the facility in Dublin. We have a police van to drive her to the airport, where she'll be 'flown' to Oakland and transported to the facility."

"Good," Judge Watkins said.

"We'll need to make it look good," Simmons said. "TMZ and the paparazzi have been stationed around the station for days."

"They have?" Jessica asked.

"You're popular," the judge said sarcastically. "It's making our job harder."

The prosecutor nodded. "They're photographing everyone going in and out, so we're going to make a big deal of using the police van. Lots of deputies, police escort to the airport, etc. Along with our announcement, we're sure they'll give chase."

The judge passed Jessica a piece of paper, and she took it, reading.

MILLS TO BE INCARCERATED AT OAKLAND-AREA FACILITY

August 5, 2012

Jessica Mills will be remanded to the custody of the state correctional facility in Dublin, California on the afternoon of April 6 following a judgment of ninety days in connection with her involvement in a car accident that resulted in the injury of two members of the public. Along with reckless endangerment and public drunkenness, Ms. Mills was charged with possession of a controlled substance. Her counsel pled guilty to all charges and agreed to allow Mills to be remanded to the Dublin facility to begin serving her term, where she will be segregated from the rest of the prison population. Mills will be eligible for release on October 29 of this year.

Simmons continued. "We'll lead them on a merry chase, I assume. The van will take surface streets to the airport, along with an escort, making lots of noise along the way. Meanwhile, Ferrara will start on the makeover here in the courthouse. When she's ready, she'll meet up with my deputy and head east. Jessica will be traveling in another vehicle. Your honor will be helping out with that."

The judge nodded. "Okay, sounds good. Aaron?"

"I'm heading out to make my speech." He turned to Jessica. "I'm going to make a scene and complain about you being incarcerated. I'll be talking about prison overcrowding and such. Between that and the police van, everyone will think you're in the upstate facility."

Jessica nodded.

The judge looked at Ferrara. "Young lady, can you step up here? You need to sign a few things."

They went through the details. Ferrara and Jessica had to agree to a number of items: Ferrara had to sign for Jessica, taking personal responsibility for her. Jessica had to follow the rules and wear a police ankle monitor. She also had to agree to stay with Ferrara's family, follow the directions of the female deputy who would be traveling to Ohio with them, and to abide by the agreement with the prosecutor's office.

Jessica was surprised that Ferrara had to sign any paperwork, but it made sense: she was vouching for Jessica in the most personal way. She was taking her out of state, taking her home to spend time with her family, and agreeing to be responsible for her.

Chapter 24
Makeunder

Ferrara was nervous.

Everything she was taking home to Ohio was packed in the rental, a Honda Pilot rented by the LAPD from an agency at LAX. She was ready to go—she'd spent the past week prepping for her "vacation." A friend would be crashing at her place to keep an eye on her apartment.

Ferrara had arrived at the courthouse on time, parking in the basement lot, and met up with Aaron at the security desk. She visited Jessica first, and when Aaron joined them, they made their way to Judge Watkin's chambers for their final conference.

Signing all the paperwork in the judge's office had been nerve-wracking, as was following the guard down the hallway to a bathroom with a "closed for cleaning" sign hanging on the door. Inside, the bathroom was cold and antiseptic, but at least it was private. She'd been worried she'd have to do Jessica's makeup right there in her jail cell for everyone to see. It was still nerve-wracking, but once she got to work, Ferrara relaxed. It was time for Jessica's "makeunder," as she was calling it. And this was at least something Ferrara could control.

"Okay, let's do this," she said, balancing her makeup and hair kits on a sink. "You ready?"

Jessica nodded, lowering herself into a folding chair that someone had put in the middle of the bathroom floor. "Never been more ready. I can't wait to get out of here."

Ferrara got to work, laying out her haircutting kit first and getting to work trimming Jessica's hair. It was a shame to see so much of her long, blond locks come off, but it would need to be short for the wig to work for an extended amount of time. Blond hair fell all around Jessica's seated figure.

"You ride in with Aaron?"

Ferrara shook her head. "We met at security. Paparazzi followed him from his house—they've staked it out. He was doing some last-minute coordinating with the airport."

"Did the rats bother you?"

"Nope, thank God," Ferrara said, snipping at Jessica's hair. "They followed me home a couple of times but then lost interest."

Jessica bit her lip. "Christ. Sorry about that."

"It's fine," Ferrara said. "Sort of exciting. Not sure how you stand it every day."

Jessica didn't say anything. Ferrara finished trimming Jessica's hair then handed her a mirror and got busy sweeping up hair from the bathroom floor. It reminded her of sweeping up hair at the salon in Cooper's Mill. She'd worked there for years, and there was a fantastic pizza place next door named DMs. She and the other stylists had spent many an afternoon gorging on pizza and watching TV. It was a wonder Ferrara wasn't fat.

"Wow, that's short," Jessica said, running her hands through her hair.

Ferrara finished bagging up the hair and rolled up her hair kit, one she'd had since back in Ohio. "I always wanted to get you into a bob," Ferrara said. "I finally got my wish."

"You did," Jessica said, handing back the mirror. "Okay, what's next?"

Ferrara opened her wig kit, a metal case with compartments for wigs and other hairpieces. Ferrara had started out as a stylist, of course, but moving into wigs and extensions was a logical step, especially after she started in the industry. One part of the wig case held a package of mustaches and sideburns, while a tray at the bottom held the glues and powders necessary to hold wigs and hairpieces in place.

"Oh, I know that one!" Jessica pointed at a reddish/pink wig at the bottom. She'd worn it on "Five Minutes to Midnight," her third film. She'd played a woman lost in a post-apocalyptic wasteland. Not her best work, Ferrara thought, but it was mostly the fault of the script.

"Yup, but here's what I'm thinking." She took out a dark brown wig. "Awesome."

They spent an hour getting her transformed. Ferrara used the wig, carefully applied to her hair once it was pressed down with a skull cap, and makeup, with Ferrara trying out several different things. Jessica itched at her arms, but Ferrara didn't mention anything. Aaron had said the coke withdrawal would be well underway by now.

The port-wine stain was the most obvious change, a large reddish mark that ran down part of Jessica's neck. "I've been practicing this for days," Ferrara said. "It's supposed to draw attention away from your face."

Jessica changed into a set of clothes Ferrara had brought, a baggy sweater and a ratty pair of blue jeans that were at least a size too big. "Thank God you brought a belt," Jessica said, cinching it up.

"The judge said they needed to be loose to cover the ankle thing," Ferrara said, adjusting the jeans. She stood back and looked—the overall effect was perfect.

Jessica looked at herself in the mirror over the sink. She turned, taking in her new look. "Where'd you get these clothes? They're terrible."

"I know, right? Wardrobe from some show," Ferrara said. "We'll buy you new stuff in Ohio, but nothing too conspicuous. Oh, and here."

Ferrara handed her a pair of glasses—Jessica thought it might be too much, but it finished off the bookish, shy look Ferrara was going for.

"I look smarter."

There was a knock at the bathroom door, and the guard let in Aaron, who arrived with a tall, bulky woman who looked like a younger version of Linda Hamilton from "The Terminator" movies. The woman looked like she worked out ten times a day, and sported a short, mannish haircut. She wore jeans and a leather jacket over a white t-shirt and was carrying what looked like a thick beeper in her hand.

"You guys ready?" Aaron asked.

Jessica turned around and Aaron stopped in his tracks.

"Whoa, Jessica? I know it's you, but wow. Great job, Ferrara."

"Thanks," she said with a smile, fiddling with Jessica's hair. "We're just wrapping up."

"Good," Aaron said, pointing at the woman with him. "This is Officer Leslie Davis, LAPD. She'll be with you on the trip, undercover."

Leslie's shoulders looked even wider close up. Ferrara thought she looked like a linebacker.

Jessica put out her hand. "Hi, Officer Davis."

"Yup," Leslie said, nodding and shaking Jessica's hand. "Leslie is fine. Or officer, for now. Ms. Mills, good to meet you." She turned to Ferrara, shaking her hand as well. "And you must be Ferrara. So, this is your crazy plan? Have to say I've never heard of anything like it before."

Ferrara nodded, backing up. "Jessica needed my help. Rehab

wasn't working, and I didn't want to see anything happen to her."

Jessica looked at Leslie. "So, you're my bodyguard?"

Leslie smiled. "I guess. But mostly I'm here to keep you in line."

"Are you packing?" Jessica asked.

Leslie pulled her jacket open, revealing an empty holster. "Not in here, but I will be. And I'll be monitoring the ankle bracelet," she said, waving it for them all to see. "You so much as wander off to pick flowers and I'll be all over you."

Jessica nodded, fiddling with her hair before Ferrara smacked her hand away good-naturedly. "Leave that alone," Ferrara said.

"It's in my face."

"I know."

Leslie took a set of photos on her phone of Jessica, getting shots from all sides. "Remember, it's my way or jail. As long as you remember that, Jessica—and follow my lead—we'll get along great."

Aaron nodded. "Okay, now that we have the formalities out of the way, we need to get moving. It's going to be a long day."

"What's the plan?" Jessica asked as Ferrara busied herself by putting away her gear.

"You don't really need to know, do you?" Leslie asked, stepping forward. "Like I said, just follow my lead. A lot of people are jumping through hoops today to get you out of town unseen."

Jessica looked at Aaron, who shrugged.

"Hey, I'm in the same boat, doing what I'm told," he said. "I have no interest in going to jail either."

Leslie knelt in front of Jessica and, for a moment, she looked like she was about to propose. Instead, she pulled up the pant-leg of Jessica's jeans and strapped the tracker around Jessica's ankle, notching it tight.

"Ow," Jessica said.

Standing, Leslie took a thin metal device out of her pocket—it looked like a TV remote. Leslie clicked it, and the ankle monitor chimed once, then three times in quick succession.

"Okay, we're good."

Jessica shook her leg. "It's heavy. And uncomfortable."

Leslie nodded but didn't say anything.

"Better than jail," Aaron added. "Right?"

"Shut up," Jessica said. "You're supposed to be my advocate. Remember?"

Leslie turned to them. "Okay, we ready?" The group nodded, and

Leslie turned, stepping out into the hallway. She said something to the guard, who moved off, and then Leslie started down the hall.

Jessica and Ferrara and Aaron followed, Ferrara leaving Jessica's discarded jail jumpsuit on the sink. Jessica glanced at it as they were leaving, and Ferrara could tell exactly what the woman was thinking: she was probably hoping she never saw this place again.

Chapter 25
Time to Go

Jessica followed Aaron and the big woman, her new "best friend," through the jail and onto the elevator. She saw few guards and no civilians. Aaron hit the button for the parking garage.

"I wish I knew what was happening," Jessica said.

"You need to get used to following orders," Leslie answered, waiting for the doors to open. "Let's just say we're doing some diversionary tactics."

"We?"

"The LAPD. And your people, too."

The doors opened on the parking lot level and they got off. A group of people was waiting for them near a large police van that was parked near the doors, the back open. The prosecutor Simmons and Judge Watkins were waiting nearby. Jessica didn't recognize the judge right away. It was the first time she'd seen Judge Watkins in civilian clothes, and she looked even smaller than before.

"Okay, that's impressive," Simmons said to Jessica and Aaron. She looked at Ferrara. "Wow. Great job."

The judge nodded, looking Jessica up and down. "Okay, maybe this could work. But I'm not holding my breath."

Aaron spun Jessica around, showing her off. "We'll make it work, judge. Don't worry."

Watkins nodded, dubious, but didn't answer.

Jessica and the others followed Watkins and Simmons to the back of the police van, which was standing open. Inside, Jessica saw a young blond woman, roughly the same build as Jessica. Looking at her, Jessica recognized what she was wearing.

"Hey, that's my shirt. And those are my jeans."

The blond girl turned around. Her hairstyle was nearly identical to Jessica's—or what it had looked like two weeks ago.

"We found a look-alike for you," Judge Watkins said. "Took some doing."

Jessica nodded, unsure of what to say.

"Okay, here we go," Leslie said, helping Aaron into the back of the police van, where two other officers were waiting. "We're behind schedule." Aaron sat down on a bench in the van next to the blond girl.

"Where are you going?" Jessica asked.

"We gotta make it look good," he said with a smile and nodding at the decoy version of Jessica. "I'm going with her. But I'll be in touch."

Leslie nodded and slammed the back doors, banging on them twice. The van started away, moving up the ramp out of the garage and into the sunlight.

"Lots of paparazzi out there, waiting to get pictures of you," Simmons said. "Hopefully, this will work. Aaron and the girl are going to the airport, where we chartered a plane to take them to Oakland. The paps will follow them, we hope, though a few of them might not take the bait."

Jessica nodded. "Okay."

"A 'thank you' would be more in order," Judge Watkins added. "You think you're worth all this? All these people jumping through hoops?"

A sharp reply leapt into Jessica's throat, but she stifled the urge to sass. "I hope so, ma'am."

"I'm leaving, too," Ferrara said. "With Leslie. We'll meet you at the rendezvous on Tatooine."

No one reacted, but Jessica smiled.

Ferrara continued. "Sorry, couldn't help it. Try not to fiddle with your hair too much."

Jessica hugged her, not excited to be alone with the prosecutor and the judge, and was surprised when ADA Simmons also excused herself, helping Ferrara with her cases. Jessica watched them walk towards a Honda Pilot nearby, which they loaded up.

Leslie nodded at Watkins. "Your honor."

"Keep an eye on this one for me, Officer Davis," the judge said, nodding at Jessica. "She's annoying."

Leslie nodded, handing the judge something, then walked off, following Ferrara and the prosecutor, who was helping Ferrara put her bags in the Pilot. It looked like a rental.

"You've got some great friends," Judge Watkins said, walking away. "Come on."

"I'm going with you, your honor?"

"Yup."

Jessica, confused, hurried to follow. The jeans were baggy and loose and made it hard to hurry. The weight around her ankle wasn't helping.

"You'll get used to it," Judge Watkins said, noticing Jessica's limp.

They crossed the parking garage and stopped in front of an old Ford Taurus. Watkins popped the trunk and held it open.

"Okay, get in."

Jessica scowled. "What?"

"Get in," Watkins said. "I'm not driving you out of here in the front seat like we're going to get ice cream together."

"You're driving me?"

"Yup."

"But I don't want to ride in the trunk. And how far? Where are we going?"

Watkins crossed her arms, a look Jessica remembered from the courtroom. "You're pushing me, young lady. But don't worry—I probably won't make you ride in the trunk all the way to Palm Springs. Or maybe I will. It depends on how much you piss me off."

Jessica looked around—there was no one else in the parking garage. This whole thing seemed very sketchy, but apparently, she had to trust the woman. Making a face, Jessica climbed in.

"Promise me you won't slam—"

Judge Watkins slammed the trunk lid.

The last thing Jessica saw was the look on the judge's face. The old woman was grinning from ear to ear.

Chapter 26
Worst Uber Ever

Jessica rode in the trunk for what seemed like forever, the car bumping around. Jessica braced herself against the impacts. Every time the car took a turn, she hit her head on the inside wall of the trunk. This whole thing was a disaster. Her arms itched even more. Soon after leaving the courthouse, Jessica had felt the car accelerate loudly, then the ride got smoother, as if they were driving on a highway.

After an hour, Jessica was starting to feel the need to use the restroom when the car slowed down. It came to a stop, then accelerated, making a series of turns before stopping. She heard the engine turn off and the car door open and keys at the trunk lid.

Finally, the lid lifted. Jessica covered her eyes against the brightness.

"You dead?"

"Not yet, your honor," Jessica replied. Several other sassier responses leapt into her mind, but she ignored them, climbing from the trunk and looking around.

They were in a mall parking lot, across from a Starbucks. It was warm out and she could see the heat coming off the mall parking lot pavement. The mall had a theater and a JC Penney and a World Gym.

"Where are we? That was like the worst Uber ride ever." Jessica rubbed the back of her head where she'd bumped it over and over.

"Couldn't be helped," Watkins said, taking out a cigarette and lighting it. "Want one?"

"Yeah, thanks, your honor."

Watkins handed her a smoke and the lighter, and Jessica lit up, enjoying the first inhalation as she handed the lighter back.

"Did Aaron and the others get away okay?"

"I did see the paparazzi tailing the police van," Judge Watkins said. "The blond girl sat near one of the windows with Aaron, and the photographers all piled into their cars and chased after them."

"Okay. So, where are we?"

"I'll give you a hint," Watkins said with a smile. She pointed at the parking lot around them. "88 miles per hour."

Jessica looked around, shaking her head.

Watkins sighed. "What about Libyans? Does that ring a bell?"

"Nope."

"Marty and Doc? Delorean?"

"'*Back to the Future?*' The movie?"

Watkins nodded, pointing at the wide parking lot. "This is the Puente Hills Mall, where they filmed the time-travel scenes. You know, Marty and Doc in the parking lot, testing out the Delorean. The Libyans showing up, Marty jumping in the Delorean, racing away. Doc Brown getting killed." She turned and pointed toward a road. "That's were Marty skateboarded down and saw himself driving off in the Delorean."

Jessica looked around, recognizing parts of it. "Wow. Cool."

"Not just cool, Jessica," Watkins said, looking at Jessica. "It is cool, of course, and a reminder that anyplace, no matter how ordinary, can be famous."

"Nice."

"But that's not why I brought you here."

Jessica turned and looked at the nearby highway, cars speeding off into the distance. "Bathroom break?"

"No, it's time for you to make a choice. Like Marty. Are you going to live your life, or let other people decide things for you? You've surrounded yourself with useless people."

"I guess so," Jessica said. "But having a career is difficult, and I have a lot going on. HAD a lot going on. Lots of moving parts. I need people who can help me—"

"Is it their job to keep you IN trouble?"

"No, it's not."

"Do they know that? If you got sober and healthy, you wouldn't need them as much. Aaron's all right, and Ferrara. But your publicist is a piece of work. What about your business manager, or those two bimbos who score you coke?"

Jessica smoked her cigarette and thought about it. She wasn't wrong—having people to run her errands was nice, but half of it was just her trying to distance herself from the world. "You might be right."

"I am right, believe me," Judge Watkins said. "Ferrara seems like a good sort. And Officer Davis will keep you in line. But you could get away if you wanted to," she said matter-of-factly. "You're being tracked, but it wouldn't take much work to get that ankle monitor off. You could be free and clear."

Jessica looked at her and suddenly wanted to run. Right here, right now. Sure, they could track her, but Jessica was young, and she and the judge were alone in a parking lot in the middle of nowhere. And the strap on the ankle monitor didn't look that thick. Jessica could run and get away, find someone or something to get the monitor off, and be free.

But would she be free? Really? Everyone knew who she was, or would as soon as she shed this stupid "disguise." Jessica might get away, but she'd never act again. Jessica scratched at her itchy arms.

"DTs?"

Jessica looked at her. It had been seven days since her last hit, and she was jumpy. "Maybe."

"They'll get worse before they get better," Watkins said. "Okay, time for a test." She pointed at the Starbucks and handed Jessica $10. "Go inside and use their restroom, then order something for yourself. I want to see if you get spotted."

"Are you kidding?"

"No, I'm not. I can tell it's you, no problem. But maybe this will work. If not, I can turn the car around and we can head back to the courthouse. I'll contact Officer Davis and call this whole thing off."

Jessica took the money.

"Remember, you can run if you want too," Watkins said quietly. "But if you do, you'll never really be free."

Jessica nodded and started inside, her mind a riot of thoughts. What if she was spotted? How could anyone in the Starbucks NOT recognize her? And what if she DID run—how long before she was recaptured?

Breathing deeply, Jessica put her hand on the door of the Starbucks and pulled, heading inside. The air was cool. Jessica looked around— it had been a while since she'd seen the inside of a Starbucks.

Usually, people got her coffee for her.

"Can I help you?"

Jessica turned and looked at a woman behind the counter, and suddenly realized how nervous she felt. Would this woman recognize her?

"Yeah, I need to use the restroom," Jessica said, dropping into the flat Texas drawl that she and Ferrara had worked out for her "character," Sydney Green. She held up her money. "And then I'll buy something."

"Oh, that's fine, dear," the woman said, waving her away. "People come in all the time just to use the bathrooms. Do you want me to get something started for you?"

"Sure," Jessica said, reminding herself to use her accent. It still sounded fake in her mouth and needed more work. "Triple Venti White Mocha?"

"Oh, that's a good one," the Starbucks lady said. "I'll get it started and you can pay when you get out."

Jessica nodded and headed for the bathroom, finding the LADIES room with no problem. Inside, she locked the door and stood at the sink for a long moment, breathing and looking at her reflection.

She didn't look like Jessica Mills.

Well, sorta. She looked like a weird Halloween version of Jessica Mills, a cheap knockoff. The glasses and the clothes and the hair made all the difference. And the port-wine stain was bigger than it had looked in Ferrara's little mirror. Jessica realized it covered half of her neck. It was hard not to look at it—that was the point. Jessica resisted the urge to touch it. Instead, she did her business and dabbed a little water on her face after washing her hands. She tried to not smudge the makeup.

Back in the lobby, Jessica got out the money and paid for her drink. The lady behind the counter thanked her and asked her to wait at the end. Jessica slid down the railing and waited near a newspaper display.

No one said anything to her. No one even looked at her. No one asked for her picture or whispered her name as they talked about her.

Instead, "Sydney" stood at the counter, just like any other person, and waited for her drink. She looked around at the other people in the shop. They were just going about their business. One person looked at her, glanced at her neck, and then looked away.

This might actually work.

"White Mocha?"

Jessica turned around to see a very skinny man behind the counter holding up her drink. He had a weird tattoo above one eye and the whitest teeth she'd ever seen.

"Yup, that's me."

"Sorry, there's no name on it."

"Thanks," Jessica said, and took the cup, smiling at the man. She started to ask him a question, but in the next moment, Jessica was amazed to see the man's attention slide away from her face and go back to his work. He was making drinks for other customers—there was a drive-through as well as indoor customers—and he needed to get back to work.

Smiling, Jessica decided to press her luck. She sipped at the coffee—it was excellent—and walked back over to where the woman was working who had taken her order.

"Thank you."

The woman looked up from the register. "Oh, no problem, dear. Have a good day." Jessica expected the woman to keep talking to her, or whip out her phone and ask for a selfie with Jessica.

Instead, she turned away, looking to another customer and ignoring Jessica.

Ignored her.

It was glorious.

CHAPTER 27
New License

It was Monday, just after noon, August 6th, and the day had been quiet so far. Frank had seen Laura and Jackson off—she was heading to work and had dropped Jackson at a friend's house—and now he was sitting at Laura's computer, checking on his P.I. license. Her cheap little laptop was frustratingly slow, and the keyboard was too small for his fat fingers.

Frank waited for the page to load, glancing around at her apartment. He knew that every empty space was piled with his cardboard boxes. Stacks of his stuff threatened to take over the place, along with the jumble of his furniture piled behind her ratty couch. Jackson's room was even stacked with boxes of his clothes. More boxes stood in the hallway, the contents of his kitchen and bathroom from down in Birmingham.

Everything Frank owned in the world was here or stuffed in his car. All of it in a perpetual state of waiting, some kind of stasis. Living out of cardboard boxes. Living off his daughter. She'd put him up, of course, but it was time to get his own place.

The State of Ohio web site finally came up—Laura apparently could only afford the cheapest level of Internet available—and told Frank Harper, P.I.-to-be, the same thing it had been telling him for a week: his license was "pending."

He'd applied for a private investigator license even before he'd moved to town, on the advice of Chief King, back when he was still speaking to Frank. Now, it looked like Frank needed to get on the phone and call someone about it in Columbus.

Originally, it had looked like getting a license was no big deal, but maybe he'd missed something. Frank read the page again, scanning it more carefully than he had the first few times. He was having trouble understanding what the hold-up might be. It was a bunch of government-speak, that special language of legalese that government folks used to discourage business, Frank guessed. But wasn't it their job to help him out if he needed help?

Finally, Frank found the part about Ohio's Concealed Carry (CC) licensing rules and realized he'd screwed up something on the original application.

"Crap."

There was a section for writing in whether or not you had an Ohio-issued CC license (he did not) or if you had an equivalent permit or license from another state (he did). The website then went on to explain that if you had an out-of-state CC license, you had to get a letter from that state to verify the license was current. There were also training requirements and exceptions for former members of military branches or police departments.

He found the appropriate number on the website and called in, waiting on hold until someone came on the line to talk to him. Frank asked about his pending application and explained what he thought he might have done wrong. The lady on the other end was very nice, and she found his in-progress application.

"Let me take a look at this for a second," she said. "Do you mind?"

"No, that's fine," he said, waiting.

She walked Frank through his entire application and confirmed why it had been delayed in their system—it wasn't clear where his current concealed carry license was from. She also said it was unclear if he was currently a police officer or retired. Frank explained the situation quickly and she corrected it on the application for him.

"Retired?"

"Yes, ma'am," he answered. "New Orleans PD. I moved to Alabama and worked cold cases for the ABI for a while. My last gun permit was from Alabama and is still current."

"Ah, okay, that makes sense," she said. He could hear her clacking away at her keyboard, presumably in some government office building in Columbus, the state capital of Ohio. "It was held up. I'll put in a call to the Alabama office of the ATF. They'll fax over your work records and the CC license. That should do it."

"Sounds great," he said, crossing his fingers.

"And I'll check with my boss—you might need to re-up your license at an Ohio range," she said. "But the 8-hour training will likely be waived—there's an exception for retired police officers. I'll call you and let you know. But with these corrections, I see no reason why they wouldn't approve this. So, what brings you to Ohio?"

He explained quickly about his daughter Laura and her son Jackson and his efforts to reconnect with them. It was strange, telling a complete stranger about something so personal.

"It's a nice story, Mr. Harper. Most of the time, people are just calling in to complain."

"Sorry to hear that," Frank said, wondering if staying on the phone with this lady and chatting her up would expedite his application—or make it take longer.

The woman started talking to someone else. "Hold on a second, Mr. Harper."

There was muffled conversation for long enough for Frank to think she'd forgotten about him before she came back on.

"Okay, sorry about that," she said. "My supervisor walked by and I talked him through it and he approved your application. I'll get the P.I. license into the mail today to you. Actually, it's a whole package of information, including a binder of regulations."

Surprised, Frank nodded even though she couldn't see him. "Wow, thanks. I didn't expect anyone to answer or help me, never mind the sitting on the phone and correcting the form for me."

"Not a problem," she said. "I'll get back to you about the CC license. Good luck, Mr. Harper."

He said thanks and hung up the phone feeling great. With his license on the way, he could start taking some of the jobs he'd passed on. He'd also heard from the folks in Alabama that his pension was kicking in starting August 31. With more money coming in, he could think about getting an apartment of his own. Laura was a dear to put him up, but he could tell he was starting to wear out his welcome.

Plus, Frank was used to being on his own. While he loved his daughter and grandson, there were times when he just wanted to sit in the dark and watch football or baseball on the television.

Getting an apartment would be a big help. It was a good thing Frank was friends with local landlord and entrepreneur Jake Delancy. Frank had helped Jake out with a sticky situation a few months ago, so Jake owed him one. If anyone could find Frank an apartment in this little town, it would be Jake.

Chapter 28
Palm Springs

"Sydney Green from Houston, Texas" walked out of the Starbucks with more spring in her step than she could remember. She looked around at the wide parking lot and tried to picture where the Delorean raced in the movie, chased by a van full of crazed terrorists, if she remembered it right.

She pointed. "So, over there? And then they drove up that way?"

Judge Watkins turned and looked at where she was pointing. "Yup, that's about it." She was leaning on her car and smoking another cigarette. "So, how'd it go?"

"No problems at all," Jessica said, holding up her coffee and passing back the change. "But it felt odd, like an out-of-body experience," she said, looking across the parking lot. "It's been a long time."

"Since you ordered your own coffee?"

"Yeah. But that's not it. It's strange, not being accosted."

"Going unnoticed?" Watkins asked. "Like a regular person?"

"Yeah."

Watkins dropped her cigarette to the ground and stubbed it out with her foot. "Well, I'm hoping you can get used to it, at least for a while," she said, pointing at Jessica's wig. "With this getup, you might blend in. But remember, you're an actor. ACT like someone else. If you're any good, people might believe you."

"Maybe."

"Okay," Watkins said, pointing at the car. "Get in."

Jessica pointed at the trunk and scowled.

"No, you can sit up front."

Ten minutes later, they were on the 10 highway, heading east.

"Palm Springs?"

Watkins nodded, not taking her eye off the road. "Ferrara and Officer Davis are meeting us there. Davis rented you guys a Honda Pilot to take cross country."

Jessica frowned. "We're not flying? I just assumed we were headed for some out-of-the-way airport—"

"Nope, I couldn't justify the costs. Getting you through security would be a nightmare, and violate federal law. The only other option was to charter something. Besides, I think it will be good for you to see some of the world."

Jessica looked around at the countryside. Highway 10 led up and out of the massive "bowl" that was taken up by Los Angeles proper. The wide road headed straight east into the mountains that ringed the valley.

She turned back to Watkins. "I'm not a shut-in, your honor. I have seen other parts of the world."

"Oh yeah?"

"And you know my history, ma'am. I wasn't born in LA. I'm from St. Louis."

"True, true," Watkins said. "But you came out pretty early, right? Second grade? 'Fun with Jane' made you famous by the time you were ten or eleven. It's probably most of what you remember."

"I've been on movie shoots, been to other countries, your honor. Places you've never been to, I'll bet."

"Maybe. And movie shoots, yes, you've done a few. Did you leave the sets and travel around?"

"Security is always a problem," Jessica said, sipping at her coffee. It was hot and glorious, her first Starbucks in a while. "They have restrictions on what we can do in our downtime. The insurance guys are always harping on it. 'Stay safe, don't go out.' That kind of thing. Has to do with the completion insurance."

"What's that?"

Jessica launched into a description of the insurance that films and TV shows took out to guarantee the completion of the project. Films often bought a "completion bond" or similar insurance, paying premiums in case something happened to shut down the production—weather, union troubles, cast or crew injuries, or natural disasters. Most of the time it was "personnel issues"—some star on the shoot would hold up production. They might derail the project by getting arrested or, worse, overdosing. It happened more than people knew. Completion bonds were big business in an industry where many of the "big names" were unreliable and addicted to one substance or another.

They drove through the mountains, Watkins watching the road and Jessica enjoying chatting. The conversation turned serious about the time they passed the exit to San Bernardino.

"You know this isn't what I wanted," the judge said quietly. "I wanted you to go to jail. Actual jail."

Jessica nodded, unsure if she should disagree or not.

"How does that make you feel? You can say."

Jessica shook her head. "I don't really want to. At this point, pissing you off seems like a bad idea."

"It's okay. Speak your mind."

Jessica sighed and looked out the window. They had been driving and the eastern horizon was darkening. "I don't think I deserve to go to jail."

"You deserve much worse, Ms. Mills," the judge said, staring straight ahead. "You're privileged and entitled. And no one in your life ever tells you 'no,' right? You've surrounded yourself with 'yes men.' I think you're a little snot."

Jessica turned and looked at her.

"I'm not being mean, if that's what you're thinking," Judge Watkins said quietly. "And I'm not jealous of you. I'm worried about you, about the path you're on. I'm giving you a final chance to turn things around. I might get into trouble when this all comes out, but I'm betting you can change. Can you?"

"I...I think so."

"You better, or your friends will pay the price," she said quietly. "If this doesn't work, your attorney's going to look like an idiot for proposing this insane plan. I will too, probably. That's the reason I'm personally driving you to Palm Springs. I need to make sure I'm fine with this whole arrangement, and I figured a private talk might set my mind at ease."

Jessica nodded, not saying anything.

"If it doesn't work, you will go to jail. 'Real jail,' as you called it," the judge said. "It won't be pretty, but no one will blame me. Murderers go to jail."

Jessica looked at her. "What?"

"Murderers go to jail. They have to pay their debt to society."

"I'm not a murderer," Jessica said quietly. "I've done drugs, yes. I caused that accident. But I've never hurt anyone."

"You know that woman in the accident?"

Jessica nodded.

"She died this morning," the judge said.

Jessica's hands were suddenly sweaty, like when she was on set under hot lights. The lights were always three times brighter than they seemed like they needed to be.

"What?"

The judge nodded. "The accident was worse than we let on, I'm afraid. We'd hoped the woman would recover, but they took her off life support this morning. When I get back, I'll add one count of involuntary manslaughter to your charges."

Jessica didn't answer. Her mouth wasn't working. The air in the car suddenly felt stifling. Jessica didn't know what to say, so she only nodded.

"Good," the judge said. "I'm glad we agree. You are in serious trouble."

"Yes, ma'am," she said finally. "I know."

"Well, as the kids like to say, you need to get your shit together," Judge Watkins said, looking straight ahead. "And don't mention the woman's death to anyone—we're trying to keep that quiet. Like your case needs MORE attention."

"Yes, your honor."

Watkins glanced over. "Good. Now be back in front of me on October twenty-ninth," the judge said, her voice low. Jessica could barely hear her. "In Los Angeles. Got it? Clean and sober and with a better attitude. Or you can try your luck in prison. It's your call, Jessica."

They rode in silence for the rest of the drive, each of them alone with their thoughts. Judge Watson took the exit to Palm Springs and directed her car to another strip mall, parking in front of a Barnes and Noble.

"We're meeting them here," Watkins said. "But we're early. This place has a coffee shop inside. Walk around, mingle, chat with people. Let's see if you get recognized."

But Judge Watkins was worried for no reason—not a single person in the bookstore gave "Sydney Green" a second look. Jessica wandered the store, picking out a stack of tabloids and magazines and bringing them to the lounge area next to the coffee shop, joining Judge Watkins at one of the tables.

"What am I supposed to do for money? I don't have my purse, or even ID."

"Officer Davis will have all of that for you. She was getting IDs made up from the photos she took. You'll get a fake ID and a credit card in Sydney's name, just in case. As for money, she or Ferrara will pay for everything. Get ready to live the high life—you might even enjoy living on less than $100 a day."

"What?"

"That's the limit I gave Officer Davis for each of you. Ferrara's paying her own way. Hope you can get used to McDonald's and cheap hotels."

The judge went back to her newspaper and Jessica sat back in her chair, digging into the magazines. She always read the tabloids. Jessica thumbed through "People" and "TMZ News" and "Entertainment Weekly," looking for news about her projects and her industry friends.

When she was done, she read through the newspapers. It wasn't something she really cared about, but it had been days since she'd had contact with the outside world.

"Oh, that reminds me. Can I get my phone?"

"No."

"What, your honor?"

"Nope," Judge Watkins said with a smile. "No phones. No internet, no Instagram, no Facebook."

"What? Why?"

"Can't risk you slipping up and talking to anyone as yourself. If you need to see something, Officer Davis is authorized to show you on her phone."

"It feels weird, being out of touch. What about my mother?"

"We'll put out a statement in the next day or two," the judge said. "You're under lock and key, as far as the world is concerned. If there is an emergency, or someone MUST get ahold of you, it will get forwarded to me and I'll make the call."

"Okay," Jessica said, going back to the newspaper. Instead of being in jail, a serious threat to her physically, she was going to disappear from the earth. Would people still be talking about her in three months? How many parts will she miss out on? How many auditions and callbacks would she have to pass on? And say nothing of promoting "Knights of the Temple." The movie folks would be furious.

Leslie and Ferrara arrived a few minutes later in the Pilot. Jessica could see that Ferrara had done up her hair in a style she never wore, getting into the spirit of things. They came inside, and Ferrara walked over and hugged Jessica.

"You okay?"

"Yeah."

Ferrara looked at her funny. "Where's your accent?" she whispered.

"I thought you were from Texas."

"Yeah, I'm fine," Jessica said, drawing out her words. "Don'tcha worry 'bout me."

Ferrara smiled.

Officer Davis talked to Judge Watkins, filling her in on what had happened. At the airport, Aaron and the young blond woman had gotten onto the private jet and flown away, heading north. Davis had seen some of the paparazzi desperately booking flights out of town, chasing Aaron and the decoy to Oakland. And Officer Davis, unknown to the paparazzi, had left the airport and met up with Ferrara at the courthouse.

"Did you have any trouble, ma'am?"

Judge Watkins shook her head, then took something out of her pocket and handed it to Officer Davis. It was the ankle remote. "No, nothing. She went into a Starbucks earlier with no problems. And no one here has said a thing." She glanced around the bookstore.

Officer Davis looked at her watch, a fat, square Apple Watch. "We'll get to the hotel, then hit the road in the morning. Any new instructions?"

"Nope," Judge Watkins said. "Just keep me and your superiors informed via that encrypted text group we set up. And call her 'Sydney' in all your communications. Can't have this get out." She turned to Jessica. "Remember, this only works if you make it work. I'm pulling for you. Don't disappoint me."

Jessica nodded, and then Judge Watkins said her goodbyes and left the store. She got into her Taurus and drove away.

When she was gone, Officer Davis sat down and pointed at the chairs across from her.

"Please."

Ferrara and Jessica sat down.

"First, let's go over the rules."

They both nodded. Jessica knew this was coming.

"I know this whole situation is like something out of a movie," Officer Davis said. "We're gonna make the best of it, and that means we have to stay aware of our surroundings. Jessica, our top priority is your anonymity. Got it?"

Jessica nodded. "I know."

"It's important that you're not outed, okay?" Officer Davis said quietly. "If you are, we'll immediately return to LA and this 'plea bargain' arrangement ends. If you want this to work, you need to be careful. Keep it top-of-mind all the time. You can't afford to let your guard down, not even for a second."

"Okay."

"Here's what I want—whenever we're in public, you need to be 'Sydney.' Like now."

"Now?"

Officer Davis nodded. "We don't need to be whispering your 'real' name or giving people a reason to be suspicious. When we're in public, you're Sydney. Got it?" she asked, crossing her arms, waiting.

Jessica shook her head and opened her mouth and the dumb Texas drawl came out. "I gotcha, Officer Davis ma'am," she drawled. "Like we say in Houston, you're running this wagon train. What do ya say, PARDNER?"

"Don't push it," Davis said. "Just stay in character. After a while, it should become second nature. Ferrara, you need to stay on top of her look. If one thing is out of place, it could be a giveaway."

Ferrara nodded soberly. "I will."

"Okay," Davis said. "The other thing is I want you to call me Leslie in public. Not 'Officer Davis' or 'Officer' or ma'am. We're all just regular lady folks, okay? Leslie."

"Leslie," Jessica said. "Gotcha."

"Right," Ferrara agreed. "Leslie."

"Good," Davis said. "Judge Watkins authorized an expense account, which I will be managing. She said to go on the cheap. Nothing fancy. And everything we buy, every penny we spend, has to be backed up with receipts."

"Got it," Ferrara said. "Gas, motels, food, souvenirs. Anything else?"

Davis shook her head, then looked around. "We need to tread lightly, ladies. I don't want us to be in any one place for long—the more people see 'Sydney,' the more likely someone will figure things out. Agreed?"

They both nodded.

"Good," Davis said, glancing at her Apple Watch. "We're booked at a casino hotel in Indio, about twenty minutes east of here. Big place, busy, lots of people going in and out. They're all gambling, not looking for Hollywood starlets. Should be the perfect place to test out your look. We'll get an early start in the morning. Okay?"

"Yup," they said around the table. Davis stood and started for the door, and Ferrara and "Sydney" followed, stepping out into the Palm Springs night air.

Chapter 29
In the Office

On Tuesday morning, Frank was up early and sitting in his "office," going over his notes and waiting for his next appointment. Space was a little cramped at his "desk," so he slid his breakfast over and opened up his notebook to write down what had just happened.

His main appointment had turned out to be a bust. The young man was getting harassed at work and wanted someone to step in and defend him or, better yet, get something on the bully and get him to quit.

Frank had told him he didn't do that kind of work, and the kid had left, frustrated.

It was not technically true—the job description of a private investigator could be stretched to fit nearly any morally-ambiguous situation. But Frank hoped to avoid getting sucked down the rabbit hole of nasty jobs like that. Of course, if the pipeline of potential paying jobs dried up, he might have to reconsider and call the kid back. Money was money. For now, he'd told the kid to go to the cops and file a complaint. You never knew when something "bad" might happen.

And he'd written it down. He'd started writing down things lately. It seemed like, since moving to Ohio, he had a lot more things to keep track of. Potential cases, leads, people he talked to, things he needed to get done. It had started out as a list of things he needed to do to get qualified for his PI license and grown from there.

"More coffee, hon?"

He glanced up at the waitress, a new one he hadn't met yet. His "office" was Booth #3 at the Tip Top Diner, his favorite restaurant in town. They had great food and even better coffee.

"Yeah, sure. What's your name?"

"I'm Polly," she said with a smile. "And you're Frank Harper. The other girls were telling me about you. Said you helped out one of the other waitresses when she had some trouble with her cop husband."

"I did," he said, opening his book and jotting that "case" down as well, even though it was closed as far as he was concerned. They were adding up.

"What's that?"

"Oh, I'm a private investigator. Figured I'd better start writing things down."

She nodded and moved on, not saying anything. Some people were like that—cops made them nervous. Maybe they didn't want people in their business. Of course, cops were rarely looking for MORE work—they usually had plenty on their plates, even small-town cops like here in Cooper's Mill.

After Frank was done jotting down his notes about the meeting with the kid, he kept writing, putting down everything going on with his divorce case. It didn't take long—that case was just getting started. Last week's three stakeouts had his first "official" tasks, other than doing the usual internet and social media searches. Frank jotted down what he had done so far, using a new page for the divorce case and sipping the last of his coffee.

He went back to his list as he finished his omelet. It had occurred to him that he needed to come up with a filing system. He'd started his list of the "cases" he'd worked on in Ohio, numbering them in order: the Martin kidnapping, his involvement with the Northsiders Gang, investigating Joe Hathaway. He quickly sketched out each "case" but didn't go into much detail. He also worked up another list on a different page, "leads" for future cases, writing down that Jake Delancy had called and left a message yesterday about a potential case.

He flipped the yellow pad to his "to do" list for today, August 7, 2012. He had two appointments with prospective clients, both here at the diner, plus another meeting with Mrs. Robinson. This place had become his de-facto office, to the point that now, when he came to eat, there was usually a message or two waiting for him from people who needed his help.

The rest of the to-do list was pretty boring. "Get a place" was at the top of the list, followed by a bunch of errands: he needed more clothes, and to meet with Jake Delancy and look at apartments. "Finish PI license" was on the list, along with "re-up CCL" and some pie-in-the-sky notes like "rent office" and "hire bookkeeper."

There were a few reachable goals, of course, and Frank would just have to work through them methodically. The "CCL" item was his focus today. He'd been putting it off, but it was something he could no longer delay.

But he wasn't looking forward to going to the range. He wasn't worried about his skill with a gun—he'd always been a good shot. He and his ex-partner Ben Stone had spent a lot of time at the range when they'd worked together down in Florida, and while Ben was always the better shot, Frank could come pretty close. Ben was always the better shot—fat lot of good it ended up doing. He'd been gunned down in a dark alley in Coral Gables, his trusty gun still in the holster.

But this wasn't about Ben. Frank wasn't looking forward to using the particular range he'd been told was the only one in the area that could certify him. Although he'd never been there, the place would certainly hold reminders of a person Frank would rather forget.

Frank sat back and glanced around at the interior of the Tip Top Diner. The place was in desperate need of an update—it looked like the place had been built and decorated in 1978 and never updated. They needed new paint and new carpet and, most of all, take down the yellowing brown wallpaper that covered the walls. There were dusty fake plants sprinkled around, and the bathrooms were sketchy at best.

But the food was great.

Currently, the place was decorated for fall and celebrated the upcoming "Mum Festival," a festival held every year at the City Park just north of the downtown. It was one of the biggest festivals in the area and had been held annually for something like forty years. Here at the diner, they had copies of most of the official festival t-shirts hanging on the walls, going all the way back to the very first Mum Festival. Apparently, the woman owner collected the shirts, and had been buying them since the start. Every year she got them out of storage and displayed them on the walls, each shirt folded around a square of thick cardboard and hung on the wall. She'd told Frank last week how she was only missing four of the shirts and often searched local thrift shops for the missing ones.

The Tip Top Diner was homey, and his office, for now. They never rushed him out the doors or made him feel like he needed to leave, and when he'd started having work meetings here, they never even asked. Frank got the idea that a lot of people had meetings here over lunch or over coffee—maybe they'd been hosting meetings here for decades, like a small-town Panera.

It was good they let him meet here. Right now, renting an office was out of the question. He glanced at the door and reconsidered kicking the bullied young man to the curb. Money was money, and Frank wasn't above kicking the crap out of some loudmouth if the job paid well enough.

Frank pushed the to-do list aside and went back to reading the local paper. The Cooper's Mill Gazette was written and printed locally and his new obsession since moving to town. There was no better way of getting the lay of the land in a new town then by reading the local paper. He was learning all the names of the important people in town, or at least those who were good at getting their names in the paper. He was also getting up to speed on the local organizations and businesses.

The most interesting part of the paper, far and away, was the police blotter, which was broken into two sections: one for the Cooper's Mill police department, the other for the Miami County Sheriff's Office. The MCSO listings were arrests and other incidents that happened outside the city limits. Frank read through both police blotters with interest, getting up to speed on the local criminals, troublemakers and those involved in domestic situations. Frank also recognized many of the names of the police officers; until recently, he'd been on very good terms with the local PD.

The little bell rang on the door and Frank glanced over, seeing Fran Robinson enter, looking out of place, dressed a little better than anyone else in the diner. She looked around for a second and then saw Frank and nodded. He waved her over and stood as she joined him at booth #3.

"Hi, Mrs. Robinson," Frank said. "Thanks for meeting with me."

She looked around and then shook his hand. "Hello, Mr. Harper. I've got to ask again—do we have to meet somewhere so...public? My situation is...delicate, as you know."

Frank nodded and sat, directing her into the booth across from him. "These are the best kind of places to meet, actually. Lots of people coming and going, lots of noise. It's hard to overhear a conversation in a place like this. Believe me, I've tried. Coffee?"

"No, thanks," she said, sitting and looking around, grimacing at the dusty decorations just as she'd done at their first meeting. She set a delicate little purse on the table between them.

Frank waved over one of the waitresses, Tina.

"Can I get more coffee?"

She nodded. "Brewing a fresh pot—be just a second."

Frank nodded and folded up the paper, then took his yellow pad and turned to a new page. "Okay, Mrs. Robinson, I've got good news. I tailed your husband three times last week, and you were right."

She nodded, her hands playing with the purse on the table in front of them, clasping and unclasping the latch. "I knew it. I just knew it. I saw the pictures you sent."

Frank went over what he'd found so far, showing her more pictures on his phone. Taylor Robinson had indeed been visiting a woman's home.

"I have pictures of him leaving on two of the nights, with timestamps," he said, showing her before setting the phone down. "I sent those over, but here are more. It's clear he's going to her house regularly. How would you like to proceed?"

She looked at her purse for a long time, saying nothing as Tina refilled Frank's coffee. Finally, Mrs. Robinson glanced up at him. "I wish I knew why," she said. "I thought we were happy. We were talking about going back to Mexico for our twentieth. It's coming up in October."

Frank didn't know what to say— "congratulations" seemed wildly out of order—so he just nodded and sipped his coffee and waited. Sometimes, the best way to get people to talk was to just let the silence stretch. People didn't like silence and rushed to fill it, even if they were nervous. He'd learned this technique years ago as a cop—sometimes, the best way to get people to talk was just to listen.

Finally, she sat back. "I need more."

"What?"

"More pictures," she said. "More proof. I can't divorce him for that," she said, nodding at the phone. "I'm suspicious—he's been so distant lately. Always 'working late,' that kind of stuff. But there's no proof, right?"

Frank shook his head. "Well, it's true. But that's all I've been able to find. And your retainer went to that," he said, tiptoeing around the subject of money. "If you want me to stay on the job, I'll need more retainer to—"

"Oh, that's not a problem," she said. She unsnapped the little purse and took out an envelope, sliding it across the table like they were in a movie or something. "$1,000 more. What does that buy me?"

Frank smiled. People watched too many movies. But it would work. He opened the envelope and checked the contents. "Twenty more hours, Mrs. Robinson. How would you like it spent?"

"Can you tail the woman?" she asked, looking around as if someone in the busy restaurant were listening, Frank thought. "Find out more about her? And follow Taylor. I want to know what...what they're doing."

Frank nodded.

"I'll see what I can do."

She leaned forward. "To divorce him, I'll need other pictures. You know what I mean? Pictures of them...occupied. Doing stuff. You know?"

Frank did.

She thanked him and left, scurrying out of the place like she thought she might catch something from the old wallpaper. Frank lingered, finishing his coffee and making more notes on the "Robinson case." It made it sound much more glamorous than what it was—trying to snap some photos of Taylor and his "chickie" in a compromising position. Frank wasn't sure how he was going to make that happen, but he was certainly going to try.

Frank left, making his way out to the Camaro. It sat gleaming in the sun, the only nice thing he owned in the whole world. The rest of his dingy crap was in boxes in Laura's apartment, but this car was something he could be proud of. He'd always wanted a nice vintage car and had spent the entirety of his reward money from solving the Martin kidnapping to buy it.

He got in and started it up, enjoying the purr of the engine. He'd almost lost the car during that whole mess with the Northsiders'. Frank glanced over at the nearby Vacation Inn—members of the gang had arranged to kidnap him from the hotel. And they'd taken his car as well. He'd been happy to get it back.

Frank ran his hands along the dashboard with a smile, then put it in gear and left the parking lot, taking the turn onto the highway, headed south. He was not looking forward to his next errand, but it was best to get it out of the way.

Chapter 30
Road Trip

They were traveling in the Honda Pilot, a surprisingly-spacious SUV. The back third of it was taken up with suitcases and a cooler, but Jessica had the large second row all to herself.

"A detox will be good for you," Ferrara said from the front seat. She was reading a book and riding up front with Leslie, who was driving. "That's what the judge said. No social media, no phone. No Jessica Mills. For a while," she said with a smile. "She said the world could use a break."

Leslie glanced in the mirror at Jessica. "What would you post about anyway?"

"I don't know," Jessica said, crossing her arms.

Leslie looked at Ferrara and faked enthusiasm. "Did you see that? 'OH MY GOD, we just passed the biggest cactus. It was so LIT.'"

Ferrara giggled.

Leslie glanced in the mirror. "I'm sure your fans would find it fascinating. It would be at about their level."

"Why can't we fly? I already hate this trip."

"That's the point," Leslie said.

"I think it's going to be fun," Ferrara said. "You'll love Ohio, Jessica. I promise."

"Oh, I can't wait."

"You will," Ferrara said over her shoulder. "It'll be fall soon. Everything is so pretty once you get out of LA. Other places have these things called 'seasons,' where the weather actually changes depending on the time of the year."

Jessica looked around at the scrub outside the SUV. "Oh, you're right. It's so amazing out here."

"We know you're not excited," Leslie said. "The judge doesn't think this plan will work either," she said. "But if you don't go with the program, this whole thing is over."

Jessica looked at her but didn't say anything.

"You want to fly? If this falls through, we'll get you back to LA on the next flight. Then I'll personally escort you straight to jail. Be happy to do it." She turned and looked at Ferrara. "Oh, I forgot to ask. Do they even have flights from Dayton to Los Angeles?"

"Of course they do," Ferrara said, shaking her head. "It's like you guys have no clue about the rest of this country. We have Starbucks and FedEx and everything you guys have in LA. But with fewer homeless people. And weather. Maybe you'll both learn something on this trip."

Jessica went back to staring out the window. They were in the middle of nowhere, traveling through western Arizona. The flat desert was broken only by the road they were traveling on and occasional clumps of cactus. A black buzzard sat on one of the saguaros until the approaching SUV made it take flight, flapping lazily into the heavy air.

An hour later, Leslie stopped in Yucca, Arizona for lunch and gas. They went to a roadside truck stop called "Dewey's," and Leslie let Jessica enjoy a smoke before the three of them headed inside.

It was another test of her new disguise—she had the short black hair, and the glasses, and the realistic looking port-wine stain on the left side of her neck. Ferrara had created a dozen thin latex patches, teaching Jessica how to apply it early this morning in the bathroom before they left. Ferrara said there were people in the industry with small port-wine stains that they kept covered with concealer.

But the point of the stain was to draw attention away from her face, and as Jessica reached the doors into the restaurant, she could see her reflection. Jessica crossed her fingers that this whole thing would work. The last thing she wanted was to go to jail. It would be the end of her career. No matter what some people thought of her, she still wanted to be an actress. It was all she'd ever wanted to do, or be, as far back as she could remember.

Jessica sighed and pulled the doors open and walked inside. Back into the "real world." She stopped at the "WAIT TO BE SEATED" sign and looking around. It was a typical cheap restaurant, with booths ringing the outside walls, edging up against the windows that showed the vast, boring desert outside. The place was busy—most of the booths were filled, and waitresses hurried from table to table.

A woman was walking toward her, and Jessica swallowed. This was it. This was the moment when she'd be discovered. Yesterday at Starbucks had been a fluke. Jessica's hand started quivering and the woman looked at Jessica and her neck and her glasses.

"How many?"

"Oh. Three."

"Follow me," the woman said, grabbing menus and leading Jessica to a booth by the windows. "Debbie will be your server."

Jessica sat and picked up the menu, glancing around. People looked at her and looked away. Did they not know who she was? Jessica was used to being noticed everywhere she went. It had been fun at first.

Ferrara leaned over and whispered. "Don't forget your accent, Jessica."

Leslie shook her head.

"'Sydney,' Ferrara. Don't forget."

Ferrara nodded as a woman approached the table.

"Hi, I'm Debbie. Something to drink?"

Jessica lowered the menu and looked straight at the woman, waiting to be recognized. The young waitress only looked at her neck and then looked away.

"Yeah, do ya have tea?"

Lesli seemed confused. "Um, you mean iced tea?"

"No, like hot tea."

"Oh, I don't think so. I'll go check."

Jessica watched her turn and scurry away, then looked at the others. "Nobody has a clue who I am."

"Quiet, please," Leslie said. "Keep it down, okay?" She pulled out a map and looked at it. "Okay, six hours from Indio to Flagstaff. We'll hit the canyon in the morning, then on to Colorado. Seven, eight hours tomorrow. Long drive, but it's good to make progress."

Ferrara looked at the map. "Flagstaff tonight?"

"Yup," Leslie said, pointing. "But we're making good time."

"It's good to have a break," Ferrara said, then looked at Jessica. "And it's the desert, Sydney. Nobody orders hot tea out here."

"I don't know," Jessica said. "How am I supposed to know what place carries what? And I thought you didn't care if this worked? Aren't you just a casual observer of this little experiment?" Jessica asked with a smile.

"I do care," Leslie said. She leaned forward so only Jessica and Ferrara could hear. "I want this to work out. But if this whole thing goes to pot, you're the one that will pay the price." She sat back and grabbed a menu. "Doesn't affect me one way or the other, Missy."

The waitress came back to the table. "Hi. Um, I looked for the tea but our boss says we don't have any hot teas. Just iced. We used to have a box of 'em, hot teas, different flavors, but we ended up pitching them. Sorry."

"That's fine," Jessica said, trying to sound like she was from Texas. "Can I just get a Coke?" Ferrara and Leslie ordered drinks, both getting Cokes and waters. When she was gone, Ferrara shook her head.

"Just stick with Coke, okay," Leslie said. "You can jog it off later. Keep your food and drink selections simple, no customization or asking for trendy stuff. Servers hate that. Keep it quick."

"Remember your back story," Ferrara said quietly, putting her menu down. "The disguise works, but Sydney's background will be the thing that sells the character."

"Okay," Jessica said. "Got it."

Leslie looked at her. "You should learn some Texas slang, too," she said. "I'll get you a list. I did notice that you sometimes call people 'cowboy' as a nickname. You need more of that."

Jessica looked at her, holding her eyes for a moment. She wanted to hate this woman, but it was difficult when the woman made it so clear that she just didn't give a shit. After a second, Jessica nodded and looked down at the table.

The waitress returned with their drinks and took their orders. Leslie put away the map and ordered a hamburger and fries. Ferrara got a chicken salad wrap and chips. When it came to Jessica, she resisted the temptation to order something off the menu and just got chicken fingers and fries.

"Good," Ferrara said. "That was good. Don't offer any suggestions about how they should prepare their food. It's insulting."

"Yeah, but what if it's gross? Can I send it back?"

"No."

"Why?"

"Normal people don't do that," Ferrara said. "Take what you get and be happy about it. Growing up, my Mom always said, 'you get what you get and you don't throw a fit.'"

"Great," Jessica said.

"Troublemakers draw attention to themselves," Leslie said. "They need or want attention. You need to avoid that."

Jessica didn't say anything.

"And your walk," Ferrara said.

"What's wrong with my walk?"

"You need to work on it," Leslie said. "You're still walking around like you're rich and famous. Like you're the queen or something."

Jessica made a face. She didn't feel like the queen of anything.

"Slump your shoulders a little, like you're trying to make yourself appear smaller," Ferrara said. "Act like you're sad all the time and no one will pay attention to you."

The table grew quiet. Jessica assumed they were all thinking what she was thinking—this trip was a waste of time. Doomed to failure. She would be discovered, either on the road to Ohio or very shortly after she arrived. Someone would shout out her name and Jessica would turn to look and this charade would be over. If that happened, she'd be back in front of that judge in a matter of hours. And this time, Judge Watkins would throw the book at her.

If that happened, no number of clever ideas would keep Jessica Mills, Hollywood starlet, out of jail.

Chapter 31
Making a Plan

In a dark room in an old mansion in the most affluent part of New Orleans, several computer monitors were situated on a desk. One of them was playing a movie, some kind of teenage drama. Three young women were arguing on the screen, including a younger Jessica Mills.

"No, there's no way I'm doing that," the young Jessica said on the screen. She was dressed in rags, and she and the other two women were clearly in some sort of post-apocalyptic situation: a rusted car hulked behind them, and they were standing around a barrel with flames flickering inside.

"You have to, Melody," one of the other young women said to Jessica. "You're the only one of us who's strong enough."

"I'm not strong enough for that," Jessica said, shaking her head. "I just want to get out of here, go back to where we were."

The third young woman nodded. "Me too. Cassidy, can't we just switch off?" she says, and started moving her hands around her face as if she was feeling around an invisible helmet. "Where's the off button?"

The second girl, Cassidy, shook her head. "No, Tawny. We can't leave. You can't feel the helmet in here, and there's no 'off' button anyway."

"I know," Tawny said, dropping her hands, disappointed.

"Look," Cassidy said. "We're trapped here in the Construct. We can't get out unless someone goes into the tower and finishes the game. It has to be Melody," she said, looking at Jessica, who shook her head.

"No. I can't. I can't face him. You know that."

"Then we'll be trapped here in this digital nightmare," Cassidy said. "Trapped forever."

They all looked terrified, and then the movie went to commercial. The screen read "Five Minutes Until Midnight, starring Jessica Mills, will return in a moment," and then faded. A commercial for cereal began playing.

Taped to the walls behind the computer monitors were several large movie posters, films that starred a younger Jessica Mills. The poster of "Five Minutes Until Midnight" read "Three girls trapped in a virtual nightmare—can they find their way to safety?" It looked like a standard post-apocalyptic action movie, with the Jessica Mills character holding up some kind of glowing stick.

The other walls were taken up with similar posters and photos from movies and TV shows that Jessica Mills had appeared in. "Bacon Tastes Good," with Jessica in overalls and holding up a muddy pig. "Fun with Jane," her breakout TV show; on the poster, she was much younger and shrugging, with a caption that read, "I guess it's break time!" The last was "Door Girl," another TV show with Jessica as a bellhop for a fancy apartment building in New York City.

On one wall was plastered a huge, six-by-six-foot grid of photos. The huge photo of Jessica, made up of individual sheets of paper taped together in a grid to show her smiling face, took up half the wall. Underneath the giant Jessica hung more printouts, lists of the TV shows she had appeared on and printouts of interviews. There were copies of each of her police reports, photocopies of her birth certificate and driver's license, even a copy of a credit card receipt with her signature on it. Dozens of other documents related to Jessica and her life were taped or pinned to the walls.

In the middle of the chaos sat Blake Oleander, hunched over his computer and staring at a map of Los Angeles, ignoring the other screen as "Five Minutes to Midnight" came back from commercial. Jessica and her two compatriots walked through a gray wasteland, moving toward a tall, ominous-looking tower in the distance.

On the next computer screen, an aerial view of several streets and houses appeared. A mouse moved across the screen, zooming in on the aerial map and centering on a particular street filled with mansions.

"Pepperidge Lane," Blake said. "Okay, there's your place in the Hollywood hills." The screen showed a large home with a circular driveway. "But you're not there?"

Blake moved the mouse and the map on the screen scrolled, stopping on an aerial view of the Los Angeles County Courthouse. The detail was remarkable, and it was easy to see the buildings and the parking garage next door.

Spread out on the desk in front of him were several tabloid magazines with headlines: "JESSICA MILLS IN CAR CRASH SHOCKER" and

"JESSICA MILLS ARRESTED AFTER CAUSING NEAR-FATAL ACCIDENT" and "MILLS HEADING FOR JAIL!!" Blake looked back and forth between the screen and the tabloid photos.

"Okay, that's where you were being held for the week..."

He flipped open a People Magazine, which showed pages of photos of Jessica's move from the temporary holding facility to her flight out of Los Angeles. The photos, all taken from far away, showed her exiting the Courthouse parking area and being taken by van to a nearby airport. Blake compared the photos to the overhead view, then, using the mouse, retraced the path that the police van took from the Courthouse, traveling up Interstate 5 through Los Angeles and Glendale to Burbank and the Hollywood-Burbank airport.

Switching to another screen, Blake looked up the Wikipedia entry on the airport and found that it was also known as the Bob Hope Airport. It was built to handle smaller aircraft than the main Los Angeles Airport, LAX.

He studied the layout of the airport and compared it to the photos from the People Magazine, which showed a blond woman, Aaron Skilling (Jessica's attorney), a county prosecutor, and several LAPD cops getting into a small plane. Switching to another screen, he pulled up a YouTube video of the loading process—the people got on the plane, which subsequently took off. He'd read some speculation online that the blond woman in the video was not Jessica Mills, but it looked like her to Blake.

Even the local news here in New Orleans had carried the update: Jessica Mills goes to jail. There were plenty of pictures and news stories about her being sentenced to a 90-day "stay" at a minimum-security prison in northern California, someplace called Dublin.

But the speculation on Reddit and Facebook was that the LAPD and other officials would never send her to an actual jail and had "put on a show" for the paparazzi. Some thought Jessica had been sent to one of the many rehab facilities in the LA area.

"Okay, so you left the courthouse and traveled to the airport," he said to himself, looking at the screen. "If that happened, you're in Dublin." He pulled up photos of the jail, shaking his head. "No way I can get to you there. But if you're in jail, you might be getting help. That's good. You need it."

He flipped back to Reddit and skimmed the conspiracy theory. The main story was titled "What if Jessica Mills ISN'T in Jail?" He skimmed the story, which stated that the woman didn't look like

Jessica (in this writer's opinion) and that the fake-out was to cover Jessica Mills' transportation to a local rehab facility. "She's already been to all of them," the article quipped, "except for Daystrom."

Curious, Blake searched for "LOS ANGELES DRUG REHAB CENTERS" in a new window on his internet browser. He scrolled through the list, clicking on each in turn and checking the address, then opened each in a map window.

The last place on the list was a place called simply "Daystrom." It was located south of Los Angeles, on a rocky coastline that overlooked Santa Catalina. Blake searched for an address and put it into the map, which showed the location in a coastal town called San Pedro.

He pulled up the website for the facility and read aloud: "We offer the most private and successful drug and alcohol treatment facility in the Los Angeles area. Our guests are pampered and treated with respect. While no addictions can be cured in five days, guests of Daystrom can return to their normal lives after a short visit, comfortable in the knowledge that addiction can be cured. To arrange for a private tour of the facility, please call the number listed below."

"Sounds great," Blake said to himself. "If you're here, you'll get help. Get healthy. That's a good thing."

Blake sat back and clapped his hands. "Daystrom, Daystrom, DAYSTROM!" He shouted and stood and he wasn't wearing any pants. He jumped up in the air and screamed in pleasure. "JESSICA!" He shouted her name again and again, jumping in the air next to the desk. He picked up an orange and threw it at the wall and it splattered, juice running down the large mosaic of Jessica's face.

"You'll get help, and then we can be together. I'll drive out to see you again, and you'll remember me from last time. And then we can be together."

He turned and skipped to the door, then threw it open and ran into a large hallway.

"Together!"

Blake, naked below the waist, ran down the corridor, still shouting her name. Wallpaper peeled in pieces from the dirty walls of the hallway, the corners filled with cobwebs. He came to a large set of stairs that led down into a beautiful foyer where a dusty, glass-paneled door led outside. He scampered down the stairs, giddy, and it looked like he was going to go straight out the front door but, at the last second, he turned, running the other direction.

He ran, passing several closed doors, and ended up in the dated kitchen with a view out into a dark, overgrown garden.

"You're gonna love it here, you're gonna love it here," Blake began to sing. He went to the fridge and pulled it open, smiling and laughing. "We'll have all your favorite foods and drinks and everything! We can do scenes from your movies, or whatever! And then, when you're ready, you can SIT AT THE TABLE!" The words came out in a sing-songy fashion, as if he heard them in song in his mind and was just joining along with the tune.

He jumped around the kitchen, pulling ingredients from the fridge and making himself a sandwich. He threw the items on the central island and used a large pointy knife to slather mayonnaise on slices of bread. Throwing the sandwich together with abandon, Blake grabbed it and ran off, heading through the set of double doors into the dining room.

The dead people were all still there, all aligned around the table. The room stank of putrefaction, but Blake had grown used to it and didn't even smell it anymore. His whole family was here, along with the newest additions. Penny, his latest girlfriend, was nowhere to be seen, and the chair at the foot of the table sat open, waiting for the next guest.

"When you're ready, you can join us," Blake sang, dancing. "I'll sit at the head of the table, and you at the foot and you'll be able to see all of my photos of you!"

He ran up one side of the table and down the other, circling the people whose lives he had ended. Blake stopped and kissed each of them on the back of their heads, smiling. He avoided the ax in his father's head and kissed Gertie on her shoulder because her head was missing. Down the other side of the table, Blake kissed each of his exes on the backs of their heads and even gave the Fed-Ex man a peck.

Stopping at Becca, the first girl from the group home, Blake leaned around and kissed her full on the mouth. "You're going to love Jessica, Becca. She's amazing. I've been watching her forever! I even met her once. If you can believe it, I carried her in my arms!!"

Becca did not answer. She had been dead for several months and was not in the mood to be part of the conversation.

"Oh, it's okay. Don't be jealous!"

Blake laughed and ran around to the foot of the table, adjusting the empty chair. "She's going to love it here."

Turning, he grabbed his sandwich and scampered off, heading

back up the stairs in the foyer, singing loudly the whole way. He started in on the theme song from "Fun with Jane," Jessica's long-running kid's TV show. Blake sang it all the way up the stairs before disappearing back into the computer room that had become a shrine to Jessica Mills.

Even with the door closed, he could still be heard singing.

Chapter 32
CCL

Frank got off the highway in Huber Heights, a town south and east of Cooper's Mill. Huber was bigger and busier, nestled in the corner of I-70 and I-75, and sported many national stores that Cooper's Mill didn't have. They had the closest Target, for instance, and Lowe's and Walmart, along with the area's only multi-screen movie theater. It seemed like Frank was regularly running to Huber to grab something he couldn't buy in Cooper's Mill, or Laura was sending him to the Target to pick up something.

Like something out of a science fiction movie from his youth, his phone was sitting on the dashboard and giving him spoken directions to an unfamiliar location in Huber. Laura had instructed him on how to use Google Maps, another app that had come with his iPhone. She showed him how to put in his destination, and then it read off directions to him. What would they think of next?

The Camaro cruised up the off-ramp and Frank waited for the light to change, making a right at the White Castle. Huber also had a K-Mart—it was looking pretty run down—and more restaurants and shops than he could count. Google Maps was taking him west, passing the shops and leaving town. Frank passed trucking companies, a self-storage facility, a gravel company and several massive piles of dirt and construction equipment. He was in an area he'd never visited before, a dead zone between the highways and the river. Thank goodness for his smartphone.

But if he was going to be operating in the area, or God-forbid chasing people, he really needed to become more familiar with the towns that encircled Cooper's Mill. Google Maps took him south on something called Rip Rap Road, which curled along a wide river. Was this the same one that ran through Cooper's Mill? The same one Joe had used to disappear? Frank didn't know. The directions had him slow and turn west, crossing the river on an unfamiliar bridge, then turning north, passing an asphalt and paving company.

Soon, Frank found the shooting range and slowed, turning into the busy parking lot. Gathering his paperwork and weapon, Frank headed inside.

All gun shops smelled the same, a sharp, unique combination of cordite and cleaning supplies. Frank looked around at the racks of guns and piles of ammo. On the walls were competition banners and targets hanging in a "WINNER'S CIRCLE," displays of shot targets and photos of past competition winners. Several banners featured Joe Hathaway, along with a "BEST SHOOTER" listing. Joe's photo smiled back at Frank from the wall, making Frank's skin crawl. This psycho had killed a man and kept his body frozen in his garage. He'd killed a pregnant woman, arranging for her car to go off the road, making it look like an accident. He'd been responsible for Deputy Peters' death, threatened the lives of Laura and Jackson and a dozen other people. And the people at this range celebrated him? It made Frank's blood boil.

"Can I help you?"

Frank turned to see a clerk behind the counter. Half the wall behind him was taken up with security camera monitors, while the other half displayed the latest in "TOP HANDGUNS" and other equipment.

Frank nodded and walked over.

"I need to qualify for my Ohio CC. Is there an instructor here who can certify me?"

The young kid nodded and reached for a binder marked "CLASSES."

"Yup, we can get you signed up for the licensing course, which takes eight weeks. That's assuming you want to skip the beginner course, which is another eight weeks."

Frank patted the gun at his waist.

"I'm not interested in any classes. I already have my Alabama CC, and talked to the state folks the other day," he said, putting some papers on the counter. "I'm retired from the force, and the lady said it exempted me from the course. She said I just need to shoot with an instructor and get qualified in Ohio. I think that's how it works."

The clerk shook his head. "I don't know, but I can get Pat over here. He's the certifier. You wanna talk to him?"

"Okay."

Frank wandered over to look at the guns while the kid made a call. There was a great display of Glocks, including several 17's and a 22, like his service weapon. The Glock 22, also known as the G22, was used by many law enforcement agencies, including the U.S. Marshalls and the FBI.

This place also had a good selection of shotguns and long guns, along with an impressive number of glass counters filled with handguns and other equipment. It looked like this place really catered to the hunting crowd—they carried lots of camo, along with hunting blinds and camping gear. Frank was looking at a portable camping stove when he heard some doors open and the sounds of a shooting range beyond. A burly man with a nametag walked over.

"You looking to qualify?"

Frank nodded and took out his Alabama CC license, which showed he was ex-police and qualified to carry. He also showed Pat the other paperwork he'd brought. "I was on the job in Louisiana before that. I had to carry in Alabama and qualified at the police range."

The man looked over his card and paperwork and nodded, handing them back. "Good to meet you, Frank. I'm Pat Mendoza. I run both ranges. You want to qualify now? I have a class going on, but it will be over in a few minutes. You're welcome to observe while I wrap up."

"Sounds good."

He followed Mendoza past the front counter and through a set of thick doors into an indoor range, where three people were waiting. Beyond them, Frank could see three targets at the far end of the enclosed range.

"Sorry about that," Mendoza said to the students. "Go ahead and pick up your weapons and fire, taking turns. Here," Mendoza said to Frank, handing him ear protection. Frank pulled on the thick headphone-like ear covers and waited as the amateurs finished up their class.

Mendoza was walking them through basic shooting, including the most important lesson: "never point the gun at anything you don't want to kill."

The students, each firing in turn, all looked like gun newbies to Frank. They were wearing headphones and firing small handguns and missing the mark widely. Two of them were a younger couple, man and wife by the looks of it, and they were both trying intently, firing from the ready position with both hands on the gun. The woman was bracing her legs, leaning against the counter, and her husband was reloading his pistol with new cartridges from a small box of ammo.

The other student was a woman who was clearly not listening to Mendoza. She wouldn't brace her firing hand with the other, so all her shots were one-handed and went high, missing the distant paper target.

The students fired for another five minutes, using all the ammo they had been given, and then Mendoza collected their guns. He pushed a set of buttons and the paper targets, which had been at the far end of the range, began moving in their tracks toward the shooting area. When they arrived, Mendoza reached up and unclipped them each in turn, passing them out. Frank saw that the one woman's target only had a single hole in it, well above the outline of a person's head, but she seemed very pleased with herself.

"That's the best I've ever shot," she said with a smile.

"Great job, everyone. If you want to collect some of your casings as souvenirs, that's fine. Just watch it—they might be hot. Had one go down a woman's shirt last month, and she got burned. See you next week."

The students gathered up their belongings and some paperwork from another table and left as Mendoza cleaned up the area, sweeping the spent casings on the floor into a bin.

"You want to shoot in here or on our outdoor range? This one's a little better."

"I'll shoot in here, if that's okay."

Mendoza finished up his sweeping, nodding. "Yup. You bring your own weapon?"

Frank patted his side and slowly unholstered his gun. It was just habit—and common sense: you didn't want to frighten someone by pulling your weapon quickly. That was a good way to get shot.

He undid the holster strap and slid the gun free, then spun the barrel away from them and handed it to Mendoza, who took the gun and looked it over. Frank glanced around at more banners and targets that had been hung out here in the range, seeing several more with Joe Hathaway's name on them. There was even one he'd autographed, like he was a celebrity or something.

"G22," Pat said, removing the full magazine and then expertly working the top of the gun to eject the bullet from the chamber, catching the round in one hand. Pat handed it back, then looked over the weapon. "Nice. Looks like you know how to take care of it. Recently cleaned?"

"Yesterday."

Pat nodded, appreciating the weapon. "Let me get you some targets and fresh ammo. It's $99 for the test. You okay with that?"

Frank nodded and Mendoza left, taking Frank's gun with him. Frank wasn't worried—Mendoza would be inspecting the weapon, weighing it and making sure it hadn't been modified. You couldn't qualify with a modified weapon. Some people filed down their barrels to bring up the bullet speed or changed out the firing pins to make the gun "BANG" louder. Frank's gun was standard issue.

Mendoza came back after a few minutes. "Okay, you're good to go." He was also carrying a pair of paper targets, which he set aside, along with two empty magazines and a box of ammo for the gun. He set them and Frank's weapon on the table, then waved Frank over.

"Let's get you set up—it's two targets, one in each lane. You'll shoot a full magazine, fifteen rounds, at each target. You'll need at least 70% in the black to qualify, so 21 out of 30."

"Okay."

"You have to use our cartridges and magazines. Here are the magazines and the ammo, but you'll need to load. I have to observe that process. Start whenever you like."

Frank set his gun down, then picked up the first provided magazine and expertly loaded fifteen cartridges from the box of ammo. He did the same for the second magazine, setting them down on the table. Pat watched him closely and nodded.

"Good. Very good. You're quicker than half of my staff."

Frank smiled. "Thanks. Lots of practice," he said. "Maybe too much."

Pat picked up the targets. "Okay, you have a lane preference? If not, we can just use the middle two."

Frank shrugged. "I don't care."

Mendoza hung two targets, one in the middle lane and one in the one next to it, then hit the button. The targets traveled down their lanes, flapping in the air, before settling to a stop half-way down. Frank stepped up to the lane and adjusted his hearing protection.

"Okay, that's twenty yards, Ohio CC license distance. Ready when you are," Mendoza said, holding up his wrist and showing Frank his watch. "You'll have thirty seconds per lane."

Frank waited for a moment, then started. He took the magazine from the railing in front of him, snapped it into the gun, chambered one round, then stood, feet shoulder-width apart, gun braced, and aimed at the target. The Glock 22 was so familiar, it felt like an extension of his own body, and he fired, fifteen shots with a pause between each shot. Fourteen hit the target, with a nice grouping of five right in the center.

He ejected the magazine and set it on the railing, then stepped to the next lane and repeated the process, hitting with thirteen of fifteen. When he was done, he ejected the magazine and set it and his weapon down on the railing before stepping back.

"Well done, Frank," the man said, going to the button and pushing it. "Looked like twenty-seven out of thirty." The targets rattled to a stop and Pat took them down, counting. "Yup, 27. Great grouping as well. You certainly qualify."

"Thank you," Frank said, picking up his weapon and returning the loaded magazine to his gun, sliding the safety on and putting the gun back into the holster, admiring the comfortable weight of it at his hip.

"Okay, let's get you checked out." Pat led him back inside and up to the counter, where Frank paid the clerk with a credit card. Pat worked at another computer, inputting the test results. "Okay, you're all set up. Once it goes through the state, the license will be active. Here's a temporary permit," he said, handing Frank a printout with all of his information on it, including the shooting scores and a notation that read "PASSED."

"Thanks."

"No problem," Pat said. "It will take a few days to get the real one—it's gotta go through the state, and then the local PD has to sign off. They're pretty quick, usually. After that, you'll get your card in the mail."

Frank thanked them and left, happy to get out of there. Mendoza was nice, and the shop was good, well stocked and professional. But Frank didn't like being surrounded by photos and other reminders of Joe Hathaway. He wondered if Pat Mendoza had helped train Joe. How many times had Hathaway shot on that indoor range? Surely he had he practiced there. Had he pretended to shoot Frank, visualizing it in his sick mind? Frank pushed the thoughts from his mind and climbed into his car, driving away.

Chapter 33
Assignment

Leslie looked at the two women sitting across from her at the diner and wondered, not for the first time, how she'd ended up on this detail. She was doing a favor for the prosecutor, Leslie told herself. She'd been telling herself that a lot.

Leslie Davis had always been a no-nonsense kind of woman, genetically incapable of tolerating any kind of bullshit. She told things the way she saw them, most times, unless it was a HEARTILY bad idea. And, even then, the truth always came out. That's why she hadn't been able to mask her concerns—or keep her mouth shut—when the prosecutor asked for her to babysit some snot-nosed LA starlet.

The first thing Leslie had done was complain to her superior.

"This is bullshit," she'd said to Captain Timmons.

He was her commanding officer and one hell of a good leader. He ran nearly one-tenth of the LAPD, overseeing several squads that covered narcotics, drug trafficking/smuggling, and vice and prostitution.

Her most recent assignment, as part of the smuggling squad, had just wrapped up with a raid that had followed four months of in-depth investigation of an LA-based restaurant chain. The Asian restaurants had been very lucrative, too lucrative to be believed, and, at the start, there were only suspicions that something untoward had been going on.

She and four other LAPD deputies had been tasked with looking into the chain, and the investigation had proceeded apace. They soon learned that the high-end perishable foods being imported from Japan also contained some "extra" ingredients: guns. Coordinated raids at four restaurants brought the full scope of the operation to light, and Leslie had been pleased to be sitting in the courtroom when five of the principal defendants in the case, along with nine other employees, were all convicted of gun trafficking and evading US import laws.

It had been a great case, open and shut, but exhausting. Timmons had promised her a break after it wrapped, tasking Leslie with some desk work. She was to write up the entire investigation as a "case study" to be published internally by the LAPD. Her captain had told her to take a month or two on it, a chance to recuperate from the 80-hour weeks she'd been putting in for the past four months.

She'd only just gotten started when she was called into the prosecutor's office with a new assignment. Technically, it wasn't an "assignment." ADA Tara Simmons had called it an "opportunity," but that was the same thing—if you wanted to move up, you did the hard work. You put in the hours, you pulled the wacky shifts, you kept your paperwork spotless and always turned it in on time, or early, if possible.

And when a County of Los Angeles ADA called you in to discuss an "opportunity," you sat and you listened and you took the gig, no matter how crazy it might sound to you. And you kept your complaints to a minimum.

"This Mill assignment is going to suck," she'd told Captain Timmons as soon as she'd gotten back to her station. "She wants me to babysit a famous drunk for 90 days. And it's an out-of-town gig to boot—we're going to someplace in Ohio. Or Indiana. I forget where."

Timmons nodded, setting his paperwork aside. She knew that meant she had his full attention, even if there was nothing he could do about it.

"There's nothing I can do about it," he said. "You know that."

"Sir…I can't be out of town for 90 days. I have that write-up you wanted me to do, plus I have plans."

Timmons shrugged. "I don't know what to tell you. They requested you, and you know what that means. People who pass on assignments get passed over for promotions. This is an incredibly-high-profile case, and you'll be running the show. I'm sure the prosecutor's office will appreciate it, and back your application should you ever apply for detective."

Leslie had thought about it and sat down, the fury evaporating. It could be a plum gig, even if she hated people like Jessica Mills, people who thought they were above everyone else. It was one of the reasons she'd gotten into law enforcement, as a way to stand up for the overlooked and underprivileged.

And Jessica Mills? She was the definition of privileged.

Now, as she sat across from the LA starlet in a crowded diner in Arizona, Officer Leslie Davis wondered if this would work. The young woman looked so completely different, it was hard to reconcile the "two" Jessica Mills in her mind. One was a spoiled superstar, appearing in every magazine. The other was a down-on-her-luck drunk. Going through coke withdrawal, jonesing for a smoke every half hour, targeted by unscrupulous friends and stalkers and paparazzi. Jailed, wearing an ankle monitor, every move monitored.

And now, to add insult to injury, the starlet had had her good looks taken away. Bad wig, glasses, an unflattering wardrobe, a huge birthmark.

Leslie wondered if she'd rise to the challenge or give up. But either way, Leslie was here to see it through. She would do the job, if only so she could get back to her life as soon as possible.

Chapter 34
Arizona

Jessica noticed Leslie staring at her, but didn't say anything. The female cop reminded Jessica of Sarah Connor from the "Terminator" movies, stoic and unflappable.

Being out of LA made Jessica feel lost, unprotected. She was used to being surrounded by her posse, the group of "friends" that always seemed to be by her side. She didn't go anywhere "Team Jessica" tagging along.

Over time, the group had grown, evolved. Agents, publicists, lawyers, drivers, security guys, stylists. She liked them well enough, but it got annoying, them spending her money and living at her house. Jessica wasn't exactly sure how it had happened, but at the beginning, it had been nice to have a friend or two to talk to. People she trusted, for the most part, and people who could act as her hands and arms in the real world. When she needed coffee or blow, she had someone to send out in her place. She was too important to be out in the real world, negotiating over drugs or picking up her own dry cleaning. Everywhere she went, people were stopping her, yelling at her, needing her. It got to be too much.

It was nice to have a layer of people between her and the world.

Jessica remembered the scariest moment of her life. It had happened only eighteen months ago, but it had spun her mind into a level of paranoia she'd never known before, one that she didn't even know could exist.

Her stalker, long lurking in the shadows, had finally come for her in real life.

The man had sent her letters for years, flattering her right along with the rest of the fan mail. But his letters were different. From the beginning, they were more personal, more sinister. The writer, a man named "Blake," would say things like "I'm watching you" or "I can't wait for us to be together." The letters, along with a few others, had been creepy enough to warrant involving the police. And the cops had failed her. They'd "looked into it," of course, but it led to nothing.

The letters kept coming, with frightening regularity. They got worse, becoming too familiar, too intimate. Blake told her the things they would do together, the sexual things he would do to her. He wanted her to meet his family. After months, she'd finally stopped reading them. She thought that, if she ignored them, the problem would go away.

Instead, in the spring of 2010, things turned insane. Jessica had been out with a friend for lunch when she'd encountered the huge balding man with the scary eyes and the scar on his face. It was a face she would never forget.

He'd tried to grab her at a restaurant on Sunset. He'd come out of nowhere, throwing Jessica over his shoulder like a sack of potatoes and running for the street and a nearby car, where the trunk stood open. If it hadn't been for a bystander, who ended up getting injured, Jessica might have disappeared for good, right then and there.

Those minutes, when a clearly-crazy man had tried to abduct her, were forever etched into her mind. The cops never figured out who "Blake" was or where he'd come from, which made matters even worse. She could only refer to him as the "stalker." For months afterward, she'd been scared to go out of her house. Every loud noise made her scream and jump—and run for the nearest bottle. It had been nearly two years, and she was still frightened to be out on her own. Maybe having a blood-sucking entourage wasn't the worse thing.

Ending up in that weirdo's trunk would have been ten times worse.

She looked up at Leslie, who had gone back to studying her map, sketching out their path to Ohio. If Jessica had to leave LA, leave the safety of "Team Jessica" and traipse across the country, at least she had this new lady to watch out for trouble. Not that Jessica was going to thank her or anything.

The food came and Jessica kept her head down.

Ferrara thanked the waitress, who walked away. Jessica felt weird—whenever she did get out for a night on the town, she always spoke to the waitresses and other help, dazzling them with her smile. She knew they were just happy to be in her presence for a moment, and it made their day to be treated nicely by one of the most famous people in Hollywood. It felt strange. She usually said "thank you" in her sing-songy way, buttering up the help so they would say something nice on Instagram about her.

The three women continued quietly discussing the back story that they'd invented for Sydney. "So, what do we think?" Ferrara asked.

"It's okay," Jessica said, pointing a French fry at the cup of honey mustard. "It's way too sweet. Too much sugar."

"I meant what do we think about your cover story? About Sydney."

"Oh."

"I think you should work for me," Ferrara said. "Maybe a hairdresser in training?"

"Oh, you'd love that," Jessica said, suddenly angry. "You get to boss me around, tell me what…"

"I get to do that anyway," Ferrara said with a smile. "Judge said so."

"People," Leslie hissed. "Stop talking about what happened in California? We need to get past this and get to Ohio and get you settled into your new life," she said, tapping the map.

"Temporary. Temporary life," Jessica said with a scowl, picking at her fries.

"Right," Ferrara said. "Sorry."

"I guess that might work," Jessica said, pointing at Ferrara. "I might learn a thing or two."

"Maybe," Ferrara said. "Of course, you'll learn some stuff. But it makes a good cover. You can just hang around with me all the time, and no one will ask why."

"Okay, so you're back for a visit in Ohio, and what, I'm your lackey?" Jessica asked. "Why would I come home with you?"

"Yeah, and who am I?" Leslie asked, putting down her hamburger. "Are we lovers?"

Ferrara choked on her sandwich and smiled, putting it down. "Oh, that would be rich. Nothing wrong with it, of course, but it would still be the talk of the town."

The conversation continued, and Ferrara was telling Leslie how she got started in the industry.

"So, how did you end up in Los Angeles?" Leslie asked.

"I'd been cutting hair for years," Ferrara said, pointing around them. "I'm good at it, I've been told. Good at figuring out what people need to look their best. Worked at a string of salons in Ohio, working my way up to senior stylist."

"Is that a thing?" Jessica asked.

"Yeah, it's a thing. Anyway, people started requesting me, and telling me how amazing my work was. I got recognized a few times by the industry, and then worked on a local movie set."

"I didn't know that," Jessica said. "Which movie?"

"Didn't end up mattering," Ferrara said. "The movie never came out. They couldn't get enough funding, and it died half-way through production. But one of the women on the shoot was impressed. She was an actress from LA, flown in to do the film and give it a little star power. She raved about my work and said I should come out to "the coast," as she kept calling it. I assumed she was full of it, but months later, after the film died, she called me up. Offered to fly me out to do her hair for a commercial shoot. Said I did it better than anyone she could find in Los Angeles."

"Wow, that's pretty cool," Leslie said.

They continued chatting, Leslie asking about Cooper's Mill, this town they were crossing half the country to visit.

At some point, Jessica realized the conversation wasn't about her, and it was a nice change. Jessica was used to people talking about her all the time, even when she was sitting right in front of them. Often, it was Hollywood types talking about her career. They'd be sitting at some conference room table, or in the office of some studio executive, and they would be talking about her—fighting over her—and she wouldn't be able to get a word in.

At some point, it had finally dawned on her that they were fighting over her because she wasn't a person. She was a commodity, a thing to be leveraged and bought and sold. Her celebrity was worth much more than Jessica herself. Her name on the poster went farther toward selling a movie, or even getting it made in the first place, than her actual acting. It had felt strange at first, the studio heads arguing with Hank Jennings, her agent, over Jessica's "power" to bring people to the box office. After a while, she'd gotten used to it.

Maybe she shouldn't have.

That had only worked when she was younger, coming off a string of cutesy teenager movies and shows with Jessica playing characters in their late teens. There were plenty of roles for someone with her looks and her ability to act goofy.

Things had changed when she'd aged out of those teenage roles, and now she was attempting to make the difficult transition to adulthood. Many young actors and actresses had failed to make the same transition. They ended up spending their later years in some small, obscure bungalow in the Hollywood Hills, living off the royalties of a short-lived career. Or they gave up the life entirely and moved away, ending up on a ranch in Wyoming to get "back to real life" and spend the money they'd earned on that one show they'd done twenty years ago.

Jessica didn't like the sound of that. She wanted to act, wanted to challenge herself with difficult roles. She'd set out to become an actress, not a teenager most famous for her roles as a goofy sidekick or a young woman trapped in a virtual world where she needed to learn a valuable lesson about herself to break free.

Or maybe that's what this was all about—it was like that movie she'd been in. Maybe years of taking teenage roles and being surrounded by her party friends was like being trapped in the virtual reality of that dumb movie. She needed to break free, grow up. Take herself seriously. If she didn't consider herself a grown-up, would anyone else?

"Okay, so you're Sydney Green, and you work for Ferrara as a hairdresser," Leslie whispered. "And I'm Leslie, a producer friend of Ferrara's who's visiting. Thinking about shooting something in Ohio. Scouting locations, that sort of thing. Nothing too complicated."

Jessica realized that she'd tuned out and missed part of the conversation.

"Oh, yeah. That's fine," Jessica said. "You'll love being a producer. They've got all the power. People can throw themselves at you for a change."

The rest of the meal went well, and they got out of there without incident. Leslie paid and made sure to ask for a receipt, pocketing it as they went out to the SUV.

Ferrara drove the next stretch—she and Leslie were taking turns. Jessica wasn't allowed to drive for several reasons, not the least of which being that Leslie apparently didn't trust her. And she didn't have a driver's license, in case they got pulled over.

Nope, she was just along for the ride. Literally and figuratively. Other people were running the show now.

Jessica didn't feel like driving, anyway. The itching was getting worse, and she'd scraped her arms raw. The greasy lunch sat queasily in her stomach. She wondered if she would be able to keep it down.

Ferrara directed the vehicle back onto the highway, and they settled in for another stretch of lonely road, getting further and further away from Los Angeles with each passing mile. Jessica hadn't yet decided if that was a good thing or a bad thing.

Chapter 35

Progress

They spent the rest of the day traveling east, the sun going down behind them. They crossed the Arizona desert, then made a detour to see the Grand Canyon before heading into Flagstaff to spend the night.

Jessica had never seen the Grand Canyon. She'd been stunned speechless by the sheer size of it. It was one thing to see pictures of it, she said, or have it described to you in a generic way. But it still blew her mind, seeing the massive scale of the canyons, or how they stretched off to the horizon in both directions. The young starlet, dressed down and unrecognizable, stood by the canyon edge for a long time, staring off into the setting sun.

To Ferrara, the canyon was scary. The sheer sides and the massive open space below made her instantly nauseous, something that she'd rarely experienced before.

A park ranger noticed her reaction and made a comment, saying it was quite common. "Lots of people find out they're scared of heights right here," he said, pointing at the rickety wooden railing that guarded people from what looked like a thousand-foot fall. "People who've been up in planes and tall buildings and swear they ain't scared of heights? Those people will come to this exact spot and lose their lunch," the round man said with a smile. He leaned closer. "Nature's a bitch, huh?"

That night in Flagstaff, at a hotel near the eastern edge of town, Ferrara unpacked Jessica's bag, laying out everything she'd brought for her on the trip. The first night, in Indio, she'd left most of it in the car, but Jessica's "new" wardrobe had been selected by Ferrara, who'd shopped at several thrift stores she frequented in Hollywood when she was looking for a particular look. Ferrara also included a small number of Jessica's personal items and toiletries. Of course, all the clothes were in Jessica's "new" style, dressing like "Sydney

Green." The jeans and blouses and sweaters weren't flattering, to say the least, and all black or brown or gray. Ferrara included a baggy oatmeal-colored waffle sweater of Jessica's, found far back in the closet. It would be great if the weather was cool in Ohio.

"I dug it out of storage."

"You should have left it there," Jessica said, looking at the sweater with distaste. "I had it hidden in the back of my closet for a reason."

Ferrara explained that the wardrobe had been approved by Judge Watkins with an eye toward blending in. Jessica's face scrunched up as she'd taken each item out of her suitcase (it was actually Ferrara's spare suitcase) and held it up to her.

"Yuck."

She'd been much happier about her toiletries, a few personal care items that she had done without for a while. Her toothbrush and toothpaste, some of her underwear, the face scrub she swore by, and a few of her favorite t-shirts to wear under her new wardrobe. And two bottles of her favorite shampoo, which was too fancy for Ferrara—the stuff was like $80 a bottle.

Ferrara also brought along some work for Jessica, two stacks of scripts to read. It might help, or it might remind her of what she was missing. It was a gamble.

Wednesday was more of the same—desert. They left early and made their way across Arizona, passing the Hopi Reservation and through towns like Gray Mountain and Tuba City and Mexican Water. They stopped for lunch in a place called Kayenta, then took another break at the Four Corners Monument, where four states intersected. Leslie and Ferrara switched off driving, keeping the Pilot at top speed as much as possible. Leslie said she was determined to put as much space between them and Los Angeles as possible the first few days.

As it started to get dark, the Rocky Mountains reared up in front of them. Bordering the Ute Mountain Reservation, Ferrara saw the sharp lines of the foothills against the darkening sky. Leslie was driving, directing the SUV north through Cortez and then east on 160, passing the Mesa Verde National Park and arriving in Durango after dark.

That night they all shared one hotel room, the first time they'd done that. Jessica said she found it awkward, but Ferrara liked it. It felt like a fun sleepover. She tried to keep everyone's spirits up by playing up a fun, "hey we're on vacation" vibe. Jessica carried her own suitcase into the hotel room and flopped down on the bed, letting out a sigh and complaining about the clothes Ferrara had packed for her.

"Dinner?" Leslie asked, grabbing her keys. "I'm heading to that bar next door."

"I'm tired," Jessica said. Ferrara didn't say anything. There wasn't anything to say. They'd spent the whole day talking already. Now it was time to let everyone relax.

"Bring me back something, will you?"

Ferrara nodded and left with Leslie, hitting the bar next door. The food wasn't great but the music was loud, and she and Leslie played pool. They brought back food for Jessica, but she was curled up on the bed with one of the scripts, sound asleep.

Ferrara smiled. Maybe this whole thing would actually work.

Chapter 36
Journal

Thursday morning, they headed north and east, driving through the Rockies. Jessica sat in the back, as usual, the latest from a pile of uninspiring scripts on the seat next to her. She stared out the window like a little kid on a car trip with her parents. The mountains were beautiful, but she was bored.

Jessica went back to her journal. In Arizona, she'd decided that so many strange things had been happening to her lately, she needed to write them down. At a rest stop in Colorado Springs, she'd convinced Leslie to buy her a nice leather journal, and now she was jotting everything down. As she rode in the back seat of the Honda Pilot, she filled page after page of recollections about the trip so far. When that was done, she went back and wrote a few pages about her time at the different treatment centers she'd attended.

It was a long day, exhausting. The longest day of driving—or riding, in her case—so far. Ten hours through the mountains, then into Denver and east from there, a straight shot to the Kansas/Colorado border and some tiny town named Colby. Jessica had watched the distant skyscrapers of Denver slide off to the left of the SUV and slowly fade into the distance behind the car as they headed east, the city silhouetted against the sharp line of mountains that pushed up against the sky.

Passing Denver, she wondered if Blake the stalker lived there. He could be anywhere, the big man with the facial scar. He could live in Denver, or Seattle, or New York. There was no way of knowing. He didn't live in LA, she was sure of that much, or else he'd be turning up at every event. But where was he? Was he planning another assault? Would she even know it was coming? She remembered the syringe in his hand, stabbing it into her neck, the world going fuzzy. She'd come to later, rescued, the man long gone. She'd rubbed her neck, where the needle had jabbed her, and listened as people told her what happened. She was lucky to be alive.

She spent a lot of time thinking about Blake—too much time.

Pushing him from her mind, Jessica scribbled in the red journal, writing about the months she'd spent shooting "Knights of the Temple" in Atlanta. The time travel movie had her traveling back to medieval England. She'd seen so little of the area that it felt like she'd never left the hotel, traveling only to the set and back. Jessica wrote about the last year and all the things that had led up to her passing out drunk behind a dingy LA club and laying in the rainy street in a $5,000 dress.

It felt good, getting it all out of her head. Putting down her thoughts on paper seemed to give the memories more permanence. At the same time, she was able to let go. Maybe her mind just didn't want to forget.

That night they stopped in a tiny town in western Kansas. The hotel was so quiet she could hear a pin drop. The town had a grand total of three restaurants, and two of them were fast food, and it reminded her of some of the small towns around St. Louis, where she'd grown up. They ended up at a mom-and-pop diner, where she got one of the best cheeseburgers of her entire life. The fries were off the charts as well, dusted with some kind of garlic powder that had her licking her fingers like a cretin.

The food was great and the conversation lively—the three of them were getting used to each other by now, remembering to call Jessica "Sydney" without prompting. The conversation turned to their lives, and how each of them had all ended up in Los Angeles, following the old saw that no one was actually "from" LA but came from somewhere else.

They debated the tax credit some states gave film companies to lure business out of Los Angeles. Ferrara led a whole conversation about makeup and whether or not women should "have" to wear the stuff. Leslie asked Jessica some probing questions about her drinking situation and when it had "gone off the rails," at least according to her.

Normally, Jessica would have been put off by the bluntness of her questions, but out here in the nowhere that was western Kansas, she tackled the questions between bites of her amazing cheeseburger. She hadn't always been a drinker, but she'd gotten an early start and was, apparently, a natural.

They discussed her past visits to treatment centers and what went wrong. A few times during the conversation, Jessica started feeling pressured and maligned and got quiet. She didn't want to NOT answer the questions, or make these women mad. Jessica tried to be truthful, where she could, and admitted that much of the fault was her own.

"I have a question for you, one I've been meaning to ask for a while," Ferrara said. "Why do you have 'Team Jessica?' You know, a crew of people who follow you around and live off of your money?"

"What are you talking about?" Jessica said quietly, relieved to be off the drinking topic. "You're part of that crew. Team Mills all the way," she said.

"Ha. I do your hair and makeup, but I don't buy you coke. And I work for other people. I have actual skills. What do those other people do? All Carrie and Gina know how to do is party. Aaron's good at his job, but Scott and Hank seem like they're just making it up as they go."

Jessica started to explain it away, then stopped. She felt herself starting to make excuses for her posse, but there was no one here to lie to. Jessica didn't need to defend anything.

"I like them. They keep me company."

"And spend your money," Leslie chimed in, pointing a garlic fry at Jessica. "Enablers, probably. Do you think they're looking out for your best interests?"

Jessica shook her head. "Not always. Especially the girls. They're in their mid-twenties, so they're not looking out for anyone but themselves. But Hank's been a friend for years."

"Yup, I know," Ferrara said. "And there's nothing wrong with having friends. I have friends. I'm sure Leslie here has friends," Ferrara said, turning to Leslie. "You have friends?"

"Yes, I do. A few."

"You get together and party?" Jessica asked.

"We go out and have a good time," Leslie said quietly. "Within reason. One of them has a substance abuse problem. I'm working on her."

"Wow, a cop?"

"It's not that crazy, really," Leslie said. "It's the most stressful job in the world. Some people need help coping. I'm not condoning it, and if they weren't getting help, I'd make sure she was taken off active duty."

Ferrara shook her head. "Still scary."

"My friends aren't the issue here," Leslie said. "But we all pay our own way. It's not centered around one person with an infinite bank account. Do you think those people would still be your friends if the gravy train ran dry?"

"That's a good point," Ferrara said. "Where are they now?"

"Well, you're here," Leslie said with a smile.

"Seriously, I'm not part of her circus," Ferrara said to Leslie. "I have a job to do that doesn't involve spending her money and getting tans with her and going to the gym with her."

"You've been to the gym with me—and I paid!"

"Oh, she's got you there, Ferrara," Leslie said with a smile.

The rest of the meal was quiet—it seemed like they'd maxed out that conversation and everyone just wanted to think. It was fine with Jessica, who was nagged by the same questions Ferrara had brought up. Did people like her for "her" or for her mansion and her money? You could tell when a new person was sniffing around, trying to get "into" the group. Those people, mostly women, were obvious gold diggers.

But what about the others, people she'd known for years? Some were fellow actresses, or friends she had made since her move to LA. Would they still be friends with her if she retired tomorrow? Were they drawn to the "business of show" and the reflected light of her "glory?" It was hard to tell.

Maybe she was too loose with her money. It might explain why cash always seemed tight. She needed to hire a serious Hollywood accountant, a guy from one of those firms that managed every star's money. She needed someone to get her finances in order, set up accounts to accept the incoming funds instead of the way she did it now, with all the checks going into an envelope for Hank or Scott to take to the bank once every two weeks. She needed a money manager—and not Hank, her agent—to get her on the straight and narrow, get her accounts and property in order. Maybe set up a very generous spending account for her to draw upon.

And no cash. Jessica didn't need it, but the "sugar twins" did. Dealers didn't take credit cards, even the fancy ones in Hollywood that made house calls and delivered whatever you needed, day or night.

Chapter 37
Jake

Thursday afternoon, Frank had an appointment to see Jake Delancy. The young man, one of Frank's only friends in town, was involved in a bewildering number of ventures, the primary being the owner and landlord of dozens of rental properties in the Dayton area. If Frank was looking for a place of his own in or near Cooper's Mill, Jake was a good place to start.

The young man lived by himself in a house on South Second Street in downtown Cooper's Mill. On his way, Frank admired the large Victorian houses that populated streets around Cooper's Mills' historic downtown shopping district. He wasn't close to buying one, not by a long shot. But he could dream, right? It'd be amazing to find a place big enough to serve as an office, or at least something he could share with Laura and Jackson. But his pension hadn't even kicked in yet.

Those ornate homes on Main Street started at $200K and went north from there. He passed dozens of spectacular homes with large, well-kept lawns, and not just the ones on Main.

He'd assumed all the nicest homes were arrayed along Main, being the showpieces of the town, but since he'd moved here and started driving around, he'd marveled at the homes on streets like Dow and Broadway and Walnut. Big homes with columns and ornate front porches and inlaid stained-glass windows. One house on Dow had white columns and gold numbering in above the front door. Another on Broadway near the school featured a turret on the third floor that looked like something out of a fairy tale.

Maybe one day, if he played his cards right, he would be able to own a place like that.

Jake's house, located on South Second near Main Street, was another Victorian, but this one had seen better days. Some of the shutters were missing, and the yard was a mess. Worst of all, one of the windows on the second floor was boarded over with plywood. Frank could tell, even from the outside, that the whole house probably needed work. From the street, it looked like Jake's own home sat at the bottom of the list of places he was working on. Frank had heard it before. What was the saying? The cobbler's kids have no shoes? Jake was probably so busy fixing up other places, he never got around to his own.

Frank parked and got out, making sure to shut off the interior lights. The Camaro featured an interesting detail: the headlights were covered with small doors that slid open and closed to cover the headlights.

Unfortunately, the left light was messed up: the doors would stay open when they were supposed to close. And whenever the doors were open, the headlights stayed on. He'd found them on during the daytime on a few occasions. Unlike modern cars, these lights were supposed to be used only at night. Once, the lights had been on all night and drained his battery, forcing him to get a jump from Laura's car. He needed to get it fixed, but he couldn't afford it right now. All he could do was check to make sure he turned off the lights.

Frank pushed aside the fence gate, scraping up more grass, and walked up the sidewalk to the front of the house. There was a random red wheelbarrow full of roof shingles near the side of the house. Frank knocked, standing to the side of the front door out of habit. Cops were trained to never stand facing a closed door—one gunshot could take you out.

Habits were hard to break.

"Coming!" Frank heard from inside, and then the door rattled and opened. It was Jake, looking more tired than usual. The situation with the Washington family looked like it had added a few years to the young man's face.

"Frank, good to see you," he said, holding the door open. "Thanks for dropping by—sorry about that front gate. It's on my list. Come on in for a sec, and then we'll head out. You mind driving?"

"Nah, that's fine."

Frank followed him into a living room that had also seen better days. Like the rest of the house, it was a work in progress. Both lights over the fireplace were missing, but the mantle looked beautiful, ornate and hand-carved. There was furniture everywhere, including a table stacked with papers along one wall. Above the table, tacked to the wall, was a numbered list of his ongoing projects: homes and apartments he was remodeling, side projects for other people, a list of beers he was apparently brewing somewhere, and a note at the bottom: "Farmer's Market next year - sell cheese and honey?" At the bottom, as predicted, the list read "Finish Second Street renovations/sell."

"Looks like you're mid-renovation," Frank said, sitting down. "You selling this place?"

Jake looked up and saw Frank was looking at the work list. "Not for a while, at this rate. I have to write everything down or I forget."

Frank nodded. "Yeah, I've been doing that lately," he said, waving his red notebook.

Jake sat in a chair opposite him, next to the fireplace. "You know how it is. I just can't seem to get things finished. There's always something else to work on. And I've been concentrating on the upstairs," he said, pointing up at the ceiling. At that, Frank heard someone moving around upstairs.

"You have company?"

Jake smiled. "Yeah, thanks to you."

"Me?"

"Rosie," Jake said with a smirk. "She helped me out with the Washingtons," he said. "Remember?"

Frank nodded. "Not something you forget."

"She helped me work out how much to tell the cops, and helped me get the Washingtons set up in Columbus after the thing with the Northsiders blew over."

"Glad that's over," Frank said quietly. The whole situation had turned uglier than anyone involved could have possibly imagined. The Washingtons, one of Jake's tenants, had had a nasty run-in with the Northsiders, a Dayton street gang. They retaliated by burning the family's house, Jake's rental, to the ground, the Washingtons escaping with their lives. When Frank had investigated the fire, he'd been drawn into a nasty situation with the gang that nearly cost him his life. Meanwhile, Jake had put the family up in a hotel in Columbus, far out of reach of the Dayton gang.

Jake nodded, not saying anything more about it. "She helped a lot," Jake said, glancing at the ceiling. "She's staying here a few nights a week."

"Congrats. No wonder you need to fix up the upstairs."

"Yeah. I was fine with a partially-working bathroom that had a hole in the floor and occasional hot water. Rosie, not so much," Jake said with a smile. He grabbed some papers off a small table.

"How's her bar doing?"

"Good, good. They're expanding, adding seating out the back."

"Good for them," Frank said. "You ready?"

"Yup. ROSE!" Jake yelled at the ceiling. "I'm heading out!"

"See you later," she yelled from somewhere upstairs, and Jake smiled at Frank as they left.

Chapter 38
St. Louis

The three young women in the Honda Pilot drove on, leaving Colby, Kansas very early on Friday morning, driving into the rising sun. They grabbed a fast-food breakfast and were heading due east before seven a.m. Jessica was getting sick of the back seat and had taken to switching sides each day, so today she was seated behind the driver.

They made good time, cruising through Kansas and crossing rivers and passing through endless small towns that nestled up to the highway like creatures seeking attention and nourishment. Nothing fancy, nothing exciting. And nothing tall—she had gotten used to the mountains that encircled Los Angeles, used to the tall buildings that jutted up from the downtown. Even the palm trees were tall. Once they got away from the Rockies, everything got flat, and the horizon stretched off into the distance, flat as a pancake.

Jessica sat in the back seat and looked out the window, her head leaning on the cold glass, and wondered why people would want to live out here in the middle of nowhere. I mean, why would someone choose to be surrounded by nothing? In LA, nothing stretched off into the haze but the ocean. It painted the western horizon a flat line, dark blue on light blue.

They reached Kansas City around 1 p.m., stopping for lunch. It felt good to get out and stretch—Leslie avoided stops unless they were absolutely necessary, saying something about avoiding public eyes. Jessica thought she was crazy, and grumbled every time Leslie called for them to hit the road again.

Four hours later, they approached St. Louis, Missouri, winding through suburbs and passing the airport. The downtown was dotted with tall buildings and Memorial Arch, and Ferrara, driving, took an exit that led into the busy downtown.

It all looked very familiar—Jessica had lived in the area until she was eight years old. She'd grown up in O'Fallon, Illinois, a small town less than twenty miles east of St. Louis. She remembered it positively:

riding bicycles with friends, walking to school and kicking the fall leaves. A backyard that looked out on a dusty cornfield. Singing and dancing in school plays and musicals, finding her talent at a very early age. Jessica recalled a bakery she loved in town, but now the name escaped her.

It had all changed when she was eight. She still remembered her parents' fights. Sometimes Jessica would go to her room and cover her ears to block out the shouting. Some of it was over Jessica and her "prospects." After her parent's divorce, Jessica and her mother had moved to Los Angeles in support of Jessica's nascent acting career.

Her dad had stayed behind. A few years later, he'd taken his own life.

And now, Jessica was back. Maybe she'd look for that bakery—they had the most amazing brownies she'd ever known. Too bad she couldn't remember the name of the place. Her mom might remember, if she ever sobered up.

The three women stayed at a fancy hotel in downtown St. Louis, one built as part of Union Station, an old-time train station that was now a massive, covered indoor mall. They got settled into the hotel, which was the first place Jessica had seen "valet parking" in almost a week.

They set out to walk around the city. It was your standard Midwestern city, with lots of friendly people and interesting things to do. It was also somehow combined with a big city feel, with tall buildings and taxi cabs and a few people rushing around and acting a though they were more important than everyone else.

For a second, she was taken aback by one man's behavior. He didn't feel like waiting for a cab and shoehorned his way to the front of a line of people waiting. When the people in line yelled at him, he flipped them off and jumped into the cab anyway. And while she was surprised by his behavior, she was more surprised by the people in line—they shook their heads and smiled after the man left.

"Big city folk," one woman said, and the others laughed.

"You can't beat 'em," a man said. "And you can't kill 'em."

Big city folk, Jessica thought with a smile. She was the epitome of that concept, even though she had grown up in a small town 20 miles from this very spot. Jessica made more money than everyone standing in that taxi line combined, probably by a factor of a thousand. And yet, they all seemed happier than her. And better able to shake things off when they didn't work out.

While Ferrara and Leslie led the way, Jessica was quietly taking things in and enjoying a few smokes. The coke withdrawal seemed to be dissipating, and the smokes helped. They walked three blocks to the Gateway Arch, a ribbon of steel that stretched into the sky above the Mississippi riverfront. She remembered it from her childhood, but still, she stood there, agape.

The thing was just so HUGE, so much bigger than she remembered. It swooped up into the blue sky and curled over and reached back down, two sturdy legs supporting an archway that looked like a strange, alien portal. They called it the "Gateway to the West," and it lived up to its name.

"Wow," Jessica said. "That is impressive."

Ferrara turned and spoke, keeping her voice down. "You can't be that impressed. I thought you grew up near here." She'd given Jessica crap about never seeing the Grand Canyon, either. "You're the richest person in this state, probably. You should get out more."

Jessica nodded, not answering. It wouldn't do any good to defend her position. Instead, she lit up another smoke and dragged on it, ignoring Ferrara.

They walked along the riverfront and watched huge boats and smaller craft move on the wide stretch of water, flat cargo ships and tugboats. An old-fashioned steamboat moved past them, a huge paddlewheel turning behind it. It pushed the boat forward, churning up the brown river water. It looked like something out of an old story, and it was: Jessica realized that the boat was named the "Huck Finn" after Mark Twain's famous character and the book of the same name. She realized she'd never read that or any of Twain's books. She really needed to start a list of things she wanted to do on her Ohio "vacation."

They elected to not go up in the Arch—the wait was over an hour—and instead, walked the banks of the river, which stretched nearly 2,000 feet across, at least according to a series of signs located nearby. Fifteen football fields could fit in the space stretching across to the Illinois shoreline.

Across the river, Jessica saw a collection of riverboats tied to the docks and realized that they were casino ships, where tourists and locals could gamble.

One of the signs mentioned an interesting incident that had happened a few years before. One of the early casino boats, the *Margaret,* had come loose from its moorings and crashed into the footings of a bridge downriver. Jessica read the metal plaque that showed an etching of the *Margaret*—apparently, it had been owned by two Italian brothers who had fought over their business.

It didn't say so on the plaque, but she got the sense that they were criminals, or at least one of them was. They had some type of shootout with a third party and the empty *Margaret* had come loose with the brothers aboard. The casino boat had been pulled downriver by the current, finally crashing and breaking up as it plowed into the massive stone footing of the Eads Bridge.

"That's a crazy story," Leslie said, pointing at the plaque with the Margaret. "Did you read about the brothers?"

Jessica nodded. "I remember hearing about it as a kid."

Ferrara looked out at the river. "I can't believe how wide it is."

"Almost a half-mile," Jessica said. "Sometimes it floods. I remember one time, all these steps were underwater, almost to the top," she said, pointing. "It was on the news. They had to close the arch."

"Did it flood?"

"No, but it came close."

"What I want to know is how did they build this thing?" Ferrara was looking up at the graceful curve. "I mean, it almost looks like something you would grow, not build, right? Did they use scaffolds and stuff?"

Leslie shrugged. "I don't know. Another thing is the fact that it got built in the first place. They could never build something like this now. No way it would be supported by the taxpayers, or get the proper permits. People like this kind of stuff but don't really want to support it with their money, I'm betting."

The women headed back in the direction of the hotel. Passing through the lobby, they continued out into the enclosed mall and got an early dinner at an upscale Italian eatery. Jessica sat down, eager for some good food after all the cheeseburgers and road food. Soon she was enjoying an outstanding plate of Chicken Marsala and a simple yet excellent spinach salad.

St. Louis turned out to be one of the highlights of the trip east, and nicer than she'd remembered. It was filled with strange stories, like the one about the riverboat brothers. All these people out here in the middle of nowhere, just doing their thing and living their lives, not caring one whit about what or who was fashionable in Los Angeles. None of these people cared about the latest film scandal or which star was shooting a new picture for an up-and-coming Chinese studio, making people worry about the future of film and TV production in southern California. These folks gave very little thought to who was dating whom and who was seen out with whom at the trendy clubs and hotel bars of "La la land."

These people were happy just doing their thing.

Chapter 39
Rental

Frank drove the Camaro while Jake rode in the passenger seat, giving him directions to the first rental home.

"So, how are you doing? Getting settled in town?"

Frank nodded. "Laura's letting me crash on her couch, but my time is running out. I've got boxes taking up her whole apartment. She'll be glad to see me get a place of my own."

Jake thought about it. "Well, Cooper's Mill is always short of rentals or houses to buy. Nothing sits on the market long. I've seen houses change hands without even coming to market—sales are done through friends or contacts. The downtown is just too popular."

"Okay, but I just need a little place."

"I have a couple, but they might be out of your price range. $400 a month?"

"Yeah. Where to?"

Jake directed him around Cooper's Mill, pointing where they needed to turn. They went to one of Jake's downtown rentals, getting out and going inside. The place was $700 a month, well out of Frank's budget, but he walked the apartment anyway. It was half of a duplex, an old home converted into two adjoining units.

"I was sorry to hear about Deputy Peters," Jake said.

Frank looked at the parquet floor of an apartment he couldn't afford. "Yeah. The funeral was hard." Actually, it was worse than just losing the only friend he had in town. Now he was on the outs with Chief King and the rest of the local police force.

"Things will get better," Jake said quietly.

They headed to the next one, another downtown apartment, this one $650. Frank liked it, just as he liked the large home they drove past—it had a $1,100 monthly rent—but Frank could only shake his head.

"These are nice, but pie in the sky for me, Jake," Frank said as they stood near the car. Frank wasn't excited about any of the rentals, and he felt weird about walking through people's apartments when they weren't home.

"I know you said $400," Jake said. "I was thinking you and Laura might go in on it," Jake said. "With your combined money, you could—"

"Laura's getting sick of me," Frank said with a smile. "That might work down the road. For now, I just need a little place of my own."

Jake nodded. "Okay. Sorry."

"It's fine," Frank said. "I just don't want to waste your time. Do you have anything else?"

Jake nodded. "I have a couple, but they aren't in the downtown. I thought that's where you wanted to be."

Frank shrugged. "I'm fine with driving a little."

They got back in the Camaro and visited two more small places, one on a road that headed north out of town towards Troy. Frank remembered driving the same road before—it had all been a blur. He'd been chasing Joe Hathaway on that cold day when Joe tried to kill Frank and Deputy Peters on the lake ice. It had been a thrilling chase, with Chief King on Frank's speakerphone, giving Frank directions. But now Peters was dead and King wasn't talking to him. Frank didn't want an apartment that would remind him of that every day.

"This is a good price," Frank said. "Anything else?"

"I have one more place in Cooper's Mill. You might like one I have up in Troy as well, but I can't show it today. It's part of a four-plex. Cheaper. The last tenant bailed in June, and I've been doing repairs."

"I was hoping to stay in town. How much is the Troy place?"

"It's $450 a month, half of what it would run here in town. Troy has a lot more inventory."

Frank nodded. "That might work. Is it small?"

"One bedroom, bottom floor," Jake said as they walked back to the car. "Nice place, once I get it back to the state it should be in. Why don't people take care of rental properties? I've increased my security deposits to $1,000, and they still trash the place. Every single time."

"Let's see the last place."

They headed south, back into town, and Jake caught Frank up on some of the local gossip. Most of the town was worried about next year's construction project, which threatened to close down the entire downtown area for several months over spring and summer. The construction project would replace Main Street—and all the utilities under it. The spring and summer of 2013 looked to be a difficult time for the business owners in the downtown, and rumors were the construction might even extend into the fall. The official target date for completion was the 2013 Mum Festival, the town's biggest event, which took place every September.

Jake said everyone he'd talked to was freaking out, especially the business owners. Some of them had banded together to make plans and print flyers to warn shoppers. People were already predicting that some of the less-successful small businesses in the downtown wouldn't make it, put out of business by the construction or decreased customer traffic.

"They're doing what they can to help," Jake said. "But I'd avoid an apartment in the downtown until Streetscape is done," using the project's official name. "It starts in April."

They turned west when they got back to Main, heading toward the highway. This part of town was busier, more commercial, and Jake had him take a couple of turns through a residential area before stopping in front of a small duplex.

Inside, the place was nice. Small, but perfect for him. It was located in the "uptown" area, near the town's only grocery store, the police station, several restaurants and gas stations, and other businesses located near the off-ramp. He recognized the grocery and Burger King and the liquor store, all of which he'd visited on previous trips to town. Maybe Frank was finally getting the lay of the land.

The apartment was $500 a month, more than Frank wanted to pay, but it kept him in town. And Frank wanted to stick with Jake as a landlord for now. The devil you know.

Besides, the place was bigger than his old apartment in B-ham. The view wasn't nearly as good—in Birmingham, his apartment building had overlooked the city. This place looked out on the back of the strip mall that contained a Domino's, a bank and the liquor store. He could see a young man standing outside the back entrance of the pizza place, smoking and talking on his phone.

Well, at least getting pizza and beer would be easy. Maybe it was karma, locating so close to the liquor store. It would either be a blessing or a curse. But then, lately, his life had been full of both.

"Looks good, Jake. When can I move in?"

Jake smiled. "I'll get the paperwork started. Three weeks? September 1?"

"Sounds great," Frank said, looking around at the place. It was all he needed right now, and he'd be out of Laura's hair.

They walked out to the car and drove off.

"Thanks, Jake. Glad I could find a place."

"No problem. I'll get it fixed up and try to get you in early, if that helps."

"It would. You also said you might have some work?"

"Oh, yeah. I forgot about that," Jake said. He started feeling his pockets, looking for something. "You remember the Russian family, the one who owed me money until you got them to pay?"

Frank nodded—it was hard to forget. Jake had done some custom cabinetry for a Russian house flipper and his two sons, but then they'd stiffed him, trying to get out of paying him for the work. Jake had asked Frank to look into it. A fight had ensued, as they sometimes did when Frank was involved, and the Russians had all ended up in the hospital. Frank had gotten some cuts and bruises, sharp words from the local cops—and Jake's money.

"They messing with you again? I'm surprised you would work for them—"

"No, nothing like that," Jake said. "They were impressed by you. One of the sons came by two weeks ago, asked if you had been around."

"They probably want a rematch."

"Nope," Jake said. "The guy seemed in awe of you. You did kick their butts."

Frank didn't say anything.

"I've got his info here somewhere. They're having trouble with one of their suppliers, I think," Jake continued. "Something about paying for materials that never got delivered."

Frank drove back to Jake's house and stopped out front. "Well, they say karma is a bitch, right? Sounds like they're getting stiffed back."

"Yeah. But I don't think it's as simple as that," Jake said. "He said his old man didn't want to go to the cops, but I don't think it's anything illegal. They flip houses, but they have a side business, shipping cigarettes in from Russia. It's all legal, I think, but something happened and there where a shipment that got seized. At least that's what I think he said—his accent is crazy. I always worked with the dad because I couldn't understand his sons."

"I will reach out to them."

"Finally," Jake said, finding a post-it and handing it over. The only thing written on it was an address. "The Resnikov kid said he'd pay you $1,500 if you could help out."

Frank smiled. "Maybe I should negotiate with you on the rent. I help you out with all your 'situations,' and you give me free rent. Sound good?"

Jake shook his head. "I'm keeping my head down. No situations for me anymore," he said, lifting his arm. When he was having issues with the Russians, he was jumped one night and pushed down a hill into the local canal, sustaining a broken arm. "It's hard to run my kind of business with one arm."

"I'll bet," Frank said, waving the post-it. "And I'll drop by, see what they want. Thanks, Jake."

Chapter 40
Flyover States

On Saturday morning, they left St. Louis early, and Jessica talked Leslie into exiting the highway in Illinois for a quick tour through O'Fallon, the small town where Jessica had grown up. She showed off the town, driving them past what places she could remember—the high school, the view of the distant St. Louis arch. The drove up Dartmouth Drive, to see the house where she'd grown up, but she was astonished to find the house was gone. There was no 209 Dartmouth, just a vacant lot and a big maple tree she remembered in the back yard. Beyond, she saw the fields of corn she remembered staring at as a child.

"There?" Ferrara asked.

"Yeah," Jessica said. "That's so weird. I can remember the house so clearly, and now it's gone. When I was six, I fell down the stairs and broke my leg." She looked around, thinking maybe she'd gotten the streets wrong, but this was where the house had been. "I'll have to find out what happened to it."

They drove on, and Jessica directed them through the cute little downtown, with its stores and train tracks and a red caboose, a local attraction. They also found the place Jessica was looking for, "Wood Bakery."

"Can I drop in?" Jessica asked.

Leslie looked at her. "I don't think that's a good idea. You might be recognized."

"Look at me," Jessica said, pointing at her face. "I don't even recognize me."

They parked in front of the bakery and discussed it for a few minutes. Leslie was against the idea, but Jessica pled with her. She hadn't really asked for anything else the entire trip, and could tell Leslie was wavering.

Finally, Ferrara offered to go in with her. "Just as a buffer," Ferrara said. Reluctantly, Leslie nodded.

They climbed out and went inside. Crossing the lot, Ferrara asked about the significance of the red train caboose.

"I don't know," Jessica said, nervous. She was a big talker, thinking nothing could go wrong, but as she approached the front of the bakery, memories came rushing back at her. Coming here with her father. Walking around the downtown, including the nearby library. It had a clock that stuck out over the road, she remembered, and it was always getting knocked aside by vehicles passing through the narrow downtown.

Ferrara hesitated, her hand on the door. "Ready?"

Jessica wasn't, but she swallowed and nodded. "Yup. No problem."

Inside, it smelled exactly like she remembered. It was a bakery, first and foremost, but they also stocked candy and toys. The place was a kid's dream, and a perfect snapshot of a Midwestern store, even down to the bell that rang when then entered. It tinkled quietly like something out of a 1950's TV show.

"I'll be right there," someone called from the back room.

Jessica and Ferrara wandered the store, picking things up and showing them to each other with a smile. They made their way up to the wide glass cases, which held an abundance of cakes, cookies, donuts, and brownies. Jessica spotted the chocolate chip cookies with a smile.

"There," she pointed. "Those. Will you order a bunch for me?"

Ferrara nodded. "Yup. I'm gonna get a few brownies, too—they look great."

"Oh, they are," Jessica said as a woman came out of the back and walked over, drying her hands off.

"Can I get ya something?"

Jessica looked away—the woman looked familiar. Very familiar.

Ferrara smiled at her. "Yes, we'd love some brownies. Six, please. In one of those little boxes, if you don't mind."

"No problem," the woman said, getting out a small pastry box with a clear lid.

"And two dozen of the chocolate chip cookies, too. Thanks."

"No problem," the woman said, glancing at Ferrara and Jessica. She seemed to linger on Jessica for a moment, looking at her face, then the port-wine stain, and then back to her face. She reached in and picked out six of the frosted brownies, carefully placing them in the box.

"You folks from out of town?"

"Yup," Ferrara said. "Passing through. Heading to Dayton."

"Ah," she said, looking at Jessica again. "You heading home?"

"Yup." Ferrara glanced at Jessica, who was trying to look busy studying the different donuts in the case. There was something familiar about—

"Sorry, do I know you?"

Jessica looked up and the woman was looking right at her. AT HER, not past her, like everyone else had been since Jessica had adopted her new "I'm hideous" façade.

"No, I don't think so," Jessica said, drawing out her words. "I'm from Texas. Never been to Illinois before."

"Hmm," the woman said, handing over the brownies. "Let me get those cookies. You look a lot like Jessica Mills," the woman said, pointing at the wall behind them. Ferrara and Jessica turned to see a large poster of Jessica's face—she'd not noticed it coming in, and had inadvertently been standing right next to it. The poster was from one of her movies, "Bacon Tastes Good," and the Jessica on the poster had mud on her face and was holding up a pig. A handwritten sign arced across the top of the poster: "JESSICA MILLS, GREW UP IN O'FALLON. HOMETOWN GIRL MAKES IT BIG."

"You've got the same outline," the woman said, studying Jessica. "You could be the spittin' image of her. Your hair looks different, but you have the same eyes." She reached in and grabbed up cookies, bagging them and looking back at Jessica. "It's uncanny, really. I've seen all her movies. Grew up with her, went to preschool together. Wow, you could be her twin."

Ferrara looked suddenly uncomfortable and spoke up. "If she had different hair, and no birthmark, right?" Ferrara said, playing along. She looked on the edge of panic. "Sydney, you DO look like her, don't ya?"

"A little, I guess," Jessica drawled, mortified. She edged toward the door.

Ferrara stepped between them to block the woman's view.

"What do I owe ya?"

The woman tore her eyes away from Jessica. "Um...eight for the brownies, six for the cookies, so fourteen." She turned to look at Jessica again. "I grew up with her, you know.

Jessica backed all the way to the door, feeling it with her hand. "I wish! I'd love to be that rich, and famous. Bye!" She pulled the door open and stepped out into the sun, walking away quickly. She walked down the sidewalk, passing an insurance company and a wallpaper store, trying to get away from the bakery windows. She stopped and leaned against the wall to wait for Ferrara.

"That was close," she said to herself. "Too close."

Ferrara exited the bakery and walked straight to the car. She glanced over and waved at Jessica, pointing her to the SUV. Jessica hurried, and they both climbed in. Leslie was looking at them.

"Let's get out of here," Ferrara said. "Quick."

Leslie, ever the cop, had the vehicle in gear and out of the parking lot before turning to Ferrara. "Why? What happened?"

Ferrara glanced back at Jessica. "She knew."

"What? No way she—"

"After you left, she started grilling me. Where were you from in Texas, how long had you been in town, where did you grow up," Ferrara said, looking at the road behind them. "After she said the port-wine stain looked fake, she went to get her cell phone from the back. Was heading out front to find you, take a picture of you. That's when I got out of there."

Getting back on the highway, they headed east and north. Jessica was quiet. They were all quieted by the close call, each alone with their thoughts. Jessica set the cookies aside—suddenly, she wasn't hungry—and thought about growing up in the small town.

And the poster in the bakery. She thought about it for the next hour, barely talking to Leslie and Ferrara. The people in O'Fallon celebrated her time. She was a local celebrity, of course, but she'd also "made it big." They were proud of her, proud of their "hometown girl." Were they still proud, with her "in jail?" Did it make them feel proud to know how much coke she had had in her purse that night?

The poster made Jessica feel strange. Unworthy.

They drove on in silence. Dayton was five hours away, so they'd arrive at Ferrara's family home sometime this afternoon. After a time, the two women in the front seat began discussing the "normal people" who lived in the "flyover states."

Jessica had heard that term a million times. It had come up in meetings ever since she'd been old enough to attend the production meetings that came with every movie and TV show. People in Los Angeles loved to talk about people in LA and New York and Chicago. Those were the cultured people, the literati and glitterati they strove to entertain and impress.

But the meetings also often mentioned the "simple folk," those people unfortunate enough to live in the middle of the country.

They were the rubes from places like Peoria or Dayton—in fact, the question often came up: "but how will it play in Peoria?" It was all the same shorthand for an unspoken, shared belief that the people in the middle of the country were too dumb to handle anything subtle. "But how will it play in Peoria?" really meant "is this project vanilla enough so the dummies in the middle of the country won't get upset and start a protest?"

It was assumed that the big cities were the "leading edge" of culture. The coasts set the tone, creating everything that was fashionable and valued and "new." From there, the skinny jeans and spinning classes and obsession with the Kardashian clan would filter down to the unwashed masses of the flyover states. And by the time folks in Peoria were enjoying some trend, it was already on its way out.

Jessica recognized just how condescending that attitude could be. The folks in "flyover country" were just people, living out their lives, going to work every day and trying to raise their kids. Like those folks in line for a cab in St. Louis.

Occasionally the "flyover states" or the "folks in Peoria" would raise their collective ugly heads and fight back, especially if Hollywood or New York presented something that was too "out there" and progressive. The thinking was they clung to their "guns and bibles" and were deeply threatened by anything new or different. Few things frightened Hollywood executives more than a boycott springing up organically from the Midwest. It was the reason Standards and Practices existed, to rein in the industry, too keep it from going "too far too fast," whatever that meant.

Maybe the "flyover states" were getting tired of it. Maybe these people were just tired of being told to "like" this and "hate" that by someone else. How would the people in Hollywood feel if someone else came in and said "hey, smoking a pipe is now the 'in' thing to do" and then relentlessly made fun of them if they didn't fall in line with the new "fashion?"

It was officially the last day of the road trip, and the conversation in the front seat progressed as they discussed plans for the day. Jessica tuned them out, jotting down her thoughts and ideas in her journal. She made another list, this one a little more painful: "Industry Peeps to Reach Out To." She'd called the list by that title, but it actually meant something much worse—it was the list of people she'd screwed over.

It was essentially a list of the people she needed to apologize to.

People who had helped her out, or taken a chance on her, only to have Jessica disappoint them. At least two of the people on the list had left the industry because of her and her actions. She'd gotten one of them fired from a set and, as far as she knew, he didn't work in Hollywood anymore. She'd heard he'd moved overseas.

"Let's stop in Richmond," Ferrara said hours later, pulling Jessica out of her journal. "You'll like it, and we can get a late lunch."

The place advertised the "world's largest candle," but it was disappointing—the candle turned out to be nothing more than a round extension of the showroom for a company that made candles. They had a factory and everything—it was strange to realize how many things were actually still made in this country. They ate lunch at a picnic table nearby, and Jessica saw that while the top of the "candle" flickered, the "flame" was nothing more than a yellow light.

They drove on, passing over the border into the state that would be her home for a while. Jessica waited to feel something different, but nothing changed. It was the same flat land and the same cars and the same sky. Dayton, Ohio, looked like every other city in the Midwest—a few tall buildings, a tangle of highways.

"What do you think?" Ferrara was pointing at the downtown.

"It's fine, I guess."

"I know, not a lot to look at," she said. The highway curled north, and Dayton fell behind them. "But there are lots of things to do, and the people are nice. You'll like it."

The car moved through a complicated cloverleaf, where this highway crossed another one, and the scenery was taken over by trees and fields.

Jessica looked out the window, suddenly depressed. The place wasn't what she'd hoped for—it was all strip malls and industrial areas. "I thought your family lived in the country."

"They do."

Jessica started seeing signs for "Cooper's Mill" and wondered what it would be like. A fun place to live, or a ninety-day prison?

"Okay, this is it," Ferrara said. They left the I-75 freeway, taking "Exit 68 – Cooper's Mill." There was a group of businesses and restaurants gathered around the freeway exit, McDonald's and a diner, two hotels, and three or four gas stations. Not very impressive. At the top of the ramp, there was a sign that pointed east toward the "Historic Downtown," but Ferrara had Leslie turn the car left, west, passing over the highway.

"The other way is downtown. We'll go into town soon—you'll like it," Ferrara said, grinning. She was clearly happy to be back. "It's a cute little town. My family's house is out this way."

They passed a hotel, some fast food places, and a small restaurant called the Tip Top Diner. It looked like a few of the places they'd stopped during the road trip. A little mom-and-pop restaurant with low prices and great food. Heading west, they passed a few more businesses and then, after another intersection, they were suddenly in the country. Fields lined either side of the road, separated by lines of trees. The crops stretched away into the distance.

"That's a lot of something," Jessica said.

"Corn," Ferrara answered. "Okay, we're almost there," Ferrara said, pointing. "Up on the left."

Jessica watched the fields whiz past the car and realized that there was nothing out here but fields and squat houses and empty roads. No mountains, or hills, or ocean. Just miles and miles of flatness.

Chapter 41
Billing Questions

"So, to what do I owe this honor?"

It was Saturday morning and Frank's daughter sat across the table from him. They were at the Tip Top Diner, but Frank wasn't here to meet with potential clients. He had some news.

"Well, I just wanted to take my favorite folks out for breakfast," he said, handing a crayon to Jackson. "Can't I do that?"

The little kid was busy scratching all over one of the paper kid's menus the waitresses handed out, along with a plastic cup of crayons. This wasn't like one of those fancy restaurants, where each kid got a new, unopened box of three crayons to go with their printed kid's menus. Nope. Tip Top passed out photocopied menus and a plastic cup of broken crayons and stubs that traveled like vagabonds from table to table.

She nodded. "Sure, but we just went out last week, and I know money is tight."

"Well, I've got news," he said, then glanced at Jackson, who was absorbed in coloring in what looked like a circus train. "I found a place," he mouthed, barely saying it out loud. "Half of a duplex. Here in town."

She understood. "Oh, Frank. I told you you could stay as long as you liked, didn't I?"

"I know, I know. But I'm in your space and wearing out my welcome. Plus, I don't know, I guess I need my own space. It's been a long time since I roomed with someone else."

Jackson looked up. "What does that mean, 'roomed with someone?'"

"It means staying at a friend's house," Frank said.

"You are my friend," Jackson said. "I'm glad you're staying at our house."

Frank looked at him and then at Laura, who only shrugged. He turned back to Jackson.

"Well, I'm not planning on living there forever, you know," he said.

...uff, and it's taking up your mom's whole place." He ...Laura. "Anyway, I looked at a few places with Jake ...nice apartment in my price range behind the Domino's. ...o be in the downtown, south of you, but he didn't have ...I could afford."

...ra started to say something but, just then, the waitress brought ...their food: an omelet for Frank, French Toast and bacon for Laura, ...and a clown pancake for Jackson—a plate-sized pancake with candy for the eyes and nose, a Twizzler for a mouth, and whipped cream for hair.

"That sounds nice," Laura said, nodding. "That's not too close to the liquor store?"

He looked up at her. "I was actually thinking the same thing. It's good we're on the same page."

"So, how's that whole thing going?"

It wasn't something they talked about often, not since the summer and his forced detox. He'd been kidnapped and held by a Dayton gang, and they hadn't been supportive of his vices. Sometimes he joked about it: "it was the cheapest rehab I could find."

"Better, better," he said. "That Oxy was scary," he said quietly, keeping his voice down. "But the drink—I'm managing it."

"I'm glad to hear that," she said. "All this stuff with Deputy Peters is hard. And you on the outs with Chief King. Just wanted to check, see if you were backsliding."

"Not yet," he said, truthful.

It wasn't like he didn't think about it. Frank Harper thought about drinking every day. Sometimes he wanted nothing more than to wander down to one of the bars in the downtown, a place like Ricky's, maybe, and knock a few back. He missed the drink, and the friends that drinking afforded him, like the friends he used to have in Birmingham. Groups of 'friends' whose friendship centered solely around going out on the town and getting shit-faced.

What Frank didn't miss was that feeling of disconnectedness that came with the bourbon or the six-pack of beers. He didn't miss that feeling of untethered weightlessness.

Well, sometimes he missed it.

But he was also enjoying control over his life, making decisions based on moving forward. Perversely, he had the Northsiders gang to thank for this new level of control. Frank was pretty certain he'd end up drinking again in the future. For now, it was under control.

Nothing was dictating his direction other than himself.

"You okay there?" Laura asked.

He glanced up and nodded. "Yeah, yeah. Just deep in thought."

"I can see that."

He took another bite of his omelet. "So, like I was saying, it's a nice place. Small. And I've got my eye on a bigger place downtown, once I get the money. My half-pension hasn't kicked in yet—they said it starts in September, so I have to watch the spending. I'm just living on what I bring in from these cases."

"How's that going?"

"Good, good," he said. "I usually meet the people here. I'm working a divorce case, and I'm meeting with a group of folks today on another job." He tapped at his journal on the table in front of him. "I started writing everything down, numbering each case."

"You have enough cases to number?"

"Yup."

She thought about it for a moment. "How many cases you think you could work in a year?"

He calculated. "Maybe two, three a week. Lots of overlap. Some cases would be wrapped in a few days, while others could take years."

"Then I'd number them with five-digit codes, starting with the year. So your divorce case would be something like '12001' and so on. First case of 2012, right? And then starting in January, switch over to '13001' and go from there. That would help with billing, too."

Frank nodded. "That makes sense. I can number what I've already done. I was also tracking earlier cases, like the whole mess with the Northsiders. You know, writing down what I could remember. But some cases might go on for months. Some might never be solved."

"But you don't know that going in," Laura said. "What made a 'cold case' cold?"

"Usually the cases were worked by cops or detectives for a year. If they weren't solved in that time, we shelved it, revisiting the case on a regular schedule."

Laura nodded. "Makes sense. I'd still order them in some system, and using numbers seems the easiest and cleanest."

"Okay, I'll give it a try."

"How are you billing?"

"Well, so far, I've just gotten paid up front. No invoices or anything."

"Are you giving receipts?"

"No, not yet," Frank said, sitting back. "You think I should be?"

.d. And you probably want to bill people—that way, on. What you're doing, what you're getting paid for."

ed open his journal to a list entitled "SETTING UP PI and jotted it down.

.n, you are collecting information, right? Name, address, stuff like that? For taxes. You can invoice people pretty easy. ubooks is good."

'Fresh Books?"

"One word," she said, looking at his list. "Online billing, invoicing, that sort of thing. I think it starts out free."

"Good."

"How do private investigators make sure they get paid? I'd think doing any of the work before you got paid would be a risk."

"It could be. I knew a couple of guys in Birmingham that did PI work on the side. They always tried to get paid up front. At least half."

"What about jobs that take months? Is there a payment schedule?"

"Hmm, never thought about that. I guess you'd ask for money at the start of each month. So far, the divorce lady paid me up front, like a retainer. Now she's paying me hourly, when I ask."

Laura thought about it as she finished her French toast. "Sounds like you need to be billing people at the start of the job, then again monthly until the case is closed or they ask you to stop, right?"

"Yeah, makes sense," he said. "I haven't figured all that out yet. I did do some research on how other PIs do it."

"I can help you out, if you want," she said. "On the house. Get you set up with a billing system, invoicing, stuff like that. And I can look into how other folks do it."

"I couldn't impose."

"Oh, you're not imposing," Laura said with a grin. "I'm getting my foot in the door. That way, when you have enough paying clients to afford an actual accountant, you'll call me first."

He looked at her for a moment and smiled. "Sounds good. I'm not quite there yet. A few more jobs and I'll need it. And the new apartment—you're fine with that?"

"More than fine," she said. "I can't wait to get my living room back," she said with a smile. He loved her honesty, a trait she inherited from him. Her mother, Trudy, never cared for talking about anything important, not the issues in their marriage or his problems at work. After a while, he'd just stopped sharing with her. Even near the end, when the divorce seemed inevitable, she'd never really cared enough to discuss their problems.

But Laura was different. She had a natural inquisitiveness about her, and never looked away from the truth, no matter how uncomfortable it got. The same trait in him had always seemed like a curse, but, in Laura, it seemed more like a blessing.

Chapter 42
Skybar Paparazzi

Bill Hanford was a tough son-of-a-bitch.

At least, that's the way he liked to think of himself. He was tough, a go-getter. Good with a camera, and never taking no for an answer. Even if that meant sneaking into someone's yard, or climbing over an occasional fence, he'd get the picture. The tabloids paid top dollar for photos of celebrities, the dirtier the better. Compromising positions, coming out of a lover's home the next morning, stumbling drunk from a vehicle that had just plowed into a tree somewhere. If someone famous was out on the town, Bill Hanford was there with both of his cameras, snapping away.

It was a dog-eat-dog industry, the land of paparazzi, and Hanford had to be tough if he was going to hang in there. Most people couldn't hang in there. They got tired, or overwhelmed, or started to feel sorry for the "targets," as the rich and famous were known. Rarely were these "targets" called by their actual names, especially between paparazzi, whose entire income was based on their ability to find the most salacious photos for their "targets" before another pap could swoop in and steal the shot.

And Bill Hanford was one of the best. He and his shock of red hair showed up wherever they could, easing in from the sidelines, snapping the photos that brought in the big bucks.

His last big photo had paid his wages for five months. It had been of a wreck like the one described, a single-car accident where a famous actor had driven his brand-new Porsche into a tree near the corner of Sunset and Olive. The actor and a young woman—not his very VERY famous wife, by the way—had stumbled from the smoking car and staggered away, coughing and gagging.

Hanford had gotten it all on film and video.

He'd been following them, hanging back far enough to see the car swerving. If he'd been a responsible citizen, he'd have called 911. Instead, Hanford followed, waiting for the inevitable. Finally, the car had fishtailed going around a sharp corner near the Mondrian Hotel on Sunset. The Porsche tipped up on two wheels before it straightened out and plowed right into one of the trees that lined the sidewalk in front of the hotel.

"DAMN!" he'd yelled to himself. "DAMN!"

Knowing instinctively where to park his car to keep it out of the shot, Hanford had jumped out, dragging both cameras. One he hurriedly set up on the hood of his car, pointing it at the scene and recording video. Then he'd grabbed the other camera, his best, and run over, snapping photos of the couple just as they climbed out.

As they staggered away from the car, he took more shots of them and the car, its hood crumpled against the base of the tree. It was leaking something, a puddle running out from beneath. He'd hoped it was gasoline—how cool would it be if the car exploded? Unfortunately, it looked green, so it was probably just wiper fluid.

"Can you...can you help me?"

It was the young woman who had been in the car with the famous actor, a man Hanford had seen recently in one of those superhero movies. The woman was bleeding from the forehead, dazed, confused. Her dress was torn, with half of one of her boobs exposed.

Hanford stepped toward her. She put up her arms, as if he were going to help her, but he lifted his camera and snapped away, grabbing another hundred photos in a few seconds before she turned, confused, and stumbled towards the hotel lobby. People were streaming out of the Mondrian, now, gasping and looking at the smoking wreck. Bill followed the injured woman and got a great photo of her tumbling to the ground. She curled up in a ball near the curb, bleeding from the head.

It was a magical photo.

He'd later sold it and the others for nearly $80,000. But the video of the incident was even more lucrative. He'd sat on it for a week, teasing it out with little snippets of the video to his sources, letting them know he had it and was "fielding offers." The top one came in from HollywoodThrills.com for just under $200,000, and he'd happily sold it.

Bill didn't care about the "targets." All he cared about was getting paid. And, he rationalized, if he didn't take the pictures, someone else would. It was an industry that was fed by photos of the celebrities at their best and worst.

Like the incident two weeks ago with Jessica Mills.

She'd stumbled drunk out of Liquid, a trendy club in West

Hollywood, and fallen in the street, causing a near-fatal accident. To avoid running over her, a couple in a vehicle had swerved and crashed into a brick wall. Mills had gone to jail for it. No paparazzi had gotten photos of the incident or her arrest. There weren't even any photos from the common folk who might have been in the alley that night. Apparently, the cops had put the scene on lockdown.

Bill didn't feel sorry for the rich and famous. Some of the other paparazzi did, occasionally. Those photographers didn't last. You couldn't feel sorry for the rich and famous—they lived off their celebrity, good or bad. They lived in the limelight, and it was the risk they took.

Two weeks after Jessica Mills' incident, Bill Hanford was nursing a scotch and soda at Skybar, the smallish rooftop bar located at the Mondrian. He drank here a lot, enjoying the small booths and the windows that looked out over the rooftop pool and West Hollywood beyond. The place was quiet, now; it wasn't even noon yet, and there were only a few people swimming in the luxurious pool. The place was usually packed at night, especially on the weekends, when the rich and famous crowded around the pool to be seen.

Bill loved the bar, and this hotel: the rich stayed here often, so he knew the place well, but it had also become a personal favorite watering hole, a place to rest between all-night chases and stakeouts outside mansions. He'd gotten to know the staff pretty well—he was good at making friends and cultivating contacts, usually through tipping well. Because of that, he was welcome to drop by any time he wished, even though the bar was ostensibly reserved for hotel guests after 1 p.m.

Today, he was relaxing in one of the booths, sipping his drink and flipping through the TMZ website on his phone. He didn't notice Steven Zachary, or his intern, walk in, or see them looking around. But Steven spotted Hanford and walked right over.

"Drowning your sorrows?"

Hanford looked up and rolled his eyes. Steven Zachary was a class-A prick and one of the best paparazzi in the business. He routinely outsold Hanford, getting into places that no one else seemed to be able to access. Backstage at the Oscars last year, even. How did he manage that? Zachary was so successful, he'd started an actual business for shooting photos of celebs—he had an office and everything. The guy called it SZ, Inc. He should have called it "Sleaze, Incorporated."

"Just taking a break," Hanford said as Zachary and the kid with him slid into the booth across from him.

Hanford gave Zachary a look. "No, please, sit down."

"Ha, ha, that's funny," Zachary said, settling into the booth and wiping off the table. He turned to the kid. "What do you think you're doing?"

The kid looked at Zachary, then at Hanford, then back to Zachary. "Sitting down."

"No, you don't sit," Zachary said. "You're an intern. You haven't made me enough money. Go get me a drink and bring it to me. Then go sit at the bar like a good boy and wait for me."

The kid scampered off.

"Wow, you've got him trained. Can he roll over and play dead."

"Yeah."

"You're taking interns now?"

Zachary nodded. "You should get some interns, Bill. Really. They're very handy. Especially the girls."

Hanford didn't say anything.

"So, anything for me?" Zachary asked. "What do you know about Jessica Mills?"

Hanford looked up. Paps never worked together unless they were desperate, and Zachary sounded desperate.

"Nothing."

"Come on, Bill. I know we're rivals and all, but no one's heard a thing. She went into that minimum-security place in Oakland. Dublin. After that, nothing."

"What have you heard?"

"That she's not even there."

Hanford thought about it. "You got someone on the inside?"

"Nope," Zachary said. "Too far away. You know how cultivating contacts goes. Gotta stay in touch regularly."

Hanford nodded. He spread around plenty of money, hopefully to the right people. People who got him leads or got him in doors he couldn't get in on his own.

"You think she's not there?"

"I don't," Zachary said. "What have you heard?"

"Nothing."

"Well, I've heard different. I heard the whole Oakland thing was a ruse. People are talking."

"Saying what exactly?"

"That the blond wasn't even her. That the lawyer was just window dressing and flew back that evening. That Jessica Mills isn't in that jail in Oakland, but instead she's at a rehab facility in San Pedro, the one that looks out over the ocean. You know it?"

He did, in fact. "No, haven't heard of it," he said, running a hand through his shock of red hair. "What is it?"

"Daystrom. Rehab center. Named for some science fiction place, I heard. All futuristic. Anyway, they say—"

His intern plopped a very large frozen strawberry daiquiri down on the table in front of them. Zachary looked at it, then looked at the intern, who was awaiting a response.

"What?"

The kid looked nervous. "Is that...what you wanted?"

"Of COURSE it's what I wanted. Have you ever seen me order something else? Now get out of here."

The kid scampered off as Zachary guzzled down a fourth of the frozen drink in one sip. Hanford wasn't sure how he did it—when Hanford drank that much of a cold drink at once, he'd get a brain freeze.

"Where was I?"

"You were telling me why you don't think Jessica Mills is in the Pedro clinic," Hanford said, pronouncing Pedro like one of the locals: "Pee-Dro." They pronounced it wrong on purpose, he was convinced, as if calling it by the non-Spanish "Americanized" pronunciation somehow made it better. Less ethnic.

"Yeah. So, no one's seen her, and the clinic isn't that big. I don't think she's there either."

"Then she's in Oakland."

"I don't think so."

"Why? You got someone on the inside?"

"'On the inside?' Come on, Bill. It's a drug treatment center. People come, people go."

"And?"

"And I talked to a few patients. Folks that have come out in the last week. No one's seen her."

Hanford shrugged. "That could mean anything. Maybe she is in Oakland. Or maybe she's at Daystrom and they have her on lockdown. Maybe she's not interacting with the civilians. Maybe they've got her in their 'rich and famous people' wing. I don't know the place."

"I do," Zachary said. "WOW. That's cold. Anyway, I don't trust the

LAPD. Her transportation to the airport seemed overly-complicated."

Hanford shook his head. "Look, I don't know what to tell you. As far as I know, Jessica Mills is doing her time in that place in Oakland. Dublin. I heard the judge, Watkins, wanted to throw the book at her."

"But real jail?"

Hanford shrugged. "She was sick of the 'revolving door,' I was told. The Shuffle. But the DA's office didn't want to put her in GP."

"Jesus, that would have been a mistake. She'd get shanked in a day."

"Yup, that's what they were worried about," Hanford said. He sipped from his drink, thinking. "But if they did send her to rehab, and the Oakland thing was a fake-out, Daystrom is a good choice. It's off the beaten path. And it's one of the few she hasn't already been to."

Zachary thought about it for a minute, then finished his drink with a flourish. He abruptly stood up.

"Thanks, man," he said. "Let me know if you hear anything. And thanks for the drink!" He turned and scooted out with a smile.

Hanford cursed under his breath and watched him go, followed by his little lap dog. But Hanford stayed, watching them set out things to prep for the lunch crowd. He sipped at the rest of his drink and thought about Jessica Mills.

When the bill came, there was a charge for one obscenely-large daiquiri on there for $18. Of course, the bar staff had added it to Hanford's tab—Zachary had been sitting with him, and they'd had a long conversation. The bartender probably hadn't thought twice about it. Hanford cursed, paid the bill, and left.

Chapter 43
Homestead

Jessica was watching the fields speed by, thinking about what it would be like to live out here in the middle of nowhere, when Ferrara had Leslie slow the car.

"It's right up here," Ferrara said.

Jessica looked and saw that Leslie was slowing to turn into a driveway. Beyond was a large grassy lawn and, at the end of the drive, a sizable home at the top of the hill. It wasn't a mansion or anything like that, but the home was large and sat in the middle of the huge, well-tended lawn that looked as big as a football field, crisscrossed with mowed lines. On either side of the lawn stretched large fields of tall corn, the stalks moving in the August heat.

The Honda Pilot started up the asphalt driveway, curving toward the house. Leslie slowed to pass through a wooden fence, driving over a bumpy series of white pipes.

"What was that?"

"It's called a cattle guard," Ferrara said. "The fence keeps any animals inside, obviously, but there's a break for the road. The cattle guard is a series of metal pipes welded together with gaps in between. The pipes are close enough to drive over, but horses and other animals can't walk on them. Spooks them. Keeps the animals in without having to use a gate."

"The little pipes—they would fall through and break their legs?"

"No, the pipes just spin, scaring them," Ferrara said. "The animals slip. Puts the fear of God into them."

"You guys have horses? You didn't tell me that."

"Not anymore. But the cattle guard kept them in when this was a horse farm. Now it keeps the deer out."

They continued up the driveway and Jessica got a sense of how big the place was. She saw a sizable pond to the left as the driveway curved around, leading up the hill to the house. The pond was much larger than it had appeared from the road. There was a treehouse on the far side, and picnic tables and seating areas near the edge of the water. A short zip-line stretched across the lake, leading from a platform on one side to the other. A fountain in the middle of the lake threw water into the air.

"Spent a lot of time in that pond," Ferrara said with a smile. "Swimming all summer. Dad set up those kiddy zip lines for us, and the pond has a filtering system—all the water from the creek runs through a small patch of reeds and plants, cleaning it. Clearest pond you'll ever see. Made us quite popular in school—we hosted a lot of parties and end-of-season sports banquets."

Jessica looked at the pond—the zip-line looked fun. Hopefully, this place had some things to do—she was going to be spending a lot of time here.

"No way to count how many trips I took down that zip line. Sometimes I'd ride it to the other side, but it was more fun to just drop off into the water. It's only a hundred feet long, so you don't get going too fast," she said with a smile. "You're gonna love it."

The house appeared again on their right, looking bigger than it had from the road. They passed the columned home and drove around the side, pulling into a paved parking area behind the house. The parking area sat between the house and a large red barn.

Leslie parked the car and they got out, looking around. The house was two stories and rambled away from her, looking like it had been added onto several times since it was originally built. There were parts that looked obviously different from the "main" house. Back here, the house was one story, but with a second story facing the road. The barn was large, and from here, Jessica could see a large window near the top and a computer desk inside. Behind the pond and next to the barn was another huge lawn, this one the size of half of a soccer field. Someone had built a regulation-size soccer goal and had used the lawn for practice.

"My brother, Joel," Ferrara said. "He left for Ohio State last week. Soccer scholarship."

They started unloading bags and suitcases. "Let's just get enough to carry now," Leslie said. "We can do the rest later."

"You'll get a whole tour from my Mom," Ferrara said, heading for the house.

She knocked, but there was no answer. Opening the screen door, she tapped a code into the keypad, unlocking the windowed door and stepping inside. "The code is 9987, just so you guys know," she said. Stepping inside, Ferrara set her bags down. "We're here!"

Jessica stepped inside, crowding in behind Ferrara. There was a breakfast nook off to her left, along with a large kitchen. To her immediate right was a large dining room with doors that led off to the rest of the house. Directly in front of her was a sunken family room, decorated with the family's memories crowding the wood shelves that lined the room.

"Hello! We're here!" Ferrara yelled, but the house was silent.

"Is anyone here?" Leslie asked, pushing in behind them.

Ferrara shook her head. "Oh, I'm an idiot," Ferrara said. "I forgot. My family won't be back until tomorrow afternoon—they went to Indy today for a Colts preseason game in the morning. They're staying over. You guys want the tour?"

Jessica and Leslie followed Ferrara around the home, which somehow seemed larger on the inside than it should. On the main floor, there was the mudroom, kitchen and dining room, which led to the wood-paneled sunken living room.

"Watch your step," Ferrara said. "Can't tell you how many times I've tripped."

The space inside the home was broken up in a weird way—it was like a collection of smaller rooms instead of one cohesive house. There were two rooms off the mudroom, including an office and a pantry, and off the large living room was a massive bedroom with a hard floor.

"This used to be a garage, but someone converted it to a bedroom at some point," Ferrara said. "That's what happens when you have an old house—rooms get remodeled, and there's no flow."

They took the hallway off the living room that ended in a large foyer and the big double front doors, each a slab of glass and wood. Through the windows, Jessica could see the grassy lawn stretching all the way down to the road. It must take one hell of a riding mower to keep that grass tamed.

"Upstairs?" Ferrara said, pointing at a curved staircase behind them. They followed her up, where another collection of rooms awaited, three bedrooms, a bathroom and a hallway. Ferrara nodded into them. One bedroom was decorated with Indianapolis Colts posters and other gear.

"Welcome home," Ferrara said. "These are our rooms—mine's to the right, at the front of the house. You two can fight over the other two guest rooms. I'm the Colts fan."

Jessica and Leslie walked into both and looked around. The

first guest room was closer to the bathroom and noticeably larger, but Jessica liked the smaller guest bedroom better: it was cozy and featured a window seat that looked out over the lake. "I'll take this one, if that's okay."

Leslie nodded. "Yeah, I want to be closer to the bathroom. But this one is tiny. You sure?"

Jessica nodded. "Yeah."

"Good?" Ferrara asked? "There's more this way." She led them down a hallway. "This was the new addition. They call it that, even though it was built in the 1960s. My folk's room and Joel's."

The hallway led to another group of rooms, a pair of large bedrooms, a bathroom, and another door, which Ferrara opened. They walked out onto a large, flat terrace, which overlooked the pond and soccer field.

"Very nice," Leslie said, admiring the seating area and a hammock. "Bet you spent a lot of time out here."

"I did," Ferrara said. "Okay, what's next?"

Jessica looked at Leslie, who nodded.

"Okay, let's get the car unloaded, then let's meet in the kitchen. I need to go over some of the ground rules. And then dinner?"

Jessica nodded. "And a bath. I really could use a bath. I always feel gross when I travel."

Chapter 44
The Russians

Eager for a lead on a potential case, Frank drove to the address Jake had given him for the Reznikov's. A job was a job, he was learning, and money was money.

The last time Frank had "chatted" with the old Russian, Oleg, and his two daft, barely-intelligible sons, they'd gotten into an "altercation." Frank had been there to negotiate on Jake's behalf over some money and equipment they owed the man. The conversation had devolved into fisticuffs, as the old-timers liked to say, which had sent the three Russians to the hospital.

Frank had only gotten a couple of scratches.

But the fight had gotten Frank into hot water with Chief King, who didn't like the idea of Frank "freelancing." Frank had said he'd been helping a friend, but he doubted King would take that excuse again.

Frank looked around the interior of the Camaro. It was getting messy—he did most of his work out of the car, or the diner, and the passenger seat was filling up quickly with his paperwork, receipts and the like. Laura was right—he needed a filing system. But it wasn't just paperwork and notes cluttering up the car. Frank had been on several stakeouts, which inevitably led to a passenger floorboard littered with magazines and food wrappers and empty coffee cups.

Frank found the house with ease and parked in front. It was a large old house on North Seventh street, just a block up from Main. It looked to be in fair shape. Once he got out of the Camaro, he could hear banging and hammering coming from inside. Out front, a green dumpster hulked near the curb, full of broken plaster and splintered boards.

He knocked on the front door, an ornate glass affair inlaid with a metal seam that ran around the glass. It looked like the kind of front door someone would install in a castle.

"Da! Coming!" he heard from inside. Someone came toward the door, heavy footsteps. They kicked something and cursed in what sounded like Russian. The door opened—it was one of Reznikov's huge, surly sons. He had been smiling but his face immediately fell as he recognized Frank.

"You. I remember. What are you doing here?"

Frank smiled. "Nice to see you, too," he said. He glanced inside—the place was a gutted mess. Frank looked back at the man and put out his hand. "No hard feelings?"

The son, whose name Frank couldn't remember, looked down and finally shook Frank's hand, dwarfing it. For a second, Frank was worried the man might simply squeeze Frank's hand off, but finally, the pressure lessened. Maybe it had been a battle of wills, or a Russian thing. It was hard to tell.

"I'm here to see your father," Frank said, rubbing his hand. "Is he around?"

"Da, kitchen," the boy said. "I'm Semyon."

The hulking Russian—Frank could swear that he'd somehow gotten even bigger in the last year—led Frank through the house. They were clearly remodeling the place, taking down old plaster walls and replacing them with studs and drywall. Jake had mentioned that a lot of these old houses had walls made of strips of wood and plaster and chicken wire, and that's what Frank saw here. He also heard more banging and cursing coming from upstairs.

They passed through a finished dining room—at least it looked finished—and into the kitchen. It wasn't as far along: new cabinets and countertops were interspersed with gleaming appliances, but one wall was still nothing but studs. A huge, gleaming refrigerator had been installed. It looked brand new and still had the stickers and energy efficiency label on the front.

To the right was a breakfast nook area, with doors that looked out onto a large backyard and some trees beyond. Oleg was seated at a round table in the nook, talking to someone on his phone. Architectural plans spread across the table, and one of them had a coffee stain ring smeared across it.

When he saw Frank, the elder Resnikov did a double-take and then waved him over, pointing at a chair across from him.

"Sit, he says," Semyon said.

"Yup, got that. Thanks," Frank replied.

Semyon turned and left and Frank walked over and sat down, waiting for Oleg. Frank looked around at the kitchen and nook—the rooms looked beautiful. Professionally renovated, to Frank's inexperienced eye. King had said these guys were slipshod and usually raced through their jobs; maybe they were getting better.

Oleg was on his phone but Frank couldn't understand what he was saying. It sounded like Russian or something. The old man's wrinkled hands moved over piles of paperwork on the table, pointing at things, and then, finally, Oleg ended the call and hung up.

"Sorry that," Oleg said. "Ukrainians. Never trust them."

"Okay," Frank said. "This place looks great," he said, pointing at the half-finished kitchen. "Your place, or a client?"

"Client. We are behind the schedule," Oleg said, putting his phone down. "My sons can be, how do you say it? 'Distract?'"

"'Distracted?' Hard to get them to focus?"

Oleg nodded. "Yes, that is right. They also have other jobs. Girls too. Hard to get them to help me."

Frank waited, but the old man didn't add anything.

"My friend Jake says you guys might need some help?"

Oleg looked confused, then nodded, pointing around him. "With the house? You have experience?"

"No, nothing like that," Frank said with a smile.

"I need good painter."

"He said you were having trouble with a supplier," Frank said. "Business? They didn't deliver something you needed?"

Oleg finally understood. "Da, da. No, we got it all worked out. The droogs owed me for some materials. Late. They make it up on the next shipment."

"Oh. Okay."

"Da," Oleg continued. "We are 'good,' as you Americans like to say. Good."

"So, you don't need any help?"

Oleg smiled and pointed at the kitchen. "Not unless you can hammer," Oleg said. "It's hard to find help."

"Okay," Frank said, sitting back. Another job that turned out to be a dead end.

"You are disappointed? Yes?"

Frank nodded. "A little. But if I hear about anyone who needs construction work, I'll send them over."

"Spasibo," Oleg said. "Painters, especially. Pay by the hour work is hard to find people. My sons prefer the weights. And the girls."

"They are big boys," Frank said with a smile, not sure where this conversation was headed. "They go to the gym a lot?"

Oleg nodded. "What you do now? To work?"

"Um...well, I help people out when they need help," Frank said, trying to boil down what he was currently doing to as few words as possible. "Private investigations."

"Good," the old man said. "So, you are like police?"

"No, not really. I help people, investigate things the cops won't, or already did."

"I don't understand."

"Find missing people, track down things. Check up on husbands who might be cheating."

Oleg laughed, a hearty chuckle that sounded like Santa Claus. "You follow men around and take the pictures, da? The girlfriend pictures?"

"Sometimes," Frank said. "I'm an investigator. Like the police, but for less important things."

"Good, good," Oleg said. "You live in town now?"

"Yes."

Oleg nodded and looked at him. "That is good to know. And you are good in fight," he said. "Never know when that might come in helpful."

Frank nodded and stood, passing one of his business cards to Oleg, who looked at it.

"In case you need anything," Frank said. With a nod, he turned and made his way through the half-finished house, showing himself out.

Chapter 45
Ground Rules

A half-hour later, after they had unloaded the Pilot, the three women gathered in the dining room. Ferrara pulled out sandwich stuff from the fridge and various cabinets and put it on the table in front of them, along with some plates and chips and dip.

Leslie wanted to take a moment to get them together and go over the "rules" again. There could be no messing this up if they wanted to get through the next few weeks without any issues. So, while Ferrara made them sandwiches for dinner, Leslie reviewed the situation to make sure they were on the same page.

"Okay, here's how it's going to go," Leslie said, spreading out some papers on the old wooden farm table between them. "Judge Watkins gave me a certain amount of leeway in this matter, like your cover and our expenses. But there are some hard and fast rules she said we had to follow. Okay?"

Ferrara and Jessica nodded, both tucking into their plates of food.

"Good," Leslie said, finding the house-arrest paperwork that Jessica and Ferrara had signed in front of Judge Watkins. "Okay, here we go: first, Jessica, you're on house arrest. You agreed to that and signed. So no leaving this house or the grounds without my permission."

"Okay," Jessica said, and nothing else. Apparently, Jessica had decided this was one of those times when she should just listen and keep the talking to a minimum. Leslie was fine with that. They had done a LOT of talking over the last five days.

"Rule number two: I'm in charge," Leslie said, looking at them both. "What I say goes. If I don't like how things are going, we'll fly back to Los Angeles. You both answer to me and me alone."

"Yup, got it," Jessica said.

Ferrara nodded, having just taken a bite of her sandwich. "Yup, gotcha," she said, her mouth full.

Leslie nodded and looked at Jessica. "Third, Jessica, you're here to learn. And you'll work, either helping out Ferrara in some capacity, or we'll find you a job in the area. Hopefully, something with a low profile."

Ferrara nodded. "My mom texted me last night. She said she lined up a job for Jessica at the grocery store, if that works."

"Good," Leslie said. "As long as she's not interacting with the public."

"My mom's a manager there," Ferrara said. "Jessica would be stocking, I imagine. Working nights with one or two other people."

"Okay," Leslie said. "We don't want to push our luck. That okay with you, Jessica, doing a job like that?"

The starlet nodded, keeping her mouth shut.

"Ferrara, you will need to introduce Jessica around town, of course, but we need to keep that to a minimum, okay?"

"Yup. Gas station, coffee shops, that's it. Keep it short and sweet."

"We want Jessica interacting with the minimum number of people, okay? And maintain her cover as Sydney Green."

Ferrara nodded. "Yeah. I'll 'train' her to help me with some stylist gigs, maybe pick up a few shifts at the salon downtown, if the grocery thing falls through. We need a couple of new wigs, and I need more skin paint and prosthetics for the port-wine stain."

Leslie jotted it down, making a list of supplies. "And me? We decided I'm a producer, looking for Ohio locations?"

"That's right," Ferrara said. "I'll give you a list."

"Producers are always looking for new places to shoot," Jessica added. "You're Ferrara's industry friend. She invited you back here to scout this part of Ohio for potential shoots."

"Okay. I'll have to maintain that story as well, travel around and look at locations, right?"

They both nodded.

"Okay, we'll go from here, make it up as we go." Leslie grabbed another sheet and started reading. "Jessica Mills, I'm your court-appointed supervisor. Do you hereby agree to these rules as stated and, further, acknowledge that you are under house arrest?"

"I do."

"Will you promise to not make any attempts to leave these premises without my permission?"

"Yes, I will. I mean no, I won't," Jessica said.

"Good," Leslie said, closing her folder. "Watkins is counting on us to make this work." She looked at the wall behind Jessica, studying it, and Jessica turned—it was a calendar, a large one from a local insurance salesman.

"Okay," she continued. "If things go well, I'll check in with Judge Watkins mid-October and find out how she wants to proceed. She wants us to be back in LA in time for your hearing."

Jessica nodded and looked at the calendar as well, not saying anything.

"Of course, that's all contingent on your disguise holding up," Leslie said, looking at Ferrara, who nodded.

"We'll do our best."

"I know. So, assuming we're back in LA on the 29th, we'll need to leave...around Tuesday the 23rd. Gives us almost a week to drive back, same as getting here. Good?"

"What about flying home?" Jessica asked.

Leslie shook her head. "Probably not. Judge Watkins was clear—we don't fly unless there's no other choice."

"What about expenses?" Ferrara asked. "Do I pay for everything here?"

"Stuff for you, yes. Jessica and I are on my dime," Leslie said. "The State of California, County of Los Angeles. If it's something questionable, just give me your receipts and I'll decide."

"And me?" Jessica asked.

"I'll give you pocket money, and pay for anything we do off-premises. You shouldn't need a lot of money."

Jessica nodded, keeping her opinion to herself. Leslie wondered if the young woman was learning to keep her mouth shut every once in a while.

"I need some more toiletries, and I'd like to get some foods that I like," Jessica said. "Would that be okay?"

"Sure," Leslie said, adding it to her supplies list. "We can go to the grocery tomorrow."

Jessica looked outside. "Can I go for a walk?"

"Sure," Leslie said.

Jessica stood, but Ferrara spoke up.

"You both should let me show you around first," Ferrara said. "You need to get the lay of the property." She looked at Jessica. "Then I'll leave you alone."

"Good," Leslie said, standing and gathering her papers. "I need to check out the security situation before I check in with Judge Watkins."

Chapter 46
The Farm

Jessica walked outside, glad to be alone, if only for a moment. She waited for Ferrara and Leslie to join her, thinking about the ground rules Leslie had gone over. It was starting to feel real, this whole "house arrest" thing. This farm, as big as it was, would be her only home for the next few weeks.

Well, she thought, looking around. At least it's better than jail.

Ferrara came out of the kitchen door, followed by Leslie, and the three of them started off. Ferrara pointed out things of interest around the property, starting out with an overview of the house and environs.

"This is for parking, obviously. House, barn, soccer field," she said, pointing. "Joel and I spent a lot of time out there trying to 'bend' the soccer ball like David Beckham. No idea how many times I got kicked in the face."

"Quick question," Leslie said. "What about the perimeter? Is it all fenced, all the way around?"

"Yes, six-foot fences all the way around. I asked Dad to check everything."

"And outside is just fields?"

"Yup."

"What do they grow?" Jessica asked.

"Mostly corn," Ferrara said, pointing. "And that's the lake. It started out as a small pond, but it got expanded over the years. We added a fire pit, some seating areas, a treehouse." She pointed out a small building Jessica hadn't noticed. "That's the 'pool' room, although it's not really a pool. They keep the toys in there, model boats and floating stuff, plus towels. Some of my old swimsuits are probably still there, if you want to take a swim."

Jessica didn't ask any questions—all she wanted right now was to be alone. Maybe if she didn't talk, Ferrara and Leslie would get bored and go away. Jessica needed to clear her head. Maybe some alone time on this homestead, surrounded by fields covered in tall corn, would be a good idea.

"When will they plow the fields?" Leslie asked.

"It's called 'harvest.' The corn's getting high now, I'd say. There's a saying: 'Waist high, fourth of July.' Now it's August, so it's over six feet in most of the fields."

"That's a lot of corn," Leslie said, looking at the fields.

"Yup. They'll be running the combines in late September—until then, it'll just grow. Sometimes it feels like you're just driving down a tunnel, the corn gets so high on either side of the road," she said. "Across the road are some soybean fields—they're shorter."

"If you don't mind, I'm going to walk the perimeter of your yard," Leslie said. "I need to check on all the fences, take pictures. We want to feel secure here. Plus, I have to document everything for my report. I'll catch up with you guys later."

"Okay."

Leslie headed off. Jessica didn't say anything. When she was gone, Ferrara turned and asked Jessica to follow her to the barn, where she pulled the door open and they went inside. The space was huge—it looked like an aircraft hangar. Horse stalls lined both walls of the barn, each stall ten by ten feet. Rows of tables took up the interior of the barn, all covered with tools and car parts. The tables surrounded a car in the middle of the barn—or the shell of a car, missing most of its insides. Along the eastern wall, a set of stairs went up.

"The previous owner kept horses," she said, pointing at the stalls. "We had a couple ponies when I was growing up, but Dad sold them when they got to be too much work. He uses this for his cars now, obviously," she said, pointing at the equipment. "He's been working on this one for at least six months. Since my last visit. Honestly, it looks exactly the same as it did in April," Ferrara said with a smile.

She turned and looked at Jessica. "I know you're probably scared," she said. "You're way out of your comfort zone, and none of your other friends are here."

Jessica didn't answer. Instead, she picked up one of the car parts and turned it over in her hands.

"But remember, I'm here," Ferrara said. "If you need anything, talk to me. Seriously, about anything. I don't want to see you go to jail. I want to see you get better."

Jessica swallowed, not sure of what to say. Instead, she just nodded.

"Look at this like a vacation from your life," Ferrara said, taking the car part out of Jessica's hands and setting it aside. She held Jessica's hand. "You need a break. Ever since I've known you, you've been go go go. Do you remember where we met?"

"Sure," Jessica nodded. "It was the set of 'Third Times a Charm.' You were doing my hair and the hair for that other young woman. I can't remember her name. She was mean."

"Actually, she was nicer to me than you were," Ferrara said with a smirk. "She asked about my day, complimented me on her makeup. You were hung over—and short with me."

"Sorry. Sounds about right."

"All I'm saying is this is your chance to take it easy," Ferrara said. "No drama, no worrying. A vacation from your life."

Jessica looked at her, not sure what to say.

"And we'll get you a job, something low-key," Ferrara said. "And when you get bored, read your scripts. But being bored would be a pretty good thing, right?" Ferrara said, dropping her hands. "I'm off to shower. If I don't see you inside, have a good sleep, and I'll see you in the morning."

Ferrara turned and left, heading back toward the house and leaving Jessica alone with her thoughts.

Chapter 47
Blake Plots

Blake Oleander loved their family mansion.

He was surrounded by his friends and family, no matter how quiet they were. His family—and his girlfriends—were happy to sit around and listen to him talk about whatever he wanted. Blake often found it difficult to be around other people. He just wasn't used to it.

Out in the world, nobody let him speak. He was just too awkward, and the scar didn't help. He'd learned a long time ago that the best way to get along with people was to just keep his head down and stay quiet. The more information people knew about you, the worse they treated you.

But Jessica Mills was different.

He could tell from her movies and TV shows that she would understand him more deeply than any other person ever could. Whenever he watched her on-screen, it was as if she was speaking to him directly, calling to him. She was the summation of all of his hopes and dreams. He'd written her so many letters, he'd lost count. Someday, he'd make her understand that there was no one else in the world for her except him.

Blake would rescue her from her life. Together, they'd be unstoppable. She'd make the biggest movies in the world, and he'd be there, cheering her on.

But their love had to wait, for now. She was in the minimum-security facility in northern California, and there was no getting close to her there. Blake would have to bide his time, using it to plan his next trip to Los Angeles.

This time, nothing would go wrong.

Blake heard a low rumble from somewhere else in the house. It sounded like an animal, trapped in the basement, a low, howling moan. He ignored it and thought about his plans for Jessica. This time, he was planning to drive to Los Angeles. The other two times he'd been to Los Angeles, he'd flown out, leaving disappointed.

On his first trip, he'd found Jessica's mansion with ease. It had only taken a few hours of careful internet searches to pin down her home's exact location in the Hollywood Hills. She had famous neighbors, and Blake wondered if they treated her with the respect she deserved.

Arriving at her mansion, he was taken aback by how big it was. The place looked more modest on Google Maps, but now he saw it was a huge place, ringed with high bushes. There was a tall gate at the bottom of the driveway, and he considered climbing it before learning that Jessica was in London, filming "Five Minutes Until Midnight." He should have done more research on her schedule. Blake stuck around a few days, hoping she might come home for a visit, but she did not. After a week, he'd finally flown home, dejected.

And over the week in Los Angeles, he'd managed to meet a few other women, but none of them had left him satisfied. None of them were ample replacements for Jessica Mills. He'd gotten angry and the women had died. Blake had left the women's bodies in obscure places in Los Angeles. He wondered if they had ever been found.

On his second trip, he'd made sure to do his homework first. He'd verified that she was in fact in southern California and had flown out there to meet her. He'd rented a car and practiced driving the Los Angeles roads to make sure he could escape as needed. He sat outside her house, watching cars come and go.

And then he saw her.

The gate that led to her driveway opened and he'd shrunk down in his seat and THERE SHE WAS, driving the little VW bug he'd read about in some tabloid. She'd gotten it as part of her compensation from one of the movies she'd made. She was with a girlfriend and they were laughing and talking and motioning at the vehicle. She looked beautiful, happy in the California sun, and Blake knew he had to have her. No one else could have her.

No one. He would convince her to love him.

The VW had pulled away and he'd followed, staying close. The car was easy to follow—there weren't too many VWs around, and none of them were that shade of lemon yellow. Blake followed, waiting for his chance. Jessica Mills was in that car, and it was all that mattered.

The VW had parked at a small restaurant and the girls got out and went inside. Blake parked as close to her car as possible and put on his disguise, a form-fitting bald cap and a baggy tracksuit that made him look at least forty pounds heavier. He also removed the plates from the rental, putting them in his car, swapping them with the ones from the next car over.

Unfortunately, the snatch didn't go as planned. He had it all worked out in his head, but it didn't matter.

Blake had waited, watching the two women eat through the windows of the restaurant. When they were finished, Blake had gotten out and waited by her car. But she must have stopped off to go to the bathroom, or had been waylaid by autograph seekers, because several minutes passed before they came outside. It delayed the plan and heightened his nerves.

It had started clean—the two women had come around the corner and he was waiting. He'd maced the girlfriend, sending her screaming to the ground, then stepped up to Jessica, who was just starting to form a scream. Her face was so perfect, her skin looked so soft.

Blake embraced her and when she pushed him away, he spun her around and shoved the needle into her beautiful neck.

Jessica went limp, reminding him of so many other women he had known. He lifted her from the ground and carried her toward his car and the open trunk.

That was when the plan went to hell.

"Hey, what are you doing?" It was a big black guy wearing an apron. He stepped from the back of the restaurant, a cigarette dangling from his lips. "You put her down."

Blake shifted her weight and pulled the gun from his waistband, pointing it at the fat man. "Mind your own business, retard!"

The black man stopped and put his hands up. "Okay, but you can't just snatch a woman off the—"

Blake pulled the trigger. The bang was louder than he'd expected. The black man's hand jerked in the air and blood spilled out of it, the man screaming, his nerve evaporating. The man dropped to the ground and started crawling around like a little baby.

"Mind your own business!" Blake yelled at the man and rushed to the rental car, Jessica still tossed over his shoulder. More people came around the corner, drawn by the girlfriend screaming and pawing at her face. Two men rushed at Blake, grabbing at the unconscious woman on his shoulder. Blake shoved them away—his mom always said he was big and strong—but one of them managed to pull Jessica off. Blake turned and shot at the men, hitting one in the leg. Blake grabbed for Jessica, but the other man pushed her away. He punched Blake hard in the face, and Blake's gun skittered away into the street.

Blake shoved the men away and paused, unsure of what to do next. Jessica was behind the man Blake had shot in the leg, so there were now four people on the ground around him, all writhing in pain except for Jessica, unconscious. Blake wanted to grab her and pick her up and run, but the man turned and leapt at Blake, forcing him back.

Blake ran, grabbing up the gun and scampering into his car.

It was already running, and he floored it, flying out of the back of the parking lot and racing away, getting several blocks away from the commotion before slowing to a normal speed.

He thought it best to put a few miles between him and the restaurant. A few minutes later, he stopped in a poor neighborhood and switched the license plates again with a parked car, then drove another couple miles and repeated the procedure near a busy restaurant.

Blake remembered getting back to his hotel room. He'd still been shaking. The cops might have a description of his car, but he thought he was safe—he was nowhere near Hollywood. He'd decided to stay at a nondescript hotel in the Simi Valley, a county over from Hollywood. He was miles away from her house and the restaurant.

At his hotel, Blake decided the mission was over, and packed up and checked out. He drove straight to the airport, stopping at a nearby McDonald's and putting the original plates back on the rental. At the airport, he watched over his shoulder the whole time until the plane taxied away from the terminal and took flight.

This time he went to Los Angeles, he wasn't going to take any chances. He didn't want a repeat of that trip. This time, he'd arrive in Los Angeles with a car that couldn't be traced back to a rental place. And he'd stake out her home until he was sure she was alone. And he wouldn't try to snatch her off the street—this time, he'd get her coming to or from her house. That way there'd be no bystanders, no one who could jump in and help.

Blake Oleander stood back and looked at the map he'd pinned to the wall of his room. It showed his path to Los Angeles. He leaned in and giggled, tracing the path with his finger. Security was too tight at the jail in Oakland, of course, although he'd been reading rumors on Reddit that she wasn't even there. People on the Internet were saying she was at a rehab facility in Los Angeles. Blake had considered driving out and trying to grab her from there, but it was too complicated.

No, this time, he was going to make it as simple as possible. The fewer things that could get screwed up, the better.

He'd wait until she was home—and then he'd start his drive. Get to Los Angeles, grab her up, head home. Maybe by the time they got back here, she would have learned to love him. Or not. Either way, she'd be with him, and he'd be happy. She would be his, and no one else's. They could watch her movies together, over and over. She could act out scenes for him. Or she could just lay there and relax and enjoy his attention to her every need.

Either way, it would work out.

CHAPTER 48
Search History

Jessica Mills walked around the inside of the large barn, exploring. She looked over the car-in-progress and the tables of parts, and then she wandered the horse stalls, which still smelled of hay and animals even though there was no indication that either had been here for years. Each stall was stacked with boxes of car parts and bags of lawn fertilizer and chemicals. Near a large pair of barn doors, she found a big green John Deere riding mower.

Backtracking, she passed the car-in-progress and headed up the stairs. On the second floor, she found a finished room full of recreation equipment: a ping-pong table, two old pinball tables, a stationary bike, a treadmill, an old weight bench and some weights, and a large flat-screen TV. A large window looked out on the parking area and the house beyond. Next to the window was a desk with a computer and stacks of paperwork.

She bit her lip, then walked over and sat down at the desk and turned on the PC, booting up the internet and doing some quick searching on herself. She wasn't supposed to, but she couldn't help herself.

She started with her name.

Most of the news outlets reported that she was at the prison in Oakland. She nodded—that was good. A few other sites were putting out the theory that she was at a rehab center in San Pedro, someplace called "Daystrom." She'd heard of it but never been there.

Apparently, the paparazzi were staking out both places, trying to get pictures of her. One site, notorious for inventing their news wholesale, reported they had photos of her taking daily walks at the Daystrom facility. They also reported insiders were saying that Jessica was "getting better."

That made Jessica smile. It was only more proof that, if they didn't have any news, the paps and the media were happy to just invent news out of thin air. Maybe there was someone who looked like her taking walks at Daystrom. Maybe the paps were watching the rehab grounds through their long-range cameras and getting confused. Maybe the cops were feeding the paps fake information to keep them focused on the rehab center so they wouldn't look elsewhere. If word ever got out that she'd been moved to a location out of state, the whole "taking photos of people at their worst" industry would collectively lose its shit.

Jessica bit her lip, glancing out the window, but didn't see Leslie or Ferrara. Going back to the computer, she quickly got caught up on industry and casting news. A few casting announcements had come out, including a few roles she'd been up for.

Jessica needed serious roles, ones that people could see her in and start taking her seriously. Transitioning from kid star to serious actress in Hollywood was always difficult. There was just something about the public—once they knew you for your childhood roles, they just couldn't accept you as a grownup. Maybe the kid's movie industry spent too much time making everyone "cute."

Some of it might be the Hollywood culture as well—once an actor was established, it affected how the industry saw them. Most kid actors were handled by agents and publicists and managers, and many studio executives couldn't get past the idea that the "ex-child" was now speaking for themselves. Or they had new representation that was looking for more "mature" roles. It was nearly impossible to shed that little kid image.

She looked for information on her entourage. Carrie and Gina had not slowed their active social lives, although Jessica wondered who was footing the bill now that Jessica was temporarily gone. The two women were all over Instagram, posting shots of them at a gallery opening, drinking all the cocktails.

At least there weren't any photos of Jessica, sitting in the middle of a wet street in a torn $5,000 dress, looking drunk off her ass.

That was a good thing. Maybe if she went a few weeks without an incident, people would start paying attention to someone else. There was always another scandal breaking, or some story about who had slept with who to get a certain part. Maybe, when the light was off her, Jessica could finally get her act together.

This place might help. Or maybe it wouldn't, she thought as she deleted the internet history before shutting off the computer. Maybe the problem wasn't where she was, or who she was with. Maybe the problem was her, and it had been her all along.

She headed back downstairs and outside, crossing the parking lot as she lit up another cigarette. The coke was out, and the smokes were in, fellas. Stop the presses, shout it from the rooftops. Trading one vice for another, she thought as she walked across the lawn and started for the pond.

The sun was setting, and it was starting to get dark, so she hurried.

The lake was larger than it seemed, and Jessica could get no sense of how deep it was. One cigarette turned into two, and then a third, as she circled the body of water. She passed the boathouse and peeked inside—there were indeed floaty inflatable items, along with a curtained area for people to change clothes. She saw a stack of towels and a basket with swimming trunks and suits. One wall of the boathouse was taken up with shelves holding pool equipment, but two of the shelves held small wooden and remote-control boats. She ran her hands over them, curious about how they worked.

Leaving the boathouse, she continued around the lake, passing under the kiddy zip-line. It looked sturdy, a metal cable wrapped around a large tree. The line stretched across the lake and ended at a wooden platform on the other side. The sun had fallen behind the horizon and she felt a chill. It felt different, seeing the sun set behind trees. Jessica was used to seeing the sun sink into the Pacific.

Jessica passed a gravel seating area that sat on a rise above one end of the lake. It featured a pair of chairs and a sign: "Bob's Fishing Spot." Starting back up the other side of the lake, she passed the wooden zip-line platform and the padded backstop to catch people who didn't let go in time.

Lastly, she approached another seating area, this one obviously the one they used the most. There were two couches and several chairs, all covered with outdoor cushions, arrayed around a large fire pit covered with a metal screen. Off to one side, a large grill and two small tables stood under a pergola. It looked like they grilled out here a lot. She could imagine attending a cookout for thirty or forty people here. Folks grilling hot dogs and hamburgers while the kids splashed in the lake or took turns on the zip-line. Sounded pretty nice.

"You getting cold yet?"

Jessica jumped. She hadn't even noticed Leslie sitting in one of the chairs near the fire pit.

"Yeah." Jessica walked over and sat down. "How are the fences?"

"Why? You wanna run?"

Jessica shook her head. "Too cold. Besides, if I wanted to run, it would've been in Arizona. Or Denver or St. Louis." She sat back and looked around. "This place doesn't suck. I can think of worse places to spend a couple of months."

Leslie nodded, bumming a cigarette off of Jessica, who lit it before handing it over.

"Don't worry," Leslie said. "You'll do fine. Keep your head down, and you'll be back in LA in no time. Back to your entitled life."

Jessica looked at her. "You really don't like me, do you? What did I do?"

Leslie looked at the lake, puffing on her cigarette. She took it out and flicked the end of it, dropping ash into the grass. "It's not just you. It's all of you."

"All of us? There's only you and me—"

"Rich, entitled, spoiled folks. I agreed with Judge Watkins—I hate the Hollywood shuffle. It encourages bad behavior."

"Maybe," Jessica said.

"I thought they should throw the book at you. Make an example."

Jessica didn't say anything.

"No sassy response?"

"No, not really. You're right—some of the people I know are into some serious shit, and they never get caught. When they do, it's a slap on the wrist."

"It's been that way for a while," Leslie said. "An uneasy alliance. But the LAPD is going to have to rethink how it handles the rich and famous. Or at least the famous. Maybe they need their own jail, separate from the GP. I don't know."

"You think I'll make it all 90 days?"

Leslie looked up and nodded. "If you make the effort," she said, standing and stubbing out her cigarette. "It will impress Judge Watkins, and it will impress me. Believe it or not, I'm pulling for you."

"Thank you," Jessica said, meaning it.

"Yup," Leslie said. "I'm cold. See you inside."

Jessica nodded and Leslie walked off. But Jessica stayed. She finished three more cigarettes, deep in thought, before the sun was completely gone and she got too cold to stay outside any longer.

Chapter 49
Welcome

Jessica and the others spent Sunday getting settled into their new digs. Ferrara's family wouldn't be home until two or three p.m. Leslie sat at the dining room table and worked on her laptop, typing up a report on the road trip they'd just completed and going over the receipts. Ferrara had disappeared early, heading into town to meet up with some friends for lunch.

Jessica set up her room, arranging her meager possessions with a frown. She only had the items that Ferrara had brought for her, along with a few things Jessica had acquired during the trip east. The guest room had an empty dresser, but her clothes and underwear only took up a tiny bit of it. All in all, the skimpy selection of clothes looked sad. Jessica put the stack of scripts on the windowsill and arranged her few toiletries in the bathroom before settling onto her bed with her journal, getting to work.

She flipped back through all the days of the trip, jotting down more details. She added more on the Grand Canyon and the afternoon at the St. Louis Arch. Jessica smiled, thinking about the wide river and her memories of growing up in the area. When she was finished, she flipped to a blank page and started making a list of the scripts she'd brought with her, noting her thoughts on the ones she'd already read.

Part of Hank Jennings' job as her agent and business manager was to keep her stocked with stacks of crappy scripts to read. They were the same scripts everyone in LA was reading, stories that often made no sense or usually involved aliens or superheroes. Jessica kept telling him she was looking for meatier roles, something she could really dig into.

But he disagreed, reminding her she needed a payday...or three. Her finances were rocky, to be sure, but Jessica wanted more out of her acting. She wanted a British drama, or some kind of project that could raise her status as an actress and yes, even as an artist. Every other actress got a chance or two at an Oscar-worthy role—why shouldn't she?

Hours later, Ferrara returned, saying her parents were on their way. Not long after, a minivan pulled up in the driveway and all hell broke loose. Ferrara ran out of the kitchen door while Leslie and Jessica waited in the dining room. The minivan parked outside, and Jessica heard a flurry of footsteps and shouting before Ferrara's mother and sister burst into the kitchen. Both Ferrara's sister, Jillian, and their mom, Simona, were awestruck in meeting Jessica, even though she was as dressed down as she had ever been in her life and nearly unrecognizable.

"I loved 'Fun with Jane'," Jillian said, gushing over Jessica. "You can stay in my room if you want!"

"It's okay," Ferrara said. "She's already set up in one of the guest rooms. Mom, this is Leslie. Officer Davis. She's overseeing the whole situation."

Simona greeted Leslie, shaking her hand, then shook Jessica's as well. "We're so happy you've come to stay with us. Both of you," she said. "Please, let us know how we can help."

Just as things started to settle down, Ferrara's father came in, starting up a whole new round of greetings and hand shaking. The man seemed intimidated by Leslie, who waited for them to finish.

Leslie nodded. "Just remember, Jessica's not on vacation," she reminded them. Ferrara had already worked out the whole situation with her family, warning them about what would be expected if they agreed to host Jessica. "No photos, and no talking about the situation with anyone." Leslie looked at the youngest girl. "Especially no social media."

Jessica thanked them all. "I know this is going to be weird," she said, touching her neck. She didn't have a port-wine stain on today, but the area was itchy anyway. "I'm going to do everything I can to stay out of your way."

"Just remember, folks, she's not a circus freak," Ferrara added. "She's my guest, and a person. Jessica will be around here a LOT, bored out of her mind. Dad, can you give her some stuff to do around the farm? Teach her how to run the Deere? And Mom, we're gonna need that part-time job we talked about."

"Gotta keep me busy, right?" Jessica asked with a smile.

Simona nodded. "It's okay. We've got it. And we'll keep quiet."

"You can't talk to anyone, or brag about it," Leslie added. "Any of you. You can't even hint about it. Okay? The main thing to remember is that Jessica is incognito. As far as everyone else on the planet knows, she's at that minimum-security prison in California. The judge and the cops have agreed to work with us on this to maintain her cover. Any hints that that's not the case, and the press and paparazzi will be here in hours," Leslie added.

"You look very different," Jillian said.

"We've altered her appearance as much as we could," Ferrara said.

"I think you look great," Simona added. "But you don't look like yourself at all. I could pass you at the grocery and not recognize you."

"That's the plan," Ferrara said.

"Thank you," Jessica said. "And thanks for letting me stay here. I know it's a lot of trouble."

"Don't worry about a thing," she said. "We're happy to have you."

CHAPTER 50
Paparazzi at Marineland

On Sunday morning, Bill Hanford was back on the job, staking out the Daystrom treatment center in San Pedro. Maybe Steven Zachary knew what he was talking about for once, or maybe he was just trying to throw Hanford off track.

But Hanford had also seen the rumors floating around that Jessica Mills wasn't actually in the "actual" jail up in San Francisco. Maybe she was here, at this new state-of-the-art facility that overlooked the ocean and Catalina Island.

He'd researched the place, which had an interesting history—it was built on the old grounds of an abandoned theme park. The old marine park had been built in the location overlooking the ocean in 1954, and at the time was the world's largest ocean-themed amusement park and animal sanctuary. Known as "Marineland of the Pacific," the park hosted thousands of tourists every day and included tanks for dolphins, sharks, pilot whales, and killer whales, including the famous Shamu, before he was transferred to the Marineland facility in Miami.

The place was a popular, thriving theme park right up until 1987, when the company was bought out by a rival and the park abruptly closed. Word was that the animals were trucked out in the middle of the night—and to ensure that no one reused the facility for another water park, concrete was poured down the drains.

The location sat abandoned for many years, a popular destination for urban explorers and folks who got a thrill from visiting burned-out locations and abandoned factories. The Marineland Ruins, as they became known, were one of the most popular stops on any Los Angeles urban explorer tour. The property was used to shoot films, as well, especially those who needed an ocean background. In fact, the first three "Pirates of the Caribbean" movies were, in part, shot on the former Marineland grounds.

In 2006, the property was bought and what remained of Marineland was torn down to make way for a huge, upscale resort and golf club spreading along the hills and cliffs to the east back towards San Pedro proper. The resort, which included cabanas, restaurants and even private bungalows, offered beautiful views of both Santa Catalina to the south and the famous Point Vicente Lighthouse to the west.

But the old parking lot served another purpose—it was bulldozed and turned into a state-of-the-art rehab and treatment center, one of the most advanced in the country.

Bill Hanford sat in his car, bored. He couldn't care less about the history of this place. All he knew was that the buildings all looked like they had been built too close to the edge. One good quake, or even a decent landslide, and the whole thing would go over into the water far below.

He sat in his car on the other end of the parking lot, the safe end, far away from the facility and closest to the road that lead east to San Pedro and west, around the point, to the old lighthouse at San Vicente.

His phone buzzed. It was a text from Anita, his office manager.

"Anything?"

He shook his head and texted back.

"Nothing here. She's NOT here I guarantee."

He waited, but nothing came back. He was talking out of his ass, of course—there was no way to really know where Jessica Mills was holed up. Sending her to actual jail seemed like overkill, so it made sense the LAPD was playing them. This facility was a perfect place to stash her—the place had high walls and no access from three directions. All he could see from this parking lot, or from any of the nearby bluffs, was the same view: walls.

If Jessica Mills was in there, no one was getting any pictures.

Hanford only had one move at this point—make friends with someone who worked inside. He nodded, putting away his camera, and sat up, putting the car in gear. There weren't a lot of places around here to drink. The resort had several upscale restaurants, but he guessed that anyone working here would seek out a local dive bar. Hanford remembered passing a dingy bar on the way out from Pedro. The Salty Wench, or something like that. It was nearing 5 p.m., and he could see some of the staff leaving the clinic and heading to their cars. A few stopped to make small talk and, he hoped, plans to go out for a drink.

Taking a gamble, he put the car in drive and slowly left the parking lot. When Hanford got to the road he turned east, looking for the bar.

Chapter 51
Frank and Taylor

Frank thought maybe he might be getting the hang of this.

He was waiting for Taylor Robinson to leave his place of work. Frank was ready to snap more photos. It being Sunday evening, Robinson shouldn't have been at work at all, but here he was. Frank sat up and stretched in the car, checking to make sure the keys were in the ignition. When you were involved with domestic situations like this one, things could move pretty fast, and with little warning. You had to be ready to go.

Sometimes stakeouts could be tedious, but lately, he'd been enjoying them. It was good money, usually, and rarely ended up in any kind of altercation. Robinson's wife was still paying him, of course, to gather more photos on her wayward husband.

One of the things on his "Work To Do" list was to buy a real camera. He'd done two jobs so far where he'd been called upon to get photographic evidence. All he'd had to take photos with was his iPhone. It had been okay, and gotten the job done, but a nice camera with a telephoto lens would let him stay further back, out of harm's way, and get the photos he needed.

People cheated. That was just the honest truth. And because some people cheated, and some other people didn't like it when those people cheated, there would always be a call for the services that Frank could provide, services that included "sneaking around with a camera" and "parking in dark alleys for hours at a time." Oh, and don't forget the always-popular "spying on your spouse for you even though, in a healthy relationship, you would just talk to them."

Of course, unhealthy relationships made the world go round.

Frank was parked outside of an office building, several rows back from the entrance. He didn't want to park too close, just in case the building had cameras or recording devices. Most buildings didn't, but if they did, the cameras were always trained on two places: the lobby and the main entrance. As long as you stayed back a dozen yards or so, you were usually fine.

Cars came and went. A few people went in and out of the front doors. The company Robinson worked for, Power Suites, took up the entire four-story building, at least according to the records Frank had pulled from the county tax department.

This case was unusual, and Frank was getting an odd vibe from the wife, Mrs. Robinson. She kept paying Frank to follow her husband, even though he'd already provided her with the photos she'd said she'd wanted at the beginning. Maybe women who thought their husbands were cheating on them couldn't get enough information. Mrs. Robinson wanted everything documented: what time her husband went out, where he went, how long was he there, who was the woman he kept visiting, etc. Maybe Mrs. Robinson was a glutton for punishment. Or maybe she was having Frank gather more information than necessary to delay the inevitable confrontation she needed to have with her husband.

Either way, Frank would be there to take the photos—and to get paid.

Chapter 52
The Salty Wench

The Salty Wench turned out to be a bust. Bill Hanford hung out in the dirty bar for a while, but none of the people who wandered in looked like they worked at Daystrom. If they did, he didn't see them. He set up at a table with a nice view of the door and the bar, staying an hour and sipping at his mediocre beer and checking his phone.

He and Anita texted back and forth, killing time. She said that, so far, none of the other paps had found Jessica Mills, so at least there was that. If no one was getting pictures, then all the paps were even.

No one was getting pictures up in San Fran either. Hanford wondered how the corrections officers were keeping Jessica safe in jail. Had there been any incidents? Was the LAPD happy with their decision to house her in a minimum-security women's facility instead of doing the usual Hollywood Shuffle and letting her spend her time in a posh rehab facility?

After an hour, Hanford gave up and packed it in. But he filed the Salty Wench away in his mental list of quiet places to meet potential clients and sources. He had a selection of bars like this one in his head, all over the southern California region. Perfect places to meet up and not be recognized by anyone.

He left the bar and looked out to the south. It was an unusually-clear day, and Santa Catalina stretched across the southern horizon. "Twenty-six miles across the sea." The old song leapt into his brain. The island lurked in the ocean like a distant creature, sulking in the water.

Chapter 53
A Month in Cooper's Mill

The next month passed slowly, at least for Jessica.

The weather was great for the last half of August and the first part of September—warm, mostly dry, with a few heavy rains thrown in for good measure. One storm featured lightning and thunder, a phenomenon rarely experienced in Los Angeles. She sat on the covered front porch, between the columns, and watched the storm march across the landscape, punctuated with bolts of lightning that arced to the ground. It was scary and thrilling.

Ferrara's family left Jessica, for the most part, to her hobbies and her thoughts. Judge Watkins had evidently mandated that Jessica be bored most of the time. The woman was probably taking some kind of gleeful joy from Leslie's regular reports, which recounted just how frustrated Jessica was with the situation.

Leslie and Ferrara were often out, buying supplies or driving around Dayton together to scout locations for Leslie's cover. Ferrara spent a lot of time with her local friends, attending lunches or catching up with people she'd been close to before she moved to LA.

But Ohio turned out to be pretty chill, Jessica thought.

She ate and relaxed and worked out as best she could and read her scripts. No spin classes or going to the gym for her, so she spent a lot of time walking the farm, stretching and lifting whatever she could find. She helped around the farm, mowed, helped dredge the pond.

She also began tracking her step count, jotting it down in her journal, and tracked her weight. She also wrote down ideas for movies, and plans for her future, and little stories that people told her.

Ferrara's family made Jessica feel welcome. They accepted Jessica into their home and rolled with the restrictions Leslie put on them, including calling Jessica "Sydney," even when they were alone. The family studied "Sydney's" biography and back story until they had it memorized, Leslie drilling them on it often.

For the first month, she rarely left the "compound," as she began to call the family farm. No Starbucks, no restaurants, nothing fun. Lots of meals around the dining room table with Ferrara's family, and lots of television. LOTS of television.

Every so often, and only when everyone was out of the house, Jessica would sneak off and use the computer in the barn to surf the internet. So far, no one had figured out that Jessica was, in fact, not even in California.

And, even though she wasn't interacting with the public, Jessica and Ferrara spent an inordinate amount of time on Jessica's appearance. Ahead of Jessica getting a job, Ferrara did more applications of Jessica's new makeup in the small upstairs bathroom they shared with Leslie, working to perfect the fake port-wine stain. She made newer versions that last longer than the ones from the road trip, which had faded quickly and needed touching up several times a day.

On the road, the edges of the fake birthmark were always getting smudged. Ferrara worked to make it darker and more permanent. She used a combination of dark makeup mixed with beet juice, something she'd learned on the Internet. Movie people used it for fake burns.

"Once you start your job, it's going to have to last longer," Ferrara said.

"Why not just use regular makeup?"

"That's what we did during the trip. Too easy to rub off, or sweat off," Ferrara said. She finished the mixture and applied it to Jessica's cheek, creating a noticeable and natural-looking reddish birthmark from her eye to her ear. Jessica followed along in the mirror. It was weird, seeing someone alter your appearance again and again.

Next, Ferrara gave her the world's worst manicure—she cut and trimmed the nails to give them a misshapen look, then painted them with a horrible teal color. "It looks like you did them yourself—and that you have no idea how to do nails."

Jessica held them up. "God, these are worse than the ones from the trip."

Ferrara went back to the makeup and added a couple of small fake zits to Jessica's forehead. Working on a new version of her makeup, or trying out new wigs, was at least less boring than sitting in the house all alone, watching endless hours of TV.

All the changes to her appearance, Jessica could handle. She was used to it, used to people painting her up—it happened on every movie set. She'd made her money on her looks and on her ability to act, and now it was necessary for her to act like she had no looks at all. The whole thing was just bizarre. Her "new normal," as Leslie liked to say.

But the other restrictions were a challenge. And of course, there was no clubbing, no drinking, no fun of any sort. Jessica was used to going out nearly every night, used to doing what she wanted. The road trip had been different enough for her to let it go, but now that she was settled down and sleeping in the same bed every night, she was itching to get out. But Leslie and Ferrara were adamant—no leaving the premises. After a few days, Jessica had started calling it "the compound" and it had stuck.

And getting off the coke was the worst part of it.

Jessica wasn't a "hardcore" user, really, just getting bumps here and there. She'd gone stretches without it, certainly, but not weeks at a time, not like this. Going cold turkey proved very difficult. She often went to bed early rather than sit up late and night, scratching at her arms.

Things started to improve in mid-September. Leslie stayed out of Jessica's way, and the Cortez family was out most of the time. Jessica learned to drive the big Deere lawn mower and spent countless hours mowing the large lawn that stretched from the front of the house all the way down to the road.

She also pitched in with a hobby enjoyed by Ferrara's father and sister Jillian: raising Monarch butterflies. They tended a line of small cages behind the barn, raising the butterflies from the eggs, which were so small they could hardly be seen with the naked eye. After a couple of weeks of eating voraciously, the caterpillars grew to be nearly two inches long, and Jillian loved to hold them, watching them walk over her hands. Soon after reaching full size, the caterpillars started spinning an adhesive filament and sealed themselves in an enclosure, a green chrysalis with a distinct gold line around the upper section.

Roughly nine days later, the chrysalis became transparent and, usually the following day, the caterpillar emerged as a somewhat shriveled butterfly. Once free of the chrysalis, the butterfly would grow, the wings drying out, before taking flight.

Jessica helped out with three generations of the butterflies, enjoying the process and marveling at the beautiful creatures that eventually emerged.

Ferrara was enjoying an extended vacation with her family, re-connecting with her parents and her sister. And Jessica got to know "the compound" very well. After a few weeks of walking the grounds, Jessica knew the place by heart. In the morning there was fog, often, before the rising sun burned it off. In mid-September, the farmers started mowing the surrounding fields on big Deere tractors, harvesting the tall corn or soybean crops from the stretches of dirt that surrounded the Cortez home.

At night, when she walked, it was impossibly clear. And quiet, so much quieter than in Los Angeles. And dark. She could see every star in the sky, like someone had turned up the brightness.

One night, about a month after she arrived, Ferrara joined Jessica for her regular night-time walk. The Cortez family knew she walked every night after dinner, and they usually left her to it. But tonight, Ferrara had some questions.

"Hey, thanks for letting me walk with you," Ferrara said as they pulled on jackets from the closet in the mudroom.

"It's your house, girl."

"I know," Ferrara said. "But we've been giving you your privacy."

"I miss Instagram," Jessica said, stepping outside. The sun was almost all the way down and it was cooling off. She'd taken two other walks today and was getting pretty good at predicting the temperature. Jessica set off toward the lake and Ferrara followed.

"I know you've been using the computer in the barn," Ferrara said quietly. "Don't you look at all the feeds?"

"I have to stay informed."

"Reading's fine, as long as you never post. I won't tell Leslie."

"Thanks," Jessica said. "I miss sharing my life. I'm down on the farm again, this time for real."

"We'll have to get you some pigs, like in the movie."

Jessica smiled as they passed the zip-line and sat in the two chairs at "Bob's Fishing Spot." It had become her new favorite spot to sit, as evidenced by the cigarette butts on the ground.

"The sunsets here are nice," she said, nodding at the horizon. The sun was gone, of course, but the western sky was awash with pinks and yellows and deep reds.

"How is your…recovery?"

Jessica looked at her and nodded. "Good, good. Better, though I'm back on the cigarettes full time now."

"It's fine," Ferrara said. "They're an improvement, in my thinking. Oh, my father said to thank you with the lawn." Jessica had been conscripted on several occasions by Ferrara's father to help around the farm, including doing the mowing. He'd also had her help clean out the barn, making her lift everything because his back was acting up.

Jessica made a fist and showed Ferrara her bicep. "No problem. He's my personal trainer, especially since there are no spin classes around here," she said with a smile.

"Oh, there are," Ferrara said. "You just can't attend."

Jessica looked out at the dark lawn. "Well, at least I'm getting good at doing those zigzag lawn patterns."

They sat awhile in silence, and then Ferrara spoke up again.

"Well, I'm glad things are going well. So, my mom wanted me to ask about work. Are you ready?"

Jessica nodded eagerly. "Yeah. I think so. It's been a nice break, but I think I'm burned out on TV. And I've read all of those scripts at least three times, along with every book in your house."

"It would be good to get started, as it's a condition of your house arrest," Ferrara said. "Leslie's been asking. She's worried about you being out in public."

Jessica pointed at the ankle monitor. "She thinks I'll make a run for it?"

"No, of course not. She's worried you'll be found out."

"Well, I'm not going to spill the beans." She pulled the wig down over her eyes. "There. Now no one will know it's me."

Ferrara smiled. "Mom has it all set up. If you're good with it, you can go in tomorrow."

"Good," Jessica said. "Maybe I'll finally get a look at the rest of this little town."

"Oh, that's right," Ferrara said. "We promised you a tour of Cooper's Mill. The downtown, the parks, all of it."

"I'm starting to think there is no town and you're just making it up."

"No, it's there," Ferrara said. "We'll drive you in tomorrow, maybe get some lunch."

"That would be nice."

"You know, I worked at that grocery for two summers," Ferrara said. "Those biceps will come in handy, I'm telling you."

"Um, can I ask you something? Who's running my social media now? I didn't see a lot of posts."

"Scott, of course," Ferrara said, shaking her head. "Hank has him posting stuff about the movie, of course, and updates about your shows, but nothing about you. Judge Watkins told him to pipe down."

"I need you to take more pictures," Jessica said. "Me here, on the farm. Sunsets. I need a camera. I want to post stuff when this is all over."

Ferrara bit her lip. "Maybe. You'll have to ask Leslie."

"I know. So, any changes to my look for the new job?"

"I might cut the wig shorter, give you some bangs."

"Bangs? Nobody wears bangs."

"I know."

"You're obsessed with making me ugly, aren't you?"

"It's fun," Ferrara said with a giggle. "Don't you think? Not everyone gets a chance to completely change their appearance, or wander around the world hearing people talk about them."

"It's like I'm invisible."

Ferrara nodded. "Yeah, you could look at it like that. Or you could pretend it's a secret power. You're a ghost, gliding through the world. Like when you dress down and go to movie premieres and sit in the back to hear what people really think."

"That's true," Jessica said. "You do get a different reaction than at the premieres where everyone is—"

"—kissing your behind," Ferrara said with a laugh. "When this is all over, you might want to rethink your 'posse' in LA. Some of those people aren't good for you."

Ferrara was right. Leslie was always talking about Jessica's 'enablers.' It was in their best interests to keep Jessica right where she was. Any self-improvement on her part was a threat to their lifestyle.

"You need to run your life like a business," Ferrara said. "Those folks are sucking money out. Think of them as an experiment you tried. It failed, and they need to go. Or they're taking you down."

Chapter 54
Downtown

On Tuesday, September 4th, Jessica left the Cortez farm for the first time in nearly a month.

That wasn't exactly true: Jessica had convinced Leslie to let her out a few times, always at night and always as part of a grocery run or something very low key. Jessica had stayed in the car, of course, so this trip out on Monday would be her first interaction with any people in weeks.

Simona drove the minivan through Cooper's Mill, and Jessica drank it all in.

It was a cute little town, that much was certain. The downtown was a stretch of four blocks or so with little shops and restaurants on either side. Simona explained that this was the entire downtown—a block in each direction filled with old Victorian homes or standard American Four Squares, whatever those were. Jessica didn't ask. But they parked and Jessica followed Ferrara and her mom as they did some light shopping, stopping into a pair of clothing shops, an ice cream store, a toy store, and an antique store.

They all held their breath, but no one recognized Jessica.

Of course, if she'd been dressed as herself, the folks here in Cooper's Mill—or anywhere else on the planet— would have spotted her in a second. They weren't idiots or rubes. But it was the drastic changes to her hair and makeup, the fake accent, the non-prescription glasses that covered half her face. Clothes that she wouldn't have been caught dead in, with the added benefit of making her look like she'd packed on a few extra pounds.

Leaving one shop, she was stunned to see a flatbed truck rumbling through the downtown, loaded to the brim with tomatoes. As the truck turned onto a side street, a few tomatoes rolled off and into the gutter.

Ferrara saw her looking. "They can tomatoes in town. There's a cannery over on first street. About this time every year, you'll see the trucks." She leaned in close. "It's going well, I think. Not a hint of recognition from anyone, right?"

Jessica nodded. It was strange, not being noticed. It was the plan, of course, but there was also a pang of sadness. Was her fame really that easy to disguise? Or eliminate?

"Okay, this way, girls," Simona said, waving them over. "Sydney, Ferrara, this place has lots of everything."

It was an antique store and, as far as Jessica could tell, it did NOT have "lots of everything." It did have lots of junk, piles of stuff that belonged by the curb with the garbage.

Jessica picked up a stack of old pictures and flipped through them. Faces of people smiling, faded vacations by some stretch of water. Three people grinning in front of an old car that looked shiny and new. A kid dangling from the low branches of a tree. A wedding, with pictures taken by one of the guests, the bride and groom saying their vows on a dock overlooking a small lake. The preacher had his back to the calm water.

Who were these people? Where had they gone? Were they all dead?

"What did you find?" Ferrara walked up, glancing at the pictures. "Something interesting?"

"No, not really," Jessica said, passing over the stack of pictures. "It's kind of sad. Who buys all this stuff?" She looked around the place.

"I don't know," Ferrara said, glancing at the photos and handing them back. "Mom loves these places. Me, not so much."

"Me neither," Jessica said, dropping the pictures where she'd found them. "Feels like a museum."

"Sometimes I find interesting wigs in places like this. Old furs from the 1950s too, sometimes."

Finally, Simona was done browsing and they left. Jessica followed them out, wandering behind them. Not too long ago, she'd been at a Hollywood premiere for her newest film. "Bacon Tastes Good" wasn't a cinematic masterpiece by any measure, but it had been fun. She'd played a rich city girl going to live on a pig farm as part of going into hiding after witnessing a murder. The whole "fish out of water" thing had been played for laughs, of course, and she'd never liked the tone of the movie—one minute there's a murder, the next, she's falling down in a muddy pigsty.

But now, Jessica was living that movie for real.

She followed the other two down the street and they all had lunch in a small restaurant. The entire meal, Jessica tried to keep her eyes on the table, desperate to not be recognized.

When the meal was over, they made their way back to their vehicle. Jessica climbed in, sullen. The little town had no clubs, no Starbucks. The closest one was two exits away on the highway. They did have two little coffee shops in the downtown, but Jessica wasn't holding out hope the coffee would be any good. Jessica felt like she was trapped on a remote island, with nothing else to do but go mad.

The van pulled away and they drove back through the downtown again, heading west toward the grocery store. She was starting to recognize her directions, now, and knew they were heading home.

Well, not "home," of course.

CHAPTER 55
Food Town

Jessica shouldn't have been excited about getting a job in a grocery store, but she found that she was nearly shaking. Maybe it was the month of boredom. She found herself leaning forward as they drove to the grocery.

"Remember, it's not a glamorous job," Simona said as she drove. "It's stocking shelves. Stock clerk, it's called. But you should have little or no interaction with the public."

"That's good. Okay, let's review," Ferrara said. "Where are you from?"

"Houston," Jessica said in her best Texas twang.

"And the thing on your neck?"

Jessica reached up and then put her hand down. "Birthmark. It's called a port-wine stain."

"Is it contagious?"

"No."

"Why are you in town?"

"Staying with you, learning makeup, I'm interning with you in LA, looking for a job in the biz," Jessica said, repeating it yet again. She had it down, no problem.

"At Food Town you'll be making new friends," Ferrara said. "People who will see you day after day. To convince those people, you have to stick to the back story. Got it?"

"Yeah, I got it."

Simona directed the car off Main, turning at the Burger King. The minivan pulled into a strip mall that they had passed earlier. Jessica saw a Subway, a Family Dollar and a large grocery store: Food Town.

They crossed a parking lot pitted with a hundred potholes. The car shook and bumped, and Jessica put her hand on the ceiling to brace herself.

"Someone should fix these potholes," Ferrara said. "It's been bad like this for years."

Jessica leaned forward. "Why don't they fix it?"

"Money, I guess. It's always money. For normal people, money doesn't just fall off the trees."

"Watch it," Jessica said. "I work for every penny I make."

They parked in front of the grocery store, which looked run down and old. "This place? Really?"

"This place is great," Simona said. "They just don't have a lot of money to keep it fixed up. But you'll like it, I promise." She put the van in park. "Okay, here we go."

"Couldn't I work in one of those places downtown?" She meant back in the historic shopping district. "At least those places were cute."

"Come on," Simona said, walking inside. Ferrara and Jessica hurried after her.

The inside of the grocery was even less impressive than the outside, if that was possible. Food Town was located in a strip mall near the I-75 interchange with Main Street and the only grocery in Cooper's Mill. The place was always busy, with people pushing carts out to their cars from opening until late in the evening. Even in the blistering heat of summer or when the parking lot was covered with five inches of snow, there were customers at Food Town.

Inside, the store looked like any other small-town grocery in the United States. It had the low ceilings and simple design of a grocery built in the 1970s. The economy and a dozen other reasons had kept the owners from updating the store to match the tall ceilings and bright lighting of the big-box grocery stores like Kroger or Wegmans.

"Remember, don't let anyone take your picture," Ferrara reminded Jessica. "Even by accident." Leslie had beaten that concept into Jessica—even showing up in the background of someone else's selfie might be enough to let the secret slip out.

Ferrara's mom led them to the office, where a large man was standing, counting money.

"Hey, Wally," Simona said.

The man turned and glanced at them. "Oh, hey. This the new girl?"

Ferrara's mom nodded. "Yeah, I'll get her started this week. Just wanted you to meet her." Jessica knew they were taking a chance—Ferrara's mom had said something about using a fake social security number on the application, something that could get her in trouble down the line.

Jessica walked over and shook his hand. The guy started to look at her face and body, but his eyes were drawn to the splotch of red on her neck. Score one more point for her "birthmark." After a second, he shook her hand again and let go.

"Stocker?"

"Yeah, if that works. She wants to earn some extra money while she's in town."

"Sounds great."

They turned and left, and Simona walked them through the store, pointing out all the most exciting parts, Jessica thought sarcastically. OHH they make their own CHICKEN SALAD? Stop the presses, alert the media. Will the world ever be the same? Oh, and they cut up their own meat in the butcher shop in the back. OH MY GOD.

It looked like any other grocery store to Jessica. Not that she had seen the inside of many—Carrie and Gina did most of the shopping. They also always managed to buy themselves a bunch of stuff in the process. More people spending her money on themselves. She hadn't been in a grocery store in years, but it looked the way she remembered.

The store was laid out like other groceries, Simona explained. Produce, meats, deli counter, and dairy all laid out around the large aisle that ran the perimeter of the store. It was called the "racetrack" in the grocery industry. The most perishable stuff went around the perimeter, where the departments could be serviced and maintained by back rooms full of more product, all kept at the correct temperature. Boxed goods, processed foods, and packaged bakery items took up the middle of the "racetrack," along with frozen goods, canned goods, packaged drinks and household products.

"Here's something I've always wondered," Jessica said. "Why is the milk in the back? Is it so people have to walk more?"

Simona shook her head, explaining that it was common for people to think that the meat and bread and milk were as far away from the front doors as possible to encourage shoppers to walk through most of the store to get to the items they really needed. And while this was helpful—it never hurt to run the hungry customers through the cookie aisle—the real reason was that the dairy department, like the others, required vast walk-in refrigeration units to keep all the products at the right temperature.

"You'll be back there," Ferrara's mom pointed at the doors between the produce and deli departments. "Unloading shipments, organizing stuff in the back, rotating product, etc. Don't worry, it's easy work, though there is a lot of lifting."

"It's like a workout," Ferrara said, trying to make it sound fun.

"Most of what we do here is stocking," Simona said. "Most groceries don't employ that many people out front. The bulk of them stock and maintain the shelves, unloading trucks of goods into the back rooms."

They wrapped up the tour at the checkout lanes. As with most stores, customers went in a circle, coming in the front doors and exiting the same way.

"The big trucks come on Tuesday and Friday mornings, but we need people every day," Simona said. "Does that sound okay?"

Jessica nodded. At this point, she'd agree to anything. Even if Simona was trying to hire her to be a lion tamer, she would've considered it. At least she'd be out in the real world.

Chapter 56
Antsy

On Wednesday evening, Blake sat in the mansion's living room, watching television.

He preferred watching TV down here, on the big screen, instead of up in his office on the second floor or in his bedroom. Sure, he had three screens in the office and could watch several shows at the same time, but Jessica looked better on a big screen.

It was Monday night and he was relaxing on the couch, nude, enjoying a plate of pizza rolls and what was probably his two-hundredth viewing of "Bacon Tastes Good," Jessica Mills' adventures on a farm. It was his favorite film of hers, and he said the words along with the movie, knowing them by heart.

Blake watched in rapt attention, waiting for his favorite scene, which was fast approaching. In the film, Jessica played a young woman who witnesses a murder and has to hide out on a farm to protect her identity. It was a dumb plot, to be sure, but it gave her a chance to do some great acting, in Blake's opinion. He didn't understand why Jessica Mills had never been nominated for any acting awards.

The best part of the film was her arrival at the farm, carrying way too many bags, and she realizes the farm is tiny and they don't have room for all of her stuff, which she has to put in this big barn. Anyway, it's a pig farm, and the pigs get into her suitcases and drag out her fancy clothes. Soon, Jessica is chasing the pigs around the farm, trying to retrieve her clothes and falling in the mud. A pig runs around carrying one of her bras. At one point, she falls head-first into a puddle of mud. She looks up at the screen, wiping the mud from her face, and says her signature line from the movie: "Well, at least it's not pig poop!"

He laughed along with the scene, smiling and repeating it over and over. He stood up, the blanket dropping away, and danced around the living room, repeating the line again and again.

Blake paused the movie and grabbed his empty plate and walked back into the kitchen to make more pizza rolls. He heard the animal sounds again, coming from the basement, but ignored them. He loved walking around the big mansion naked. He had the whole place to himself, unless a guest was visiting. And although his entire family was in the next room, they didn't bother him. Blake made another plate of pizza rolls and popped them into the microwave.

Waiting for them to cook, Blake looked out the kitchen windows and noticed the expansive greenhouse and the broken window. He hated that window. Hated how it made him feel, of course, but worse than that, Blake hated the window because of what it had caused. The fight with his father, the glass pane, his sliced cheek. After that, his mother had never looked at him the same. She was always harping about how he looked, how he'd never have a girlfriend or a wife with a face like his...

He pushed the memories from his mind, thinking about Jessica Mills instead. He hoped she was getting better, whether she was in jail or a rehab facility. Blake couldn't wait to see her again. She would be better, happier.

Maybe Blake could help her, once they were together. He was smart—he could help her pick out her roles and visit the set with her. Blake could help her pick out her outfits and go with her to the premieres and be that doting boyfriend on her arm. She would smile for the cameras and then turn and smile at him—completely in love with him, of course—and then extend her hand, calling to him.

"Come here, Blake. I want you. I need you."

The microwave beeped, bringing him out of his reverie. He got the pizza rolls out and carried them back into the living room, repeating the beautiful words she would say to him at some future movie premiere.

When he sat back down and restarted the movie, Blake knew they would be happy together. Happy forever.

Chapter 57
Background Checks

Frank Harper was busy going through stacks and stacks of personnel files. A week before, he'd been hired by Anderson Tool & Die for a delicate case that required some skills that Frank was comfortable with—and a few he was not.

Anderson Tool & Die was missing money.

The owner, a middle-aged woman named Jill Anderson, had contacted Frank and asked to meet him. The voice mail message had been cryptic, but that had been just the start. Jill had insisted on meeting Frank in a location up in Piqua, a town twenty miles north of Cooper's Mill. He didn't know the town, so she'd suggested the food court of the small local mall.

Arriving, Frank had made the immediate determination that the mall had seen better days and needed either a serious infusion of cash—or a wrecking ball.

Jill had shown up, at least, and that was a good start. She was clearly very nervous as she walked him through the situation with her business, one she'd inherited from her father at his passing three years before.

Someone was stealing from the company. Jill was convinced it had been happening for years, as the business had never been a money-maker despite the fact that it was incredibly busy all the time. The police had investigated the situation for her, as well, finding nothing suspicious. She said she'd always wondered why the place hadn't been more profitable, she explained as they sat in the Piqua Mall food court, Frank sipping on a milkshake from Dairy Queen and Jill nibbling on a bag of chocolate chip cookies.

"They're my weakness," she'd said.

Jill walked him through the finances, providing him with a printed copy of their books for the last ten years. At least she was thorough, he thought. He'd followed as much as he could, but he didn't have a head for numbers and took her word for it when she explained the amount of money missing: at least a half-million, spread over ten years. He decided to get Laura involved—he needed someone to go through the books for him and tease out any discrepancies.

"Wow," he'd said, sitting back.

"I know," Jill agreed, eating another cookie. "Father said it bothered him, of course. He suspected someone in the company was stealing." She looked at the table. "I'm convinced he died still thinking it."

"Do you mind if I ask..."

"Oh, sure," Jill said. "Car accident. His eyesight was going. I don't know why he was still driving. But he loved his cars—it was part of the reason he got into the tool & die business in the first place, to make car parts and machinery. He loved his cars—growing up, he'd cover the seats with plastic. Us kids weren't allowed to bring food into his cars. Never."

"Sounds like a riot," Frank said.

"He was fun. He really was," she said, her eyes shiny. "I miss him. But he ran a good company, good people. Hard workers. I hate to think one of them is stealing, but there's no other explanation. Can you help?"

Frank agreed to look into it. Jill wanted new background checks run on every employee, with special attention paid to anyone who'd been there for the ten years.

And she wanted the old-timey employees followed.

Frank had explained that he was a small operation and that it would take some time to go through the background checks and follow all nine of the employees that had been there at least ten years, but Jill hadn't blinked. She'd offered him $5,000 up front to get started, banking a hundred hours. Frank had nodded, taking the job.

Now, three weeks later, he was starting to regret it.

Doing background checks wasn't difficult. Once he'd gotten his PI license from the State of Ohio, he'd contacted a company that did background checks and gotten the ball rolling. Jill had provided Frank with personnel files on her people, including Social Security Numbers. The background checks were in progress now, starting with the employees who had been there the longest. While that was happening, Frank had started following the first person on the list, a woman accountant who'd been with Anderson for twelve years.

But Frank was only one person and spread thin as it was. He needed to chat with Laura on the financials, to be sure, but he also needed other help.

The door of the coffee shop jingled as someone walked in, and

Frank looked up. He was at the Perks Coffeehouse on Main Street, the same place where he'd met with Deputy Peters for the first time. The young deputy had brought Frank a pile of folders to look through after Frank had offered to help out on a child kidnapping case.

But tonight, Frank was meeting someone else.

He stood and waved at Monty Robinson, who had entered the coffee shop and was looking around at the decorated interior. This place always went crazy with the decorations. Monty saw Frank and smiled, walking over.

"I'm surprised this place is open in the evening," Monty said, shaking Frank's hand. "They do other stuff besides coffee?"

Frank nodded, sitting and offering Monty the other chair at the table, which was stacked with folders once again. "Yeah, sandwiches, pastries, stuff like that." Frank looked around. "And decaf coffee. I guess there aren't a lot of places to socialize in the downtown."

Monty looked around. "That's about right, unless you want to be drinking. So, how can I help ya?"

"Well, I need a hand with a job. You free?"

Monty smiled. "I was hoping you'd say that."

Chapter 58
She Works

Late on Wednesday evening, "Sydney Green" officially started her job at Food Town.

Simona drove her to work, grilling her the whole way. They reviewed "Sydney's" back story yet again, to the point where Jessica could probably repeat it all in her sleep.

"Are you going to get in trouble?" Jessica asked. "The fake social security number?"

Simona shook her head. "I doubt it. I'll get the police involved as soon as you go back to Los Angeles, explain the situation. They're pretty good. I'm sure between them and Judge Watkins, we'll get it worked out."

"Judge Watkins?"

"Yeah, she sent along a letter with Leslie. I'll give it to the cops. Explains why you're here in town, etc. Should hopefully fix any 'issues' they might have with my slight violation of employment law."

Jessica looked around at the parking lot when they arrived—it was dark and nearly empty. Only the McDonald's across the street seemed busy this late at night.

"I'll drop you off here in the front, but we normally park around back," Simona said. "Find Wally when you get inside, and don't forget to clock in. And good luck."

Jessica nodded and climbed out of the car, heading inside.

It was weird, how nervous she was. This was nothing like showing up to an audition or going on set and acting in front of hundreds of strangers—and yet, her heart was pounding. Was she worried about the disguise? Or her ability to "act" like a normal person? What if she'd forgotten how to be normal?

Inside, she found Wally with no problem. He was cashing out, he called it, counting all the money they'd taken in for the day, it looked like. He glanced up at her and looked at her face and then at her neck and went back to his counting.

"Ah, there you are," he said. He looked out the doors. "Where's Simona?"

"Dropped me off and left. She'll pick me up at 6 a.m."

"Okay, that sounds good," he said. "You know, there are a couple of employees that live out on Peters Road. None in tonight, but they'll be on the schedule. They might be able to give you a ride."

Jessica nodded. "I'll mention it to Simona."

"Good," he said. "Okay, the day crew will be leaving soon, and we'll lock up the front. It'll just be you and Cheryl and Roger."

Jessica nodded, not saying anything.

"You don't talk much, do you?"

"No, not much," she said, remembering her Texas twang.

"Okay, let me show you how to clock in." He found a blank timecard and wrote her name on it, then showed her how to use the clock to punch in and out. "It's important that you don't forget."

She nodded.

"Okay, come with me." Wally walked away and she followed. "Cheryl's in charge of the night crew," Wally said, leading her through a set of doors into the back of the grocery. Jessica followed him inside, entering an expansive room that was stacked to the rafters with boxes, shipping crates and packaging materials. "She'll get you up to speed."

They passed more boxes and emerged at a loading dock, where a semi was backed up to the open doors. Three other people were unloading the truck—well, two guys were unloading the truck and a very large woman was standing nearby with a clipboard, checking things off. They walked over.

"Cheryl, this is Sydney Green. Simona's friend. She's starting tonight," Wally said, pointing at Jessica.

Cheryl shook her hand and Jessica couldn't avoid looking at the waves of fat jiggling from her outstretched arm. "Nice to meet you."

"Hi," Jessica said. "I don't have a lot of work experience. Hope that's not a problem."

Cheryl shook her head. "Nah. We'll be fine. Let's just get you up to speed, okay?" Cheryl said. "Thanks, Wally."

The man nodded and left.

"Okay, you're gonna be unloading and processing incoming merchandise," Cheryl said, sounding bored. "I'll tell you where to take it. After the truck leaves, we'll be rotating in the new stock and purging anything expired. Does that work?"

Jessica nodded, not saying a word. She wasn't sure how convincing her accent was.

"Okay, start grabbing boxes off the truck. Follow Roger's lead. Call out what you're unloading, and I'll mark it off the sheet," she said, waving the clipboard. "Once we're done, I'll get you working on stocking."

The next four hours went smoothly. Roger, the only other Food Town employee present, greeted Jessica without saying a word. Soon, they were working in tandem, unloading the back of the large truck.

The driver of the truck, whose name Jessica did not catch, was also unloading but stopped frequently to check in with Cheryl over quantities and product names. They squabbled in a good-natured way, as she accused him of short-changing the grocery or he chastised her for ordering too much of the wrong things.

Jessica and Roger piled box after box around the backroom or stacked items on the shelving units the covered every wall. Some of the boxes went right out onto the grocery floor, arranged in the middle of the aisles. Roger stacked some of the heavier boxes onto a dolly and wheeled them away.

Jessica's arms and legs and back warmed to the task, and soon, she was sweating and focused completely on her work. It was like a trip to the gym, but they paid you instead of the other way around. She stacked boxes and shouldered packages of produce and stopped for an occasional drink of water or to wipe the sweat from her face and neck.

Once most of the crates were unloaded, the truck driver used Food Town's mini-forklift to pick up a series of heavy-looking crates and stacks of boxes on pallets, backing them off the truck and out the doors onto the main floor.

They finished emptying the truck just before midnight. Cheryl came over to Roger and Jessica, who were both wiping their hands. Some of the boxes had leaked unknown substances.

"Roger, get started in the frozen foods section. Both of those pallets that went out are good to go—just unpack and stock. But first, get Sydney here started in produce. Unload that banana pallet first—they looked soft."

Jessica followed Roger out onto the main floor and was surprised to see most of the lights were out.

"Yeah, they turn the lights down at night," he grumbled, noticing her look. "Saves money, I guess. Makes me feel like a vampire."

They walked to the produce section and Roger pointed at the top box in a stack on a pallet.

"Okay, you're starting with the bananas," he said, pointing at the box of greenish-yellow bananas. "Check them for bad ones—leave those in the boxes. Pull anything from the shelf that's bad too. Put out the good stuff, bad stuff in the box."

"Okay."

"And rotate. New product in the back, old product up front. That way it sells sooner. Bananas are easy—the green ones are new, right? Squishy is bad. Grapes after that," he said, pointing at another stack of boxes.

Jessica nodded. It made sense. She got to work, and Roger watched for a minute and then left.

It wasn't that hard, really. The store was cold, as was the produce she was unboxing, but her arms and legs warmed quickly. She sorted out the bad bananas on display first, setting those aside. She moved the current bananas up front, closest to the customer, and then grabbed bunches of green bananas from the box and arranged them along the back of the display. Last she put the "bad" product back in the box. When the bananas were done, she got started on the grapes, repeating the process.

A half-hour later, Roger came back over.

"How's it going?"

"Good, I think," Jessica said, brushing her forehead. She was working up a sweat. "Can you check those?"

He went through the banana box, pulling out a couple that she hadn't been sure about. He put them back on the display and eyed it, adjusting a few things.

"Good work," he said. "Just don't pull anything that's borderline. Cheryl or Wally check everything before we open, so it's better to have them pull something from the floor. They'd rather take something out themselves than have us throw away good product."

Jessica nodded as Roger looked over the grape display. "Bananas looks good. Grapes too. Keep going. Peaches next. Be careful with those—they get really soft. Then just work your way through these boxes," he said, pointing at the stack in the aisle.

"Sydney" worked, getting into a rhythm. Her shoulders grew sore, but she pushed through it. When the displays were full, she took the rest of the boxes back into the large refrigerator room behind the produce department. One whole box of avocados looked bad and

Jessica showed it to Cheryl, who agreed, testing several by twisting them open.

Soon, Jessica was surprised to see the sun was coming up outside. She glanced at the clock on the wall and couldn't believe it read 5:50.

"Time flies when you're having fun," Cheryl said with a smile. "Right?"

Jessica nodded. "Went quick."

Cheryl looked over the produce section, her hands on her very ample hips. "You did good, Sydney. You can take off. And don't forget to punch out."

Jessica smiled and went to the front of the store. She glanced outside and saw Simona waiting in her minivan, the engine running. Jessica clocked out and Roger let her out, locking the front doors behind her. She walked to the van—it was chilly this morning. The sun was coming up, and Jessica could see her breath in the air. She got to the van and climbed in, greeted by a yawning Simona. "How'd it go?"

"It was kinda fun."

"Fun?"

"Yeah. And the night just flew."

CHAPTER 59
Stocker

The next two weeks went well, with Jessica putting in as many shifts as she could at the grocery. She worked every night the first week and several the second week, keeping her head down and making a few friends and following all the rules that Leslie and Simona and Judge Watkins had put in place to protect her identity.

In the end, it wasn't even her fault.

Jessica did everything right. But the whole situation was like a knife, balanced on its edge. Eventually, something would give. Something would happen, and a series of events would begin to occur, a trickle that would, soon, become a river. But it actually had nothing to do with Jessica or her whole situation. No, it was about something else entirely.

On Monday night, September 17th, Jessica was back at work at Food Town. It was just before closing and she was digging through the cases of frozen food, separating out the expired product and setting it aside ahead of tonight's incoming shipment. Roger had wandered off to chat with Cheryl: the truck would arrive just after the store closed at 10 p.m., and there was some confusion about what was coming in tonight on the truck other than a crap-ton of frozen food.

A few final customers wandered the grocery aisles, picking up items or a last-minute case of beer or gallon of milk. Jessica ignored them, sorting some frozen foods. Jessica was stacking the frozen potatoes—tater tots and French fries—when a woman customer ambled up to her.

"Oh, can I get past you?"

Jessica turned to see a middle-aged woman standing nearby. She had a half-full cart of groceries, but the thing that was really striking about the woman was that she was wearing sunglasses, even though she was inside a building and it was pitch-black outside.

"Oh, sure." Jessica stepped away. "Sorry about that."

The woman nodded and grabbed out three small bags of tater tots, tossing them in her cart. "I hate shopping late at night, but sometimes it's the only time I can," the woman said. She slid her sunglasses aside and eyed Jessica. It felt like the woman was looking right through her—or looking right through her disguise.

"You're Sydney, right? Staying with the Cortez family?"

Jessica nodded, breaking eye contact. "Yes, ma'am. I'm up from Texas."

"Oh, what part?"

"What do you mean?"

"Which part of Texas? I know some folks down there."

"Oh, Houston," Jessica said, grabbing some bags of potatoes and rearranging them. "South side, near the airport," she said, remembering what she could about her cursory study of Houston and the surrounding areas. Leslie had gone over it with her, just in case, but little of it had stuck in Jessica's head.

"Oh. Down by Waco?"

Jessica nodded. "That's right."

The woman was staring at Jessica's port-wine stain. "I can understand why you're up here—Texas is way too hot this time of year."

"It can be," Jessica said.

"You been to San Antonio?" the woman asked. "I love the Riverwalk."

"No, can't say that I have."

"What?" The woman eyed her seriously. "Never been to San Antonio? I'm Tina, by the way, Tina Armstrong." She saw Jessica looking at the glasses and she tapped them. "Photophobia."

"What's that?"

"Extreme sensitivity to light."

"Oh, I'm sorry," Jessica said before looking at the open freezer case. "I have to get back to it."

Tina nodded and pushed her cart away. "It was nice chatting with you, Sydney."

The woman left and Jessica got back to work. She reorganized the freezer, and when the truck got there, she and Roger unloaded it, integrating the new product with the old. Cheryl even helped out a little, making Roger smirk. She never helped out, but everyone knew you only had a limited amount of time to put the frozen stuff away before it had to be staged in the freezers in the back.

Jessica worked, trying to concentrate on her job and put the strange encounter with the sunglasses woman out of her mind. But Tina Armstrong had studied her. She'd looked at Jessica strangely. Actually, it was the opposite of a strange look.

It was one of familiarity.

Chapter 60
Curious

The offices of the *Cooper's Mill Gazette* were sparse, to say the least. It was a one-woman operation, literally. Tina Armstrong ran the "local paper" with an iron fist, whether it came to negotiating deadlines with her stringers or the printers up in Troy who printed her weekly black and white paper. Not only was she the editor, she also laid out the paper for print, arguing with the InDesign software and struggling to make the words fit into a limited space. She also did payroll, ad sales, hiring and firing, advertisement design, and a dozen other jobs. And she'd changed the name of the paper to give it more of a hometown feel.

On Tuesday morning, Tina Armstrong was on the phone. She was sitting in her dark office, the overhead lights off, the only light penetrating the office a series of thin bars of light struggling to get in through the closed blinds.

Her computer was on, but it was hard to tell. Next week's nearly-finished paper was displayed on a screen so dimmed it was barely legible. She had an odd medical condition, one she'd suffered with since middle school, and she blamed it for her inability to get close to people. It was an excuse, she was sure, but a convenient one. No one questioned her when she explained why she wore sunglasses all of the time. And, while it made her job more challenging, it also gave her a ready excuse to be short with people.

"I don't care, Phil. You know this is one of my biggest weeks of the year," she said into the phone propped on her shoulder. "Said" wasn't quite the right word, not forceful enough by a stretch, but she wasn't yelling. Not yet. Her words were clear and concise. Tina was not to be misunderstood. She listened to the other side of the conversation, then cut him off.

"Look, you know what time we go to press. Normally it's Tuesday nights, but this is early. This week's paper, plus the special edition on the Mum Festival. That's why I sent everything last night, Monday night, instead of waiting until this morning. Now I need it by 3 p.m.

so I can distribute it today. Call me when it's ready."

She hung up, not waiting for an answer. She didn't have time for this. Mum Festival week was always crazy around town, and, being the 50th anniversary, this one was even crazier. Normally it was a three-day festival celebrating the mum flower. Could you have anything more Midwestern? All the towns around here held their own annual festivals. There were apple festivals and sauerkraut festivals and chocolate festivals. Troy, the next big town north of Cooper's Mill, held a week-long strawberry festival every year at the start of the summer, and they tinted the big fountain in the middle of the town square red.

Here, in Cooper's Mill, they celebrated the chrysanthemum flower. It had something to do with a big greenhouse company located in town that used to be the world's largest grower of mums.

This year's festival was ten days long to celebrate the anniversary. It would kick off on Thursday, September 20th, and end on Sunday the 30th. A week of parades, marathons, car shows, and other stuff, along with the eight-day festival grounds set up in City Park with over 200 booths selling food, drinks, crafts, antiques, and knick-knacks. It was another reason this week's special edition of the *Gazette* had to go out—locals were getting confused about the festival schedule.

Tina went back to her desk, which was strewn with a dozen piles of paperwork, half-finished documents, printouts, and a copy of today's Dayton paper. It always helped to keep on top of the other local news, but she didn't have time today. Too much going on.

She'd been here late last night, finishing this week's paper and special edition and getting it to the printers by midnight. Why they were having trouble getting it printed today, she had no idea. And she didn't really care to hear their excuses.

The special edition had to be distributed to all the local locations today—it had the Mum Festival schedule in it, along with the parade route, lists of events and activities, and information on the related marathon and motorcycle rides.

But the most important part of the special edition, for her at least, was the advertisers. The rest of the special was taken up with ads she'd spent the last three months selling. If it didn't go out, there'd be hell to pay.

Tina put it out of her mind and checked her email inbox again, probably for the hundredth time today, but there was nothing new. Now that the special had gone to print, she was putting together next week's paper, which would go out on Tuesday the 25th. It would be mostly stories about the first few days of the festival, photos, and updated schedule information.

Of course, there would be other stuff in the paper, as well, including the police blotter and sports. She still didn't have anything from Darrell, her sportswriter. Sometimes his column came in on Monday, but most of the time he sent them early unless it was covering a game or something happening over the weekend. Sighing, she picked up her phone and dialed his number from memory.

"Darrell? Got anything for me yet?"

She waited, listening.

"Okay, send it Monday. The 24th. But don't forget, I need time to edit your copy. Get it in by 4:00 or it doesn't run. The printers charge extra if they get the files after 5:00. If you send me something late again, I'll just take the money out of your check." She waited, listening, and finally nodded. "Yup," she said, hanging up.

Tina turned back to the dark computer monitor. It was too dark for most people to read, but it suited her just fine. She got back to work on next week's issue, dated SEPTEMBER 25, moving headlines and blocks of text around on the screen, dragging and dropping them in the InDesign software, filling in holes. She left room for the festival updates and stories and set aside four pages in the middle for photos. The masthead stayed where it was, of course—it was the banner at the top of the first page that said the name of the paper, per-copy price, print date, etc.

Finally, after another half hour, it looked ready. She saved the file and put it aside for now.

She looked around the empty office. She was used to working alone—people couldn't handle her or the dark office. Tina had tried having other people working in the office with her, but it was just too difficult. They couldn't get used to the dim lighting conditions.

But the paper was a success, knock on wood.

Tina ran a tight ship and pinched every penny. She'd bought the failing paper back in 2007 and turned it around, probably because she did almost all of the work herself. Her writers were great—she had Darrell on sports, a woman named Maggie who did all the committees and government articles, and a few other stringers who wrote garden pieces or opinion columns.

One guy, a local writer, submitted four different columns every week—the man could crank out words, to say the least. He had a tech column and one on healthy living, but his most popular contribution was a local opinion/commentary column called "Talk of Cooper's Mill," which discussed local goings-on along with events in his own life. It wasn't Shakespeare, but people loved it.

Lately, he'd been pitching an anonymous gossip column to be written with another person in town, but Tina had been resistant to the idea. Cooper's Mill wasn't Los Angeles or even Dayton. You couldn't gossip about people in town when everyone knew everyone, a lesson she'd learned the hard way. Not long after she'd moved to town, she'd been talking too loudly at one of the local coffee shops about a run-in she'd had with a local doctor. She'd said a few things that she later regretted. Of course, the doctor's cousin had been in the coffee shop at the same time and Tina's words had gotten back to him. It reminded her to be more aware of her surroundings.

While others wrote the bulk of the newspaper, Tina liked to handle the investigative journalism side of things. It was what had drawn her to being a writer in the first place, and she was feeling that familiar "tickle" in the back of her mind when there was something bothering her.

Shuffling the papers on her desk, she found a note she'd left herself. Something curious was going on at Food Town, the grocery store. A contact at the police station had mentioned that a couple of the employees were shady, possibly even dealing drugs out of the location. Tina hadn't heard anything concrete, but she was smart enough to write everything down just in case.

And now there was that strange girl.

She seemed so familiar to Tina, somehow. There was something about her, about the shape of her face, that Tina's mind kept returning to. Even as Tina had driven home that night and put away her groceries, she'd thought about the girl. Tina was sure she'd seen her before, met her somewhere.

Tina was curious, and her curiosity had served her well over the years, breaking more than her fair share of cases. The new girl, Sydney, had a strange port-wine stain on her neck. Could she have been involved in the drug angle, or was there something else going on?

That was usually how her best stories started: with the tickle. Tina saw something, or someone would say something in passing, and it would get her mind going. Tina would jot it down, think about it, and then start digging around the edges. It was how she'd uncovered the fraud at the local animal shelter, where they were charging for services they weren't carrying out.

Tina didn't know what to do about the Food Town situation, other than to keep picking at it. Dig around the edges, try to talk to the young woman again. It was a start. Maybe nothing, or maybe the start of something.

Chapter 61
Jessica Mills

In the end, it all happened very quickly.

If this had been a movie or something, it would have been much more interesting. She would have gotten herself in trouble, somehow. Maybe hitting up one of her new co-workers for coke or something like that. Jessica could have come up with a good plot: she was strung out, agitated. It had been several weeks and now she was running through almost two packs a day to keep her nerves steady. Jessica would grow desperate and set up a buy with one of her co-workers. She'd flirt with him, as best she could dressed like a weird Texas troll, and he'd produce a small amount of coke. They'd share it and maybe get up to some kissing or something and then the cops would appear and the whole gig would be exposed. Her in cuffs—again—and the wig pulled off and cameras flashing, her ruse exposed. A ruse that could never have worked anyway, really.

But reality was far less impressive. It involved waffles, a Journey cover band, and a merry-go-round.

Jessica had heard about the local Mum Festival and was fascinated by the idea of attending it. Everyone was talking about it, and Jessica had asked Ferrara and her family. Even the people at the grocery couldn't stop talking about it.

To Jessica, it sounded like a fun, ten-day small-town party running from the 20th to the 30th. There was a festival area, with food and drinks and shopping, along with a parade and a car show and other events. It all sounded like fun, and a chance for Jessica to see some of what they got up to in town.

Jessica begged to go. She'd been so sick of being cooped up—except for the occasional rides with Ferrara or Simona to run errands, Jessica was ALWAYS either at the farm or in the back of the grocery store, unboxing produce. She'd become something of an expert on fruits and vegetables, pretending it was a job for her next TV show. She would be the BEST at sorting fruits and veggies and maybe win an EMMY. Ha.

Two days before the festival began, Jessica had begged and pleaded and Ferrara and Simona—and Leslie—had finally relented. It was Leslie's decision in the end, and something Jessica said must have worked.

On Saturday morning, September 22, Jessica and the others headed to the festival.

Cooper's Mill City Park was crammed with booths and tents, people selling everything under the sun. There were dozens of large food trucks and trailers selling hamburgers and hot dogs and something called a "Texas Tenderloin." A kid's area had been set up on the park's tennis courts, with inflatable bounce houses, games, and an obstacle course. In the center of the festival, a large bandstand had been set up, and musical acts and other demonstrations were scheduled for all week, leading up to a fireworks show on Sunday, the 23rd. The festival would continue for another week, of course, ending with a parade on the 29th and more festivities on the 30th to wrap things up.

Jessica and Ferrara wandered the festival grounds. Looking back on it, they were just setting themselves up for failure. But Jessica was happy, and Ferrara was excited to shop for fall-themed decorations to take back to Los Angeles.

After some shopping, they'd walked to the center of the fairgrounds and Ferrara had wandered off to get a "waffle" from a booth set up by the local firefighters. Evidently, they only made and sold their famous "Fireman's Waffles" once a year and only at this festival. Ferrara had pointed out the line before, doubling back on itself several times when they passed it.

"Oh, it's short right now," Ferrara had said.

Jessica had shot her a look. "Short?"

"Yeah, usually they have at least fifty or sixty people waiting. Some people buy a huge pack and freeze them," she'd said, explaining how they were impossible to get anywhere else.

So Ferrara had gone off to buy Fireman Waffles.

Seriously, you couldn't make this up.

Jessica stood near the bandstand and watched a great Journey cover band. They did "Separate Ways" and "Open Arms," and the lead singer was pretty good. He hit all the high notes, even the ones at the end of "Wheel in the Sky." Jessica watched the singer and noticed fans taking pictures, lots of pictures. She should have known better and turned away, but she was caught up in the moment.

If she'd been planning a big "reveal," Jessica would have jumped up on stage and pulled off her wig and started singing along with the cover band, surprising everyone. The audience would have gasped, then applauded.

What happened was much more ridiculous.

When the band launched into "Don't Stop Believing," Jessica wandered over to the nearby playground, passing a merry-go-round crowded with kids and a climbing area that looked like natural rocks. Jessica grabbed one of the playground swings and sat on it, enjoying a quiet moment surrounded by normal people.

Jessica didn't see the lady from the local paper, who had been taking pictures of the cover band. The woman had seen Jessica walking alone and followed, snapping photos of the kids in the park and the merry-go-round and "Sydney" on the swings.

Then it all went to shit.

Jessica got on the swing and started moving back and forth. Soon, she was swinging high, leaning and kicking her legs. It felt great, like freedom. Wind in her hair, wind on her face, kids playing all around her. It was a beautiful, brief respite from the charade.

But there was too much wind in her "hair."

Her wig came loose and flew off. Now, if she'd been standing on the ground and a sudden breeze had lifted her wig off, it would have been a simple fix: lean down, pick it up, hope no one noticed. Plop it back on, straighten it, then look around and make excuses if anyone had seen.

But here, in the park, her wig went flying, flapping to the ground like a wounded squirrel.

Jessica panicked, gasping loudly, drawing even more attention to herself. Everyone in the area turned to look, and kids stopped playing and pointed.

Desperate to stop the swing, Jessica dragged her feet in the dust, slowing her speed. It sent up a cloud of dust and dirt and made too much noise, drawing more attention. She jumped off, coughing and taking her fake glasses off to rub the dirt and dust out of her eyes. Jessica stepped from the cloud and looked around for the wig. There were so many eyes on her, a feeling she'd forgotten.

A kid had walked up and picked up the wig and was handing it to her, and the lady from the paper was snapping photos.

That's when it happened.

Jessica heard her name.

Her real name.

"Wait. Is that...is that Jessica Mills?" Someone asked a friend. Jessica turned—it was a teenage girl, talking to another girl. The second girl nodded, and, in a flash, they both had their phones out, snapping photos.

Jessica stepped towards them. "No. Please."

They backed away, and Jessica heard her name again, several times. More people snapped photos, not bothering to get her permission.

They never did.

Jessica turned and saw the sunglasses woman taking photos as well, both of her and of the people around her. A rush of recognition rippled through the crowd. The Journey cover band stopped playing, the notes of "Don't Stop Believing" dying mid-note, the lead singer pointing at her from the stage.

The playground area swelled with people, rushing in, snapping photos. Kids and teenagers crowded around Jessica, saying her name, touching her. They asked for selfies with her, shouted at her, asked her what she was doing in Ohio.

It was overwhelming.

She was used to planned publicity events, of course, and public "meet and greets" where she could rub up against the "common folk." But this was overwhelming—suddenly, this Midwestern crowd had a huge Hollywood star in their midst. All decorum evaporated with the first "Is that REALLY Jessica Mills? Here in Cooper's Mill? What the hell?"

The crowd jostled her, and someone grabbed the wig and ran away. Jessica grabbed after it but faced a wall of faces of little kids and teenagers and adults, all suddenly thrust into proximity with fame.

Finally, a hand from the crowd put their arm around her.

"Okay, okay! That's enough!"

Jessica had her head down, looking at the dust and shuffling feet. It didn't sound like Ferrara. Where was Ferrara? Jessica glanced up and saw the sunglasses woman. She had her arm around Jessica and her big camera was slung around her neck, forgotten.

"Okay, people! That's enough! Back up! Let us through!"

Tina Armstrong walked Jessica away from the crowd, moving toward a group of vendor booths. The crowd was like a wave—as Jessica and Tina moved in one direction, the wave surged after them, trailing them.

Tina stepped under a tarp and into a booth, confusing the vendor who was in the middle of selling a pair of sunglasses to a customer. The vendor and the customer both stopped their conversation mid-word, mouths open, staring at Jessica.

"Okay, we need to get you out of here," Tina said to Jessica. "Follow me. What the hell are you doing in Ohio? I thought you were in rehab."

Jessica nodded, tears streaking her face. "I...I need to find my friend. Ferrara. She has to be here somewhere."

"No time for that," Tina said, glancing at the vendor. People were peeking into the booth, and Jessica could hear a low rumble of conversation outside. "We have to get you out of the park." She grabbed the pair of sunglasses off her face and put them on Jessica, squinting at the bright light. "And put this on." Tina slipped off her jacket and put it over Jessica's shoulders.

They headed out of the booth, Tina grabbing another pair of sunglasses from the vendor's table. "I'll be back to pay for these," she shouted over her shoulder. Dragging Jessica, Tina made her way to a group of food trailers and behind them. Back there, someone had set up some tables and chairs for the vendors to relax. Several were eating and looked up at Jessica.

"Come on, this way," Tina said, walking quickly.

Jessica nodded at the vendors and followed Tina, who led her behind the trailers. Jessica felt naked without her wig and tried to pull the jacket up over her face.

They stepped over thick electrical cables that ran to a nearby building. Jessica followed Tina into the building and out the other side—it was a pair of restrooms, one on either side, with an open corridor down the middle. Emerging from the other side, they were near a fence that ran around a football field. Jessica had seen it before—the City Park was located next to the local High School's field.

"My car's over here," she said. "They let me park with the cops and firefighters."

They got to a fenced-off area filled with a smattering of cars, and Tina jumped into a Volvo that had seen better days. Jessica, with no other options, looked around for Ferrara and then climbed in the Volvo.

"Okay," Tina said. "At least for now, we've lost the crowd. I can get you out of here, but I want an exclusive."

"What?"

"You know. Why you're here, in Ohio. The disguise. Everything. Agreed?"

Jessica nodded. There wasn't anything else to say.

Tina reached for a tape recorder on her dashboard and started it taping.

"Okay, let's get out of here. I'll ask you questions on the way."

"Where are we going?"

"We need to get out of the park and find your friend," Tina said, starting the car. "Duck down, and speak up so the microphone gets it. This is a huge story, you have to know that."

Jessica leaned over, nodding. "Yes, I know. But it is court-ordered. All of it. Anything you print will have to be approved."

Tina bit her lip as she negotiated the cars in the lot. "That's fine. That's fine. We'll go to my office, work from there. Call Ferrara, have her meet us there. Do you have a phone?"

Jessica shook her head. "No."

"You don't have a phone? Everyone has a phone."

"Not me."

"Okay, you can call her from my office."

Jessica felt the car turn sharply and accelerate. They were on a road now, not bumping over dirt ruts. They were leaving the park area, and Ferrara had no idea where she was. Jessica was on her own.

"So, court-ordered? Like part of your rehab? I've been following the story. Everyone has. You're supposed to be in a jail in San Francisco. So, what do you mean court-ordered?"

Jessica bent down and ducked out of sight, praying that no one else could see her. She couldn't see anything other than the floorboard of Tina's car. Papers and copies of the local paper, the "*Cooper's Mill Gazette*," jostled around her feet.

"So? We don't have long," Tina said. "Those selfies are already on Instagram, the ones those teenagers took. I have to get to the office and post something or other outlets will beat me. So, what do you mean court-ordered?"

Jessica sighed, gripped her legs, and started talking.

Chapter 62
Good Fortune

Tina couldn't believe it. Literally couldn't believe it. People used that word all the time, but they didn't mean it in the way it was supposed to be used. Tina would be at some event or sitting in the audience at a City Council meeting, waiting for it to start, and someone behind her would say something stupid like "oh my God that literally kills me."

No, it doesn't, Tina would think. Or you'd be dead. Literally means it's actually happening. Not might happen, or feels like it's happening, but actually happening.

This was actually happening.

Tina had been at the Mum Festival, snapping pictures. She didn't like paying for photos, but she understood the draw. People wanted to see themselves or people they knew in the paper, so she tried to include as many photos as she could in each week's paper.

She'd been snapping photos of kids playing on the playground, action shots of people shopping, fun photos of vendors selling their wares. These were the easy gigs, usually, and much better than running grim photos of car accidents or mug shots of criminals. People loved their happy stories, and Tina tried to oblige as much as possible.

All morning, she'd been taking pictures at the festival. She'd snapped over three hundred photos, kids eating ice cream and people trying on hats and some great photos of a local older woman's clogging group, who performed a few numbers in front of the bandstand, shuffling and clogging along to the music.

The Journey cover band was one of the highlighted musical acts, so Tina had gotten there early and gotten some fun shots of the band members setting up and playing for the crowds. She was just wrapping up when she'd spotted the young woman from Food Town wandering the festival grounds alone.

There was something about her.

It was more than the fact that the woman was new in town. She'd appeared out of nowhere, as newcomers did, but she'd also gotten a job at the grocery almost immediately. Who did she know? Tina had asked around and no one knew her. Literally, no one knew who she was, other than she was up from Texas visiting the Cortez family, staying at their large home west of town.

Tina had done a story last fall on the Cortez boy. He'd gotten a full ride to OSU after leading the Cooper's Mill High School soccer team to an appearance in the state finals. They'd lost, sadly, thoroughly pissing off Darrell, Tina's sports columnist. But the appearance had gotten the Cortez boy a scholarship to one of the best schools in the state.

Seeing the Sydney girl alone, walking through the park, Tina had followed. It wasn't an instinct, per se, but Tina had learned to follow her gut when it told her something was happening. The same thing had happened two years ago when she'd broken the story at the animal shelter. Something just felt "off" about the couple that worked there.

Tina followed the girl, casually trailing her and snapping photos. She got a few of the children on the play equipment, and some older kids playing together on the merry go round. The sounds of "Journey" played in the background. Maybe Tina could get her alone, ask her some questions. There was something about the way she carried herself. Maybe there was a story there, a young girl with an interesting background...

And then things went crazy.

The girl lost her hair.

It took a moment for Tina Armstrong to realize the young woman was wearing a wig. She'd been on the swings and the wig had flown off.

The girl scrambled off the swings in a panic, grabbing for the wig. She looked...so familiar.

The initial surprise washed over Tina, and she recognized the Hollywood starlet in an instant.

Jessica Mills.

Here, in Ohio. In Cooper's Mill.

She was here, in town, staying with friends. Disguised, for some reason that would, probably, make for an excellent story.

If Tina could get it first.

Things suddenly made more sense—Tina remembered that Simona's girl, Ferrara, had been a hairdresser here in town. She'd moved to California and worked in the film industry. She must know

Jessica Mills, maybe does her hair. Somehow, they'd become friends? And Jessica had gotten invited to stay at Ferrara's family's home, here in Ohio?

The most heartbreaking part was seeing the young woman's reaction to being outed—she'd stood there, shocked, overwhelmed. Clearly, the young woman had been counting on her disguise to keep her secret, but she'd been betrayed by one particularly boisterous ride on a set of swings. And now she was mobbed, surrounded, dumbstruck.

Tina stepped in, whisking Jessica Mills away to a quieter part of the festival.

Of course, some part of her wanted the story. But another part, a stronger part, couldn't stand to see the young woman in pain, overwhelmed, confused. She needed help, and Tina might have been the only person in the entire park who was able to set aside her awe and get to work getting Jessica out of the situation.

On the ride from the park, Tina had gotten most of the story: the Los Angeles judge, the fake jail sentence. The crazy idea put forth by Jessica's hairdresser. The judge and the prosecution in Los Angeles relenting, agreeing to it. Her trip east, her handler, a fearsome woman named Leslie. And her weeks undercover in Ohio, working and getting clean and taking a much-needed break from her life in Los Angeles—and her army of enablers and "handlers."

They had driven to the *Gazette* offices and hurried inside, and now Tina sat at her desk, typing at her computer. She was trying to get the whole story down quickly, getting every detail she could into this first draft, shouting out occasional questions to the young woman across the room, who stood by the windows, looking out.

"And the trip west—you said you went through Denver?"

Jessica Mills turned from the window and nodded. "South, first. The Grand Canyon. That was amazing. Then north and across." Jessica ran her hands along a stack of last week's newspaper, then played with an old piece of photographic development equipment. Tina never used it anymore but kept it around just in case. The other two desks sat empty. "You have other employees?"

"No, not really," Tina said, pointing up. "No one likes the low lights."

Jessica looked up at the dimmed fluorescents. Tina had only put one tube in each overhead fixture instead of four. Even that had been too bright, so she had half of the fixtures off. "Your eyes?"

Tina nodded, typing, distracted. She really only had time for one draft and then this would have to go on the website. She also needed to warn her hosting service—a story like this could crash her site. And she had dozens of photos ready to go, watermarked with her name and the name of the paper. They would go to AP first, along with the story, and they'd have first dibs to bid on the story. After that, Tina would likely spend the day doing paid interviews. Hopefully.

"What was it called again?"

"Photophobia," Tina said, hitting SEND on the email. She stood, stretching. "My eyes are overly-sensitive to light. Always have been. In here, I can control the light level, but elsewhere, it's very painful."

"At night too?"

"Sometimes," she said, walking over to the window. There was a small crowd gathered on the street outside, and people were taking photos of the windows above. Crazy. "Bright lights are bad. Really bad. I have to wear sunglasses when I'm at the scenes of car accidents. The police lights."

"I couldn't stand that," Jessica said. "I'm at so many events, with lights flashing. Camera flashes, all kinds of stuff. It can get overwhelming."

They stood together, looking out through the drawn blinds, which kept the light out. They watched the street below—Tina had called the police, and they were keeping people from coming into the building or up the steps to her office.

"Your friends?"

"I don't see them yet," Jessica said. She reached to open the shades further but stopped. "There's another TV crew."

Tina looked—it was Dale Bumpers. She knew him from other local stories: he was obese to the point of it being a joke. How he got around, she had no idea.

"Look, it's your call. But they'll hound you until you make a statement. My story just went out, so the exclusive is over. As soon as AP runs it, you'll be free to go." Tina looked at her. "And thank you for that."

Jessica nodded. "Thanks for getting me out of there. That was worse than any movie premiere—oh, I see Ferrara."

Tina Armstrong looked down and saw Ferrara Cortez talking to one of the cops. With her was a huge woman, very serious looking. That had to be this Leslie woman Jessica had mentioned several times. The woman sounded very intriguing, to say the least. After a second, Tina saw the member of the Cooper's Mill Police Department let Ferrara and Leslie through the cordon and approach the doors to the inside of the building.

Moments later, they came up the steps and Jessica rushed to hug Ferrara. Leslie glanced around the office and looked up at the dim lights.

"Are you okay?" Ferrara asked. "I went to buy waffles and you were gone. What happened to your wig?"

"Gone, gone," Jessica said to her and Leslie. "It was crazy. I lost the wig, and people knew. Like immediately. I didn't have time to react, really."

Leslie listened to her talk. "Well, the disguise was bound to fail at some point. Are you hurt?"

"No, nothing like that," Jessica said. "Just freaked out." She turned and pointed. "Tina helped get me out of there."

"In exchange for an exclusive, I suppose," Leslie said, eyeing Tina. "Ferrara told me about you on the way in. Couldn't wait to take advantage of the situation, right? You press are all the same."

Tina was taken aback. "No, I saw a girl in trouble. And yes, once I figured out who she was, I wanted to know more. Everyone does."

Jessica looked at Leslie. "I told her most of the story. I had to."

Leslie looked at Tina. "Who have you told?"

"AP."

"The wire service?" Leslie asked, incredulous. "Already?"

"This story is breaking fast," Tina said, not backing off. "Her picture is already online." She went to the computer monitor and turned it around, showing photos from local Instagram accounts. "It's taking off. If you were smart, you'd get ahead of it."

Leslie scowled. "No, if I were smart, I'd figure out a way to sit on this."

"You can read what I sent in," Tina offered. "I gave them sixteen paragraphs and eleven photos, all approved by Jessica." She clicked through screens and pulled up the article and photos. "Anything more will be follow-up and background."

Leslie walked over and Tina couldn't help noticing how big the woman was. She towered over everyone else in the room. She plopped in the chair and Tina wondered if it would hold her. Leslie read the article, grunting when she was done.

"Well, I don't really want all that information out there, but it's going to happen," she said, looking at Tina. "It reads nice, actually."

"Thanks," Tina said.

"And I liked the stuff about me."

"You're welcome."

Leslie sat back and looked at her, finally nodding. "Okay, I don't like this, but the train has left the station, as my dad used to say. All we can do is stay on track."

Tina nodded. "If I were you guys, I'd have Jessica sit down for a quick interview with one of the local TV stations. I can set it up. You can do it here," she said, indicating the office. "Channel 2 is good, Channel 4 not so much."

"I don't think so—"

"Then they'll hound you every moment until she leaves the state," Tina said, glancing at Jessica, who was deep in conversation with Ferrara. Tina lowered her voice. "This is the biggest thing to happen in Dayton since last year and the gang war at the hospital downtown. And this is a good story, for once. Local girl, friends with a huge celebrity, brings her back to Ohio for some rest and relaxation."

Leslie thought about it, glancing at Jessica.

"It's a great story," Tina said. "Feels good. And giving the interview first lets you guys set the tone going forward. I'd follow that up with daily press conferences for a few days, just until people find something else to be excited about."

Leslie thought about it.

"Okay. Set it up. A half-hour from now, here in this building somewhere. I have to make a call first."

Leslie walked away, reaching for her phone. Tina was impressed—Jessica had said the woman was formidable, but it hadn't even begun to cover it.

Tina grabbed her sunglasses and walked over to Jessica.

"Leslie approved the article," Tina said. "And I pitched her the TV interview we talked about, and she went for that as well. I'll go set it up with Channel 2."

Jessica nodded, and Tina headed downstairs.

Chapter 63
Interviewed

The television interview went well, better than Leslie had hoped.

She'd immediately hated the idea—any cop would. People like her were genetically opposed to publicity. They didn't work in the shadows, but a little darkness never hurt.

But here they were, on TV with the local Dayton affiliate, Channel 2. The story was out. Jessica and Ferrara, front and center, mic'ed up and being interviewed. Nothing to do now but try to get in front of the story. They would have time afterward to figure out where they went from here.

Most likely, they'd be on the first flight back to Los Angeles.

Tina Armstrong, the woman who ran the local paper, had pulled the whole thing together in a matter of minutes, negotiating with the TV station and their producer over the whole activity, insisting on certain payments—and making sure they were going to treat Jessica with respect. It had been impressive, and not something Leslie would ever have expected out of a member of the media. Armstrong was keeping some of the funds, but the bulk of the interview payment would be donated to the Mum Festival committee.

Leslie looked over at Tina, who was watching the interview wrap up. The woman, now wearing sunglasses as every light in the office was on, along with a pair of bright studio lights that had been set up on either side of the HD camera filming the interview. Leslie didn't know what to make of the capable, attractive woman. If this had been any other situation, or if they had been back in Los Angeles, Leslie might've taken a chance on asking the Armstrong woman out. As it was, things here in Cooper's Mill were crazy enough without getting involved romantically with a local. What was she even thinking?

Jessica had gotten right back into the swing of things with almost no hesitation. She'd had Ferrara do her makeup in the normal fashion. When the interview began, Jessica and Ferrara had been sitting there giggling like two schoolgirls when the channel came back from commercial.

The woman doing the interview seemed nervous, out of her league, but Jessica got her to warm up and soon the interview was going gangbusters. Jessica talked about her "jail sentence" and how the judge in Los Angeles that thought a break from acting might help Jessica "get her mind right."

The reporter asked all the questions that were probably on people's minds: "how did you get to Ohio?" and "why were you wearing a disguise?" and "what did she think of Dayton?" and Jessica handled all of them like a pro. She deferred to Ferrara on the makeup questions, and the young woman talked on and on about wig colors and ratty nails and bad makeup jobs to "hide the beauty underneath." That part had made Leslie roll her eyes, even if it was all patently true.

Jessica also mentioned that they weren't sure how long she would be remaining in Ohio or when they would return to Los Angeles.

The station seemed to want the interview to go on forever, but Leslie and Tina Armstrong had been clear—ten to twelve minutes, nothing more. As they came to the end of the second segment, the on-scene reporter was repeating questions she was getting from back at the station, and the last one had a sharp edge: "Don't you feel bad, lying to everyone around you?"

Jessica thought about it for a second, and Leslie leaned in, wondering if this was the moment the interview went off the rails.

"No, not really," Jessica said after a moment. "I know it's not fair—lots of people have done what I did and gone to jail. I'm just thankful that the judge took a chance on me. She allowed me an opportunity to get cleaned up. And thanks to the great people of Ohio—and my friend Ferrara and her family—I can honestly say I feel like a whole new person. Thank you," Jessica said, looking at Ferrara.

Leslie nodded. The young woman was a professional, as she had been for years. And while Leslie still thought she could act like a spoiled brat on occasion, at least today she was walking the line. The interview ended and the bright lights went off and Leslie heard Tina Armstrong sigh loudly, taking off her sunglasses and rubbing her eyes before putting them back on. Leslie went over to her.

"You okay?"

Tina looked up at her. Leslie could only see her own reflection in the mirrored glasses.

"Yeah, much better now." She tipped the glasses down slightly so Leslie could see her eyes. "And once I get all you crazies out of here, I can finally turn the lights all the way off."

Leslie glanced at the computer on the desk. "Don't you have more work to do?"

"Yeah, follow up articles. AP wants a five-part piece. Paying very well."

"Congratulations, I guess?"

Tina smiled at her. "Not excited about the word getting out? From what I've heard, you did a great job."

"I suppose."

"So, is the ruse up? Will you guys be heading back to Los Angeles soon? I was hoping to get an interview from you as well. But I can't imagine Judge Watkins will want Jessica to stay here much longer."

"I don't know," Leslie said, and it was the truth. She'd called Judge Watkins immediately, as soon as Ferrara had called with the news that Jessica had been 'outed' at the festival. Ferrara had been walking around the festival, looking for Jessica, and Leslie caught a ride into town with Simona. Leslie called the judge from the car and talked as Simona drove to the park, coordinating and meeting up with Ferrara when they got there.

Judge Watkins didn't seem surprised—in fact, she mentioned how the ruse had gone on longer than she'd imagined. Leslie had assumed they would be heading back to LA soon, but the judge asked for more time to think about it.

Jessica and Ferrara walked over to join Leslie.

"So, what did you think?" Jessica asked.

"Good, good," Leslie said, looking around. "We need to talk."

"I know," Jessica said. "I shouldn't have walked off on my own like that. Ferrara went to buy some of those waffles—"

"Don't blame this one on me," Ferrara said sharply, a drastic change from her 'smiles and laughter' on the TV just moments before. Leslie could tell that she was genuinely upset. "This is a disaster, Jessica. Everyone knows who you are, and everyone knows where you live. The farm is going to be overrun with people, trying to get in, trying to get over the fence—"

"It's okay," Leslie said. "We'll handle it."

Jessica looked at the floor as if she didn't know what to say. Leslie rarely saw her quieted. It was a good look for her, humbled, less confident than usual.

"Okay," Leslie continued. "I talked to the judge a few minutes ago."

Jessica looked up. "I'm assuming we're going home. Ferrara, we'll be out of your hair in a few hours."

"Watkins said it was up to me. And you," Leslie said, looking at Jessica.

"What?"

Leslie nodded. "She knew the story would get out eventually. We all did, right? But the judge's been impressed with you. She said we could stick it out here if we wanted, finish out the last few weeks. Assuming it's okay with Ferrara's folks."

Jessica looked surprised. "I just assumed, with the secret out, we'd go back to LA."

Leslie shrugged. "Even with everyone knowing, Watkins said this is still a better place for you."

The Tina woman walked over to join their group.

"I think the interview went well."

"As well as could be expected," Leslie said, giving her a look.

"Thanks for setting that up," Jessica said. "I know I promised you the exclusive, but they asked some stuff that I hadn't covered with you—"

Tina waved her hand. "It's all good. My site metrics are through the roof, and the AP has agreed to a five-part series, with several more background pieces on you and on the town. If you can meet with me sometime tomorrow, we can wrap those up. So I'm fine. How are you?"

Leslie looked at the woman and scowled. This woman, this member of the press, was asking Jessica how she was doing?

"I'm okay," Jessica said. "Looking forward to getting home."

"Home—where's that?" Ferrara asked.

"I mean the farm," Jessica said with a smile.

"Why don't you two head back there now," Leslie said to Ferrara and Jessica. "But take the long road home so I can coordinate things."

"We could run downtown, do some shopping," Ferrara said. "Now that the cat's out of the bag, I'm sure Jessica would like to pick up some new clothes. And the local cops can give us a little security."

"Can I get my phone now? Or my accounts unfrozen?"

Leslie shrugged. "I'll have another talk with the judge, see how much freedom she wants to give you." Leslie got serious. "But I'm telling her we're staying, at least for now. Is that right?"

Jessica looked at Ferrara, who nodded, and then back to Leslie. "Yup. Let's finish it out."

"Good," Leslie said. "I need to coordinate with the local cops, then, and get a few things set up at the farm. Give me two hours. And try to not get into any more trouble."

They smiled together and left, Jessica thanking Tina one more time for pulling her out of the crowds. Leslie watched them leave, talking to the local cops.

Tina smiled at her. "I figure you've got six hours before half of Los Angeles shows up here to chase the story. At least I've got a head start."

"It's going to get crazy," Leslie said. "Especially out at the farm."

"You can coordinate with the CMPD downstairs. I can help with that. They can assign officers, help cordon off the Cortez farm. But you're going to need more help, security people who answer to you and not the county. I know a few names."

"Thanks," Leslie said. "And thanks for helping her."

"I saw that look you gave me when I asked Jessica how she was doing. What, you think I don't have a heart?"

Leslie looked at the small woman wearing sunglasses, sizing her up. "Well, you're not going to argue that a huge story fell into your lap and that you're going to be making the most of it."

"Nope, won't argue that," Tina said. "But I don't want to see anything happen to her either. It was my first instinct to get her to safety. After that, I went for the story," she said. "Any newspaper would."

Leslie looked at her, not sure what to say.

Chapter 64
What Now?

That evening, Ferrara joined Jessica and Leslie and a guest at the dining room table.

The Cortez farm was a circus, with news vans and reporters lined up on the road outside. Ferrara had suggested her family go away, 'encouraging' them to travel to Indianapolis for a regular-season Colts game. "Or head to Chicago. Stay for a few days," she'd told her parents and sister. There was no reason for them to have to put up with the reporters as well.

"They're doing another live shot," Leslie said, looking down the driveway at the reporters gathered there.

Chief King nodded. He was seated at the dining room table as well, jotting notes down on a little yellow notepad he'd brought with him. Ferrara had never met the man, even though he'd been the head of the local police force for the entire time she'd lived in Cooper's Mill.

"My men will keep them at arm's length, as best as they can."

"What do they want?" Ferrara asked.

"More interviews, I imagine," Jessica said. "Live shots all night, with updates for all the national and international affiliates. They're not going anywhere."

"Great," Leslie said.

Ferrara could tell how upset she was and shook her head. "We should never have gone to the festival."

Leslie shook her head. "We kept her secret longer than I would have guessed."

"You did well," Chief King added. "I just wish someone would've given us a head's up." He was reading through the letter from Judge Watkins—Ferrara could see the official letterhead at the top. "I'm happy to cooperate with our friends out west, of course. But if we'd known, we might've been able to help shield her from discovery," he said, glancing up at Jessica. "Ma'am."

Leslie smiled. "It's okay, Chief. The judge wanted all this done on the 'down low,' as they say. She thought the fewer people who knew, the better."

"Well, now lots of people know," Chief King said. "And more coming. I heard the flights into town from Los Angeles are booked up."

"What?" Jessica asked, her face falling.

"Paparazzi, I'd imagine," Ferrara said, shaking her head. "Those rats will be flying in to make your life hell."

Leslie looked at Chief King. "Jessica has five weeks left on her 'house arrest.' Is it realistic to stay here?"

King shook his head. "I don't know. We can provide some security, of course, but there are only nine of us in the entire CMPD. Even working triple shifts, we couldn't cover your security needs along with our work."

"Right," Leslie said.

"You need security, really. Two men, at least, around the clock. If they travel with you everywhere you go, it should be fine." King sat back. "If our deputies were doing security for you, they'd be getting called away all the time. We can provide for traffic control out front, and patrol the farm."

"I'll also be around, obviously," Leslie said. "But if the local cops can't cover her, I've been authorized to hire local protection. Do you know anyone?"

King sat back. "A few people. One, in particular," he said, shaking his head. "He's cheap, and good. But he's got a bit of an attitude. Not sure if you guys will get along."

"I don't care," Jessica said. "I don't want to go back," she said. "I told myself I could do this. And even with the paparazzi winging in, and the local press in my face, I want to try. Leslie?"

"It's going to be rough," she said. "Cameras everywhere you go. At the grocery, if you keep the job. When you go out to eat. Everywhere."

Jessica smiled. "I'm used to it. So, Chief King, who is this person you're talking about?"

Chapter 65
Breaking News

It was getting late on Saturday and Frank was watching the local breaking news. Apparently, some young actress from Hollywood had shown up at a festival right here in Cooper's Mill. Laura had called, giving him a head's up. She was excited to hear about it and had told Frank, who couldn't care less. He'd heard of her, of course, but didn't attach much stock to someone simply because they were famous, especially in today's Hollywood.

The young woman was hiding out in Ohio, something to do with a drug rehab situation. Frank's opinion of the young woman slid up one notch when he learned she was trying to get clean, then slid back down two notches when he heard it was court-ordered. In his experience, telling someone to get clean rarely worked. They had to want it.

He was watching the local television coverage when Frank's phone rang. He grabbed it, frowning when he saw the caller ID.

Chief King.

"Hello?"

"Hey, Frank," King said on the other end. For a moment, Frank experienced a disconnected feeling, as if he'd fallen out of touch with the world. He recovered quickly.

"Oh, hey, Chief. What can I help you with?"

The conversation was awkward. At least it was short. They talked and things smoothed out quickly. Chief King needed him, and Frank said he'd be there, no questions asked.

Five minutes later, Frank was dressed and in his car, driving up Main Street. He waited on a large flatbed truck filled with tomatoes passing through the downtown, then turned west and drove out of Cooper's Mill proper, heading into the setting sun. He passed the bank and a tattoo store and the small car dealership that took up three of the four corners of Main Street and County Road 25-A.

They needed to come up with better names for these roads. The folks in Ohio seemed to have this thing where all the roads were either named one of two ways: it was a number, which sorta made sense, or they used a ridiculous system where the road was named after the two towns it connected.

It was a simple system, obviously, but seemed designed to keep visitors in the dark. It required you to know the layout and configuration of all the little towns in the area. There was "Dayton-Springfield Road" and "Anna-Greenville Road" and "Xenia-Yellow Springs Road." Whoever came up with these road names had no imagination at all. And they made it difficult for the new resident to figure out where they were going—unless you were actually in "Xenia" and planning to take that road because you were heading to "Yellow Springs," the name of the road was of little help. And it didn't even tell you which direction you were heading in.

Frank passed farms and houses grouped along the road. This was the road that connected Cooper's Mill with West Milton, he knew that much at least. But he'd only been out this direction a few times. It was amazing how quickly you passed out into "the country" and were surrounded by farms and fields that stretched to the horizon. Many farms were separated by thick lines of trees that probably followed a stream or river.

He glanced at his phone. Google Maps took him west and said the turn was coming up. King had said the Cortez family lived on an old horse farm near Robert's Road and warned that there might be "activity" on the shoulder nearby.

It didn't take long for Frank to figure out what King meant.

He saw a farm up on his left that might be it—and a swarm of reporters, accompanied by news vans with their telescoping antennae and at least fifty members of the public crowded around the driveway. A cop stood in the road, directing traffic around the congestion. Another cop stood at the end of the driveway, waving people back. There was even a food truck, selling tacos and burritos to the gathered crowd.

Frank slowed and turned in, stopping at the cop who held up his hand.

"Sorry, no visitors," the cop said, a member of the CMPD that Frank didn't recognize.

Frank showed his ID as reporters swarmed around his Camaro.

"Chief King called me, asked me to come by," he said. The cop nodded and stepped out of the way, pulling a pair of cones aside so Frank's car would fit through.

Frank headed up the long driveway, passing over a cattle guard.

Behind him, in the rear-view mirror, he could see the many reporters gathered on the shoulder of the road. One of them was doing an on-camera interview, the farmhouse in the background, while another reporter held a microphone that read "BBC."

Wow, this woman was drawing a crowd. Frank also saw three men leaning against their cars and holding cameras, snapping pictures. Paparazzi, Frank guessed, waiting for something to happen. One of them, a man with a shock of red hair, snapped pictures of Frank and his car as Frank drove up the driveway.

The paved road snaked up a hill, passing a pond, and ended at a large farmhouse. It'd looked smaller from the road—from here, it looked like a mansion. Must be nice, Frank thought. Beyond the house was a massive red barn and what looked like part of a soccer field.

He parked and got out, heading for the door closest to the cars. Frank saw the Chief's car—it was identical to the other CMPD patrol vehicles, but the plate read "CMPD 1." Down the driveway, the red-haired dude was still taking Frank's picture. Frank shook his head and walked to the kitchen door, knocking.

The door opened, and a large woman greeted him. She looked like an East German wrestler, as if that was a thing anymore. Right away, Frank could tell she was a cop.

"Frank Harper?"

He nodded. "Yes, ma'am."

The woman pulled the door open further and let him inside.

"I'm Officer Leslie Davis. LAPD. Jessica and Chief King are upstairs. Do you know him?"

Frank nodded. "Pretty well," he said, looking around at the small kitchen. The walls and cabinets and fixtures all needed updating desperately. There was no way to tell how old this house was, but Frank was pretty sure this was the original kitchen.

Leslie sat down at the dining room table in a nook next to the kitchen and offered him coffee from a tray sitting on the table. He made himself a cup and they got started.

"Well, thanks for coming out."

"No problem."

"I'm sure you've heard about everything that happened," she began.

Frank shook his head. "No, not really. Just that she was spotted in town."

Leslie gave him a look. "Do you know who Jessica Mills is?"

"Sure, I guess. Movies, TV?"

"Yes."

"Okay," he said. "I don't watch a lot of movies. Sorry. She was here for rehab?"

"Something like that," Leslie said. She ran through the story quickly, with Frank jotting down the salient points in his journal. The young woman had a history of drugs, rehab, brushes with the law. Finally, a judge in LA got tired of her crap and gave her a choice—jail, or three months away from her crew of enablers.

"I like this Judge Watkins," Frank said with a smile.

"Me too," Leslie said. "Jessica had been to almost every rehab within a hundred miles of LA. The judge didn't feel like she was making any progress."

Frank heard people walking around upstairs, and Leslie hurried through the rest of it: road trip, six weeks here with no trouble, disguises. The judge in LA worked with the police and corrections to make it appear Mills had gone to jail, so no one was looking for her outside of Los Angeles. Frank was impressed—that wasn't an easy thing to pull off. It involved coordinating a lot of cops.

Jessica had been flying under the radar for almost two months here in Ohio before someone figured out who she was. Then the incident this morning at the Mum Festival, and all hell breaking loose.

"I can't believe the press is out there already," Leslie said as she wrapped up. "National and international, along with a few of our Los Angeles paparazzi thrown in for good measure."

Frank nodded. "I saw a BBC reporter. How'd they get here so fast?"

Leslie shrugged.

"Okay, so what's the job?"

Leslie smiled. "She's under house arrest here at the farmhouse, when she's not going and coming. Judge Watkins wants us to stay here in Ohio if we can, finish out her five weeks. Let her keep working, keep as low a profile as possible. The judge is worried about her safety, first and foremost."

"Makes sense."

"But to stay here, she needs around-the-clock protection. She needs to stay focused to finish her house arrest. But Chief King said Jessica needs paid bodyguards—his troops can help, but not around the clock."

Frank nodded, sitting back. "Gotcha. You're looking for private security."

"Yeah. How's that work? I'm used to deputies covering everything. What's it run?"

"I usually charge $100 an hour, but that's for investigations," Frank said, fibbing. It seemed like an opportune moment to raise his fees. "We can start with that, see how it goes. Not sure how to bill for something that's 24/7. I would accompany her everywhere she went, and we could get a person out here to watch the house. Family owns the property around the house?"

"No, it's another farmer."

"Well, we can talk to them and get permission to keep people off his land as well. What's the judge want?"

"She said that Jessica had to be guarded and stay on her rehab, essentially. She's really only here and at her work—she's been picking up hours at the grocery here in town. Part of her rehab."

"Okay," Frank said, writing it all down. "I'll need to coordinate with the Chief, obviously, and you." It was a good thing he'd brought his notebook.

CHAPTER 66
Paparazzi

Bill Hanford heard the news about Jessica Mills on Saturday around noon. It came up as a Twitter alert, and he scanned the low-resolution crowd photos, pictures of her disguise and all the other related tweets with eagerness. It was a break he could hardly imagine.

Not only had Jessica Mills not been sent to jail, she wasn't even in California.

Hanford scrambled, paying top dollar to get the first flight out of Los Angeles. He was in the air by noon, but he was forced to connect in Denver and didn't get into Dayton International until late on Saturday evening. He rented a car and raced to the location noted on Twitter. Local people and members of the press were sharing everything publicly, so it wasn't difficult to get an exact location.

Seven hours after the story broke on Twitter, Bill Hanford was leaning up against a TV news van, his cameras trained on the small farmhouse at the end of a long driveway.

There were a couple of other shooters there already, both up from Cincinnati. Hanford was the first paparazzi in from the west coast, but he was sure he wouldn't be the last. He shot some photos of people coming and going, and lots of pictures of the house from the road. Some old guy in a Camaro arrived, and Hanford snapped two dozen photos of him as the cops let him through. Must be part of the security detail Hanford assumed the locals were pulling together.

The local cops were keeping everyone back, cordoned off near the main road. But Hanford wasn't a dummy—he started looking for a way around the police cordon moments after he arrived.

The house was surrounded by fields of tall corn. He walked down the road, passing a Mexican food truck and waited until he was out of view of the police before crossing a culvert and disappearing into the cornfield next to the home.

Chapter 67
Protection

"So, you're a PI? Ex-cop?" Leslie asked as they sat waiting at the dining room table. "Chief King mentioned—"

"Yeah. PI license here in Ohio," Frank answered. "And I worked a few bodyguard jobs when I was down in Alabama. I'll have to bring in help."

There was noise in the hallway and two people walked into the kitchen, joining them. Frank stood and shook hands with Chief King, who gave him a strange look—almost one of relief.

"Good to see you, Frank," he said. "Been too long."

Frank smiled—it was the perfect "man" apology. "Yup. Good to see you."

Chief King introduced Jessica Mills, the Hollywood starlet. A young woman, thin and pretty, with dark hair. Frank shook her hand, looking at her face and her hair. She seemed familiar—he'd surely caught a movie she'd been in at some point in his life.

"Nice to meet ya," Frank said.

"Thanks," Jessica said. "Leslie, where are we?"

Leslie asked them all to sit down and Frank took the opportunity to make himself another cup of coffee. This was turning out to be a busy evening. The Hollywood girl sat as well, curling one leg up underneath her. To Frank, she moved with a dancer's grace, but she also betrayed a haughtiness that put him on his guard.

"Well, Mr. Harper's on board," Leslie said, glancing at Frank. "He can serve as your protection for the rest of our time here in Ohio."

Jessica turned to Frank. "You ever kill anyone?"

He looked at her and smiled. "Why? Would that make you feel better?"

"Yes. Yes, it would."

Frank glanced at Chief King and back to Jessica. "Well, yes. I have."

"Really?"

"I used to be a cop," he said with a sober nod. "It happened."

Jessica leaned forward. "Tell me about it."

He looked at her for a moment, then shook his head. "Something for another time. Leslie was telling me about your situation. Do you want to stay in Ohio?"

She sat back, frustrated. "Yes. I have to do 90 days, either here or in a jail in LA. Ohio is nicer. Barely. Can you keep me safe?"

He nodded. "Sure, if that's what you want. But if you're running around like a loose cannon, you're gonna get killed."

"Why do you say that? Do you know about my stalker? Once he finds out I'm in Ohio, he'll head this way."

Frank was confused and looked at Leslie.

"Jessica was nearly abducted eighteen months ago," Leslie said. "Though there was never any proof he was a serious—"

"He grabbed me and threw me over his shoulder," Jessica said, her voice rising in volume. "Drugged me. Huge guy. He had a car and the trunk was open."

"Sounds scary," Frank said, serious. "People are crazy." He jotted it all down just to be sure.

"You're taking notes now?" King asked with a smirk. "Nice journal."

Frank nodded. "Gotta keep it all straight, right?" He turned to Leslie and Jessica. "Okay, this will work. I'll need to bring in some help to cover the hours."

Chief King looked at Frank. "Who you thinking?"

"I just brought on Monty Robinson to help me with that Anderson Tool & Die job," Frank said.

King nodded. "You're working that case? Jill Anderson's been in a few times. Nothing came of it."

"She's convinced someone's stealing from the company," Frank said, looking back at Jessica and Leslie. "But between Monty and me, we'll manage," He looked at Leslie. "It'll get rough, though—round-the-clock is tiring. Plus I've got other jobs I'm working. She'll have to tag along."

"I'm right here," Jessica said, looking at Frank. "I hate it when people talk about me like I'm not in the room."

Frank nodded. "Sorry, ma'am. I didn't mean to offend."

Chief King leaned forward. "It's just that we're stretched thin as it is, Frank," he said with a knowing look. The information passed between them without needing to be said out loud: Deputy Peters was dead, and King was down a man on his roster. "We can handle the crowds, and provide some coverage, but the up-close security isn't something we have the manpower to cover."

Frank nodded. "I know, Chief. It's fine. We'll make it work." He looked at Leslie and Jessica. "So, what's the schedule?"

Leslie looked at a stack of papers on the table—she'd been referring to them off and on during their previous conversation. "Jessica's house arrest is up on November 29. Five weeks. We have to be back in LA for the hearing, and the judge wants us to drive back. We're planning on leaving on or around the 23rd," she said. "Until then, we stick to the schedule. Jessica works nights, mostly."

"You sticking with that?" Chief King asked.

Jessica nodded.

"She needs to," Leslie said. "If we can make it work." She looked at Frank. "And then here at the farm during the days."

"I don't see that being a problem," Frank said.

Jessica scoffed. "'Not a problem?' Have you seen the reporters out there? They'll follow me everywhere. And the paparazzi? They're even worse. I can't get away from them."

"Well, Chief, I'm assuming I have your permission to shield her from them as best as I can."

King looked at him. "What do you mean?"

"She deserves her privacy," Frank said.

"Within reason," King said, nodding. "I agree."

"Those paparazzi can be pretty aggressive," Leslie added.

Jessica nodded. "They think it's their right to follow me everywhere."

"Well, maybe in LA," Frank said. "Not here. Everyone has a right to expect privacy. We'll get her away from them."

"Just be careful," King said.

"So, we're agreed," Frank said, summarizing. "I'll provide security around-the-clock, call in the chief if I need help."

"Agreed," Leslie said.

"And we do things my way," Frank said quietly. He looked at Jessica. "My way. That means we go where I say we go and we do what I say we do. Got it?"

Leslie looked at the young woman. "Jessica?"

Jessica looked at Frank, staring at him, sizing him up. Frank waited, doing his patented silence thing. Silence made people uncomfortable—he'd gotten his share of confessions and information from suspects or informants by just waiting them out. He let the silence wash over the table until the young woman finally nodded.

"Okay. I guess."

Leslie nodded. "It's either that or we head back to LA. We have to make this work, or you start over."

Jessica nodded, looking at her nails. "What about my 'disguise?' Is there any point in keeping that up? Ferrara went to bed—she was too freaked out. Can I tell her we're bagging the whole disguise thing?"

Leslie looked at Frank. "What do you think?"

"Keep it," Frank said. "It will keep her from being recognized by casual observers, right? That will cut down on interactions. And I'll figure out what to do with the photographers."

"I'm sick of being a brunette," Jessica said, playing with her hair. "It's so ugly."

"Five more weeks. You can handle it."

Jessica nodded, quieted.

Frank turned to Leslie. "I'll get a contract sent over tonight."

"What about the public running into her at the grocery—"

"Let me worry about that."

"Okay," Leslie said. "The rest of the time?"

Frank looked at Jessica. "She can tag along with me."

Jessica looked at him. "What?"

"I have other cases," Frank said. "I'm not gonna drop them for you. You can tag along so I can keep an eye on you."

Leslie looked at Frank. "You sure?"

"It's the only way. She can have meals at my house, too, if she's not too much trouble."

Jessica put her hands on her hips. "What? Are you serious?"

"Sure," Frank said, sitting back. "Welcome to my life."

Chapter 68
Cornfield

Hanford made his way through the cornfield, traveling parallel to the farmhouse and its extensive lawn. He stayed in the first couple of rows, moving south, peeking through the tall corn every once in a while to make sure he was staying even with the farmhouse. To his left, he could see the knot of cops and reporters near the road.

As he walked, he snapped more photos, using mostly his backup Canon. You never knew what the tabloids would pay for, and a comprehensive photo essay of the "Jessica Mills Hideout" might bring top dollar. He snapped photos of the lawn and a private pond, which featured a zip-line and an outdoor BBQ area.

Moving on, he got good pictures of the house, moving around it and the barn that sat behind the house, getting more photos. All the windows were closed and the shades drawn, so he couldn't get any inside, but he kept going.

Near the rear of the home, the barn doors were standing open, and he could see an old car inside, partially assembled. It looked like whoever lived here was working on the car, either building or refurbishing it.

Not one to be intimidated by unimportant things like fences or property lines or personal privacy, Hanford scaled the fence, climbing it easily and dropping to the ground on the other side. Adjusting his cameras and straps, Hanford quickly crossed the patch of yard that separated the cornfield from the barn.

Inside, Hanford took more photos with the backup Canon. Yep, an old car, broken down. There were Amazon boxes of new parts on one shelf.

Losing interest, he snapped a few photos of the parts and the car and the inside of the barn. He also pocketed several of the smaller car parts—you never knew what might be valuable. People paid big money for souvenirs from crime scenes. He'd heard from a friend that when a famous Hollywood actor OD'd on the sidewalk outside of a nightclub back in the 1990s, the syringe on the sidewalk—supposedly the one he'd shot up with—went for over $100,000 to some collector.

Working his way through the barn, Hanford came to a large window that looked out on the farmhouse and a smattering of cars parked between the house and barn—

And he saw Jessica.

She was inside the home, seated at a small dining room table. She looked sad, tired.

Hanford grabbed his main camera and started shooting. Jessica was talking to some people. One was another woman, tall and wide. Looked like Linda Hamilton from the Terminator movies. And two guys, both older. One was a cop, the other was the old dude from the Camaro.

Hanford kept snapping pictures, doing so without looking through the viewfinder. It was a talent he'd learned long ago—you never knew what your camera might catch. He moved in closer, stepping out of the barn. Scrunching down, he walked slowly over to the window, his camera trained on the group inside. They looked to be having a serious discussion about something, maybe what to do about all the reporters and—

Jessica looked up and saw him through the window.

The look on her face, captured instantly on Hanford's camera, was priceless. She stood, her mouth open, and pointed.

It was the shot he'd flown half-way across the country to get. He snapped away, calculating how valuable that one photo would be.

There was a flurry of activity inside and Hanford backed away, heading for the barn. He figured he could make it back into the shadows before anyone spotted him, but the four people rushed out of the house.

"What are you doing here?" the cop said, looking right at him.

"Paparazzi," Hanford said. "It's a free country—"

"You're on private property."

The older man approached, and Hanford suddenly got the impression he used to be a cop. He had a strange look on his face and Hanford wasn't sure—

"Give me the camera."

"No," Hanford said. "I don't care if I'm—"

The old man made a sudden, quick move, looking like he was falling to the side. For a moment it looked like the old man was tripping, but then Hanford felt his own legs swept out from under him and he went down hard. Hanford dropped the camera he'd been carrying. The old

man, perfectly fine, caught it in mid-air before it could hit the ground.
"The cop stepped forward. "Frank, what are you doing?"
"Getting those photos,"
Hanford wasn't hurt—more surprised, really. The older man had used some kind of karate move and dumped him right on his ass without a moment's hesitation.
"It's gotta have a card or something," the old man said, showing it to Jessica.
Hanford finally got his breath back. "You don't—hey, don't you touch my camera! That's private property!"
The cop looked down at him. "Oh, now you're concerned about privacy."
Jessica Mills walked up between them and looked down at Hanford with a smirk. "That's where you rats belong, Hanford. On the ground." She took the camera from the older man. "Here, let me see."
Hanford started to stand but the old man gave him a look that pinned Hanford's butt to the ground. "Just stay right there, buddy. And be glad I didn't hurt you."
"I'll sue you," Hanford said. "I'll sue you for assault."
The older man didn't seem concerned.
"I wouldn't do that," the tall woman said, looking down. Out here in the dark, she looked even larger. "This is private property and you're trespassing. There are signs all over—I checked. Chief, what do you think?"
"Yep," the chief said. "I could arrest you right now."
"Here it is," Jessica said, pointing at the SD card slot. The older man popped it out with a fingernail and pocketed the card, then dropped the camera in Hanford's lap. "The other one."
"What?"
"The other camera."
"Why?"
The older man didn't say anything. He just put his hand out, waiting. Hanford looked at the others—there was nothing but contempt on any of their faces.
Hanford stood, slowly.
"No," Hanford said. "I don't think so. It's mine."
"You sure?" the older man asked.
"Yes," Hanford said, putting his hands on his hips. "You've already confiscated my property, which is illegal. I should be able to keep the other two or three hundred photos I have with this camera," he said,

lifting the Canon and showing it to them. "It's also—"

The older man's hand moved so quickly it was hard to track. He stepped up and punched Hanford right in the eye, a soft punch that was more surprising than painful.

"Oh, Jesus!" Hanford held his eye, rubbing at it.

"Frank, watch it," the cop said.

Hanford looked at the cop, who wasn't moving to stop this Frank guy.

"Camera," Frank said, his hand out.

It was clear where this was going. Looking with one eye, Hanford could see there was no other way out. He reached up and pulled the camera strap from around his neck and handed the Canon over to the older man. It was his beat-up backup camera, and the Frank guy and Jessica started looking it over.

The cop stepped forward and started frisking him, running his hands over Hanford's pockets. "From now on, you stay off this property, son," the cop said. "I mean it. And tell your paparazzi buddies. The rules are different here in Ohio. I don't care what you get away with in Los Angeles—you guys start hopping fences, you will go to jail."

The cop pulled the car parts from Hanford's pockets.

"What the hell are these?"

Jessica looked over. "Parts. From the vehicle-in-progress. In the barn."

"Well, that's theft, right there," the tall woman said.

"Yep," the cop said. "Larceny, maybe grand theft, depending on the value. Plus trespassing. Maybe menacing, chasing Jessica down like that and taking pictures without her permission. You think so?"

The tall woman nodded. "Yes, I do."

The cop agreed, then turned back to Hanford. "And I'm sure if I stand here for a few more minutes, I could think of a few other things." The cop looked at him. "Maybe you should just take off now," he said, pointing at the fence and field beyond. "Save me the paperwork."

Hanford looked at Jessica. "My other camera."

She shook her head. "Just consider it part of doing business."

Hanford looked around and got the message. They were letting him go, but at a price. No charges, no jail, if he left. Right now. Down one camera.

Hanford sighed and took a step back toward the barn. The cop looked at him expectantly, not saying anything.

Hanford took another step back, a larger one. He hoped none of the other paparazzi were seeing this humiliating incident, but the house was blocking their view.

"I'm leaving. We good?"

The chief took one step forward and put his hand on the butt of his holstered weapon.

"It depends on how fast you can run."

Hanford backed away, slowly at first, then turned and sprinted for the fence. In a moment, he was over it and making his way back to the road.

Chapter 69
Good News...

After the photographer was gone, the group headed back into the house.

"I can't believe you punched him," Jessica said with a smile. She was carrying the paparazzi's Canon, still fiddling with the SD card to get it out of the slot.

"Yeah, you shouldn't have done that, Frank," Chief King said. "I don't need people suing us."

"Private property," Frank said, handing the other SD card to Jessica. "Who was that guy?"

They sat back down at the table and Jessica popped out the second SD card, holding it up. "Bill Hanford. He's one of the worst. He's the guy that took those really bad photos of Tyler McKenzie's wreck last year. Remember those?"

"No, not really," Frank said, taking the card from her.

"He's a movie star," she said, looking at him. "How can you not know who he is?"

Frank shrugged.

"Okay," Jessica said, drawing out the word. "Anyway, he was out with one of his girlfriends. Hanford was following them. They wrecked, crashing near the Mondrian. Hotel. Anyone remember?" She looked around but their faces were blank.

Leslie nodded slowly. "Vaguely, I guess."

"Well, Hanford got out of his car and took photos instead of helping them," Jessica said, disgusted. "The girlfriend had brain trauma, wandering around the accident scene with a head injury."

"Oh, I remember that," Leslie said. "There was talk of charging Hanford with something. But there's no law in California that says you have to help people."

"Well, there should be," Chief King said, and Frank nodded, agreeing. "It's just common human decency," the cop said. "You have to help where you can."

The table got quiet. Frank glanced around and saw they were all in thought. He slid the camera over and popped the card back in, then powered on the camera and looked at the back. He saw a VIEW button and pushed it and started scrolling through the photos.

"Wow, these are exciting." He held up the camera and showed them. "Lots of photos of the barn, the corn. A few through the windows into the property."

Jessica smiled. "You'd be surprised. Tabloids would pay big money for those."

"Hmm," Frank said. "More than you guys are paying me to babysit you? Maybe I should change professions..."

She looked up but Frank was grinning.

"That's not funny," she said.

"It's kinda funny," Frank answered.

"Okay, let's wrap this up," Chief King said. "We're all good? The CMPD will provide traffic coverage as needed, and some help at the grocery. Frank and his people—"

"Monty," Frank interjected.

"Frank and Monty will be with you 24 hours a day. Officer Davis, will that work?"

"Yes, I think so. Provided things go well, we should be able to finish out her house arrest."

"What's the end date again?" Chief King had his notepad out again, writing things down. That reminded Frank, who grabbed his journal and started doing the same again, drawing a look and a smile from the Chief.

Leslie looked on her phone. "We have to be back in LA on the 29th, so we'll start the drive back on the 23rd."

"October 23rd, right?" Chief King was jotting it down.

"Yup."

"We can't fly back?" Jessica asked. "I don't want another driving trip."

"I'll have to ask," Leslie said. "She wanted us to drive both ways."

"But that was before Jessica was outed," the chief said. "Security for a road trip like that would be a nightmare. You'll be followed all the way back to California. At least on a plane, you could lock things down."

Leslie nodded. "I'll discuss it with the judge. But, for our purposes, assume we'll be leaving on the 23rd."

They covered a few more points, details on coordinating communications between them. Chief King reminded Frank that the use of force was to be discouraged, and Frank said he'd try to keep from hurting anyone, a remark that drew smiles from everyone around the table except for Chief King.

"I'm serious, Frank," the chief said. "Your job is to protect Ms. Mills here, not beat the crap out of every paparazzi that comes to town."

"I wouldn't mind," Jessica said.

"Oh, I bet you wouldn't," Leslie added.

"Okay, so you're good here tonight," Frank said. "Stay in, don't go out. Either I or my associate, Monty, will be here in the morning. He or I will be with you whenever you're out of this house. Chief, can you let your deputies know we'll be coming and going? And give them Monty's information?"

"Will do."

Frank looked at Jessica. "Don't worry, miss. Between us, Officer Davis, and the local police, we've got you covered. This is going to work out fine."

Jessica looked at him and smiled.

Chapter 70
...and Bad

Crazy. This was all just crazy.

He had the BMW mostly packed already. Blake was rushing around, throwing things into his suitcase while keeping one ear on the news from the TVs in his office.

Jessica Mills wasn't in Los Angeles.

It had been breaking national news all day, covered by every news channel. If it weren't so shocking, it would have been a delightful day of watching his girl, Jessica Mills, on every screen and on every channel. She was all over the news—when they weren't talking about the news updates, they were showing clips from her movies and TV shows.

But what had happened in the last day was stranger than any fictional story she'd appeared in. She'd gone to someplace in Ohio to serve out her house arrest. As crazy as it seemed, she'd gone undercover, wearing a disguise and everything. Photos of Jessica in her new get-up were all over Twitter and Reddit. People in Ohio broke the story originally, posting photos of the Hollywood icon dressed down and "uglified," as one of the reporters had put it.

And while it was difficult for Blake to imagine Jessica as anything but beautiful, the disguise was pretty bad. She was wearing a horrible wig, bad glasses, and no makeup—except for a very fake-looking "birthmark" on her neck.

Blake didn't care. Jessica wasn't in some prison, or behind the walls of some guarded rehab center. She wasn't even in her mansion in the Hollywood Hills. She was staying in some regular house in a little town near Dayton, Ohio. There were photos of her at a festival, surrounded by regular folks.

And, apparently, there was no security of any kind.

It was perfect.

Blake had done the calculations while he packed. If he drove through the night, Blake could be in Dayton in fourteen hours. Or he could stay overnight in Atlanta and get into Dayton tomorrow afternoon. Either way, it would only a matter of getting Jessica alone long enough to get her into his car.

Chapter 71
Starlet

The next few days were crazy but, for Jessica, they were a relief. Her secret was out. People knew who she was and knew where she was, and it was no longer a massive stressor to keep her identity a secret. Keeping up the costume was a good idea, but they weren't putting as much effort into it. Even though people knew who she was and knew how she was dressed, it still kept the casual observer from spotting her.

In many ways, things didn't change much with her exposure to the public. She still spent most of her time at the farm and the grocery, only now she was accompanied everywhere she went by either Frank Harper, his employee Monty, Leslie or one of the deputies from the local police force.

Jessica had stopped calling the Cortez's home "the compound" somewhere along the way after she saw how it made Ferrara and her mother depressed and frustrated. At some point, Jessica had realized she was hurting their feelings—and it was only right to be nice. They were putting her up—and putting up with this huge disruption in their lives.

After the initial furor died down, the Cortez family returned from their impromptu trip to Indianapolis, but they were still forced to navigate the crowd of news vans and onlookers at the base of their driveway.

Jessica liked Frank and Monty. Things got kicked off well, with Frank taking the day shifts and Monty the night shifts at the grocery. During the days, Frank would take her around town if needed, but she mostly stayed at the Cortez farm, working on her scripts or on the computer. Judge Watkins had relaxed her "no social media" rule, and Jessica was now allowed to post occasional items to her Instagram and other feeds.

Initially, she explained what had happened, but then she took to posting photos of her "new" life—pictures from the farm, or selfies of her at work, stacking oranges or unboxing fish sticks. People seemed to love the idea that she was working at an "everyman" job, doing her time and living a "normal" lifestyle, whatever that meant.

Jessica liked it too.

Her shifts at the grocery continued as normal. Monty, a very amiable African-American man with an infectiously pleasant attitude, would pick her up at the Cortez farm after dark and drive her to Food Town. Fans were usually gathered in the grocery or just outside, and Jessica would sign a few autographs or take selfies with people before heading inside, where she'd get to work.

But her hours at Food Town were nearly identical to how they had been before: stacking, unstacking, piling up produce, culling out the bad bananas or pulling expired product off the shelves of bread.

Cheryl and Roger didn't seem phased at all by her celebrity status—on the first night back at work, Jessica had expected long conversations about her life. Instead, Cheryl made one comment when she arrived: "I hope you're still willing to work hard," to which Jessica nodded. Roger didn't say anything. He was either too embarrassed to mention it, or, Jessica started to think, it was possible that he didn't even know about it. Roger struck her as a serious stoner, so he probably had no idea why there were now groups of people outside the grocery at opening and closing, taking pictures through the windows.

The only real change: she asked everyone to call her Jessica. But she kept the wig and kept working just as hard as she'd worked before.

There was something relaxing about real work, actual labor.

It made the time fly by—her first night back on the job, after the selfies and the autographs, Jessica threw herself into stacking boxes of macaroni and cheese and sorting all of the pasta sauces. She finished her work early and helped out Roger with his. Her arms and shoulders got sweaty and she could feel the muscles in her legs and back joining in. They grew tired and, at the same time, seemed to vibrate with energy. She was getting paid to work out

Her life settled into a nice pattern as Jessica worked to finish out her days of house arrest in Ohio. Her nights were busy with work, her days filled with sleeping or reading or just relaxing, surfing the internet and reading about herself, posting an occasional comment. Most of the commentary was positive, but not all of it.

Oh, and Judge Watkins had lied.

That accident in Los Angeles, the one Jessica had caused? Both of the people in the car had survived. Watkins must've been trying to scare her, and it had worked.

Now, looking back at it, Jessica wasn't even that mad. It was a fib, one that Jessica suffered under for a few weeks. It didn't hurt anyone, other than Jessica's opinion of herself.

And looking back on it, her ego needed to come down a peg or two—or ten.

Some people on the Internet seemed to think she was getting off too easy. "A Vacation in Ohio," one article read. And it wasn't far from the truth. In some ways, Jessica agreed with them. It was not the kind of treatment she would have received if she'd been a "normal" person. Jessica would have been sent to jail, no hesitation. But Jessica resolved to make the most of Judge Watkins' leniency and try to come through this situation for the better.

And she rode along with Frank sometimes on his investigations. She pretended she was doing research for a role as a private investigator, asking him questions until he got pissed and told her to be quiet. He was not a talker, to say the least.

Jessica Mills conducted a few interviews in the days after her exposure at the Mum Festival. She sat down again with Tina Armstrong and did a long video interview, going into depth for the first time on many of the details of her house arrest, including the details of their road trip east.

Leslie Davis had insisted on driving Jessica to the interview, strangely, but then Jessica got a distinct vibe that something was going on between her and Tina Armstrong. Apparently, they'd been chatting, setting up the interview, and had been out for drinks twice. Good for them.

The interview was featured in the October 25th edition of the *Gazette*, the entire paper dedicated to Jessica's appearance in Cooper's Mill.

Jessica also had arranged for a few of the news people camped at the bottom of the driveway to come up to the house for short, on-camera interviews. They had sat at "Bob's Fishing Spot," with a great view of the pond and the house, and Jessica had patiently answered questions from folks from the BBC and NBC and Bloomberg News. Frank had made sure that the interviews didn't go on too long, and he'd taken great pleasure in bossing the news people around.

Things were pretty normal, up until Wednesday night, her night off from the grocery. For some reason, Frank and Monty had switched shifts, and a very sleepy Monty hung out at the Cortez house all day on Wednesday even though he'd been at the grocery with Jessica

Tuesday overnight.

"You look like you could use a nap," she'd told him. "Or a cup of coffee."

"You're not kidding," Monty said. "I've had three, but I could use a break. Can't wait for Frank to get here."

Jessica scowled. "Yeah, what's going on? I thought you did the nights."

"He said he wanted you to tag along tonight. He's working a case."

"What?"

"Yeah," Monty said, yawning. "Get ready for a boring stakeout."

Chapter 72
Partner

A few hours later, Frank Harper sat in his Camaro, watching the front of the house. The Robinson guy was in there, he was pretty sure—he'd tailed the guy from work, and then left for a few minutes to pick up food and his "partner." Tyler Robinson's car was still parked in front when Frank got back.

He'd also snapped a bunch of photos tonight with his "new" camera, the one "donated" to him by one pissed-off paparazzi from Los Angeles. It was a great camera, as far as Frank could tell, and much nicer than anything he could afford, even though that Bill Hanford guy had dismissed it as his "crappy backup" and been willing to trade it for his freedom.

"I'm bored."

Frank looked over at Jessica Mills. It was still bizarre, thinking that this young woman, an actress he'd seen in a half-dozen movies and TV shows, was bumming around with him in a small town in Ohio and taking part in a stakeout.

"Sorry," he said. "I'm not great at entertaining folks. There's a stack of magazines in the back."

"What are we doing here?"

Frank looked over at Jessica and, for the tenth time in an hour, regretted his decision to bring her along for his work.

"It's called a 'stakeout'."

She looked around at the houses. "I know that. But why?"

"I'm following someone," Frank said slowly, as if he were explaining it to a five-year-old. "He's in that house," he said, pointing. "We wait and watch."

She looked around and shook her head. "Still bored."

"Only boring people get bored."

"What?"

"I had a partner, Ben Stone. He used to say that. We would go on stakeouts and he would always bring something to do and sometimes I'd forget and get bored."

"Sounds like a genius. What happened to him?"

"He got killed."

Jessica's head spun around. "Really? Are you serious?"

"Yeah," Frank said, looking at the house.

"What happened?"

"He got shot," Frank said quietly. "We were in Florida, working a case. He got a lead and didn't tell anyone. Went by himself to check it out. Got shot."

She didn't say anything.

"No witty retort?" Frank glanced at her. "Nothing snarky to say? That's the problem with your generation. You're scared of everything. Criminals and the weather and animals and global warming. The international banking system."

"What? I'm not scared."

"You people are petrified," Frank said, looking at the house. "And you hide behind snide comments. Everything is sarcasm. Everything is a snotty retort. Try going a day—hell, try going an hour without saying something with a snarky tone. Bet you can't do it."

"I can do that, cowboy."

"I bet you can't."

"What's the wager?"

He thought about it for a moment. "Winner buys dinner."

"Deal."

He nodded at a stack of papers and magazines in the back seat. "Grab something to read if you're really bored. Laura, my daughter, loves Entertainment Weekly and People and gave me a stack. We could be here a while."

She started to say something and stopped herself. It looked like it physically hurt her to not retort with a "I can't WAIT to sit here for an hour" or "THANK YOU for letting me read your magazines" or whatever snarky phrase she was about to utter.

Instead, she turned around and grabbed a stack from his back seat and started thumbing through them. Laura had donated them. He'd been complaining about being bored, but flipping through her "solution" had turned him off—it was all about how vapid the movie industry had become, or was becoming. He was left unimpressed.

Jessica flipped through the first magazine loudly, as if she was trying to make a point or something. When he didn't say anything, she cleared her throat. Still nothing. Finally, she turned to him.

"This isn't any better. How long do we have to sit here?"

Frank nodded at the squat brick home three doors down. "Until I figure out what he's doing in there."

She looked at the house. "Are they screwing?"

Frank looked over at her slowly. "Wow. Thanks for being subtle."

"Well, you didn't tell me much," she said. "And Monty was too tired to explain why I'm helping you here at night instead of spending my night off as snug as a bug in a rug at Ferrara's house."

She looked at him, but he didn't answer. Frank wasn't used to having to make conversation, especially on a stakeout. It had been years since he had a partner. Maybe if he didn't talk, she'd fall asleep and leave him in peace—

"Tell me again about this case."

He looked at her and smirked. "Like I said, I'm not here to entertain you."

"I know that," she said, getting quiet. "You really don't like me, do you?"

He glanced over at her. Why was he giving her such a hard time? He looked in her eyes and suddenly knew.

"It's 'cause I was a cop."

She seemed confused. "What?"

"I was a cop."

"I know that. What do you mean?"

He sighed and rubbed the steering wheel with one finger, dislodging a mustard stain and flicking it to the floorboard. "I spent a lot of time tracking down criminals. You know."

"I don't. Not really."

"We investigate, follow leads," he said, shifting uncomfortably in the driver's seat. If he was going to be doing a lot of stakeouts, he needed to make this seat more comfortable. Maybe get one of those wooden bead thingys he'd seen in taxi cabs. Did those actually work? Did they make the hours of sitting more comfortable?

Frank looked at the house again.

She turned and looked at him. "And?"

"And what?"

"You just kind of drifted off."

Frank shook his head. "Sorry, I need more coffee. Anyway, cops track down the bad guys. But the prosecutors decide if there's a good case or not. Sounds like out in Los Angeles, certain 'folks' get away with stuff."

"Famous people?"

"You tell me."

She turned and looked at the house. "You're not wrong, cowboy," she said, using a word he'd heard her use on more than one occasion. It sounded funny, coming out of her mouth. "They let us skate. Maybe too much."

Frank hesitated, trying to decide if he should press the issue or just leave it alone. But he couldn't help himself. "Rich people don't think the rules apply to them," Frank continued. "I've seen it. They have lawyers and cash and big houses. They sneer at the 'little folk' who actually go to jail."

"I know," Jessica said quietly.

"I read up on your case a little," Frank said. "I like that Judge Watkins. She got sick of the 'Hollywood Shuffle,' as she called it. You're lucky you ended up here."

She nodded, not saying anything. He realized she was starting to cry. "Oh, don't do that," he said. "I don't know what I'm talking about."

Hollywood starlet Jessica Mills opened his glove compartment and fished out an old napkin, dabbing at her eyes. "No, you're right. You're right. And I do need to make the most of this. I do."

"What about your entourage? I'm surprised they haven't flown in—"

"Judge Watkins wouldn't allow it," Jessica said, drying her eyes. "They're not allowed to be here."

Frank thought about it. "Probably for the best."

She nodded. "Yeah. I need to cut some of them loose anyway," she said. "I need a new agent. Hank's my agent and business manager, but I need to upgrade."

"Better roles?"

"Yeah, he's not putting me up for the stuff I want to be doing. And Scott, my publicist, works for him. He doesn't book me in the right things. Plus, there are other folks I need to drop," she said cryptically.

The car got quiet, and Frank let the silence linger. Ten minutes passed, then twenty. At some point, she stopped sobbing and went back to her magazines, reading through several while Frank made notes in his book.

An hour passed. Frank stared out the window, watching the front of the run-down house. He watched cars come and go and made notes about anyone passing the house. She read, alternating between the magazines and checking her phone.

"I needed that," she said.

"What?"

"A good cry," she said with a smile. "Oh, I hate this bitch," she said, holding up a magazine. Frank looked over and she was pointing at a photo of a movie star that he recognized from a movie he'd enjoyed a few months ago.

"Really?" he said. "She seems nice."

"No, she's not," Jessica said. "She's a bitch."

"That's not very nice."

"I don't care," she said. "She stole a part from me. Had her representative call the production company and pretend to be my agent, told them I wasn't interested in the part. Swooped in and stole it."

"That doesn't make any sense," he said. "That can't be the way they do business out there."

"It is," she said, flipping angrily to the next page. "It's all word of mouth and who you know and whose ass you're kissing. Or who you're banging." She flipped a few more pages. "There's no...what's the word when you say what you mean and mean what you say?"

"Integrity?"

"Yeah, integrity."

"Well, they say it starts at home."

"What?"

He looked over at her. "Kindness, charity, integrity. Those things start with you. You have to have them first, then you'll know who else has them, right? Sounds like you're hanging around the wrong people."

The car grew silent as she went back to her magazine, occasionally talking about the different people she saw and articles she read. Frank ignored her running commentary. She seemed to think he cared about the intimate details about these people's lives. She told him where they liked to get coffee and which ones went to yoga classes and which ones had private trainers. He didn't have the heart to tell her that he didn't care. It was apparently very important to her.

Clearly, her life was full of competition with these other women. It was sad.

Jessica soon got bored with the magazines and put them aside. She started talking, telling him about her life in Los Angeles and her career. She told him about the night of the accident, and then recounted in vivid detail the incident with her stalker. It sounded scary, and he said as much.

After a bout of silence, Frank saw her looking at the house.

"Okay, seriously. Tell me what's going on with this case."

Frank shook his head and looked back at the house. "Tyler Robinson, been coming to this woman's house twice a week for two months," Frank said, nodding. "His wife is my client. She's convinced he's cheating on her, wants proof. I've gotten photos of him coming and going, of course, but nothing else. Based on what I've seen, he's probably sleeping with this woman."

"Okay," she said.

"He's not very careful, though. Drives straight here after work, and they never meet anywhere else. I've confirmed they don't work together."

"What's her name?"

Frank grabbed his book and flipped to the page on this case. "Natalie. Pine."

Jessica nodded and got out her phone, tapping on it. She'd been referring to it off and on since they'd arrived. He'd thought about asking her to put it away a couple of times, but she seemed to be judiciously using it instead of just staring at it for the hours they'd been here.

"That's interesting," she said.

Frank glanced over. "What?"

"You know what she does?"

"No," he said.

"She teaches dancing," Jessica said, turning the phone to him. "In-home instruction. Charges by the hour."

Frank took the phone, shaking his head. "No, she works in HR for some big company down in Dayton. I looked into her background, did a check."

He flipped through the photos on her phone, swiping up awkwardly. There were dozens of her in various outfits, and one with her and a male partner holding up a trophy. "What is this?"

"Instagram? Heard of it?"

"Yeah, but I don't look at it. It's for kids, right?"

Jessica flipped through the photos. "Looks like she works days in HR. Does dancing lessons at night. Won a few competitions."

Frank looked at the photos. "You're saying—"

"Could be she keeps it quiet," Jessica said, taking the phone back, doing another search. "Not the kind of hobby a person in HR should have, maybe? I don't know. There's nothing on her Facebook about it. And she doesn't have a website," Jessica said, waving her phone at him.

"That's strange," Frank said. "I did a few searches, and nothing came up. Facebook, LinkedIn, background check. Nothing about dancing. Is she really teaching or is it a cover?"

"I don't know," Jessica said. "Any reason for him to be taking dancing lessons?"

And then it clicked.

"Dammit."

"What?" Jessica asked, looking over.

"He's got an anniversary coming up," Frank said, looking at his notes. "The wife said something about their tenth wedding anniversary. She said they were planning on renewing their vows in Mexico before all this happened."

Jessica smiled. "Sounds like I cracked the case. Partner."

Frank looked at her. "I don't know about that. They could be banging."

"Wow, thanks for being subtle," Jessica said, chiding him.

"And there is money missing from their joint account—"

"Dancing lessons," Jessica said. "He paid cash so there would be no names on the credit card receipt. They share credit cards, right?"

"—and he's always leaving sweaty—"

"Dancing is hard work," she added. "I've done it for a few roles. Exhausting," she said with a grin. "You ever danced?"

Frank shook his head and looked at the house, suddenly angry. Had he wasted weeks on a case that could have been closed with a simple internet search? He didn't use Instagram, but he knew the younger generation did. Maybe having a younger partner wasn't such a bad idea.

Chapter 73
New Arrival

Tuesday night, Blake Oleander sat in Ricky's, a dirty bar in downtown Cooper's Mill, surrounded by local morons.

The place was gross, heathen-filled. Actually, the whole town was a pit, a Midwestern hovel filled with idiots. The town was tiny, and there were tomatoes in the gutters. He'd seen at least ten flatbed trucks filled with the red orbs passing through town, chugging along and losing product whenever they turned.

Today, he'd been out scouting the parade route and the whole town smelling like spaghetti sauce. Someone had said they canned tomatoes here, bringing in product from all over. He didn't care—and it didn't help when you stepped on one crossing the street, the red liquid ruining his nice shoes.

Not that he was wearing nice shoes in this dive bar. It stank of old beer and desperation. He was used to much nicer places, of course, and the swill they served here matched the décor, some tacky, dated take on Mardi Gras. It made him sick to his stomach, seeing his beautiful city and its signature celebration tainted like this. The beer was warm and cheap and never stopped, as evidenced by the advanced states of inebriation he saw in all the rednecks around him in the bar.

Blake stretched, trying to work the kinks out of his neck. He'd been sleeping in his car the last several nights, and it was starting to wear on him.

He'd arrived on Sunday, after staying overnight in some tiny town south of Atlanta, then driving the rest of the way up, nervous. He'd gotten in late on Sunday and his first stop had been, of course, the house where Jessica Mills was holed up. He drove back and forth several times, then drove the neighborhood near her new home, looking for ways to approach the house without being seen. He also scouted it on Google Maps, realizing the house backed on a bunch of cornfields, which would allow him to get very close without being seen at all.

Seeing the little encampment of news vans and paparazzi and fans, he joined them, asking around and getting updated on her situation. Most of the regular folks were fans of Jessica's, just like him, and some held up signs with Jessica's picture on it.

Blake talked to as many people as possible, finding out that Jessica had hired private security that traveled with her everywhere she went. It was disappointing. Blake also saw that the local cops were involved, providing the roadblock at the Cortez home and limiting the number of people who had access to Jessica.

Blake needed a plan.

But he didn't spend all his time at the encampment. It didn't feel right, standing out there with those other people and sharing his adoration for Jessica with them. His love for her was his own private business and something deeper, truer. Being around others that "loved" her only cheapened his experience. They didn't love her the way he did. They couldn't. He'd spent years adoring her, from afar and from close up.

He'd actually held her in his arms.

What did these "fans" and bored news reporters and angry-looking paparazzi know about Jessica? They didn't know her the way Blake did.

He loved her.

But Blake also followed his instincts, and they rarely failed him. It seemed like a bad idea to be around the TV cameras and photographers, so when he was out at the encampment, he tried to stay on the edges and out of the limelight. He wasn't interested in getting his photo taken or getting spotted on television. He needed to plan how he was going to get close to her.

Blake had spent the last few days drifting around the little town, getting the lay of the land and trying to get a sense of it and the people who lived here. He asked around, learning as much as he could. Blake visited the park where she'd been outed, taking pictures of where it had happened for his wall back home. He snapped selfies of him on the swing she'd been riding on, and of the little merry-go-round where those mean kids had been riding before they jumped off and grabbed her wig.

The festival was still going on, surprising him. Blake wandered the two hundred booths that had been temporarily set up in the City Park, a small park north of the downtown, and learned that the festival would last ten days, ending on Sunday. But before that, there would be more festivities—a marathon, a beauty pageant, and several

concerts held in conjunction with the festival in the park.
And a huge parade through the downtown.

People talked in this little town, and Blake listened. Everyone wanted to talk about Jessica Mills, who she was, how she'd come to be the town's newest resident, however temporary. Everyone shared their excitement about her presence or talked about how they'd been at the park that day when she was exposed to the world. People talked about her working at Food Town, their local grocery, but he dismissed the idea of approaching her there—she worked overnight, when the place was locked up tight. No, he needed to get her out in the open. The grocery wouldn't work, and neither would the home she was staying in.

Blake kept talking to people, chatting with anyone who would talk. They speculated on Jessica, wondering what she was doing right now. He asked how often she came out into public, and where she went. Some people swore they saw her in the downtown, shopping, while others insisted she'd been back to the Mum Festival grounds to buy souvenirs and try the famous Fireman Waffles.

Many people seemed convinced Jessica would be at the big parade on Saturday morning, October 29. It would wind through the downtown. One man said she'd been asked to be the parade guest of honor, but she'd turned it down. Others thought she might ride in the parade, perhaps on the lead float. From what Blake was hearing, no one knew anything for sure, but the whole town was caught up in the speculation.

Blake stretched again and sipped at his warm beer, waving at the barkeep to bring him another. When she did, he didn't acknowledge her or even look up. Instead, Blake Oleander surfed his phone, reading up on the Mum Festival and the parade route that would snake through the downtown.

He read about the different floats and marching bands that would be making up the bulk of the parade, and learned where the marching bands and floats were to assemble on Saturday morning before the parade started. He studied the varied, diverse groups of people who would be participating in the parade—among them a large group of Shriners, two horse-drawn carriages, various local businesses, a troupe of clowns, and several monster trucks.

He had an idea.

Chapter 74
Dancing

As usual, Taylor Robinson wrapped up his time with the Pine woman around midnight and headed home. Frank and Jessica sat in his car, watching, and Frank snapped more pictures with his "new" camera.

"What are you going to do?"

He looked at her. "I don't know," he said. And he didn't. She'd given him a lot to think about.

Frank put the Camaro in drive, following Robinson to his home in Cooper's Mill. Frank took more pictures of the man going inside his house, then put the car in gear and drove away.

"You're quiet."

Frank nodded, not saying anything, and drove her home. He passed the police cordon with a nod at the cop on duty, who moved the cones and waved him through. The news vans and paparazzi and fans were all still there, all still milling around, even though it was nearly midnight. He drove up the long driveway and stopped next to the Cortez house.

"Well, that was interesting," Jessica said. She made no move to get out. "Thanks for letting me tag along. You mad at me?"

"No, not really," Frank said, lying. "I've been a cop for too long, maybe."

"No, I don't think so," she said quietly. "But things change. Technology changes, right? You keep up with all of that, but you might miss a few things."

He looked over at her. "It's different. If you make a mistake, you miss out on something on social media. No big deal."

"No, when I make mistakes, people almost die. They drive into brick walls at full speed," she said, looking at the messy floorboard. Her shoes were resting on a Burger King bag. "You should clean up in here, really."

Frank nodded. "I know. Thanks for tagging along," he said, nodding at the house. "Get some sleep. I'll be back in the morning, and we can run to Target, if you want. You've been asking."

"That would be cool," she said, opening the door. "And don't beat yourself up, Mr. Harper. There was nothing on her Facebook about it, and it's obvious she's keeping her side hustle quiet."

"Side hustle?"

"Yeah, a job you have on the side to make money."

Frank smiled. "I'm learning new stuff all the time with you. And call me Frank."

She looked at him and started to say something else, then simply smiled and got out. "Night."

He watched her go inside and a light came on in the house. Officer Davis opened the door for her and nodded at Frank. They had an informal method of "passing her off," something Davis had insisted on. You could tell she was an active-duty cop—all by the book. Frank nodded back and drove away, heading into town.

Christ, had he really missed it? The woman, Natalie Pine, could be teaching Taylor how to dance. It made sense and explained a few things that Frank had been dismissing. Maybe Robinson wasn't an idiot for not being more careful about his comings and goings. If nothing bad was going on…

Frank pulled into the parking lot of the Burger King and got on his phone, doing several searches while the car idled. He downloaded Instagram, and it turned out they were owned by Facebook, so he used the same login and password to access the app. He scanned Natalie Pine's public photos, which clearly showed her history of dancing competitions. There were shots of her instructing several different people and even a couple of posts soliciting customers.

One of the posts jumped out at him: "Learn at your own pace. Come to my home and learn in private. No more embarrassing dance studios."

That was it.

Frank shook his head and put the car in drive, heading to her house. He didn't care if it was the middle of the night—he needed to get to the bottom of this. There was no way he could sleep anyway—if he'd missed so much about this woman's life, he'd be kicking himself.

He parked in front of the house he'd just spent hours parked in front of. But this time he got out, bringing the camera with him, and walked up the sidewalk, knocking on her door. Frank waited, nervous, and a light came on inside. Finally, he heard someone on the other side of the door.

"Yes?"

"Natalie Pine?"

"Yes," she said, her voice muffled.

"I'm Frank Harper," he said, holding up his PI license to the peephole in the door. "I need to chat with you, if you have a moment."

"It's the middle of the night," she said. "And I don't know you."

Frank nodded, sighing and putting away his license. "I know. I'm investigating Taylor Robinson, a man who has spent many evenings here with you. I have photos. His wife hired me—she thinks he's having an affair. With you, specifically. But tonight, I had another idea. I think he might be learning to dance."

There was a pause, and then he heard the door unlocking. Finally, the woman opened the door and looked at him, curious.

"What?"

Twenty minutes later, he was on his way to the Robinson house. He went over again what Natalie had said, and of course, the explanation was so simple—and so innocent—that Frank felt like a fool.

Natalie taught dancing in her home because she was just starting the business and couldn't afford to rent a space. Taylor had been taking lessons to surprise his wife. He'd told Natalie that the couple was planning on renewing their vows in Mexico in the spring. It all matched exactly what Mrs. Robinson had told Frank at the Tip Top Diner, and when stories from different people matched up perfectly, Frank knew he was on the right track.

He parked in front of the Robinson house and headed up, knocking on the door. It was past 1 a.m., but there were lights on in the house and Frank could see the flickering shadows of a TV on in the living room.

The door opened, and Frank introduced himself to Taylor Robinson, a man he knew well but had never met.

"Yes, I'm Taylor Robinson. What's all this then?"

Frank looked at him. "We need to talk. You, me...and Fran. Your wife."

He looked confused.

The conversation that followed in the Robinson living room was awkward, to say the least. Frank told Mrs. Robinson that he'd figured out what was going on, not letting on too much about her suspicions, but they quickly came out anyway. Taylor was surprised—and very dismayed—to find out that his wife thought he was cheating on her.

The wife was surprised, of course, with the explanation. Taylor had already bought their tickets to Mexico for the marriage renewal. He'd been taking dancing lessons because, apparently, she'd mentioned somewhere along the way that he needed them. She'd said their first dance as a married couple, twenty years ago, had been awkward. She still thought about it, and suggested they take lessons together to improve for the party she was planning after their marriage renewal. Fran's relief was genuine, as far as Frank could tell, masking the fact that she'd spent months—and not a small amount of money—suspecting her husband of cheating.

Soon, the Robinsons were talking to each other and apologizing and Frank felt like a third wheel. He let them talk and busied himself by looking at the muted movie on the television. It was some black and white film he didn't recognize. Monty would know it, of course—the man was an expert.

It made Frank think. Monty knew old movies, and Jessica knew social media, and Laura knew accounting. Frank needed more people around him, especially if he was going to make a go of this private investigator thing. He couldn't know everything—instead, he needed to draw on other people and their expertise.

It was a lot like being a cop, actually. Frank didn't do everything on his own—he'd relied on his partners, who knew about topics that were foreign to him. Ben Stone had been a better shot, and Deputy Peters and Chief King knew the local area in Ohio better than Frank did. Frank's various supervisors had shielded him from the organizational bureaucracy of their departments, freeing him to do his job. Other people handled the accounting, paperwork, plea deals, prosecutions, and crime scenes. Hell, if Frank was going to be a private investigator, he'd have to learn a lot of different things, even if only to know what he needed to avoid.

The Robinsons were still talking, but now they were talking as if Frank wasn't even in the room. The tone had changed, too—she seemed relieved, somehow, and Taylor's sudden indignation had melted away into understanding. Frank gave them another twenty minutes, then finally stood.

"It sounds like you have a lot to talk about," Frank said. They both stood, and Taylor, absurdly, shook Frank's hand.

"Thank you for doing this," he said. "Really. I'm glad it's out there.

It was going to be a fun surprise," he said, turning to his wife. "I didn't think it would cause this much trouble."

Fran nodded and smiled. She turned to Frank. "And we're good? The money?"

"Yes," Frank said. "I just wrapped up the hours you already paid for," he said awkwardly. It was strange, talking about finances in front of Taylor. "You'll get a final report from me on the case, but we're square, money-wise." He looked at them. "Good luck to you both, and I hope you make that trip to Mexico."

He saw himself out and walked to the car, shaking his head. If someone had told him earlier in the evening that this case would be wrapped by 2 a.m., he wouldn't have believed them.

Chapter 75
Parade

The Mum Festival parade was being held on Saturday morning, September 29th, and Jessica was excited to be attending the parade.

Jessica and the others had discussed it a few days before and decided it was worth the risk. She didn't want to seem like she was hiding from the world, and the parade would give her a good opportunity to participate in something the city was doing without overshadowing it.

The parade folks had gotten in touch with Monty, asking through him to see if she would be interested in being in the parade proper, serving as the Grand Marshall and riding in the front car. Through Monty, Jessica had politely declined, saying that, while she wanted to be involved, she didn't want to take away from the small-town celebration.

In the end, she and the others decided the best thing to do would be to make an appearance at the parade in the downtown, then find a place to watch in private. After the parade was over, Jessica would travel to the festival grounds and walk through, signing autographs and taking photos and selfies with people before calling it a day and heading back to the farm.

On Saturday morning, Frank arrived at the Cortez house early, just after 8 a.m. Monty was already downtown, staking out a location for their chairs. Apparently, getting a space for any parade in this town was part of the fun, and some folks roped off the sidewalk in front of their homes to keep an area open for them to put their chairs. Other folks even drove downtown the night before and put their chairs out to claim a spot. Some folks showed up at 7 a.m., three hours before the parade, to plop down and grab a patch of grass or sidewalk. Frankly, Jessica was amazed to learn that people cared that much—or that they put chairs out overnight without them being stolen.

Frank drove Jessica and Leslie, while Ferrara drove with her family. The plan was to head down early and get settled, watch the parade, then visit the festival and mingle with fans. Frank Harper seemed very concerned about her being out in public, especially walking at the festival, but Jessica didn't care. The secret was out now, and she only had to worry about serving out her time. Getting out and enjoying a parade sounded like the perfect antidote for weeks of being cooped up in the house.

As Frank pulled out of the Cortez driveway, news vans and paparazzi followed, a caravan of vehicles heading east into Cooper's Mill. A family Simona Cortez knew who lived in the downtown had offered to let Jessica and her group watch the parade from their balcony. Jessica thought that would work out nicely—they could enjoy the parade without people crowding around and blocking the view. And, if Jessica was out of reach, maybe the people would just relax and enjoy the parade instead of worrying about her. Ferrara and her family would follow later, meeting them there. After, they would all meet up and head to the festival.

Once Frank arrived in the downtown, things got crazy. Frank found a spot one street over from the parade route, parking in front of a beautiful white home with two columns out front and an ornate, gold-leafed single-digit number above the front door for the address.

The news vans had more trouble parking, and Frank spoke harshly to two of the paparazzi, including Bill Hanford, telling them to keep their distance or he'd "knock them on their asses," making Jessica smile. She was starting to think having full-time security was a good idea. When she got back to LA, she'd have to figure out a way to make it happen, even if she had to make up the costs by dropping others from her entourage.

Jessica followed Frank and Leslie to the private home they'd been offered, greeting the folks, who were jazzed to have Jessica as their guests. The house was located on Main and Fourth streets, right on the corner, facing north.

Jessica made a point of going around and greeting all the people at the home—the homeowners, in addition to hosting Jessica's group, was also holding a potluck. Guests had brought crockpots of warm food or trays of baked goods. Jessica and her group partook as well, loading up plates before heading up to a large balcony off the second floor that looked out on Main Street and the parade route.

"Well, this is the life," Frank said with a smile, sitting down with his plate of deviled eggs and macaroni salad. "I bet these are the best seats in town."

They waited for the parade to get started, chatting and feeling the electricity in the air. And it wasn't the only thing.

"Does anyone else smell spaghetti sauce?" The scent floated around them, and, to Jessica, it smelled like the homeowners were making sauce.

"Oh, that's the cannery," Ferrara said. "They must be making spaghetti sauce today. Smells like tomatoes and garlic."

A few minutes later, the parade got started. The downtown church bells sounded out ten rings, letting everyone know the parade had officially begun. And even as the parade began on the other side of town, the crowd lining either side of Main Street was electric—it was easy to understand their collective excitement. Soon, Jessica could hear the parade coming, music in the distance, long before the first marching band crossed the train tracks and headed into the downtown.

"Here they come," Leslie said, leaning forward.

Jessica loved the parade—it was cute, small-town, nothing like anything she had ever seen in Los Angeles. It was under-produced, to say the least. In fact, it seemed barely organized at all. The order of the floats and bands seemed random, and the entire parade ground to a halt to wait for a passing freight train to rumble through town.

Simona said the parade came down Hyatt Street from the Post Office, then turned at the Dairy Queen and came east down Main, passing over the train tracks and into downtown Cooper's Mill.

The parade route passed in front of Jessica and the others, going left to right. To their right, set up in the intersection of Main and Third, was a flatbed semi topped with chairs for local dignitaries and a podium. On the portable stage, an old guy was narrating the whole thing, mentioning each float or band. "And now, we welcome the award-winning New Carlisle Marching Bees!" The band would stop and play a little number, people would applaud, and the band would head up Third Street, following the rest of the parade. Simona said they gathered back at the Post Office, having made a big loop through town.

Jessica took pictures, borrowing Frank's "new" camera. She snapped photos of high-stepping cheerleaders and big kids carrying tubas and drums. She wished she could be down there, greeting people and saying "hi." It would be a bad idea, surely, but it didn't hurt to ask.

"I need a break," Jessica said, looking at Frank and Leslie. "I want to go out, say hi," she yelled over the marching band that was passing in front of the house. "I feel like I owe them that much. And I feel like an idiot."

"What do you mean?" Leslie asked.

"I'm sitting up here like the queen," Jessica said. "Waving at the little people. Can I walk the sidelines a little? Pose for some selfies?"

Frank looked at her and started to shake his head, but Leslie nodded. "I'm fine with it. I'll go with you. Frank?"

He didn't look excited about the idea, but finally nodded. "Okay. Take Monty," Frank said, pointing down at the area of chairs that Ferrara and her family were occupying. "I'll keep an eye on things from up here."

Jessica smiled and hugged him. "Thanks, Frank. I'll be right back."

She made her way downstairs, greeting people at the party and then walking out onto the sidewalk in front of the house. Leslie intercepted the paparazzi and Jessica found Monty, getting him up to speed. He didn't seem excited by the idea, either, but shrugged.

"Hey, you're paying the bills, little miss," he said. "Just stay with me."

She greeted Ferrara and her family, telling them she was going to work the crowd on the south side of the street for a little while. With that, Jessica turned and smiled at a group of nearby fans. She leaned in, taking a selfie with a pair of little girls, the band marching along behind them in the background.

CHAPTER 76
Snatch and Grab

Blake had been at the post office early this morning, watching the different groups assemble for the parade.

This was the staging grounds, as groups and floats and bands gathered on the streets and in the parking lots all around the post office. Blake walked around, talking to people until he was able to obtain a printout of the parade order, which had just been finalized this morning.

Out here, the different groups were getting set up, dressing in outfits or warming up their little Shriner cars. Most of the groups were represented by a float of some sort, and Blake passed a number of them, the riders and "walkers" who would accompany the floats getting ready.

In some cases, they were still doing last-minute decorations to the floats or tweaking the seating arrangements for the people who would be riding. People prepared aprons and bags filled with candy and coupons and Frisbees, items that would be handed out to spectators along the parade route. One group was giving out blue spatulas, while the local library would be handing out used paperback books. On some of the floats, large bowls of candy were arranged so the riders could scoop up handfuls and throw them to the spectators as they passed.

Blake walked along the assembly route, scanning it and comparing it with his list. He finally found the group he was most interested in. Blake greeted them, telling them he thought they were doing a great job. He made a cash donation and took selfies and photos with them before heading back to his car.

Now, two hours later, Blake was just finishing up his makeup. He could hear the marching bands and hurried, pulling on the red nose and organizing all of his hair under the goofy wig he'd bought at a party supply store in another town to the south.

The white makeup covered his face, his scar, everything. It looked nice, Blake thought. For the first time in a long time, the scar across his face wasn't the most prominent thing people would see. The white makeup, the red nose, the huge eyes—he would blend in perfectly.

Finally, finishing up, he looked in the rearview mirror again, touching up the white makeup under his right eye. Everything was in place, and he set the makeup kit aside, climbing out of the car and resisting the temptation to scratch at his face.

The Mum Festival parade moved past him. He'd found a place to park near the parade route, but it was shielded from the street by a stand of trees. Beyond them, he could see floats and marching bands making their way up Main.

He checked the list for the fiftieth time, then saw the group he'd talked to earlier approaching. They waved to the crowd and did funny stunts. Several handed out candy, and one of them sprayed water from a large fake flower pinned to his chest.

Blake walked around the back of his vehicle, opening the trunk. He gathered up the balloons he'd worked on earlier, then stepped back. The car was parked facing away from the parade route.

He left the trunk standing open.

This was a gamble, he knew. But she was out there, waiting for him. People had talked. Everyone seemed to know she was watching the parade from a house on Fourth and Main, sitting up on a balcony overlooking the parade route. It made sense, Blake thought—she could be part of the festivities and still be above them. She knew she was better than that.

Blake breathed in and out, steadying himself, and then started up the alley. He worked his way west, tacking toward the parade route, and came out near the train tracks.

"Look, mommy," a kid yelled, pointing at him. "Another clown!"

Blake smiled, a wide red grin on his white, made-up face. He did a little skip as he walked up to the kid and played with one of the balloon animals he'd made earlier. Blake made a show of petting the balloon animal, a dog, and then handed it to the little kid, who squealed with delight. The mom smiled approvingly, and Blake moved on, making his way to the parade route.

The plan was that he pretend to be one of the clowns from the group up ahead in the parade, but that he'd gotten separated from them and left behind. He would be working to catch up, but never quite getting there.

The parade moved on, continuously, and it made sense there would be stragglers. Blake worked his way through the crowd on the sideline and then stepped out into the parade route itself, walking east, following a marching band. He was all by himself, but no one seemed to care, even though the "rest" of the clowns were three groups ahead. Blake hoped everyone would assume he'd gotten separated from the group.

Blake walked the street, keeping pace with the band he was following and trying not to hurry. He waved and stopped for selfies with kids and moms along the sides of the parade route. When he wasn't taking photos or interacting with kids, he was waving and tossing balloon animals to the crowd.

He saved his last one, keeping it on his shoulder.

Blake reached into the pockets of his rented clown suit, throwing out handfuls of candy, and carefully tracked his location. He'd entered the parade a half-mile west of the tracks, walking along with the parade east. He needed to end up back near his car.

Finally, he saw the house where Jessica was supposed to be, near the intersection of Fourth and Main. His plan was to walk up and stop, then wave at her and see if he could get her to come down from the balcony to claim his last balloon.

He'd worked it all out in his head ahead of time—he'd stop by the house, in full view of her and the crowds, then show her his last balloon, offering it to her with a showy, over-the-top dance. She'd be too embarrassed to not come down, especially if he kneeled or did some pretend clown crying, shaking his shoulders and making the crowd moan along with him.

How could she resist? And then he could throw her over his shoulder and they would be together forever.

But Jessica wasn't there.

Blake had a good view of the house and the balcony, but there was only one person sitting up there, an older man. Jessica was nowhere to be seen.

What if this didn't work? What if she had left already? People had seen her on the balcony—Blake had asked as he made his way through the crowd. Maybe she had left? Walked down to the announcer stand?

Blake felt the panic rising. He fought to keep it down. Stay calm, work it out. All he wanted was to take her home, introduce her to his family. She would love them. And then they could all sit around the ornate dinner table together, swapping stories and enjoying each other's company. She would sit at one end of the table, him at the other. They would drink coffee and make plans and she could tell him how much she loved him—

Blake Oleander finally saw her.

There she was, smiling and taking photos with the regular people on the south side of the street. He angled in her direction. It didn't make sense that she'd be walking in the crowd, but there she was.

She looked beautiful, even with her strange hair. At least she wasn't wearing that horrible wig today. He could see her short, blond hair, shimmering in the October sun. Kids and adults swirled around her.

Blake followed the marching band and angled toward the southern side of the road, approaching the crowd that surrounded Jessica. He made a point of pointing and acting like he'd seen the most beautiful woman in the world. Blake put both gloved hands over his heart, as if her beauty was so phenomenal, it was causing him to have a heart attack.

He sidled up to where Jessica was talking to a group of little kids. One of them turned and pointed at Blake and smiled.

"Jessica, look, it's a clown!"

Jessica turned and some small part of him hoped she would recognize him. In actuality, that would be a very bad thing, but still, he wanted to be seen. To be noticed.

But she only smiled at him.

"Hi, clown!"

One of the kids ran over and pulled on Blake's leg. "Balloon! Balloon!"

Blake pretended he didn't hear him, making Jessica and the kids laugh. Blake looked up in the air and all around as if he'd lost it.

"No, it's on your shoulder, silly!" the kid yelled.

Blake looked around, working the crowd. He shrugged and pointed at other people as if he didn't know he had a balloon on his shoulder. Finally, he "saw" it and pretended to be surprised to find it there. He jumped in the air, nearly falling. The crowd around Blake and Jessica laughed. Then, he turned and detached the balloon from his shoulder. He kneeled, holding it out for Jessica as if he were proposing to her.

"Oh, for me?" Jessica asked, smiling. She reached and grabbed it, their hands briefly touching.

It was now or never.

Instead of standing, Blake stepped forward, staying hunched over. He put his arms around her waist, gripping her tightly. A thrill went through his body—he could smell her even over the overwhelming odor of the clown makeup. He could feel her against his shoulder.

Finally, Jessica Mills was, once again, in his arms.

Standing, he lifted Jessica into the air easily. She felt light and solid. The clown threw the Hollywood starlet over his shoulder, and the crowd laughed and pointed and smiled at the show.

Backing away, Blake the clown spun her in a circle, delighting the children.

"Oh, the clown has Jessica! The clown has Jessica!"

He danced and waved, making a show of carrying her in a circle. He slapped her on the butt and the crowd around them laughed at the sudden spectacle.

"Okay, okay, put me down," he heard Jessica say, playing along with the show.

Instead, Blake reached into the pocket of his clown suit and took out a huge handful of candy. Tossing it into the air, he turned and ran out into the parade route, running in a wide circle. Kids dashed into the street, grabbing up the fallen candy. People laughed and pointed, realizing who the clown was carrying. It was all for show, and all for fun.

Blake completed the circle and a tall woman stepped out from the crowd, putting her hands up.

"Okay, that's enough. Put Ms. Mills down. You've had your fun."

Blake ran right up to the tall woman, a woman he recognized from Jessica's recent interviews. He did not slow down. Blake knew Jessica had security—a pair of local guys—but this was the lady cop who had traveled out with her from LA. Blake had read every article, every scrap of information from every interview Jessica and the others had put out in the last week.

Blake knew everything.

He ran up to Officer Leslie Davis, not slowing, and then ran around her, making a circle as the spectators laughed along. She seemed somewhat embarrassed by the spectacle.

The blade was out in a flash.

He pulled it from another of the big pockets in his clown pants, one that also held candy and a loaded syringe, which he would need as soon as he got back to the car.

Blake Oleander slashed the woman officer across the stomach, blood staining her shirt.

The first screams happened when a few people finally realized what was happening. The big woman stumbled and fell to the ground. One of her hands went to a gun at her waist, but she was too surprised to draw.

Blake backed away, turning as a black man stepped from the crowd and leaned over Officer Davis, confused. As Blake turned, the man looked at the lady cop sprawled on the ground.

Blake didn't have time to watch. In the confusion, he turned and ran south of a group of trees. He could see his car beyond them, the trunk still standing open.

This was going to work.

PUT ME DOWN!" Jessica screamed, hitting at his back. He pocketed the knife, then reached up and rapped her hard on the head with a fist. Blake felt her body go limp.

He moved through the crowd, quickly getting away from where the excitement had happened. Now he was just a clown running up the sidewalk with a woman thrown over his shoulder, and the people smiled and pointed, assuming it was a funny joke.

The way to his car was blocked—he would have to cross the parade route, running out into the open. Instead, Blake turned and ran up the sidewalk on the south side of Main, ducking around one of the paparazzi guys he'd seen holding vigil out where Jessica was staying.

Blake turned at the corner of Fourth street, sprinting past the wide windows of a furniture store. He turned, seeing a wide, empty street lined with houses.

No crowds, nothing.

The way was clear. He could run west from here, up the alleys, then cross Main near the tracks and get back to his car.

Chapter 77
Chase

Everything went to shit in a matter of moments.

Frank was sitting alone in the balcony, feeling a little bit like Abraham Lincoln. For some reason, he'd started thinking about the old president, watching a play and getting shot in the back of the head. Frank managed to creep himself out enough to get up and look in the inside hallway that led out to the balcony.

Nope, no assassins.

Frank decided to get more food and headed downstairs. He tossed out his plate and grabbed two more of the donuts that were there for the taking. They were good—and then Frank saw the label on the box they were in: "Tim's Donuts." Those were the donuts favored by everyone in town, brought in from a store down in Vandalia, one highway exit to the south.

Deputy Peters had loved the donuts from that place.

Frank glanced around and put the donuts back. Suddenly, he wasn't hungry.

Outside, Frank heard peals of hysterical laughter and went through the front door and out onto the wide porch that looked out on the parade. The porch was crowded with spectators, and he worked his way around to the steps.

A clown from the parade was entertaining Jessica and some kids, handing her a balloon. There had been another group of clowns earlier, and this guy looked like one of them who'd gotten separated from his clown posse. What did you call a group of clowns? Frank knew a bunch of crows was called a "murder." What about clowns?

Suddenly, the clown bent over and picked Jessica up and threw her over his shoulder, running in a wide circle while the crowd laughed and pointed. He galloped like a horse, and Jessica bounced on his shoulder.

Frank remembered something Jessica had said. About her stalker, throwing her over his shoulder—

It was all good fun until someone screamed.

Frank could see Monty and Officer Davis near the street. Davis waived the clown down, but he seemed to charge her, and she fell. Frank saw a flash of silver in the crowd. A blade, he thought. Monty leaned over Davis and the clown ran away, heading west.

He had Jessica.

Frank was off like a shot, running toward the clown. Whatever had happened to Monty and Leslie, Frank's first priority was Jessica Mills. He saw the clown rap her on the head, knocking her out, and then he ducked into the crowd and Frank lost them.

Could it be?

Jessica had told Frank about her "stalker." It all sounded like hooey, but she'd obviously been freaked out enough to tell him the whole story twice, once while he was at the Cortez house and the other on the night of their stakeout. The man had been large, scooping her up and carrying him over her shoulder.

This clown was clearly a big boy. Could it be the same guy? What were the chances?

Jessica being in Ohio had made national news. Everyone knew, especially anyone who was interested or followed news about the starlet. Could he have driven here from wherever he lived?

Frank ran, racing up the sidewalk. He juked back and forth, rushing past people and diving around spectators to avoid plowing into them. Some were still watching the parade, but others were pointing after the clown or Jessica. Frank barked at them to get out of the way, or asked hurried questions.

"The clown. Jessica Mills. Have you seen her? This way?"

People nodded, or just looked confused. Frank hurried, reaching an unholstering his gun. He used a finger to blindly verify the safety was on, then ran with it out in front of him. It parted the sea of people as if he were Moses—now, people's eyes went wide when they saw Frank coming, his gun shimmering in the sunlight.

"This way? Where's the clown? Did you see him?"

Frank shouted at people as he ran past them. Sometimes he heard their answers, sometimes not. He ran, losing sight of his quarry.

He stopped, panting, looking around. The crowd had closed around the clown and Jessica and now it was just a sea of people, faces, mostly turned toward the parade, completely unaware that something terrible, horrible, was taking place right here and right now.

There was no sign of the clown. Or Jessica.

"Hey, I saw him," a voice behind Frank said. He turned and it was the paparazzi guy, the one from the Cortez farm. He had his camera out and was shooting pictures. The guy still had a black eye from where Frank had punched him.

"Where! Which way!"

The paparazzi guy pointed. "Up there, around the corner."

Frank sprinted away, running in the direction of what looked like a furniture store. Huge, floor-to-ceiling windows displayed beds and tables and other furniture inside. Frank glanced back and saw the paparazzi guy following him, snapping pictures even as they ran at a dead sprint.

Frank ran, darting around spectators and paralleling the big furniture store windows. He got to the end of the building and turned onto what looked like Fourth Street. It was a wide, residential street, lined with shops and houses stretching away into the distance. Both sides were crammed with parked cars.

Frank saw the clown.

He was half-way down the block, running along a wall of windows that looked into the large furniture store. The clown was just passing an open doorway the size of a garage door.

"STOP!" Frank screamed. He pointed the gun in the air and flicked off the safety. "PUT HER DOWN NOW!"

The clown jerked to a stop and turned, looking back at Frank. He seemed calm, almost serene. The clown looked around, saw the open garage door in the rear of the furniture store, and ducked inside, disappearing.

Chapter 78
Entrance

Bill Hanford followed the old guy, the same guy that had given him a black eye days ago. Hanford's eye still smarted, but it was forgotten now. Hanford ran, shooting pictures as he went.

The old guy got to the corner of the furniture store and turned, disappearing. Hanford cursed and ran faster, wishing he had spent a little bit more time in the gym and a little less time hanging out in bars and schmoozing waitresses. It was part of doing business in Los Angeles, but it didn't help when his job called for a quick sprint. The old guy was decades older than Hanford, but he was quick. He'd been quick that night on the farm when he'd moved so fast, knocking Hanford to the ground.

Hanford ran after the old man, racing along windows that displayed beds and other furniture, and finally reached the corner. He turned.

Fourth street was wide, with houses on either side, stretching away from the parade route. To his left, beyond the furniture store, Hanford saw what looked like a loading entrance, a garage door standing open. The old man, Frank something, was standing next to it, edging around it carefully, his gun drawn and up to the side, held in both hands like a guy out of one of those spy movies.

Hanford snapped more photos as he ran to catch up.

Chapter 79
Shots Fired

"You need to stay back, friend," Frank said to the paparazzi guy as he ran up. "Leave this to the cops."

"You're not a cop," the man said, out of breath. "I remember that much, at least."

"Close enough. Seriously, stay back. This could get ugly."

Frank Harper turned and eased around the edge of the open garage door, peering into the building, his gun up and ready.

Inside the back of the furniture store, Frank saw storage areas and doors. The one to his right was open, showing a large room filled with furniture, much of it wrapped in plastic. To his left, he saw the office of the furniture store and, through a set of wide windows, the sales floor.

The thing that surprised Frank was what he saw in the middle, between the office and the storage room: a driveway, going east into the building. He saw tire marks, as if vehicles routinely drove into the building. The driveway continued on and turned, sloping downward and to his left, disappearing out of sight.

He moved quietly to the storage room door and looked in, holding his gun aside. It was dark, and he saw no movement, just a room full of furniture. He stepped further into the building, feeling movement behind him. He turned and saw the paparazzi guy.

"Stay back," Frank said. 'I don't know where he went."

Frank looked back around and into the office, but again saw no movement, either in the office or out on the sales floor. Beyond, he could see the large glass windows and the parade, still moving down the street, ignorant of what was happening.

Frank turned his attention back to the roadway.

"What is it?" the paparazzi guy asked. "A garage? Underground?"

Frank shrugged. "Maybe," he said. He heard no sounds coming from anywhere inside the building, and suddenly wasn't excited about descending into the dark alone.

"What is that, a ramp?" The paparazzi guy was pointing past Frank.

"I don't know."

Frank turned and looked around the corner. It was indeed a ramp, like in a parking garage. It sloped down into a dark, dank, underground space.

"Christ," Frank said under his breath. He turned to the photographer. "Okay, stay here on the ramp. Shout out if he comes back this way. And send Monty or the cops down here when they show up."

The paparazzi guy swallowed and nodded slowly.

Frank turned and started down the ramp. It smelled like a cave, or an underground parking area. He slowly walked down the concrete ramp, listening intently but only hearing the sounds of his breathing and his own footsteps, echoing in the dark.

As the ramp sloped down, Frank saw a series of rounded concrete pillars, equally spaced, and a ceiling above them. Beyond, in the dark space, Frank saw dozens of vehicles parked in rows, most covered with dusty white sheets. Cars and boats and a few motorcycles, stored under this furniture store and kept out of the weather. It was bizarre, finding an underground garage in this small building in this little town.

Frank pointed the gun ahead of him.

"Okay, there's no way out of here," Frank said loudly. "Give me Jessica and maybe you get out of here alive."

He heard a chuckle from somewhere off to his left, amid the rows of tarp-covered vehicles. "Yeah, I doubt that, cop."

"I'm not a cop," Frank said, walking slowly forward. He scanned, left and right, as he passed under a rusty light fixture. "You need to let her go—"

There was sudden movement to his left and he turned. Something came out of the darkness, whizzing at his head. Frank ducked away, the wrench missing him by inches. It smacked into the light fixture behind him, shattering it, sparks flying.

Frank saw more movement and suddenly a man dressed as a clown manifested out of the shadows, slashing at Frank's gun with a wicked-looking knife. It caught him on the back of the hand and Frank's gun fell away, skidding under one of the tarp-shrouded vehicles.

Frank backed away, rubbing his hand. The clown stood still, the knife out, looking at him.

"You should just let me have her," the clown said. His eyes were crazy, matching his countenance. "I love her. I'll take care of her."

Frank backed up more, listening for Jessica. "That's what I'm worried about, pal." Was she already dead? It sounded like this guy was obsessed with her. In his experience, Frank didn't think the guy would kill her.

Not yet, anyway.

If he were going to kill Jessica, he'd do it somewhere else, somewhere private. Someplace where he could take his time.

"You love her, huh?" Frank stepped backward, looking for an opening. He watched the knife. It danced in the darkness, held aloft by a madman. It moved back and forth, from hand to hand, the clown gloves long gone. "You gonna take care of her?"

"Yeah, old man," the clown said. "I am."

"And if she doesn't like you?"

"Oh, she'll love me. She has to."

Behind the clown, Frank saw a pair of eyes peek around the corner. It was the photographer guy, easing around the last concrete column. Frank nodded slightly, hoping the guy would understand.

"She'll love my house," the clown said, stepping closer. The knife danced in the shadows, moving erratically. "My family has a great house. She'll be right at home. She'll be the guest of honor—"

There was a sudden flash of light, off to Frank's left. He looked away and looked back. The clown had turned to see what it was, and Frank moved, ducking and stepping in, using the same sweep move he'd used on the paparazzi. It was one of the most basic moves in Krav Maga, something he'd taught to dozens of people. Now, it would have to work perfectly, or else.

The clown was a big guy and went down hard, his legs going out from underneath him as Frank swept his own leg from right to left.

Somehow the big man managed to keep a handle on the knife.

Even as he fell, the clown turned and swiped in Frank's direction with the sharp blade. But there was only one direction the knife could come from, and Frank had anticipated the move, trapping the blade between his hands. The knife caught his fingers, cutting him.

They struggled for the blade, grunting, but the big guy was stronger than he looked.

He rolled on top of Frank, who was pinned against the tires of an old car, the tarp flapping around the two men as they fought. Frank shook it off and tried to pinion the knife out of the man's hand, but then the clown dropped the knife, scooping it up with his other hand, and stabbed at Frank. In the half-darkness, the knife seemed to move in slow motion, swooping at Frank's face.

Frank ducked away and the knife dug into the concrete floor where Frank's head had been only a second before. Frank grabbed the clown's arm, directing the knife up and away. He twisted the clown's hands, the two of them struggling to control the blade while pushing the other man away. Frank grimaced, turning the knife slowly, pushing, increasing the angle of the silver blade. When it was finally pointed in the right direction, Frank kicked out, hard, changing the direction of the pressure he applied. Frank rolled the clown over while simultaneously pulling him onto Frank.

Frank felt the knife sink into the man's chest, piercing the white clown suit and whatever he was wearing underneath and not stopping until it hit what sounded like bone.

The man collapsed, rolling to the side, the knife sticking out of his chest. Frank watched, moving closer, and thought about removing the knife if only to have a ready weapon in case the fight continued.

In a moment, the clown went still. Frank heard a final, ragged breath escape the man's painted lips. After that, nothing. There was no movement, no breathing. Nothing.

Frank sat back against another car, looking at the clown on the ground. He hated killing people, but sometimes it was necessary.

He heard footsteps off to his left. Frank looked up and saw the paparazzi guy, the camera around his neck, forgotten.

"Jesus. You're bleeding," the guy said, pointing at Frank's hands.

He was, indeed—the back of his left hand was gashed, and the fingers as well. Frank found a scrap of white cloth and wrapped his hand. The paparazzi guy—Hanford, Frank thought his name was—went to take a photo of the clown, but Frank grabbed the camera.

"Don't even think about it," Frank said. "Have some respect."

"Respect? For that guy?"

Frank nodded. "Yeah, even for him."

Hanford looked like he was going to argue but changed his mind. "I'll go get the cops. I heard sirens before I started down the ramp."

Frank nodded as Hanford walked away, disappearing up the ramp.

It didn't take Frank long to find Jessica.

She was slumped down behind one of the old cars.

She looked dead.

He moved to her, feeling for any signs of life, and, after an anxious moment, confirmed that she was still breathing. He sat for a moment, smiling, brushing the short blond hair from her eyes until they fluttered open.

"Frank?"

He nodded and pulled her out from behind the car, moving her into an open area. She blinked her eyes and tried to sit up, and then moaned, feeling her head.

"Ow," she said. "What happened."

Frank nodded at the floor nearby, and she turned, gasping.

"I think your stalker showed up," Frank said simply, sitting down next to her. "Big guy. Scar on his face, though it's hard to see under all that makeup. Threw you over his shoulder like you were a sack of potatoes."

"Is he...dead?"

"Yup," Frank said, rewrapping the bloody bandage around his hand.

She looked at the clown's body for a long time, until Hanford came back down the ramp and walked over to them.

"Are you okay, Ms. Mills?"

Jessica nodded, rubbing her head. "Hanford? Shocker. Of course, you're here."

"I saw the guy grab you up," Hanford said.

"He knocked me pretty good," Jessica said. "I was out for the whole thing."

Hanford nodded, looking at the clown on the ground. He had one hand on his camera, which hung around his neck. Frank could tell what he was thinking.

"Go ahead, Hanford," Frank said. "It's okay. Take a few before the cops get here."

He looked at Frank. "You sure?"

"Yeah," Frank said. "You earned it."

"What?" Jessica looked at Frank. "Are you crazy?"

"Hey, he saved your life, Jessica," Frank said. "Saw which way the guy went, pointed it out to me. Then distracted him, helped me take him out." He looked back at Hanford. "Go on. You deserve it."

Hanford looked at Jessica, who finally nodded as well, and then he stood back and began snapping photos of the body on the floor of the garage.

Chapter 80
Ninety Days

After what happened at the 2012 Mum Festival parade, the next few weeks were rather dull.

Her stalker was dead, and Jessica was okay, despite the scare. The man was finally out of her life, and she found herself relaxing for the first time in as long as she could remember. She'd stayed and watched the police swarm the scene. Even after they'd told her it was okay for her to leave, Jessica had stayed, watching the police and crime scene folks bag up the clown's body and take it away. She'd followed them up the concrete ramp and watched them put the dead man in a vehicle. She'd smiled as it had driven away.

Leslie got cut pretty badly across her stomach and spent the next three days in a local hospital before being sent back to the Cortez farm to recuperate. The doctors said she would need a month or two of physical therapy before she could go back on the job. Tina Armstrong had visited her every day, sitting in her room and telling her stories from her years as a journalist.

The stalker was Blake, the man who had written her all of those letters over the years. He was also the same guy who had tried previously to abduct Jessica in Los Angeles, nearly getting away with it. The guy had been obsessed with her, but now, thanks to Mr. Harper, was dead in the ground. It was a great relief for Jessica to know that he was gone forever.

Blake was a mental case from New Orleans. Frank was also from the same area and took a special interest in the man and his background. Investigators working in New Orleans uncovered the man's address and found a mansion full of horrors: his entire family had been murdered, along with several other locals who had gone missing. Apparently, the guy had preserved all their bodies and propped them up around his dining room table like a dinner party in hell.

In the basement, investigators also found a young woman, his latest victim, barely alive. She'd been taken weeks ago, tied up and left for dead. She'd managed to get free and, although unable to escape the home, found enough food to hold out until the cops freed her.

Frank Harper's hand injuries turned out to be superficial, and he and Monty and Jessica went back to their routine. Jessica worked hard at the grocery store, keeping her head down and staying out of trouble. Her arms got bigger as she put in her hours, stacking watermelons and organizing endless bags and boxes frozen food. She felt leaner than she had in years, and the repetitive work was routine, wonderful. By the end of her time at the grocery, she and Cheryl and Roger had become friends.

After the excitement, Leslie talked to Judge Watkins, who had been monitoring the situation closely. They'd discussed having everyone return to Los Angeles after the incident at the festival, but Leslie convinced Watkins to let them remain in Ohio.

Jessica enjoyed the rest of her stay, helping out with the Monarch butterflies and even shopping in downtown Cooper's Mill. She made some new friends and even found time to reach out to an old one: the woman Jessica had grown up with in O'Fallon, Illinois. Jessica had put in an interesting call to the young woman, who was working behind the counter at Wood Bakery. Jessica had smiled when the young woman shouted to her customers that Jessica Mills was on the phone, and Jessica even promised to make an appearance someday soon in her hometown.

On Friday, October 12, two weeks after the parade incident, Leslie looked across the breakfast table at Jessica. "Hey, can we take a walk around the pond?"

"What's this about," Jessica asked a few minutes later as they headed out. "You hardly ever want to walk, and never in the morning."

Leslie looked over at her. "It is relaxing here," she said. "Will you miss it when we're gone?"

Jessica looked around and nodded. "Yeah. I'll have to figure out a way to enjoy these same feelings back in Los Angeles. You know, relaxation. Happiness. And, of course, I can come back to visit. But I'll miss this place."

Leslie looked around. "Yeah, me too. So, you know I've been talking to the judge. I spoke to her this morning, before you got up. Sunday could be the last day of your sentence. She's thinking about commuting the last two weeks."

"Sunday? That's in...like three days!"

"Yup," Leslie said. "She wants us to fly back Sunday. Meet with her. If she thinks you've made enough progress, that'll be it. She'll change the sentencing to 'time served' and you'll be free to go."

Jessica didn't know what to say. "Wow. But why?"

Leslie smiled. "I've been keeping her in the loop, as you know. I told her you're making great progress, in my opinion. Especially these last two weeks. Head down, going to work, no drama. She was impressed."

Jessica didn't know what to say. "Thank you, Leslie."

Jessica spent Friday and Saturday wrapping things up in Cooper's Mill. She and Leslie told Frank, who was pleased for Jessica. Frank told Leslie he'd wrap up the final billing and send her an invoice in Los Angeles.

On Friday afternoon, Jessica walked down to the encampment at the bottom of the driveway, setting everyone abuzz. She announced she was returning to Los Angeles to meet with the judge in her case, who was considering commuting part of the sentence. Jessica stood in the crowd of cameras and lights, calmly answering questions from the news people and even a few from the gathered fans. She even offered to do two live interviews, one for the local Dayton news channel and another for the BBC.

Friday night, Jessica worked her last shift at the grocery, keeping her head down and doing her work. She would miss this, realizing how nice it was to have a simple goal and then working the problem until it was solved. She resolved to take that lesson and apply it to the rest of her life. She said her goodbyes to the rest of the night crew, thanking them for putting up with her and letting them take photos with her, including one of the day and night crews to post behind the front counter.

On Saturday, Jessica and Leslie and Ferrara packed while Ferrara's family said their goodbyes. It was clear that they would miss Jessica and Leslie—the two of them had become a part of their family. They shared a final family meal together Saturday evening. Jessica helped cook for the rest of them to thank them for putting her up. She would miss these people, miss the way they accepted her. Miss the way they lived their lives on their own terms, uninterested in what other people thought of them. Yeah, it was a gross oversimplification, but it was something to shoot for, right? At the beginning, they hadn't cared if she was rich or poor. The people at the grocery—and the Cortez family and the town in general—had accepted her for what she was.

Sunday morning, they left through the front doors, walking to the car. They drove away, Jessica riding in Frank's Camaro and Leslie and

Ferrara in a rental driven by Monty. At the bottom of the driveway, Frank Harper drove carefully through the massive crowd of news people and fans. Cops cleared him a path, holding back the crowd. It seemed like every person in the Dayton area was smashed together along the shoulder of this particular stretch of rural road.

Frank looked around, amazed, and then looked at Jessica. "You okay?"

Jessica nodded, not saying anything. She didn't want to cry in front of the cameras.

They headed to the Dayton airport, accompanied by a gaggle of press vehicles and well-wishers. Frank got Jessica and the others through security, which was mobbed by news people and fans saying goodbye. Frank walked Jessica to her gate and waited until the plane began to board.

"Sure you don't want to come to Los Angeles, cowboy? Be my bodyguard full time?" Jessica asked as they called her flight.

"No, thanks," Frank said. "Not my scene. Too many crazies."

She smiled at him.

"But good luck to you," he said with a wink. "And get your shit together."

They hugged, and Jessica realized she would genuinely miss him.

Chapter 81
La La Land

Jessica realized she didn't miss the crowds.

After the flight from Dayton to Los Angeles, she and the others exited the plane. The waiting area at LAX was jammed with news people and paparazzi.

"Back to the mess," Ferrara said with a scowl after retrieving their bags.

"Yeah," Jessica said, agreeing. "I didn't miss it."

Her agent and publicist met them at the airport, and she was immediately struck by how fake they seemed. They kissed her and told her how much they missed her and how good she looked. Had she lost weight? Were her arms larger, more muscular? Oh, we need to get some pictures of the new you! Oh, you look amazing!

She let their fakeness wash over her. Jessica was a rock, unperturbed by a stream of false flattery. And she made a mental note to immediately begin her search for new representation.

Upon arrival at the airport, Leslie was met by members of the LAPD, who said they would be escorting Jessica and the others straight to the courthouse. Judge Watkins wasn't wasting any time. Once they had procured vehicles, Jessica and Ferrara and Leslie were directed into the underground parking garage at the courthouse, then brought upstairs to the courtroom by waiting policemen.

The courtroom looked huge compared to how it had looked three months ago, Jessica thought. Judge Watkins was pleasant, for once, eyeing the "new" Jessica with interest. Aaron was waiting for them at the defense table, and commented on how healthy Jessica looked. She thanked him, not saying anything else.

The bailiff called order, and Jessica stood, head held high. She felt better than she had in years, and maybe it showed. Judge Watkins greeted them, then began to ask Jessica a series of questions. Aaron stood to respond for her, but Jessica waived him off. She looked at the judge and answered them all herself, her voice firm, answering them clearly, honestly.

Apparently, Watkins had already made up her mind, and just needed to hear the right things from Jessica for herself. The hearing itself was merely a formality. Satisfied, the judge waived the last few days of her sentence, commuting it to time served and closing the case. Ferrara was ecstatic, and Aaron was pleased—and surprised—by how Jessica comported herself in front of the judge.

"It's like you're a different person," he said, gathering up his materials and handed her a manilla bag of her effects. She looked inside—her purse, her phone, the keys to the VW.

"Well, we'll see," she answered. She pulled out the phone and looked at it. The thing felt foreign in her hand, a talisman of the old days.

Exiting the courtroom, Jessica didn't feel vindicated, or even that she'd won any kind of leniency from Judge Watkins. Instead, she felt like she owed the old judge a favor for letting her off early. They shared a look as Jessica left the courtroom, and for a moment, it felt like Watkins might have been pleased with her. Maybe even a little proud.

Leslie drove her and Ferrara home, dropping Jessica off first. It would be weird, not seeing these women every day. They promised to get together the next day for lunch and then said their goodbyes, making quite a scene in the driveway for Jessica's mansion.

Inside, her house was just as she'd remembered it—she hadn't been there in months, but someone had been there, of course, "taking care of it." Living rent-free, more likely, and eating all of her food. There was a hand-written note from someone on the kitchen counter, a list of things they were "out of." The place looked lived in, and not in a good way.

She walked through the halls, looking at a house that suddenly seemed too large for her. After sharing a set of small rooms with two other women for almost three months, this place felt like an airplane hangar, loud and sterile. And, of course, the rooms at the Cortez farm had been a palace compared to the jail cell she'd occupied previously.

Jessica surprised herself by cleaning the entire house, taking up much of Sunday afternoon, her first day of freedom. She scrubbed, cleaning and purging her home, boxing up stuff she didn't want anymore. She cleaned out the fridge, which stank of old pizza and stale beer. Jessica threw away all of the alcohol she could find. She'd expected to be tired, or interested in reconnecting with local friends, but, instead, she spent the evening on her knees, scrubbing a toilet.

And boxing up other peoples' stuff.

When she was done, Jessica sat alone in her living room. She needed a plan.

What would she do first? The entourage was at the top of her list of things to work on. Who would she hire to replace Hank Jennings and Scott Rubin? How quickly could she get rid of Carrie and Gina, letting them know that she no longer required their "services?"

She needed a clean slate, just her and some security. She dug out her phone and made a couple of calls, tracking down that bouncer from the fateful night at Liquid. He'd stood up to her, despite knowing who she was. That was the kind of people she needed in her life right now—"no" men, instead of "yes" men. She drove down to the club and talked to him personally, asking him to serve as her security for the next few months. He was delighted—his name was Tyler—and he put in his notice at the club.

Back at her place, she continued working on her plan. How could she move her career forward, take it to the next level? She needed to be proactive.

Jessica went to the bedroom and dug through her luggage—she needed to remember to return the suitcase to Ferrara and thank her. Really thank her. Ferrara had put her life on hold for Jessica. Was there anyone else in Jessica's life who would do that for her? She didn't think so.

Digging through the borrowed suitcase, she found the two things she was looking for: her journal, and the stack of scripts, now tied together with twine.

Jessica Mills carried them both back into the living room and sat down. She opened her notebook and reviewed the list of screenplays and her opinions on them. She read through the notes she'd made. She needed to be in charge of her career instead of waiting for roles and acting jobs to come her way.

When she was done reviewing the scripts, she flipped to a new blank page and wrote "NEW CAREER STEPS" at the top. Over the last three months, she'd thought a lot about starting her own production company—she knew a few other women in the industry who had done that. It gave them a pipeline of projects, including projects that she might not want to appear in herself but still wanted to champion.

She started writing, jotting down her thoughts on a production company and potential names for the business and what her goals were for it. Jessica wanted more say in the kinds of roles she went up for. She would be in charge of her auditions, not someone else.

And she needed to create some kind of structure where she could make money on movies she produced, even if she didn't appear in them. She made a list of other women she knew who had started their own companies, numbering them in the order she wanted to contact them.

Jessica also made a list of movie roles she wanted, starting with movies that were in pre-production now or in casting. Jessica made a list of people to contact about roles, people other than her good-for-nothing agent. She also made a list of potential new agents and agencies she could approach.

And Jessica jotted down story ideas. Stories about road trips through the American southwest and to the Grand Canyon. Stories about ex-cops investigating a cheating husband and realizing the case was about something else entirely. Stories about a scary mansion in New Orleans and one room of the house filled with long-dead bodies, propped up around a dining room table. Stories about casino riverboats, and stories about crazed stalkers chasing people across the country, showing up dressed as clowns.

Jessica filled up one page, then another, then another. She had a lot of ideas. She didn't go to bed until she felt good about the house and her plans. Then, and only then, did she take a long shower and sink into her own comfortable bed for the first time in months.

CHAPTER 82
Settled

Frank Harper sat in his new apartment, watching TV and fiddling with his new camera. Over the last three weeks, he'd gotten all of his stuff out of Laura's apartment. He'd moved the last of it yesterday, and last night was the first night he'd been able to relax in his new place.

Moving was difficult business, and it felt like he'd been moving for months. His last day in his old apartment in Birmingham had been July 20th. In a sense, he'd been "moving" ever since. It was nice to finally be settled in a new place—one that he was paying for—even it had taken three months.

And he was paying for it. Between the jobs he was doing and the windfall from providing personal protection for Jessica Mills, the money in his checking account was starting to pile up. He'd paid Jake Delancy for first and last month's rent on this place, and there was still plenty of money in the account, even after he'd paid Monty Robinson and his other expenses. It occurred to him that the Robinsons, the couple from his divorce case, shared a last name with Monty. He doubted they were related, he thought with a smile.

No, things were looking up. He was in a new place, and all of his furniture fit fine, along with a new TV he'd splurged on. Laura and Jackson had visited earlier today and complimented him on his choices. Jackson had run around like a crazed monkey, getting into everything. Frank reminded himself to "kid-proof" the place as much as possible before he started having Jackson over regularly.

Nodding, Frank dug out his notebook and added "kid-proof the apartment" to his list of things to do. He was knocking things off at a pretty good clip.

His phone dinged, and he grabbed it off the side table, muting the TV. It was an email from Jessica Mills. He'd followed her return to Los Angeles on the news. The judge had waived the last days of her house arrest, and Jessica was settling back into her life. Her email was just her touching base. She was doing fine, was starting to look for work. Wanted to know if she should try to get him cast in her next movie as some kind of tough guy. He smiled. She was still feeling indebted to him, obviously. But he'd just been doing his job, a job he'd been hired to do.

That wasn't exactly true. He had taken a liking to her, after a few days. Frank tapped at the tiny keyboard on his phone, emailing her back. He told her to be careful, have fun, and not to take life too seriously.

Frank put the phone down and went back to the TV, unmuting it. It was yet another episode of "Forensic Files," probably his favorite show. They were always using new technology to crack cold cases. Of course, some of these episodes were fifteen years old, and the "new" technology they were using was positively quaint.

Frank felt restless. The move was done, his two biggest cases had wrapped up, and there was nothing more to do on the Anderson Tool & Die case this late at night. He was still looking into the missing money and running backgrounds on the employees. He would start the personal interviews soon, try to shake something loose. People didn't like being interviewed if they were under suspicion, and they would hate being interviewed by Frank. He could sit there all day with his arms crossed, waiting for people to talk.

He glanced at his list of cases. The only other open case consisted of two words: "Joe Hathaway." There was nothing to be done about that case either, other than endlessly driving the back roads around Cooper's Mill. It accomplished nothing, but it made him feel better. The guy was out there somewhere. Or maybe he was dead. Maybe his body would turn up someday and Frank could finally cross that case off his list.

Or not. Maybe he'd reappear to haunt Frank some more.

He shook his head. It was those kinds of cases that were the worst, the ones with no resolution. Like Ben Stone's murder, or that little kid who suffocated in a cardboard box in the middle of an industrial area of Atlanta. Cases that you could never put away, cases that haunted you.

Add Joe Hathaway to the list, Frank thought. He could be out there somewhere, right now. Frank stood, shaking his head. There was no point in fretting about it. But Frank felt restless, aimless. He needed to be working on something, even though there was nothing to work on.

He heard a noise outside and looked out the windows, the ones off his living room that looked out on the neighboring strip mall. He could see the back of a pizza place and the local liquor store. A guy was standing out behind the strip mall, smoking and sipping a beer.

The thought of having a drink drifted into Frank's mind with no hesitation.

He was riding high, on a roll, and deserved to celebrate. Money was coming in, and he had a place of his own now, so he didn't need to worry about drinking in front of Laura or Jackson. Or listen to her complain, if she didn't like him drinking.

No, there was nothing wrong with it, really. He was celebrating his new place, and his new town, and his new life.

A few drinks wouldn't kill him.

Frank nodded, making up his mind. He grabbed his keys and his wallet and left the house, heading through the thin strip of woods that separated his duplex from the liquor store.

Epilogue

Jessica Mills rode in the back of the stretch limousine, traveling through North Hollywood. She was leaning against the window, looking out at the wide boulevards lined with hotels and stores, interspersed with twisty, narrow streets that disappeared up into the dark hills.

It had rained, an exceedingly rare occurrence in Los Angeles, and the dark streets reflected the storefronts and headlights and sodium streetlights like a scene from some old noir film. The dingy streets outside reminded her of that cobblestone alley behind Liquid, the club in Los Angeles where, suddenly, everything in her life had changed. At least those people in the car had recovered. Jessica wasn't sure if she could handle it, being responsible for someone's death.

It wasn't like with her stalker—she hadn't regretted his death in the least. He'd chased her, tracked her. Showed up in Los Angeles and thrown her over his shoulder to carry her away like some prize. More information had come to light about the man—he'd been to Los Angeles at least one other time, but she'd been out of town on a shoot. And the LAPD were investigating three murders of young women— women who looked like Jessica—that had occurred during the man's visits to Los Angeles. It made her shiver, just thinking about him. He'd appeared in Ohio and nearly gotten away with snatching her away from the world. She didn't even like to remember those frantic moments at the parade, or what came after.

Jessica sat back from the window and looked around at the inside of the stretch limo. Most of the ceiling was taken up by a huge skylight, outlining the ghostly shapes of buildings passing by outside. The skylight was circled by a glowing ring of blue LED light or some kind of thin neon tubing, she couldn't tell which. More blue light ran along the floor beneath her feet, ringing the soft leather couches that took up the rear and either side of the limo.

The studio had gone all-out for this, though Jessica wasn't sure if the limo was for her or to impress the fans and press who were waiting for Jessica to arrive. The studio suits were still pissed at her, so this whole show was more likely a nod to the fans and the press: "See, everything is fine. Everything is getting back to normal."

The limo was anything but "normal," at least as it had been defined in her life for the last few months. It was over-the-top, audacious. The vehicle had three flat-screen TVs, a karaoke machine, and a disco ball that could be lowered from part of the ceiling. A fully-stocked mini-bar lurked in one corner, the bottles clinking quietly together as the vehicle prowled the Hollywood streets. Each bottle was attached to the bar with a loop of blue neon.

But Jessica didn't feel like a drink tonight. Or any other "recreational" substance. She was here for one purpose only: to get her life back on track.

It was Friday night, November 23, the premier of her newest movie, "Knights of the Temple."

The studio had pushed the premier back two weeks as a result of her "unfortunate situation," the words one of the studio suits had used to summarize her whole summer. No one talked about it to her face, but she knew everyone was gossiping about it behind her back, especially at the studio where "Knights" was produced. Shortly after returning from Ohio, Jessica had made the rounds, something Aaron, her lawyer, had referred to as her "apology tour." Jessica got her face out there, meeting with as many people as possible at the studio and calming the suits down.

And word trickled out to the rest of "Hollywood." The press was rampant with rumors she'd spent the last two weeks quashing, practically since her plane had landed at LAX. Yes, there would be a glitzy Hollywood premiere for "Knights," and yes, she would be in attendance. Yes, Jessica Mills was sober. Yes, her stalker was dead and he'd killed a bunch of people and had been obsessed with her. Yes, Jessica had worked a menial job in Ohio for a few months and worn a disguise to hide away from the world. No, she wasn't still wearing an ankle monitor—she'd "paid her debt" to society and was free and clear.

Yes, Jessica Mills was back.

But she didn't "feel" back, not really. She just felt different. Older? Smarter? She couldn't put her finger on it. More mature, maybe? Jessica wasn't sure.

She spread her hands across the beautiful rented dress she was wearing, smoothing out the fabric and straightening one of the gown straps. Jessica wondered how much the ornate dress cost. She hadn't even asked—the studio had picked it out, sending it after three fittings. Apparently, people had gossiped that she'd gained weight in Ohio, eating all that Midwestern food. The seamstress who had measured her had been surprised—Jessica was trimmer than she'd been in years, and she'd even buffed out a little across the shoulder.

Jessica smiled at the thought as she smoothed the dress. It looked expensive. How many shifts would she have had to work at Food Town to pay for it? How many nights of stacking pallets of bananas and piling up bags of frozen chicken would it take to afford the dress she was wearing right now? She had no idea. Insane amounts of wealth were just tossed around out here, audacious signs of conspicuous consumption.

The limo turned sharply, and Jessica heard giggles from the other occupants. She ignored them for now, remembering one of the meetings just after she'd returned from Ohio. Another example of Hollywood being out of touch with real people.

The studio was anxious, needing to meet with her and plan the movie premiere. Jessica had been shown into a massive windowed conference room and introduced to a waiting group of studio executives, most of whom she knew. Aaron had gone with her and done most of the talking, and he and the execs discussed "Knights" and the possibility of delaying the premiere for up to six months. Some of the suits wanted to push it back to Summer 2013, thinking that the Jessica's situation would be a drag on the box office and letting the furor died down would help. Others argued to keep the film on track—they wanted to lean into the current controversy, saying that Jessica's name, plastered all over the news, would goose ticket sales.

Jessica hadn't really been listening—as usual, people talked about her as if she wasn't in the room.

But this time, she didn't get mad. Instead, Jessica spent the first forty-five minutes of the meeting looking across the room at a large table near the door, where caterers had put out a spread for the lunch meeting: sandwiches and fruits and drinks, all of which were being completely ignored by the occupants of the room.

Jessica looked at the trays of massive sandwiches and two huge bowls of macaroni salad and Cole slaw and breads and a huge tray of cookies and fudge. She wondered how much of Cooper's Mill that spread would feed. If she could magically transport the huge table of food to the Ohio town's historic downtown, maybe set it up in the parking lot of one of the churches, she could offer forty or fifty people a nice free lunch.

A black women busied herself around the table of food, straightening and organizing. She moved the food around with such care, Jessica assumed she was the owner of the catering business. Another woman stood near a separate table to pour drinks. But other than a couple of people, no one had gotten any food.

Finally, Jessica stood and excused herself, going to the bathroom. It was really just an excuse, and when she returned to the conference room, she turned and went to the food table.

"Hi," she said to one of the women, then nodded at the table of trays of food. "This all looks amazing."

The black woman smiled and straightened her apron, which read "Washington Catering."

"Oh, thank you, Ms. Mills. Would you like something?" she asked, motioning at the table.

"Yes, please," she said. "And it's just Jessica. Is that macaroni salad?"

The woman beamed. "My momma's recipe, actually. Here, try a little."

She scooped up a taste on a small spoon and handed it over. Jessica tried it and smiled.

"Mmm, that's good. Tastes like...paprika, maybe?"

"That's right," the woman said.

"Well, I'll take a ham sandwich and some more of that salad, if you don't mind."

The woman made her a plate while Jessica got a drink from the other woman, who poured up a glass of pink lemonade. Jessica thanked them both and went back to her seat at the table. The conversation had continued on without her, just as she'd known it would. Aaron and the suits had come to a consensus to push the premier two weeks but keep everything else the same, including the VOD and DVD release dates. About the time she finished her food, someone at the table thought to ask Jessica her opinion, and she agreed. It didn't really matter to her—at this point, "Knights" was part of her old life.

After the meeting broke up, Jessica went over and chatted with the caterers as they cleaned up. Turned out the older woman, Deanna Washington, was the owner of the catering company. They talked about her business, and catering movie shoots and premieres. Deanna beamed as she described all the different dishes she often made, specializing in southern food. She worked for another caterer but was starting to branch out and take on her own jobs, making Jessica smile. She was happy to chat with someone who wasn't rich and wasn't involved with the studio. She was barely in the industry. After a few minutes, Deanna offered to box up some of the food for Jessica, who accepted happily as she nibbled on a piece of the chocolate fudge.

"This is amazing."

"Oh, thanks. My brother made that—he's pretty handy. When he's not acting, he's in the kitchen with me, cranking out meatballs or oatmeal cookies."

Before she left, Jessica asked for Deanna's card, promising to book her in the future. After she left the conference room and was walking down the hall to find Aaron, Jessica heard the two women inside, giggling and happily congratulating each other. It made Jessica smile.

Perspective, she thought. Maybe that was the change Jessica was experiencing. Maybe she was finally seeing things from other people's perspective. A few inexpensive meals at a diner could do that. Or pinching pennies on a long road trip, or spending hours unboxing cartons of frozen spinach until your arms ached.

Jessica wasn't much older than she'd been before heading to Ohio. She was only a year older than she'd been in Atlanta when she'd filmed "Knights," a time-traveling romp through medieval England. The script had seemed silly then and it seemed silly now. But they'd hired her, one of the shrinking list of studios that would still take a chance on her. The shoot had been challenging. Jessica had seen nothing of Atlanta but the inside of her hotel room. The sugar twins had gone along, procuring whatever alcohol and drugs Jessica needed to stay wired and "happy." A few times, the shoot had to be delayed, prompting a discussion with the producers about her behavior.

Well, that was all about to change.

"You okay?"

Jessica looked up and saw Ferrara Cortez, her friend and stylist, sitting on one of the benches ringing in neon. She had been absorbed in doing her own makeup, for once, and was holding up a compact from the open makeup case on the seat next to her. Ferrara was also decked out in an expensive dress, something far out of her own personal budget.

Jessica smiled and smoothed her dress again. "I'm fine. It just feels...you know, weird. After Ohio. But I'm fine."

Ferrara stood and shuffled over to Jessica's couch, negotiating the moving vehicle by holding onto the ceiling with one hand. She plopped down next to Jessica.

"You don't look fine. Nervous?"

"No, not really," Jessica said with a smile. "I've done a million of these."

Ferrara looked at her.

"No, you haven't, not like this," she said. "This is big. Your first public event since coming back. I'd be nervous if I were you."

"Oh, well, thanks a lot," Jessica said, play punching Ferrara's exposed shoulder. "Some friend you are."

"I'm not gonna lie to you," Ferrara said. "I'm nervous too, and nervous for you."

"Thanks."

"But this is good, getting back to things."

Jessica nodded.

"And you look great," Ferrara added. "I can't get over those shoulders. You look like a Klingon."

Two months of actual work, out in the real world, made all the difference. One shift at Food Town was like four trips to a fancy Hollywood gym. Jessica smiled and lifted her arm, curling her bicep and making a muscle.

"If any of those paparazzi gives me any trouble, I'll put them on their ass."

Ferrara nodded. "Get 'em."

The limo slowed and turned, and Jessica and Ferrara held on as they swayed on the seat. Ferrara ducked down and looked out through the partition that separated the back of the limo from the driver. "We're getting close to the theater. You want to cancel?"

"Oh, no, she can't do that," another voice spoke up, nervous.

They turned and looked at the only other occupant of the back of the limo, Becki Newsome. The young woman clutched her little bag. Becki was Jessica's new publicist, and she'd been on the job for a total of four days. The woman was large and thoughtful, careful with her words. She had an energy that was infectious; sometimes, the young woman seemed to "crackle around the edges."

Jessica had wanted to find someone "regular," more "normal" than the usual publicists, who all seemed coked up, rail thin and hyperactive. Becki had impressed Jessica with her deep knowledge of the industry—she had interned with three other publicists and finally struck out on her own, but no one would hire her because her "look" wasn't right. Jessica had snatched her up.

Scott Rudin, Jessica's former publicist, had been fired last week. It was part of Jessica's "purge." All the rest of "Team Jessica" had been shown the door, including the sugar twins and Jessica's manager, Hank Jennings, and several other folks. She'd let everyone else go, getting down to just the two people she trusted in Hollywood: Ferrara and Aaron, her attorney. Becki was a new hire, along with Jessica's new bodyguard, Tyler, hired away from Liquid. She was still looking for a new manager.

"It's okay, Becki," Jessica said, leaning forward and putting her hand on Becki's knee. "I'm not gonna cancel. Ferrara was just kidding."

"Good," Becki said, relieved. "I want this to go well, obviously. It's good for you, Jessica, but also, it's good for your brand."

"My brand? You sound like Scott," Ferrara said. They had both been regaling Becki with stories of Scott's hyperactive nature and his tendency to treat Jessica like a "thing" instead of a person.

"Scott was an idiot, like you said," Becki said with a smile. "But he was right about one thing—you are a brand, and a valuable one at that."

Jessica nodded, agreeing. "One that should get more valuable over time."

"Right," Becki said. "And that means also adhering to any previous agreements you signed, as distasteful as it might seem. We finish those out, then move on. New gigs, new roles. Maybe a few appearances, with your approval. But I promise to not sign you up for any more of those creepy meet-and-greets, especially with handsy old men."

"Good," Jessica said. "Thank you."

"And once you start making your announcements, your stock is gonna soar," Ferrara added.

Jessica nodded. Ferrara was talking about Monarch Productions, Jessica's fledgling production company. Borne out of the trip to Ohio, the idea had been running around in her head and solidifying over the past three months. Her own production company, staffed by people she handpicked. Looking for good work to produce or champion.

The little company was just getting started, setting up shop in a tiny office she'd procured on the Paramount lot. Becki had said that production companies were taken more seriously if they operated from one of the studio lots, and Jessica had called in a favor—she still had a few left—to make it happen. The office was tiny, and nothing too fancy. She had yet to hire anyone, though she was looking at resumes. The only occupant of the office, so far, was a fiddle leaf fig Jessica had brought in from home.

But it was a start.

And, like Becki said, the smartest way for Jessica to grow her brand. She would be producing films, as well as acting in them, and have her pick of the properties that came through the door. Finally, she would have some say in what roles she was accepting, instead of just lurching along, day after day, hoping for things to get better.

"But nothing tonight," Becki reminded Jessica. "Stay on task."

Jessica nodded soberly. "Got it. No announcements tonight," Jessica said, looking at them both. "Tonight is about this film, so let's push that. I'll smile and talk nice and thank the producers and we'll see how the premiere goes. Hopefully, this is the last movie I'm in that I'm not particularly proud of."

The limo slowed and Jessica looked up, seeing the theater approach. A throng of fans crowded the sidewalk, threatening to push out into the street.

It wasn't surprising—some were here for the premiere, obviously, but many were probably there to get a look at Jessica. The whole situation with her time in Ohio, the arrest and "hiding" in plain sight, had enamored her with the public. The fish-out-of-water Ohio "vacation" sounded like a movie, making the national news. And even that was topped off by the incident with the stalker, making even more newsworthy. Now, everywhere she went, there were crowds. She tried to stop and sign autographs—they were fans, and needed to be treated with respect.

The paparazzi were also out in force tonight—she could see a dozen of them, swarming around the crowd of fans and parking themselves between the limo and the theater entrance. More were camped out across the street, their strobes flashing. But where Jessica used to dread them, swarming around her like rats, now she just smiled to herself. She remembered Frank Harper punching the one photographer in the stomach, dropping him to the ground and taking away his camera. These photographers had no power over her. At this point, all they did was make her laugh. It was hard to be intimidated by them after she'd seen the look on the one photographer's face, looking up at her and Harper from the ground, stunned and perplexed and utterly humiliated.

"Okay, here we go," Ferrara said, smoothing her own dress. She looked nervous. "I can do this, I can do this."

Jessica reached over and took her hand. "It's no big deal, Ferrara," Jessica said. "It's just a bunch of industry types, here for the reflected attention."

"I know, I know," Jessica's friend said.

Jessica's friend. Jessica thought about that for a moment as the limo slowed, approaching the theater. Ferrara Cortez was truly a friend—she'd watched over Jessica, taken her in. Invited her to live with her family, helped Jessica get clean and completely off the coke. Ferrara had stuck with her when others hadn't, and come up with an audacious plan to keep Jessica from going to prison, where she could have been hurt or even killed. On so many different levels, Jessica owed Ferrara her life.

As the limo came to a stop in front of the crowded sidewalk that fronted the movie theater, Jessica saw Tyler working the crowd, holding people back. Just seeing him there relaxed her—he was huge, and had one job, to protect her. Jessica also saw Leslie Davis working the crowd, another freelance security hire. Jessica turned and squeezed Ferrara's hand one more time, then let go.

"Thank you," Jessica said quietly, nearly drowned out by the screaming voices outside.

Ferrara looked at her. "Thanks? Thanks for what?"

"Saving me," Jessica said, looking at Ferrara. With a smile, Jessica Mills turned, breathed slowly in and out, and pulled open the door of the limo.

About The Author

Greg Enslen has published eight mysteries and thrillers, including the Amazon bestsellers "A Field of Red" and "The Ghost of Blackwood Lane." His four-book "Frank Harper Mysteries" series has received critical acclaim. He also writes original screenplays and has published twenty other titles, including in-depth binge guides for popular TV shows such as "Game of Thrones" and "Mr. Robot." His books are available from major retailers and on his **Amazon Author Page** at http://bit.ly/geauthor.

Greg lives in southern Ohio with his wife, three children, five dogs and an indeterminate number of cats. His interests include travel, reading, film and television, and yelling at various sports franchises. Greg enjoys writing late at night, after everyone else has finally trudged off to bed and the house is quiet. For more information, visit his website at **gregenslen.com** or check out his **Facebook fan page** at http://www.facebook.com/gregenslenswriting.

BOOKS BY GREG ENSLEN

Greg has written and published thirty books. Most titles available from Amazon, other major book retailers, and on Kindle:

Frank Harper Mysteries

A Field of Red
Black Ice
White Lines
Yellow Jacket
Welcome to Cooper's Mill (free companion guide, available exclusively at gregenslen.com)

Fiction

Black Bird
The Ghost of Blackwood Lane
The 9/11 Machine

Guide Series

A Field Guide to Facebook
"A Viewer's Guide to Suits," Season 1
"A Viewer's Guide to Suits," Season 2
"A Viewer's Guide to Suits," Season 3
"Game of Thrones: A Binge Guide" for Season 1
"Game of Thrones: A Binge Guide" for Season 2
"Game of Thrones: A Binge Guide" for Season 3
"Game of Thrones: A Binge Guide" for Season 4
"Game of Thrones: A Binge Guide" for Season 5
"Game of Thrones: A Binge Guide" for Season 6
"Game of Thrones: A Binge Guide" for Season 7
"Mr. Robot: A Binge Guide" for Season 1
"Mr. Robot: A Binge Guide" for Season 2
"Mr. Robot: A Binge Guide" for Season 3

Newspaper Column Collections

"Tipp Talk" 2010 Newspaper Column Collection
"Tipp Talk" 2011 Newspaper Column Collection
"Tipp Talk" 2012 Newspaper Column Collection
"Tipp Talk" 2013 Newspaper Column Collection